The Snow King's Thrall

Rory West

INDEPENDENTLY PUBLISHED

Chapter 1

M INA HUDDLED DEEPER INTO the worn, oversized sweater she'd claimed from a thrift store years ago. The sleeves hung past her wrists, frayed and pilled, but it was comforting, a cocoon against the cold creeping into her apartment. Around her, the clutter of her solitary life formed an uneven fortress: mismatched mugs bearing remnants of old lattes, stacks of books with cracked spines and dog-eared pages, and a blanket she'd bundled around her legs like a nest.

She ran her thumb over the faded gold lettering on the cover of *The Snow Queen*, the motion more muscle memory than deliberate thought. She had read the story countless times, its tale of loyalty and longing speaking to something deep inside her. Mina's lips moved silently over her favorite lines: *"And Gerda went forth barefoot and alone into the wide world."* The words were like a mantra, equal parts thrilling and wistful. How many times had she imagined herself in Gerda's place? Chasing after something—or someone—that made life worth the struggle.

The soft buzz of her phone jolted her from her thoughts. It teetered on the edge of her desk, vibrating insistently against the chipped surface. Mina reached for it lazily, expecting another email from her boss or maybe a meme from Lisa, her overly cheerful coworker. Instead, her mother's name glowed on the screen.

Call me sometime.

Mina's stomach twisted. It wasn't an unusual message, but its simplicity carried a weight that settled heavily on her chest. She hadn't seen her mother in months. Their last phone call had been strained, filled with long silences and careful questions about Mina's job, her health, her future. *When are you going to settle down? Don't you want something more stable?* The questions weren't cruel, but they cut all the same, reminders of the gap between them.

She hovered her thumb over the keyboard, considering a reply. A quick *Will do* might be enough to ease her mother's worry, but the thought of opening that door—however slightly—felt exhausting. Mina sighed and locked the phone, setting it face down on the desk. "Tomorrow," she said aloud, though the word felt hollow in her mouth. She knew she wouldn't call.

Outside, the snowfall thickened, the flakes swirling hypnotically in the dim glow of the streetlights. The city was unnaturally quiet, the usual buzz of cars and voices muffled beneath the blanket of white. Mina frowned, leaning closer to the window. Snow wasn't uncommon this time of year, but there was something strange about this storm. The flakes fell too heavily, their edges sharp and crystalline, and the cold seemed to seep through the glass as if the frost were alive. She rubbed her arms, trying to shake off the unease.

"It's just snow," she muttered, though the words did little to convince her. She shifted her gaze back to her books, piled high on her nightstand and overflowing onto the floor. They were her sanctuary, her way of making sense of a world that often felt dull and relentless. In them, kingdoms rose and fell, love burned like wildfire, and ordinary people became extraordinary. They were everything she had ever wanted life to be.

And yet, they weren't enough.

Mina leaned her head against the window, her breath fogging the glass. She thought about her last date—a well-meaning accountant who'd spent the entire evening explaining tax loopholes. He'd been nice, but nice wasn't what she wanted. She wanted passion, adventure, someone who made her feel like the heroes and heroines in her books. But the men she met seemed content with polite texts and coffee dates that ended before sunset.

"Maybe I'm the problem," she murmured, the thought slipping out before she could stop it. The hum of the radiator was her only response.

At work, it was easy to pretend she was happy. She smiled at customers, joked with Lisa, and took comfort in the small routines of her barista job. But there was always an undercurrent of restlessness, a feeling that she was skimming the surface of a life that refused to open up to her. Each day felt like a placeholder for something she couldn't quite name, as if her real story was waiting to be written.

The cold deepened, frost creeping along the edges of her window, like fingers grasping for warmth. Mina tugged her blanket tighter and glanced back at *The Snow Queen*, still open on her lap. The passage she'd been reading spoke of the Snow King's heart of ice, his endless winter. The words felt sharper tonight, cutting through the haze of her thoughts like a blade.

She flipped to another page, but the words blurred together. Her chest felt heavy, her longing for something—anything—growing sharper with each breath.

Her world felt so small, and all she wanted was a way out.

Mina closed *The Snow Queen* with a soft thud, the familiar weight of the book settling in her lap. The frost on the window had grown thicker, spreading inward like creeping vines, and the room felt colder despite the radiator's dull hum. She shivered and pulled the blanket tighter around her shoulders, her fingers brushing against the stack of books teetering precariously on her nightstand.

Something unusual caught her eye.

Nestled beneath the pile was a book she didn't recognize—a beautifully bound volume with an icy-blue cover that shimmered faintly in the dim light. Her brow furrowed as she reached for it, the book colder to the touch than it should have been. The frost-like patterns etched into its surface glinted as if catching invisible light, and the title along the spine was written in a language she couldn't read.

Mina frowned. She didn't remember buying this book. She didn't even remember seeing it before tonight.

Curiosity gnawed at her hesitation. She ran her fingers over the cover, tracing the strange script, before opening it to the first page.

The page was blank except for a single line written in silvery text: *To those who seek the truth hidden in the frost.*

The words sent a shiver down her spine, though she couldn't say why. She turned the page, her fingers brushing the edge delicately, as if the book might shatter.

On the next page was an illustration that took her breath away: a towering palace of ice with jagged spires reaching into a stormy sky. Snow swirled around its base, burying the land in a glimmering white expanse. In the foreground, a cloaked figure stood alone, their face hidden, the folds of their garment whipping in the icy wind.

Mina's heart raced as she flipped to the first line of the text beneath the illustration:

"The Snow King's heart was bound in frost, its beat silenced by betrayal and loss. His kingdom lay buried beneath endless winter, its people forgotten, its beauty preserved only in ice. And so he waited, seeking the warmth of a heart strong enough to thaw his curse..."

The words seemed to pulse on the page, their dark ink shimmering faintly. As Mina read on, the air in her room grew colder, the frost along the edges of her windowpane thickening until it formed solid sheets of ice.

She drew the blanket close around her shoulders, but her focus stayed fixed on the story. The Snow King's tale unfolded like the fairy tales she loved so much, but there was something about it that felt sharper, more vivid. The words seemed to ripple and blur as if alive, drawing her deeper into the story.

A sharp wind howled outside, rattling the windows. Mina jumped, her heart thudding against her ribs as the sound grew louder, more insistent. The room's temperature plummeted, and her breath came out in visible puffs.

Her lips moved unconsciously as she read the next passage aloud, her voice barely above a whisper:

"Come to the frost where silence grows, Where Winter's heart in stillness slows. Come to the cold where dreams reside, And solace waits where shadows hide."

The words hung in the air, resonating as if the room itself had absorbed them.

The light in the room flickered, then dimmed entirely. The frost on the windowpane began to spread—crawling down the walls, across the ceiling, and toward her. Mina gasped, dropping the book, but the cold was relentless.

A sudden, sharp pull gripped her chest, like an unseen hand yanking her forward. The frost around her swirled in a vortex, the icy-blue cover of the book glowing faintly at its center. She tried to push herself back, but her body felt weightless, untethered.

"No—wait!" she cried, her voice swallowed by the roaring wind.

The frost spiraled faster, encasing her in a cocoon of cold light. For a brief, disorienting moment, she felt like she was falling—not through air, but through something denser, darker. The world around her twisted and blurred, the edges of her reality dissolving into a wash of icy blue.

And then, silence.

When Mina opened her eyes, she wasn't in her apartment anymore.

Her first sensation was the bite of cold. Not the feeble chill of her drafty apartment, but a bone-deep frost that pressed into her skin, sharp and unrelenting. She gasped, her breath curling in the air like smoke.

Snow crunched beneath her hands as she pushed herself up, her limbs sluggish and unfamiliar.

The pale expanse around her stretched endlessly. Jagged peaks loomed in the distance, their icy spires reflecting the weak glow of a sun barely visible through thick clouds. The air was still, muffling sound, and for a brief, disorienting moment, Mina wondered if she'd stumbled into a lucid dream.

But then she looked down at her hands—and froze.

They weren't her hands.

These hands were rough and calloused, the fingers long and strong like those of someone accustomed to hard labor. Her pulse quickened as she turned them over, flexing the unfamiliar joints. The movements were hers, but the hands weren't.

Her breath came faster, fogging in the frigid air as she scrambled to her knees. Her body felt heavier, sturdier. She glanced down, her heart skipping a beat at the sight of broad shoulders draped in a tattered cloak, a sturdy frame encased in worn leather. She touched her face with trembling hands, feeling the sharpness of a jawline, the coarse stubble along her chin.

"What—" The voice that came out of her throat was low, masculine, and utterly unfamiliar.

Panic surged through her, hot and dizzying. She pressed her hands to her chest, feeling the solid weight of muscle where there should have been softness. The world swayed, her mind racing to make sense of the impossible. *This can't be real. I'm not so lucky.*

But the cold was real. The snow under her hands was real. The rasp of her breath and the steady thud of her heartbeat were real.

Her gaze darted around, searching for answers, but the landscape offered none. The snow was pristine and undisturbed, save for the shallow imprint of her body. She clutched the edges of her cloak, her fingers trembling.

"Okay," she whispered to herself, her voice rough and unfamiliar. "Think. Just... think."

Her thoughts were a jumbled mess of disbelief and fragmented memories. The last thing she could recall was sitting in her apartment, reading that strange book. The words, the frost, the blinding cold light—it had all felt like a dream. But now she was here, wherever *here* was, and her body...

She pushed herself to her feet, wobbling slightly as she adjusted to her new center of gravity. Her boots—her *boots*—sank into the snow as she steadied herself. The weight of a sword hilt at her hip made her flinch. She pulled the cloak tighter around her shoulders, bracing against the chill as she scanned the horizon.

Far off, the jagged silhouette of a village broke the monotony of the white expanse. Smoke curled from a cluster of rooftops, and faint shapes moved between them. It was distant but tangible, a tether to something resembling reality.

Mina hesitated. A strange voice whispered in the back of her mind, warning her not to trust this place. But the wind howled louder, biting at her exposed skin and forcing her to move.

She trudged toward the village, each step sinking into the snow. The terrain was rough, and her legs ached with the effort, but her unease propelled her forward.

As she neared the edge of the village, she saw weathered cottages clustered close together, their thatched roofs sagging under the weight of snow. Icy lanterns glowed dimly along the narrow streets, casting pale light on the frost-covered cobblestones.

The people—villagers, she supposed—were bundled in heavy woolen cloaks, their faces etched with weariness. A few paused to glance in her direction, their expressions wary. Mina's stomach churned under their scrutiny.

"Kai," someone muttered, the word carrying faintly in the cold air.

Her heart skipped a beat.

A man hauling firewood stopped to stare at her, his brows furrowing. "Kai," he said again, louder this time. He looked her up and down, suspicion flickering in his eyes before he shook his head and turned away.

More voices murmured her—or *his*—name as she passed. She felt the weight of their gazes, heavy with judgment and curiosity.

Kai. I'm Kai.

The realization hit her with the force of a hammer. Not only was she in someone else's body, but she was also someone the villagers clearly knew. And judging by their guarded looks and the whispered conversations, that someone wasn't particularly well-liked.

Mina swallowed hard, her mind racing. She couldn't afford to make a scene, not when she had no idea where she was—or how to get back to her real body.

She forced her expression to remain neutral, tilting her head in a way she hoped looked aloof rather than terrified. If anyone asked questions, she'd have to bluff her way through. She'd read enough fairy tales to know how quickly things could go wrong in strange villages.

As she walked deeper into the village, her nerves sharpened. This place felt old, almost timeless, like it had been plucked straight from the pages of a storybook. It was beautiful in its starkness, but the tension in the air made her skin prickle.

Whatever life Kai had lived here, it wasn't a happy one.

The village felt impossibly small as Mina—or *Kai*, she corrected herself—walked down the narrow streets. It wasn't just the tightly packed cottages with their weathered facades or the faintly sour smell of smoke from poorly ventilated chimneys. It was the way the villagers moved—watchful, deliberate, as though everyone knew everyone else's business.

He—*she? No, he*—tried not to meet their eyes, but the murmurs continued to follow him. Kai's name slipped through the air like a wisp of smoke, rising just loud enough to reach his ears but too quiet to confront.

Kai. That was his name. He could do this. This whole situation was far beyond suspended belief and Mina had always sunk into character when reading. This was more... immersive, but the same logic applied. *I am Kai...for now.* He clung to it like an anchor, a shield against the gnawing panic trying to claw its way to the surface.

He tightened the cloak around his shoulders, pulling it up higher to obscure his face. The rough fabric brushed against his jawline, a sensation so foreign and sharp it made him shiver.

You're Kai, he repeated, the words steadying him. The truth of it was strange and impossible, but arguing with it wouldn't help. He had to figure this out—starting with blending in.

A woman stacking firewood outside her door paused as he passed, her eyes narrowing. She didn't say anything, but the subtle downturn of her mouth spoke volumes. *Kai* wasn't popular here, that much was clear. The villagers looked at him like he was a storm waiting to happen, something best avoided unless absolutely necessary.

"Not exactly a charming prince," he muttered under his breath. The low tone of his voice startled him again, but it didn't sting as much this time. He was beginning to settle into it, like slipping into an old coat that didn't quite fit but still kept you warm.

The wind picked up, swirling snowflakes around his boots. He stopped for a moment, glancing down at the sturdy leather. They were scuffed and caked with snow, but they held firm. *Practical. Durable. These are someone's shoes,* he thought. Someone who lived here, worked here, survived here.

Kai—*her non-Kai-self*, whoever that even was—had always been clumsy, prone to stumbling in heels or tripping over untied sneakers. But these boots felt steady. Strong.

He ran a hand over the back of his neck, feeling the rough texture of his hair. Short, cropped, nothing like the wild curls he was used to. Everything about this body spoke of a life lived outside, in the cold and the dirt. It wasn't *him*, but it was...

"It's mine for now," he murmured, testing the words in the deep timbre of his new voice.

A sharp laugh broke his thoughts. Ahead, a group of villagers clustered near the center of the square, their breath visible in the icy air. They spoke in low tones, but their expressions shifted when they saw him approach. One man straightened, nudging his companion and nodding in Kai's direction.

"Back already," one muttered. The words were just loud enough to carry.

Kai kept walking, forcing himself not to react. It wasn't just wariness in their eyes, but something sharper. Annoyance? Disapproval? He could feel the weight of their judgments pressing down on him, suffocating and stifling.

And yet, a flicker of curiosity sparked in him. What kind of person had Kai been, to earn such a reputation? It was clear he wasn't the village darling, but there was something fascinating about that. A life with rough edges, a story steeped in conflict—something Mina's own life had never been.

Before he could dwell too long on the thought, a man stepped into the square, and the world seemed to narrow around him.

He was tall and broad-shouldered, his leather apron dusted with soot and his dark hair falling in loose waves around his face. His hands were strong and scarred, the hands of someone who worked with fire and metal, and his eyes were piercing, catching Kai's in a way that sent a jolt through his chest. *Holy hell he's gorgeous.*

The man's expression softened immediately, his brow furrowing with concern. "Kai," he said, his voice low but urgent.

The name sent a ripple of something unfamiliar through him—familiarity, warmth, something that wasn't his but felt close enough to touch.

"Are you all right?" the man asked, stepping closer. His movements were measured but deliberate, and Kai felt himself flinch instinctively. "The elders—" He paused, glancing around at the watching villagers before lowering his voice. "It's not safe for you to be out."

Kai fumbled for words, his mind racing. He knew he should say something, anything, but the man's presence was overwhelming, his gaze searching his face for answers Kai didn't have.

"I'm fine," Kai said finally, the words awkward and stilted.

I'm anything but fine.

The man's frown deepened, and he stepped closer still, close enough for Kai to feel the faint heat radiating from him in the freezing air. "What happened?" he pressed. "You never came back after the meeting—what did they say?"

The meeting. Kai's pulse quickened as he realized this man—whoever he was—expected him to know things, to *be* someone. He nodded vaguely, hoping it would pass for an answer.

The man's sharp gaze softened again, and he reached out, his hand brushing against Kai's arm. The gesture was subtle, but it lingered, a quiet reassurance that sent heat prickling up Kai's neck.

"Come with me," the man said, his voice quiet but steady. "We can talk somewhere safe."

Kai hesitated, his breath catching. For a moment, he wondered what this man—this stranger—saw when he looked at him. The man's concern wasn't just casual; it was personal, familiar, as though they'd shared something deep and unspoken. *I'm not that lucky.*

Kai swallowed hard. Whoever this man was, he trusted him.

The man led Kai toward the outskirts of the village, his broad shoulders cutting through the swirling snow with practiced ease. Kai struggled to keep up, his boots sinking into the uneven ground. Each step reminded him of how different this body was—how much heavier, how much stronger—and yet it felt like he was fumbling with borrowed tools, unsure how to use them properly. *Oh my god. I have a...* Kai stumbled, blushing even as he tried to abandon that thought and focus.

"Here," the man said softly, gesturing toward a modest stone workshop. The building's low roof sagged under the weight of snow, and the door creaked as he pushed it open. Warmth spilled out into the cold, carrying the faint scent of wood smoke and molten metal.

Inside, the glow of the forge bathed the room in a rich, amber light. Tools hung neatly along the walls, their edges gleaming in the firelight, and a half-finished blade lay on the workbench, its surface hammered smooth. The space was surprisingly tidy, each item carefully placed as though its owner took pride in every detail.

The man shut the door behind them and turned, his gaze immediately locking onto Kai.

"Are you going to tell me what happened?" he asked, his voice quiet but firm.

Kai hesitated, the weight of his scrutiny pressing down on him. The man's intensity was palpable, but there was no hostility in it—only concern, layered with something deeper.

"I'm fine," Kai said, his voice rougher than he intended. He shifted awkwardly, tugging the edges of the cloak tighter around his shoulders. "Nothing... happened."

The man frowned, crossing his arms. "Nothing?" he repeated, the skepticism clear in his tone.

Kai's mind scrambled for a response. Whoever this man was, he clearly knew Kai—knew him well enough to spot the hesitation, the cracks in the facade Mina was desperately trying to hold together.

"I'm just feeling a bit tired. I needed some air, so I went for a walk," Kai said finally, glancing away. "That's all."

The man exhaled slowly, his shoulders relaxing just slightly. He didn't seem convinced, but he let it go.

"You've been distant lately," he said, his voice softer now. "The elders are pushing harder, and the way they talk about you... It's not safe, Kai."

The way he said the name sent a ripple through Kai's chest. There was a familiarity to it, a weight that made the name feel less like an identity and more like an anchor tying him to this place, to this person.

"I can handle it," Kai said, the words instinctive, though he wasn't sure if he believed them.

The man's lips pressed into a thin line. He stepped closer, his presence steady and grounding, and rested a hand on Kai's shoulder. The touch was firm but careful, his calloused fingers warm even through the thick fabric of the cloak.

"I know you can," he said quietly, his tone heavy with sincerity. "But you don't have to do it alone."

Kai's breath hitched. There was something in the man's voice—something raw and unspoken—that made his chest tighten. Were these two lovers?

"What's your name?" The question slipped out before he could stop it.

The man blinked, his brow furrowing. "Gerhard," he said slowly, studying Kai's face. "You know that."

Kai forced a small, awkward smile, hoping it masked the sudden rush of panic. "Right. Of course," he said quickly. "Sorry, my mind's been... scattered."

Gerhard's frown deepened, but he didn't press further. Instead, his hand lingered on Kai's shoulder, the gesture grounding him in a way he hadn't expected. Kai wished he knew if this was a romance or dark fantasy. The urge he had to kiss this man was almost painful, but how could he when he didn't know what their relationship was? What if Gerhard was his brother? What a way to end a story early.

There was a warmth to Gerhard's presence that felt both reassuring and unsettling. It wasn't just the strength in his voice or the way he carried himself—it was the way he looked at Kai, like he saw someone worth protecting.

"Listen," Gerhard said, stepping back slightly but keeping his gaze steady. "If the elders are planning something, you need to tell me. Whatever they're up to, it's not going to be fair. Not to you."

Kai nodded stiffly, though he had no idea what the elders might be planning. His thoughts were a jumble of confusion and instinct, and he could feel himself teetering on the edge of revealing too much.

But then Gerhard smiled—just barely, a faint, fleeting curve of his lips—and the tension in the room eased.

"Stay here tonight," he said. "You'll be safe here."

Kai's pulse quickened. The idea of staying felt too close, too intimate, but it also felt... right. The workshop was warm, the air filled with the faint hum of Gerhard's quiet confidence, and for a moment, the chaos of the village felt distant.

He opened his mouth to protest, but Gerhard raised a hand to cut him off.

"No arguments," he said firmly, though his voice was gentle. "You're staying. I'll take care of it."

Kai nodded slowly, his words caught in his throat. He didn't trust himself to speak—not with the way Gerhard was looking at him, his eyes soft with something Mina couldn't quite place.

He wondered what Kai—the real Kai—had done to earn that kind of devotion.

Gerhard turned and began clearing a small table near the hearth, brushing aside scattered tools and a half-finished horseshoe. "I don't have much space, but we'll make do," he said, his tone casual, though his shoulders were stiff. He grabbed a folded blanket from a nearby shelf and tossed it onto a chair, motioning for Kai to sit.

Kai hesitated, his pulse thrumming in his ears. There was something in Gerhard's gaze, an intensity that made him feel exposed, like Gerhard was seeing more than what was on the surface. It was both unnerving and comforting in a way he couldn't name.

Gerhard glanced back, his brow furrowing. "You can sit, you know. I won't bite."

Kai startled, a nervous laugh slipping out. "Right. Thanks." He perched on the edge of the chair, hands gripping the edge like it might steady the strange, buzzing energy in his chest.

The workshop was small but warm, a stark contrast to the icy winds outside. The faint glow of the fire cast flickering shadows on the walls, illuminating the sturdy wooden beams and the tools hanging in neat rows. It smelled of iron and leather, tinged with the earthy scent of ash.

Gerhard approached a chest against the far wall, opening it and rummaging inside. "You can't keep wandering around in those," he said, gesturing at Kai's clothes—a patchwork of threadbare wool and mended seams that barely kept out the cold. "They're not warm enough, and they make you stand out."

Kai looked down, suddenly self-conscious. The clothes were practical enough, but they weren't *his*. They belonged to someone else—someone he had stepped into, someone whose life he was now trying to carry without fumbling.

"I guess I didn't think about it," he mumbled, his voice quieter than he'd intended.

Gerhard straightened, pulling out a thick, fur-lined tunic. "Here. This should fit." He handed it over, his fingers brushing against Kai's briefly. The contact sent an unexpected jolt through Kai, and he quickly pulled the tunic close to his chest, his cheeks flushing.

"Thanks," Kai said, avoiding Gerhard's eyes. He stood, unsure where to change.

Gerhard caught the hesitation and cleared his throat, turning away. "I'll, uh, stoke the fire. Take your time."

Kai ducked behind a partition, grateful for the sliver of privacy. He pulled off his outer layers, the chill in the room prickling his skin, and slipped into the tunic. It was soft and warm, the kind of comfort that made him want to sink into it and forget about the storm that seemed to be following him everywhere.

When he emerged, Gerhard was crouched by the hearth, coaxing the fire into a brighter blaze. He glanced up, his gaze lingering just a moment too long. "Looks good," he said, his voice softer than before.

Kai's stomach fluttered, and he cursed the way his body reacted without permission. "Thanks. It's... warm."

"Good," Gerhard said, standing and brushing his hands off on his trousers. "You can take the bed. I'll sleep here." He gestured toward a narrow bed tucked into the corner, then to the bench near the fire.

"No, I couldn't—"

"Kai." Gerhard's voice was firm, his expression brooking no argument. "You're taking the bed. You need it more than I do."

Kai opened his mouth to protest again but stopped when he saw the look in Gerhard's eyes—an odd mix of exasperation and something gentler, almost tender. He nodded mutely, swallowing the lump in his throat. "We can share it. If that's not weird."

Gerhard gave him a strange look before shaking his head. "I've known you since we were babes. It's not weird."

Kai hesitated, watching Gerhard settle onto the bed with the ease of someone who had done it a thousand times. The firelight danced across his face, casting sharp shadows over his strong jaw and the faint scar that ran along his cheek. There was a steadiness to him, a quiet resilience that felt unshakable.

Lying on the other side, Kai stared at the ceiling, his thoughts churning. There was a strange, persistent weight in Gerhard's gaze, like the man could see right through him. And maybe he could. Gerhard had known the *real* Kai. He had known him so well, had cared so deeply, that the truth must have felt like a splinter lodged beneath the skin.

The room fell silent, save for the crackling of the fire. Every so often, Gerhard shifted, the quiet rustle of fabric or the creak of the bed breaking the stillness.

Finally, Gerhard spoke, his voice low and quiet. "You've changed."

Kai's breath caught. "What do you mean?"

"You're… different," he said, his words careful and deliberate. "It's like you're seeing the world for the first time." He chuckled softly, though there was no humor in it. "The Kai I knew wouldn't have thanked me for a tunic, let alone stayed here without a fight."

Kai's heart pounded, the weight of the words pressing down on him. "People change," he said weakly.

"Maybe." Gerhard's gaze flicked toward him, his eyes dark and searching. "But sometimes it feels like you're not you at all."

The words hung in the air, heavy with unspoken meaning. Kai turned his head away, clutching the blanket tighter.

Gerhard didn't press further, but his presence lingered, steady and warm. Kai closed his eyes, but sleep didn't come easily—not with the way Gerhard's words echoed in his mind, and not with the sense that he was being unraveled one thread at a time.

The fire had burned low during the night, leaving the room steeped in shadows and a lingering chill. Kai stirred, his mind sluggish and unmoored, caught in the hazy space between sleep and waking. The weight of something solid and warm against him pulled him fully into awareness.

He blinked, his breath catching as he realized he was pressed against Gerhard's chest, his body wrapped securely in the man's arms.

For a moment, Kai froze. The rise and fall of Gerhard's steady breathing was an anchor in the stillness, his presence solid and grounding. One of Gerhard's arms was draped across Kai's waist, his hand resting lightly on his side, while their legs were tangled beneath the blankets.

Kai's pulse thundered in his ears. He didn't know how they'd ended up like this. The last thing he remembered was lying on the bed, staring at the ceiling and trying to untangle his thoughts. At some point, he must have drifted off, the tension in his body pulling him toward the closest source of comfort.

And now, that solace was Gerhard.

Kai's face flushed as a wave of heat crept up his neck. He became acutely aware of every point their bodies touched. Gerhard's warmth seeped through Kai's tunic—the one given to him earlier—and Kai couldn't help but notice the breadth of the man's chest, the strength of the arm encircling him or the faint woodsy scent clinging to his skin.

Simultaneously, Kai became aware of his own body. He felt the stirring of unfamiliar sensations in his groin as he fought to resist the urges brought about by the intimacy of their contact. Despite trying to focus on anything but the throbbing between his legs, it only amplified as he became increasingly aware of Gerhard's thigh pressed against him. Every breath, every subtle shift of their bodies teased and tormented him until he couldn't take it anymore. He gasped quietly as an overwhelming sensation washed over him, leaving him both relieved and mortified.

Kai swallowed hard, his breath unsteady as he tried to shift away without waking Gerhard. But the man stirred at the movement, his arm tightening slightly around Kai before his eyes fluttered open.

"Kai?" Gerhard's voice was rough with sleep, his brow furrowing as he blinked at the pale light creeping in from the window. His gaze fell to their position, and his arm loosened, though he didn't pull away completely. "Are you alright?"

Kai's face burned, and he turned his head quickly, desperate to avoid Gerhard's searching eyes. "I—I'm fine," he stammered, his voice pitched higher than he'd intended.

Gerhard shifted, propping himself up on one elbow and giving Kai the space to sit up. "You were shivering in your sleep," he said, his tone softer now, touched with concern. "I didn't think you'd mind."

Kai's heart twisted, guilt gnawing at him. He didn't know how to respond—how to explain the storm of emotions that had taken root in his chest. He rubbed at the back of his neck, avoiding Gerhard's gaze. "I wasn't... I mean, it's fine," he muttered.

Gerhard frowned slightly, watching him for a long moment before nodding. "Good." He sat up fully, raking a hand through his messy hair. "If it made you uncomfortable—"

"It didn't," Kai interrupted, surprising himself with the force of his own words. He glanced at Gerhard, his chest tightening at the quiet sincerity in the man's expression. "It was... fine."

The corners of Gerhard's lips quirked upward, though his gaze remained thoughtful. "Alright," he said simply. He swung his legs over the edge of the bench, standing and stretching as he moved toward the hearth. "I'll get the fire going again."

Kai sat frozen on the bed, his hands gripping the blanket tightly. His mind churned, caught between the remnants of his own vivid sensations and the memory of Gerhard's steady warmth. This body—Kai's body—reacted so strongly, so instinctively, in ways that made him feel like a stranger in his own skin.

But it wasn't his skin, was it?

Gerhard busied himself at the fire, unaware—or perhaps pretending not to notice—Kai's lingering tension. The room filled with the sound of kindling snapping and the soft roar of flames reigniting. Kai took a steadying breath, forcing himself to focus on the present, on the heat spreading through the workshop as the fire grew stronger.

His hands felt clammy as they gripped the edge of the blanket. He needed to—he couldn't—he had to get rid of the evidence of his body's betrayal. His mind raced for a solution, and then the thought hit him, absurd as it was.

"Gerhard," Kai said, his voice a little too sharp, making him wince. He cleared his throat, trying again. "Do you... have a washcloth?"

Gerhard, who had been rummaging near the hearth, looked up at him with furrowed brows. "A washcloth?" He paused, confusion flickering across his face. "For your face?"

Kai flushed. He wasn't sure why that sounded like the most ridiculous thing in the world, but it did. "Yes, um—yes, my face," he stammered, awkwardly brushing a hand against his cheek, hoping to cover his sudden discomfort. "I just—need to wash my face." He had no idea why his body felt so hot, but he was certain Gerhard could see right through him.

For a long beat, Gerhard stared at him, his mouth twitching, clearly trying to keep his composure. Then, his lips curled into a slight grin, and Kai could feel the heat flooding his face intensify.

"Alright," Gerhard said, though his voice held a touch of amusement. He turned away quickly, pretending to be focused on the firewood. "There's a cloth there by the wash basin. I'll go get more firewood. You... take your time."

Kai blinked, unsure if he was grateful or embarrassed by Gerhard's ability to read between the lines without directly addressing it. He cleared his throat again, though it didn't help his nerves at all.

Gerhard, clearly trying to hide his grin, threw on a coat over his tunic and bent down to pull on his boots, still making sure to avoid looking directly at Kai. "I won't be long."

"Right. Of course. Thank you," Kai muttered, his mind racing with both relief and the burning weight of his own awkwardness.

As Gerhard left the room, the door creaking softly behind him, Kai immediately got up and rushed to the small washbasin near the corner of the room. His hands were shaking as he grabbed a cloth from the shelf, dipping it into the water with more force than necessary. He knew Gerhard hadn't directly acknowledged what had happened between them, but he couldn't escape the fact that he had no idea how to navigate this new territory of his body—how to deal with *this* side of being a man.

He took a few moments, scrubbing his hands and the evidence of his disarray away, trying to settle the storm in his chest. But there was still a tight knot of shame and guilt, as though he had crossed some invisible line with Gerhard that couldn't be undone.

When he felt like he'd done all he could, he sighed, wiping his hands down with the washcloth one last time before folding it neatly. He placed it back on the shelf, avoiding his reflection in the water.

A heavy weight still sat on his chest as he turned to look at the fire, its warmth offering only the faintest comfort. Would it always be like this, he wondered? His mind racing with conflicting emotions and desires, each new moment of closeness with Gerhard only adding to the confusion.

But he had to push that aside. The cold wind would be back soon, and Gerhard might need help with the firewood.

The door creaked open, bringing with it a gust of icy air and the faint scent of snow. Gerhard stepped inside, his broad frame momentarily silhouetted against the pale morning light. Snow clung to his coat and hair, and he stomped his boots twice on the threshold before shutting the door behind him.

"Cold out there," he said, his voice breaking the silence as he carried an armful of firewood to the hearth. He set the logs down with practiced ease, brushing his gloved hands together to rid them of lingering frost.

Kai, standing stiffly near the fire, nodded but didn't reply. His face felt too warm, the contrast between the heat of the room and the memory of his earlier embarrassment making it impossible to focus.

Gerhard glanced at him, his expression neutral but his gaze lingering just a second too long. Then, as if by chance, his eyes drifted to the washcloth left near the basin. It was damp, crumpled slightly at the edges, and had been left sitting atop the basin in a way that clearly indicated recent use.

Gerhard's eyebrows lifted slightly, the smallest flicker of amusement crossing his face. He said nothing at first, merely turning back to stack the firewood. His movements were slow, deliberate, and far too composed.

"Hope you got everything sorted out," he said finally, the corners of his mouth twitching as he stoked the fire with a piece of kindling.

Kai's breath hitched, his head snapping up. "What?" The word came out too sharp, too defensive. He instantly regretted it.

Gerhard straightened, his hands on his hips now, regarding Kai with a faint smile. "The washcloth." He tilted his head toward the basin, his grin widening slightly when Kai visibly tensed. "Looks like it's been through a lot this morning."

Kai scrambled for a response, his cheeks burning hotter than the fire. "I—I just needed to wash my face," he stammered, the words spilling out in a rushed, uneven string. "I didn't think it'd be a big deal."

"Your face, huh?" Gerhard mused, his voice low, almost thoughtful, but there was no mistaking the teasing edge beneath it. He leaned casually against the mantle, crossing his arms as he watched Kai struggle.

Kai glared at the floor, his hands balling into fists at his sides. He hated how transparent he must look, how every nerve in his body seemed determined to betray him. "Yes. My face," he muttered. "It's not that unusual."

Gerhard's chuckle was soft but unmistakable. "Right. Not unusual at all." Gerhard didn't press further, instead focusing on removing his gloves and setting them by the hearth to dry. "Well, I'll leave you to it," he said lightly, as if granting Kai a mercy.

Then he moved to his boots, toeing them off with practiced ease and setting them neatly near the door. His coat followed, draped over the back of a chair, and for a brief moment, the room fell into an almost comfortable silence.

Kai couldn't stop fidgeting. Every small movement—the scuff of Gerhard's boots, the creak of the floorboards—made him hyper-aware of the space between them. He felt raw and exposed, as though Gerhard could see every thought stamped across his face.

Finally, Gerhard turned toward the bed, raking a hand through his hair to shake off any remaining snow. "I'm going to get some sleep," he said, his voice softer now, the rough edges smoothed out. He crossed to the bed and settled onto the far side, his back to Kai.

He shifted a little, making himself comfortable but careful not to sprawl too much, leaving plenty of space for Kai. "You should join me," he said simply, as though it was the most natural thing in the world. "It's warmer that way."

Kai blinked, heat prickling at the back of his neck. He stared at the space Gerhard had left for him, his thoughts whirling. "I—I'm fine by the fire," he stammered, though he wasn't sure who he was trying to convince.

Gerhard huffed a quiet laugh, the sound low and warm. "Suit yourself," he said, his tone carrying a note of amusement. He didn't turn to look at Kai, but his voice softened further as he added, "You'll freeze out there, though. Just saying."

Kai swallowed hard, his feet rooted to the floor. Gerhard's broad back was a solid, steady presence in the flickering firelight, his breathing already slowing as though sleep was just within reach.

But Kai couldn't bring himself to move yet. His eyes darted toward the washcloth still sitting near the basin, damp and faintly wrinkled from his hurried efforts earlier. If Gerhard had noticed it, he hadn't said anything—but that didn't mean he hadn't put the pieces together.

For a long moment, Kai stood there, caught between the pull of Gerhard's warmth and the weight of his own embarrassment. The fire crackled softly, its light dancing across the walls, and the room settled into a quiet rhythm, broken only by the sound of Gerhard shifting slightly on the bed.

Finally, Kai exhaled, willing his legs to move. He padded toward the bed, his steps hesitant but steady. When he slid beneath the covers, he kept as much distance as he could between himself and Gerhard, though the bed wasn't wide enough to make it convincing.

The heat from Gerhard's body was immediate and overwhelming, and Kai's chest tightened as he stared up at the dark ceiling, trying to will his thoughts into something resembling order.

Gerhard's breathing stayed even, steady, but Kai swore he caught a faint shift in the man's shoulders, almost like he was smiling to himself.

Kai squeezed his eyes shut, hoping sleep would claim him soon, though he doubted the storm inside his chest would let him rest easily.

Kai—Mina—stood just outside the village's modest hall, his breath curling in the cold air as he tried to steady himself. The voices inside were muffled but unmistakably tense, the cadence of an argument rising and falling. The council was meeting, and from what Gerhard had said earlier, their focus was him.

The thought tightened his chest.

He wasn't sure how much longer he could bluff his way through this charade. The truth—that he wasn't the man they thought he was, that his soul had been pulled from another world and thrust into Kai's body—was impossible to explain. Even Gerhard, with his warm eyes and gentle voice, would never believe it.

You have to play along. Stay quiet, stay small. Figure out what they want, and then plan your next move.

Mina clenched Kai's hands into fists, the calloused skin rough and unfamiliar. The weight of this body—the sheer physicality of it—was unsettling, but he didn't have time to dwell on it. He adjusted the edges of the cloak Gerhard had given him and stepped inside.

The hall was dimly lit by flickering lanterns, their golden glow casting long shadows across the weathered wood. A group of villagers sat in a loose circle near the center of the room, their faces tight with worry.

Elders, he guessed.

At first, no one noticed him. The conversation flowed in clipped, anxious tones as the elders leaned toward one another, their breath misting in the frigid air.

"The winter is worsening," a woman was saying, her voice sharp with authority. She was older, her hair streaked with gray, and her eyes swept over the others with the confidence of someone used to being obeyed. "Our stores won't last until spring if this keeps up."

"There's no proof the weather will hold," a man countered, though his tone lacked conviction. "We should wait. Maybe the snow will break—"

"And what if it doesn't?" the woman snapped, cutting him off. Her voice carried easily, crisp and commanding. "Are we supposed to sit here and starve while the Snow King holds us in his grip?"

At the mention of the Snow King, the room shifted. The air grew heavier, the murmurs quieter. Kai froze just inside the doorway, his heart pounding in his chest.

A grizzled man near the back spoke up, his voice gruff. "You're suggesting the ritual, aren't you?"

The woman met his gaze without flinching. "Yes," she said simply. "It's our only choice."

The tension in the room broke into a dozen muttered objections, disbelief mixing with anger. Kai's pulse quickened as he watched them argue, his mind racing to keep up. She knew the term—the ritual—but only from the fairy tales he had read. *A maiden's sacrifice,* they had called it. An offering to the Snow King to appease his wrath and end his eternal winter.

But that was just a story. Wasn't it?

"This hasn't been done in decades," the grizzled man said, his tone incredulous. "We don't even know if it works."

"It doesn't matter," the woman replied. "The winter is growing worse. If we don't act, there won't be a village left to save."

Kai's stomach churned. He shifted slightly, and the movement caught the sharp-eyed woman's attention. Her gaze flicked to him, narrowing. "Kai," she said, her voice cold and clipped.

The room fell silent.

All eyes turned toward him, and Kai felt the weight of their stares like stones pressing against his chest. His throat tightened, and he forced himself to step forward, his movements stiff and awkward.

"I—" His voice cracked slightly, but he cleared it quickly. "I'm sorry. I didn't mean to interrupt."

The woman's lips thinned into a line. "You should be careful where you tread, Kai," she said, her tone edged with disapproval. "You've been lucky so far to escape the Snow King's wrath."

The words stung, though Kai couldn't say why. He swallowed hard, keeping his expression neutral. "I was only... curious about what's being discussed," he said, trying to sound casual.

The room was quiet for a moment, the tension thick enough to choke on. Then the woman let out a sharp laugh, bitter and cutting.

"Curious," she repeated, shaking her head. "Well, since you're here, let me tell you. We're deciding the future of this village. While you wander around with your head in the clouds, the rest of us are trying to survive."

Kai bristled, the words biting deeper than they should have. He tightened his grip on the cloak, forcing himself not to react.

"The elders are leaning toward the ritual," a younger man said, his voice quieter but no less grim. His gaze flicked between Kai and the sharp-eyed woman. "And there's talk that..." He hesitated, his voice trailing off.

"Say it," the woman said, her tone commanding.

The man sighed. "There's talk that Kai might be the best choice."

The words hung in the air, their weight crushing. Kai's breath hitched as a wave of cold swept over him—not from the air, but from the realization sinking in.

"Me?" he managed, his voice barely above a whisper.

The woman's gaze was unflinching. "You're young," she said. "Unattached. And you've always been... different. You don't belong here, not really. The sacrifice has to be meaningful, and if the Snow King values purity, well..."

Her words trailed off, but the implication was clear.

Kai's blood ran cold. The room spun slightly as he struggled to process what he was hearing. They weren't just discussing a sacrifice—they were discussing *him*.

His breath came faster, his mind racing.

I need to get out of here.

The walk back to Kai's house was a blur. Kai could still feel the weight of the elders' words pressing against his chest, his pulse racing with the enormity of what they were planning. Snow crunched beneath his boots as he stumbled through the empty streets, the cold air sharp in his lungs.

His body—Kai's body—moved instinctively, finding its way through the narrow, frost-covered alleys. The small, weathered cottage that Kai called home loomed ahead, its roof sagging under the weight of the snow. Kai didn't remember opening the door, but suddenly he was inside, his hands braced against the rough wood of the table in the center of the single room.

His breathing came in ragged gasps, visible in the air. He pressed his palms flat against the table, grounding himself, his thoughts a chaotic tangle of fear and disbelief.

They want me to be a sacrifice. To the Snow King.

The idea was absurd. Sacrifices were the stuff of myths, of fairy tales. They didn't happen in the real world—or even in a world as strange as this one. But the grim determination in the elders' voices had been real enough. And the way they'd spoken about Kai, as if he were already half-forgotten, half-dismissed...

His stomach turned, a bitter mix of anger and panic rising in his chest. He didn't know who Kai was—what kind of man he had been—but no one deserved to be spoken of like that.

Kai pushed off from the table, pacing the small space. The cottage was modest, its few possessions arranged with a practical neatness that contrasted sharply with the chaos in his mind. A bed in the corner was covered in a rough woolen blanket, a small stove provided meager heat, and a shelf held a handful of books and tools. It was a life pared down to the essentials, stripped of anything unnecessary.

His eyes landed on a small journal on the shelf. Kai reached for them without thinking, his fingers brushing against the rough edges of the pages.

They were notes, scrawled in a sharp, angular hand. The ink had smudged in places, but the tone was unmistakable—biting, sarcastic, and laced with frustration. One passage caught his eye:

"If I had a coin for every time this village decided I was their problem, I'd have enough to buy a ship and sail far away. But no, they need me here. To fix their roofs, to chase off the wolves, to be the scapegoat for every curse that falls on their heads. Gods help me, I wish I could leave."

Kai flipped through the rest of the pages, his fingers trembling slightly as he scanned the uneven script. The writing varied—some passages were scribbled hastily, as though penned in anger or desperation, while others were more measured, deliberate. Each entry painted a picture of a man caught between resentment and resignation, someone who had been forced to endure far more than anyone should.

Another line jumped out at him:

"Today they said the storm was my fault. Because I didn't attend the last offering at the shrine. How does one man control the snow? If I could, I'd bury this place in it and walk away without looking back."

Kai's throat tightened. He could almost hear the bitterness in the words, the sting of being blamed for things far beyond his control.

He turned to another page, this one calmer, but somehow more haunting.

"Gerhard came by today. He brought me bread and said nothing about the way the others were whispering. I think he wanted to talk, but we've had that fight before. He thinks I should speak up for myself. Maybe he's right. Maybe I should care about what they think. But I can't anymore. What's the point? He doesn't understand what it's like to carry this weight, to be the one they all turn to when things go wrong."

Kai paused, his breath catching. There was a tenderness in that passage, hidden beneath the frustration. It was clear that Gerhard had been important to Kai—the real Kai—in a way that went beyond mere friendship. But there was also a wall between them, a barrier that neither of them had been able to cross.

He turned to another page, his chest tightening as he read:

"There are days I think about leaving. Packing up what little I have and walking until the cold swallows me whole. At least then I wouldn't have to see their faces, hear their voices, feel the weight of their expectations. But then I think about Gerhard. How he'd look at me if I told him I was leaving. He wouldn't say much. He never does. But the disappointment would be there. I think that's the only thing that's kept me here this long."

Kai's fingers tightened around the page. The words were like a blow, the rawness of them cutting through the haze of his own confusion. The real Kai hadn't just wanted to escape—he had needed it, craved it, but something had held him back.

Would Gerhard have looked at me with disappointment? Kai wondered, his chest tightening. *Does he already?*

The thought lingered, heavy and unwelcome.

As he flipped to the final entry, his gaze caught on a single, stark line scrawled at the bottom of the page:

"I don't want to be here."

The simplicity of it made his breath hitch. There was no anger in the words, no sarcasm—just a quiet, aching truth.

Kai sat back, clutching the journal to his chest as though it might anchor him. He couldn't imagine what it had been like to write those words, to pour out such pain onto the page. The real Kai had been desperate, trapped in a place that saw him as expendable. And now, somehow, *he* was the one standing in his place, carrying the weight of a life that wasn't his.

But if the real Kai had wanted to escape, had dreamed of it so fiercely that it seeped into every word he wrote, then maybe, just maybe, he would have wanted this chance—this trade, this *freedom*.

Kai let out a shaky breath, placing the journal back on the shelf. His hands still trembled, his thoughts a tangled mess of anger, grief, and a strange, stubborn determination.

"I'll protect this life," he murmured to the quiet room, his voice barely above a whisper. "I'll protect *you*."

His voice grew steadier with each word, the determination in his chest solidifying into something fierce. He had no idea how to escape this village, let alone how to find his way back to his world, but he refused to give up.

He moved quickly, searching the room for anything that might help. The sword by the door caught his eye—a sturdy weapon with a simple leather grip. He hefted it, testing the weight. It felt awkward in his hands, but the unfamiliar strength of Kai's body gave him a faint edge.

"We'll figure this out," he said aloud, his voice echoing in the empty room. "I don't know how, but we will."

Outside, the wind howled, rattling the windows. The storm was building again, the frost creeping further across the glass. Kai glanced at the window, the eerie pull in his chest returning.

For the briefest moment, he thought he heard something—low, faint, and distant. A whisper carried on the wind, the words too soft to decipher.

His grip tightened on the sword.

"I'm not afraid of you," he said, though the words were mostly for himself.

The frost on the window shimmered faintly, and Kai turned away, his mind racing with possibilities. Whatever this world wanted from him, he wasn't going to give it easily.

The storm descended with startling speed.

Kai stood at the window, watching as snow began to fall in thick, relentless sheets. It wasn't the gentle snowfall he was used to back home—the kind that quieted the world and softened its edges. This was something far more intense, the wind howling like a living thing, tearing through the village with a ferocity that made the walls of Kai's cottage groan.

He pressed a hand to the frosted glass, the chill seeping through his palm. The snow buried the cobblestone streets in minutes, the rooftops of nearby houses quickly blending into the endless white. The flickering lanterns outside cast dim, flickering halos of light, barely cutting through the swirling chaos.

The cold outside wasn't just physical—it had a presence. He could feel it pressing against the walls of the cottage, seeping into the cracks, settling deep in his chest. It felt as though the storm wasn't simply raging around him but *watching* him, waiting for something.

Kai's fingers tightened around the hilt of the sword he had propped against the wall. He hadn't let go of it since the meeting with the elders, the weight of it grounding him in a way nothing else could.

As the wind screamed outside, he turned back to the room, pacing to keep his body moving. He couldn't shake the sensation that something—or someone—was out there, hidden in the blinding snow.

His thoughts drifted to the Snow King, the figure he'd read about in the strange book that had brought him here. In the stories, he was a phantom, an ancient figure cursed to rule a frozen kingdom, luring others into his endless winter. The villagers' fear of him was palpable, but Kai wasn't sure if he believed the tales—or if he even had the luxury of doubting them.

His chest tightened with that same eerie pull he'd felt earlier, a faint tug deep inside him. He wrapped Kai's cloak tighter around himself, trying to ignore the sensation. "It's just nerves," he muttered, though his voice lacked conviction.

The storm grew louder, the wind rattling the shutters with violent force. For a moment, he thought he heard something within the storm—a low, mournful note, like a distant horn or the echo of a voice. His heart skipped a beat, his grip on the sword tightening.

He stepped closer to the window, peering into the swirling white. The snow was so thick it was impossible to see more than a few feet, but his breath caught as he thought he saw movement—a dark shape cutting through the storm, steady and deliberate.

Kai froze.

The figure trudged closer, its silhouette tall and broad, shoulders hunched against the wind. He took a step back, his mind racing. If it was a villager, they'd be struggling in this weather. But this figure moved with purpose, as though the storm itself bent around them.

His pulse quickened. For a wild moment, he wondered if it could be the Snow King, drawn to him by some unseen force.

The figure stepped into the faint halo of light cast by the lantern outside, and his breath left him in a rush.

It was Gerhard.

Relief flooded him, followed immediately by confusion. What was he doing out in this storm? His hair was damp with frost, his heavy cloak dusted with snow, but he moved with calm determination, his jaw set as he approached the cottage.

Kai hesitated, the tension in his chest unresolved. He couldn't shake the feeling that there was more to this storm than just wind and snow. He stepped toward the door, his boots scuffing against the wooden floor, and paused with his hand on the latch.

His mind raced. Gerhard was the one person he trusted in this strange world, the only tether he had to something solid. But the intensity of his presence earlier, the way he'd looked at him like he was his entire world—it unnerved him almost as much as it comforted him.

The latch felt cold under his fingers. He exhaled slowly, then pulled the door open.

The wind hit him like a wall, icy and sharp, forcing him to brace himself against the frame. Gerhard stood just outside, his dark hair plastered to his forehead and his breath visible in the frigid air. His sharp blue eyes met his, and for a moment, neither of them spoke.

"I told you it wasn't safe," he said finally, his voice rough but steady. "You should've stayed with me."

Kai blinked, unsure how to respond. He stepped aside, wordlessly motioning him inside. Gerhard didn't hesitate, ducking through the doorway and shaking the snow from his shoulders. The door groaned as Kai shut it against the storm, and the wind's howls dulled to a low roar.

Gerhard turned to face him, his expression a mix of relief and frustration. "You've been avoiding me," he said, his tone direct but not unkind.

Kai faltered, the accusation catching him off guard. "I haven't—" he began, but Gerhard raised an eyebrow, silencing him with a look.

"You've been acting strange," he said. "Since the meeting. Since... before that, even."

Kai's heart pounded. Gerhard's eyes were too sharp, too focused, as though he could see through him. He looked away, tightening his grip on the cloak around his shoulders.

"I'm fine," he said, his voice lower than he intended.

Gerhard stepped closer, his broad frame filling the small space. "You're not," he said simply. "But we'll talk about it later."

Before Kai could respond, a loud crack echoed outside, like a tree splitting under the weight of the storm. Gerhard's eyes snapped toward the window, his jaw tightening.

"This storm isn't natural," he said quietly.

Chapter 2

"You shouldn't be out alone in weather like this," Gerhard said, his voice low and tight. His eyes swept over him, and there was something piercing in his gaze, as though he was searching for cracks in the person he thought he knew.

"I can handle a little snow," Kai replied, attempting to summon Kai's sarcastic tone. He stepped back to give him space, trying not to let her unease show. The low timbre of his voice still felt strange, like it belonged to someone else entirely.

Gerhard shot him a look, his brow furrowed. "It's not the snow I'm worried about."

He moved toward the center of the room, his movements steady and deliberate. The firelight flickered across his face, illuminating the tension in his jaw and the way his hands gripped the back of the chair as he turned to face her.

"They're talking about you," he said, his voice dropping into a near-whisper. "At the meeting. The elders, the others... they're saying you should be the sacrifice."

Kai froze.

The words weren't a surprise—not really—but hearing them spoken aloud, in Gerhard's steady, gravelly voice, made them hit harder. He looked away, his fingers tightening around the edge of the cloak draped over his shoulders.

"They've always wanted me out of the way," he said, the words spilling out before he could stop them. They came out sharper than he intended, tinged with a bitterness that felt almost natural, almost like *Kai*. "This is just their excuse."

Gerhard frowned, his knuckles whitening as his grip on the chair tightened. "That doesn't make it right."

Kai's chest tightened at the anger in his voice—anger not directed at him, but at the situation, at the injustice of it all. He wanted to say something, to deflect the weight of his frustration, but he couldn't find the words.

"They're scared," Gerhard continued, his tone softer now. "The winter, the crops failing... They're looking for someone to blame, and you..." He trailed off, shaking his head.

"I make it easy for them," Kai finished, forcing a wry smile.

Gerhard glanced up at him, his expression softening in a way that made his stomach twist. "You don't make it easy for anyone," he said, the faintest hint of a smile tugging at the corner of his lips. "But that's not a bad thing."

The warmth in his voice sent a flicker of something unfamiliar through his chest—something almost like shame. He didn't deserve this kindness, this fierce loyalty. Not when he wasn't even the person Gerhard thought he was defending.

He stepped closer, his eyes meeting Kai's with a quiet intensity. "Listen to me," he said, his voice low. "I won't let them hurt you. I don't care what the elders say, what the village thinks—I'll find a way to stop this."

Kai's breath caught. The raw sincerity in his words, in his eyes, was almost overwhelming. He opened his mouth to respond, to tell him not to waste his energy, but the lump in his throat wouldn't let him speak.

Instead, he managed a laugh—a dry, hollow sound that felt more like Kai than himself. "You're going to take on the whole village by yourself?" he said, raising an eyebrow. "That's ambitious, even for you."

Gerhard didn't laugh. He didn't even smile.

"Don't pretend this isn't serious," he said quietly, his tone cutting through his bravado. "I've known you long enough to know when you're scared, even if you won't admit it."

Kai's stomach churned. He turned away, his hands clenched into fists at his sides. The truth was, he was right—he *was* scared. But admitting it felt dangerous, like peeling back a layer of armor he couldn't afford to lose.

"I'll figure it out," he said finally, his voice steady but thin. "I always do."

Gerhard stepped closer, his hand brushing against his arm. The touch was brief, but it lingered, a quiet reassurance that made his chest ache.

"Don't push me away," he said softly.

Kai swallowed hard, unable to meet his gaze. The words hit too close, stirring something he didn't want to name.

Gerhard pulled back, the faint tension in the room dissipating as he moved toward the fire. He stood there for a moment, his broad frame silhouetted against the flickering light, before turning back to him.

"Get some rest," he said, his voice lighter now, but still firm. "Tomorrow, we'll figure out a plan."

Kai nodded, though his thoughts were anything but settled. As Gerhard turned and opened the door, the storm outside surged, snow whipping against the frame as he stepped into the night.

He watched him go, his chest tight with unspoken words.

Morning came too quickly.

Kai stirred on the bed, the faint light of dawn spilling through the frosted window. His body ached in ways he hadn't expected, every muscle stiff as though he'd spent the night hauling firewood instead of sleeping. It took him a moment to remember why his limbs felt so strange, why his hands were broad and rough, and why the weight of the blanket pressed so heavily against a chest that wasn't his. *Hauling firewood, really?*

His breath fogged in the chilly air as he sat up, the room around his cold and quiet. For a moment, he let himself linger in the strange stillness, his mind heavy with fragments of the previous night. Gerhard's words replayed in his head, the quiet conviction in his voice as he promised to protect *Kai*.

He rubbed his face with one hand, his fingers scraping over the rough stubble along his jawline. "Get it together," he muttered under his breath, his voice unfamiliar and low.

After throwing on the thick woolen cloak he'd left by the bed, Kai stepped outside. The cold hit him immediately, sharp and bracing, but the village was already awake. Villagers moved through the snow-dusted streets, their faces drawn and tense as they went about their business. The faint hum of activity filled the air—voices low and clipped, the thud of axes splitting wood, the creak of carts struggling over uneven ground.

Kai pulled the cloak tighter around his shoulders and started walking, his boots crunching through the snow. He didn't know exactly where he was going, but staying still felt impossible.

The weight of the villagers' stares was unmistakable. People glanced at him as he passed, their gazes sharp with wariness. Some quickly looked away, as though avoiding eye contact would save them from whatever trouble they thought *Kai* would bring. Others whispered in hushed tones; their words barely audible over the wind.

He caught snatches of the murmurs: *"The elders are right." "It's for the good of the village." "He's always been... different."*

Kai's stomach churned, but he kept walking, his head held high. He didn't know if Kai had been the type to confront these people or ignore them, but he knew he couldn't let them see him falter.

At the edge of the village, he paused near a small, snow-covered market square. A group of young men leaned against the side of a building, their breath visible in the cold air. They were laughing, their voices carrying easily across the open space.

One of them, a wiry boy with a shock of blond hair, caught sight of him and nudged his companion.

"Well, if it isn't the village hero," he said loudly, his tone dripping with mockery.

The others chuckled, their eyes glinting with a mixture of amusement and disdain. Kai's steps slowed, but he didn't stop. He had no idea who these men were or how Kai might have handled them, but their taunts set her teeth on edge.

"Surprised he's not off hiding behind Gerhard again," the blond one added, smirking.

Kai froze. The words hit harder than he expected, not because they were cruel, but because they carried an unspoken truth. The villagers knew about Gerhard and Kai—or at least suspected. And in a place like this, that kind of bond wasn't just frowned upon; it was ammunition.

He clenched his fists under the cloak. For a moment, he wanted to snap back, to let his voice ring out across the square. But the weight of Kai's life pressed down on him, reminding him that he didn't fully understand the consequences of his actions here. The consequences for Gerhard, if nothing else.

Instead, he forced his shoulders to relax and kept walking, the laughter fading behind him.

The village's small blacksmith workshop caught his attention, its forge cold and quiet. Kai hesitated, glancing at the weathered sign above the door before stepping inside.

The interior was neat, the tools arranged with the same care he'd seen in Gerhard's personal workspace. The air still smelled faintly of soot and metal, but the forge itself was dark, its fire long extinguished.

Kai wandered through the space, his fingers brushing over the polished handles of hammers and the smooth surface of an anvil. He wondered if this was where Gerhard spent most of his days, working alone while the rest of the village gossiped about him and Kai.

His chest tightened at the thought. He could see why Kai might have been drawn to someone like Gerhard—a man who was steady and unflinching, who carried himself with quiet strength despite the villagers' scorn.

But Kai hadn't been easy, either. The sharp quips in his notes, the defiance in the way he carried himself—Kai could feel the tension of a life spent pushing against the boundaries of a small, unforgiving world.

He exhaled slowly, his breath misting in the cool air. "How did you live like this?" he murmured, his voice low.

There was no answer, of course. Only the faint creak of the building settling under the weight of the snow.

As Kai stepped back outside, he spotted a group of women nearby, their heads bent together in quiet conversation. They glanced at him briefly before quickly turning away, their whispers barely audible.

"...doesn't belong here..."

"...Gerhard always..."

Kai's jaw tightened, but he forced himself to walk past them without a word. He was beginning to piece together the puzzle of Kai's life—the way the villagers saw him as both an outsider and a threat, someone who didn't fit their narrow definition of what a man should be.

But what stung the most was the way Gerhard's name kept coming up, always tied to Kai in a way that felt both protective and damning. Their bond wasn't just an open secret—it was a weapon; one the villagers were ready to use against them both.

Kai's hands clenched into fists again, but this time, he didn't relax them.

They don't deserve him, he thought, the anger flaring hot and sudden in his chest. *They don't deserve either of them.*

Kai hadn't made it far through the village before a boy ran up to him, panting and red-faced from the cold. He couldn't have been older than twelve, his small frame bundled in a patched coat that seemed two sizes too large.

"The elders want to see you," he said, his voice high and uncertain. He didn't linger after delivering the message, darting off as quickly as he'd come, his boots leaving shallow prints in the snow.

Kai watched him disappear around a corner, his stomach sinking.

The square in front of the meeting hall was deserted by the time he arrived, its silence thick and oppressive. Frost clung to the edges of the windows, and the tall wooden doors seemed heavier than before. He hesitated, his hand hovering near the latch.

Stay calm, he told himself. *You're Kai. Act like Kai.*

He pushed the door open.

Inside, the elders were seated at a long wooden table, their faces drawn and severe. The same sharp-eyed woman from before sat at the head, her posture ramrod straight. To her left was the grizzled elder Kai recognized from the previous meeting, his lips pulled into a frown. The others regarded her with thinly veiled disdain, their gazes cold and assessing.

"Kai," the sharp-eyed woman said, her voice cutting through the air like a blade. "Sit."

Kai's heart thudded in his chest as he stepped forward, his boots scuffing against the worn floorboards. He lowered himself onto the only empty stool, its rough surface creaking under Kai's weight.

"You know why you're here," the woman said without preamble.

Kai met her gaze, forcing himself to keep his expression neutral. "Enlighten me," he said, the words coming out sharper than he intended. He winced internally but pressed on, adopting a tone he hoped sounded like Kai's usual bravado. "You've never been shy about sharing your opinions."

The woman's lips pressed into a thin line, but she didn't rise to the bait. "The village is on the brink of ruin," she said. "The winter is worse than any we've faced before, and if it continues, we'll all starve."

Kai's stomach tightened, but he didn't speak.

The grizzled elder leaned forward, his hands clasped together on the table. "The Snow King's curse has held this land for generations," he said. "It's time we put an end to it."

"And you think a ritual sacrifice is the way to do that," Kai said flatly.

The sharp-eyed woman narrowed her gaze. "It's worked before."

"Has it?" Kai shot back, unable to keep the edge out of his voice. "Because last I checked, you're all still here, freezing in the snow."

A murmur rippled through the group, but the woman silenced it with a raised hand. "You think this is a joke?" she asked, her tone icy. "This isn't about you, Kai. This is about the survival of the village."

Kai bit the inside of his cheek, struggling to keep his composure. The woman's words were harsh, but there was no mistaking the way she said *you*, as though Kai were already an outsider.

"You've made your disdain for me pretty clear," Kai said, leaning back in his chair. "Why not just come out and say it? You want me to volunteer because you think my life is worth less than yours."

The room fell silent.

The woman's expression didn't waver, but her eyes flashed with something sharp. "Your life has always been your own to squander," she said. "But now, it's the village's to claim. The Snow King demands a sacrifice, and you…" Her gaze swept over Kai, her mouth curling into a faint sneer. "You're the logical choice."

Kai's breath caught.

The other elders murmured their agreement, their voices blending into a low, ominous hum. He caught snippets of their reasoning—Kai's defiance, his lack of family ties, the rumors surrounding him and Gerhard—all laid bare in clinical, detached tones.

They weren't just justifying the sacrifice. They were justifying why it had to be *him*.

His hands clenched into fists under the table, his nails digging into Kai's calloused palms. "This is insane," he said, his voice low but trembling with anger. "You're asking me to throw myself to a monster for your chance at survival. A chance."

"You have no choice," the sharp-eyed woman replied, her tone cold and final.

Kai's heart pounded in his chest, his mind racing for a way out. But the elders' expressions told him everything he needed to know. They weren't looking for his consent. They were expecting his compliance.

"This meeting is over," the woman said, rising to her feet. The other elders followed suit, their chairs scraping against the floor. "We expect your cooperation. If you resist…" She let the words hang in the air, the unspoken threat heavy with implication.

Kai stood, his legs unsteady beneath him. His throat felt tight, his chest heavy with frustration and fear. But he forced himself to nod, his jaw set in defiance.

"Fine," he said, his voice steady despite the storm raging inside him.

He turned and left without another word, the door slamming shut behind him.

The cold air outside hit him like a slap, but it did little to clear his mind. The weight of the elders' decision pressed down, suffocating in its finality.

He had no idea how to fight this.

But he knew one thing: he wasn't going to let them destroy Kai's life without a fight.

Fenrir

Fenrir prowled through the frozen halls of the Winter Court, his massive wolf form moving with a silent grace. The air was sharp, biting even to him, though his thick fur absorbed most of the chill.

The throne room loomed ahead, its frost-lined walls glinting faintly in the dim light filtering through ice-covered windows. Fenrir stopped at the edge of the great chamber, his sharp golden eyes scanning the space. The Snow King was not here—not that he'd expected otherwise. His king often drifted between shadows, lost in the endless storm of his own magic.

Outside, the storm raged on, endless and unrelenting, its icy winds howling through the night like a living thing. Snow battered the castle's exterior, obscuring the landscape beyond in a swirling haze of white.

He'd walked this storm many times before. It was his constant companion, the manifestation of the curse that had bound them all. But tonight, something about it felt different.

Fenrir's ears flicked forward, his body tensing as the storm shifted. It wasn't a change in its ferocity—no, the winds howled as fiercely as ever—but there was something else. A ripple. A faint vibration that rolled through the ice and snow, brushing against his senses like a whisper in the dark.

His hackles rose instinctively, the fur along his spine bristling as he sniffed the air. The scent was faint but foreign, a trace of something warm and alive that didn't belong here. Magic. It pulsed faintly, a subtle thrum that resonated with the storm's fury but carried a note of discord, like a single warm ember smoldering within a sea of frost.

Fenrir growled softly, his claws digging into the stone beneath him. The storm had been unchanging for centuries. For this ripple to disturb its endless monotony meant only one thing: something new had entered Winter's domain. Something—or someone.

With a powerful leap, Fenrir launched himself through the shattered window, the icy winds slamming into him as he landed in the deep snow below. He shook himself, scattering frost from his fur, and lifted his nose to the air. The scent was there, faint but unmistakable. It tugged at his instincts, urging him to follow.

The storm closed around him as he began to move, his powerful frame cutting through the snow like a shadow in the night. He prowled through the frozen wasteland, his golden eyes sharp and alert as the ripple of magic grew stronger with each step.

The storm's winds screamed as Fenrir loped through the endless drifts of snow, the weight of the cold pressing down on him. The ripple of warmth remained a distant pull, faint and elusive, but steady enough to guide him through the desolation. It carried him beyond the castle's reach, far into the frozen wilds where even the storm rarely allowed wanderers to venture.

It wasn't long before Fenrir caught the scent of smoke, faint but distinct against the icy bite of the wind. He slowed, his ears twitching as he crested a ridge that overlooked a small village nestled in the snow-draped valley below. Its once-sturdy cottages huddled close together, their roofs sagging beneath the weight of ice. Smoke trickled weakly from chimneys, barely visible against the swirling snow, and the dim glow of candlelight flickered faintly through frost-covered windows.

Fenrir's sharp eyes swept the village, noting the signs of decay that had spread like frostbite. Doors hung crooked on their hinges, their wood warped and brittle. Wagons and tools were buried in snowdrifts that no one had bothered—or had the strength—to clear. The central well, once the lifeblood of the settlement, was frozen solid, its stone rim coated in a thick sheen of ice.

He moved closer, his massive form blending seamlessly with the shadows as he descended into the village. His steps were silent, his golden eyes gleaming faintly as he prowled along the edges of the settlement. Despite the storm, the air here felt stifling, heavy with despair and something darker—something that made his fur prickle with unease.

The people were ghosts of themselves. Fenrir crouched behind the ruins of an abandoned cottage, watching as a woman trudged through the snow toward the well, her frame stooped and gaunt. Her breath puffed weakly in the cold, her thin shawl clinging uselessly to her emaciated frame. She reached the well, her hands trembling as she tried to chip away at the ice with a dull, rusted knife. Her movements were slow, hopeless, as though she expected no water to come.

Further ahead, a group of villagers huddled around a small fire in the center of the square. Their faces were pale and drawn, their voices low and filled with the kind of fear that came from too many nights spent bracing against death's approach. Fenrir's sharp ears twitched as he caught fragments of their conversation.

"They say the storm grows worse each year," one man muttered, his gloved hands trembling as he held them to the meager fire. "The cold will take us all if this keeps on."

"It's the curse," another replied, his voice tight with anger and despair. "The Winter Court brought this on us. Their magic seeps into the land, poisoning it. We were fools to think we could live so close to that accursed castle."

A third voice, softer and tinged with fear, whispered, "But the ritual... the old ways... They say it appeases the storm. They say it—"

"Don't speak of that!" the first man snapped, his tone sharp enough to cut through the howling wind. "We've done enough. No more sacrifices. It doesn't work. It never worked."

The group fell silent, their faces grim as the fire sputtered weakly between them. Fenrir's ears flattened against his head as unease coiled tighter in his chest. He knew the village had always struggled against the storm's edges, but this... this was different. The Winter Court's curse had grown beyond its borders, its icy tendrils creeping into the lives of those who had no part in their tragedy.

Fenrir shifted his gaze, his attention pulled to the distant edge of the village where the ripple of warmth called to him again. He moved silently through the snow, his massive paws leaving faint imprints as he followed the trail toward the source.

As he neared, the scent grew stronger—warmer, alive. It was faint, a thread of life struggling against the frost's grip, but it carried something else too. Something that felt out of place, like a note of music played off-key.

Fenrir stopped at the edge of a small clearing, his breath misting in the air as he lowered his body into a crouch. Through the swirling snow, he saw him: a young man, his form hunched and shivering as he trudged through the drifts. His movements were awkward, uncertain, as though he were unfamiliar with his own body.

Fenrir's golden eyes narrowed as he studied the boy, his instincts prickling with unease. The storm seemed to curl around him, the frost clinging to his form but never quite touching him. And the ripple of magic—it radiated from him like a faint pulse, the warmth of it foreign yet familiar, like something Fenrir couldn't quite name.

For a moment, he hesitated. Then, silently, he began to follow.

Fenrir stalked closer, his massive form moving silently through the snow. His golden eyes stayed fixed on the figure ahead, every step measured, every muscle coiled and ready. As the storm curled and swirled, he caught glimpses of the man—a willowy figure wrapped in ill-fitted clothing, his arms crossed tightly over his chest as though trying to shield himself from the relentless cold.

Man, not boy, Fenrir corrected himself, his sharp gaze taking in the subtle details. This wasn't some fragile, naive youth. The set of the man's jaw, the determined squint of his eyes against the driving snow, spoke of someone who had faced storms far fiercer than the one around them. Yet there was an unfamiliarity in his movements, an awkwardness that clashed with the quiet strength he exuded.

His clothes, though practical, hung oddly on his frame—too loose in some places, too tight in others. They weren't tailored to him, nor did they seem like the sort of garments anyone in the village would wear. It was as though he had been dressed in haste or had scavenged whatever he could find. Fenrir's nose twitched as he took in the faint, lingering scent of magic that clung to him—chaotic, foreign, and wholly out of place in this frozen expanse.

The man stumbled slightly, his foot catching on a drift of snow. He swore softly under his breath, his voice carried faintly on the wind. Fenrir froze, his ears flicking forward as he caught the sound. There was something peculiar about the way he spoke—his tone held none of the clipped precision of Winter's inhabitants nor the lyrical cadence of Summer's. It was rougher, heavier, and unfamiliar in a way that made Fenrir's hackles rise.

The man regained his footing and pressed onward, the frost clinging stubbornly to his boots and the hem of his coat. He paused suddenly, his head lifting as though he sensed something watching him. Fenrir crouched low, his breath misting in the air as he melted into the shadows of the storm. The man turned slowly, his dark eyes scanning the trees with unease, his hands tightening around the edges of his coat.

"Who's there?" he called, his voice firm despite the tremor that edged it.

Fenrir didn't move. He studied the man intently, the ripple of warmth that radiated from him growing stronger as he spoke. This was no ordinary traveler. He didn't belong here—his presence was as foreign to the Winter Court as the Summer King's flames.

The man took a cautious step back, his gaze darting nervously over the snow. "If you're trying to scare me, you're doing a damn good job," he muttered, his breath fogging faintly in the icy air.

Fenrir hesitated for a moment longer before stepping forward, his massive form emerging from the shadows like a ghost from the storm. The man froze, his eyes widening as he took in the sight of the enormous silver wolf, its fur shimmering faintly in the dim light. For a moment, neither moved—the storm seemed to hold its breath as the two regarded each other.

"You've got to be kidding me," the man whispered, his voice tinged with disbelief. His hand twitched toward the small knife strapped to his belt, but he didn't draw it. Instead, he took a cautious step back, his gaze locked on Fenrir's golden eyes. "What the hell is this place?"

Fenrir tilted his head slightly, his ears twitching as he took in the man's words. He wasn't speaking to Fenrir, not really—his question was more an echo of his own confusion, his own disorientation.

The wolf's golden gaze swept over the man once more, noting the tension in his shoulders, the way his breath came fast and shallow. He wasn't afraid of Fenrir—not in the way most humans were when faced with a predator of his size. No, his fear was different. It wasn't Fenrir himself that unsettled him—it was the storm, the cold, the strangeness of a world that seemed to reject his presence.

For the first time in centuries, Fenrir felt something stir deep within him—something he hadn't felt since the early days of his service to the Snow King. It wasn't quite curiosity, nor was it pity. It was a pull, faint but undeniable, that tied him to this awkward, lithe man who didn't seem to fit in his own skin, much less the frozen expanse around him.

The man straightened slightly, his dark eyes narrowing as he stared at Fenrir. "You're not going to eat me, are you?" he asked, his voice laced with a mix of sarcasm and nervous energy.

Fenrir let out a low, rumbling growl—not a threat, but an acknowledgment. His tail flicked once, his golden eyes gleaming faintly with something almost amused. The man blinked, his lips parting as though he weren't sure whether to be relieved or more alarmed.

"Well, that's reassuring," he muttered, his breath hitching as Fenrir stepped closer. He didn't move to run, nor did he reach for his knife. Instead, he stood his ground, his gaze steady despite the tension in his frame. "You're... not just a wolf, are you?"

Fenrir paused, his ears twitching at the question. The man's perceptiveness surprised him, though it shouldn't have. There was something sharp about him, something that spoke of a mind accustomed to reading between the lines, to seeing what others missed.

After a long moment, Fenrir stepped back, his golden gaze lingering on the man before turning away. He padded silently through the snow, his movements unhurried as he disappeared into the storm.

Behind him, the man let out a shaky breath, his voice barely audible over the wind. "What the hell is going on?"

Fenrir didn't answer. He had seen enough. The ripple of warmth that radiated from the man, the chaotic magic that clung to him like a second skin—it all pointed to one undeniable truth.

The Winter Court had been shaken, and this man—whoever he was—was the reason.

Fenrir moved silently through the frost-laden corridors of the Winter Court, his massive silver form blending seamlessly with the cold shadows. His sharp golden eyes scanned the familiar halls, their intricate ice patterns glinting faintly in the dim light. The oppressive silence of the castle pressed against him, heavy and suffocating, as if the walls themselves mourned the state of their frozen king.

The great hall loomed ahead, its massive doors groaning faintly as Fenrir pushed them open with a single powerful shove of his shoulder. The throne room stretched before him, vast and desolate. At its heart sat the Snow King, a figure carved from ice, his frost-lined cloak pooling around him like frozen mist. He stared out over the frozen figures of his court, his pale blue eyes distant and unfeeling.

Fenrir padded forward, his movements graceful and deliberate, each step light against the frost-covered floor. His breath misted faintly in the frigid air as he stopped at the base of the dais, his golden gaze fixed on the Snow King.

The silence stretched between them like a taut string, until finally, Fenrir rumbled a low, guttural growl to announce his presence.

The Snow King's head tilted slightly, his pale eyes flicking down to meet Fenrir's golden gaze. "Fenrir," he said, his voice a cold whisper that seemed to carry the weight of centuries. "You return."

Fenrir's ears flicked back briefly before he let out a low huff, his frustration barely restrained. He took a step forward, his sharp gaze unwavering. The warmth he'd sensed in the woods, the ripple of foreign magic—it all demanded attention, yet here sat the king, frozen in his own apathy.

"The storm," Fenrir growled, his voice carrying the deep resonance of his wolf form. "It reacts to something. Someone."

The Snow King's frosted features didn't change. "And?"

Fenrir let out a sharp, exasperated breath, his claws scratching faintly against the ice as he moved closer. "I found a man," he said, his voice rumbling with urgency. "In the forest. He carries magic unlike anything I've felt before—chaotic and foreign. And the storm... it stirs around him."

The Snow King's pale lips curled faintly, though the gesture was more disdain than amusement. "A single man in the forest," he said flatly. "Hardly a matter of concern."

Fenrir bristled, his tail flicking sharply as he resisted the urge to bare his teeth. "This is not just about him," he growled, his voice thick with frustration. "The storm is spreading. It's affecting the villages—the humans are suffering under its weight. There was talk of sacrifices."

The Snow King finally moved, his frosted cloak shifting as he rose slowly from the throne. Each step he took down the dais was deliberate, the frost beneath his feet cracking faintly with his weight. His pale blue eyes narrowed as they fixed on Fenrir, their icy intensity enough to send a chill even through the wolf's thick fur.

"I don't see how this involves the Winter Court," the Snow King said, his tone dripping with disinterest. "Humans are of no consequence. Their lives are fleeting by nature."

Fenrir's hackles rose, his golden eyes blazing as he stepped closer, his massive form looming in the frost-laden air. "They should matter," he snarled. "This curse—it was yours to bear. And now it seeps beyond your borders, dragging them into your misery."

The Snow King stopped at the edge of the dais, his head tilting slightly as he studied Fenrir. "You speak as though this storm is sentient," he said coolly. "It is mine, and it does as I command."

"No," Fenrir snapped, his voice a deep growl that echoed through the hall. "It's growing beyond your control. You don't see it because you refuse to look."

The Snow King's eyes sharpened, the frost around him spreading in jagged veins. "Careful, Fenrir," he said, his voice dropping to a cutting whisper. "You tread dangerously close to insubordination."

Fenrir held his ground, his breath misting heavily as he glared up at the king. "And you tread closer to ruin with every moment you waste. What if this is a sign, my king?"

The Snow King's frosted lips pressed into a thin line, his pale features unmoving as his icy gaze bore into Fenrir. The tension between them was suffocating, the weight of centuries of loyalty and frustration clashing in the frigid air.

Finally, the Snow King exhaled a soft, disdainful sigh. "And what would you have me do, Fenrir?" he asked, his tone laced with mockery. "Chase shadows in the woods?"

Fenrir growled low, his tail lashing once before he stepped back. "Come with me," he said firmly. "See him for yourself. Feel the magic he carries. If you refuse to act, then at least witness the destruction with your own eyes."

The Snow King tilted his head, his pale blue eyes narrowing. For a moment, the frost beneath his feet stilled, the tension in the room tightening like a vice. Then, slowly, he turned away, his frosted cloak trailing behind him as he ascended the dais once more.

"I will not waste my time on ghosts," the Snow King said, his voice cold and final. "Leave me be."

Fenrir's golden eyes blazed with frustration as he watched the king retreat to his throne, his frosted silhouette blending with the ice around him. The dismissal was as sharp as a blade, cutting deeper than Fenrir would ever admit.

With a low, rumbling growl, Fenrir turned and padded from the throne room, his claws clicking faintly against the frost-covered floor. The weight of the Snow King's indifference pressed heavily against him, fueling the fire of his resolve.

As he slipped back into the biting chill of the storm, Fenrir glanced over his shoulder, his sharp golden eyes narrowing as the gates of the Winter Court closed behind him.

"If you won't act," he muttered under his breath, his voice a low, guttural growl, "then I will."

Night descended over the village, bringing with it a hush that felt unnatural. The snowstorm had faded into a stillness so profound it made Kai's skin crawl.

Kai's home was suffocatingly quiet. He sat near the fire, the flames casting flickering shadows against the walls, but even the warmth couldn't chase away the chill that had settled deep in his bones. He gripped the hilt of the sword he'd taken from beside the door, the leather-wrapped handle comforting in his hand.

The weight of the elders' warning still hung heavy in his chest. He wanted to scream, to rage against their audacity, but what good would it do? They'd already made their decision, and the villagers wouldn't stand in their way.

His gaze shifted to the frost-covered window. Outside, the moon hung low in the sky, its pale light spilling across the snow-drenched streets. A restless energy thrummed through him, a sharp pull in his chest that made it impossible to sit still.

Before he could second-guess himself, he stood and grabbed the heavy cloak draped over the back of the chair. The cold greeted him like a slap as he stepped outside, the village bathed in silver light. The snow glowed eerily under the moon, and his breath curled in the air as he started walking.

He didn't have a destination in mind—he only needed to *move*, to feel the icy wind on his face and clear his thoughts. The crunch of snow under his boots was the only sound, the village quiet as if it were holding its breath.

The snowstorm had eased, leaving the forest eerily silent. Each crunch of his boots against the frozen ground sounded unnaturally loud, the only disturbance in the heavy stillness. Kai adjusted his ill-fitting coat, wrapping it tighter around himself as the icy wind bit at his cheeks. The coat didn't fit properly—too loose in the shoulders, too tight at the sleeves—but it was all he could find.

A shiver rippled through him, but it wasn't just from the cold. The deeper he ventured into the woods, the stronger the sensation grew—the inexplicable pull that gnawed at his chest. It wasn't painful, but it was unsettling, a feeling he couldn't explain.

The air seemed to thicken as he pushed forward, the shadows of the trees looming taller with each step. The moonlight filtering through the branches painted the snow in fractured patterns, making the ground look almost alive. He swallowed hard, his nerves fraying as he glanced around, half expecting something to lunge out of the darkness.

And then he heard it.

A faint rustle, barely audible over the soft crunch of snow. His body stiffened, his fingers tightening around the edges of his coat as his breath caught. He turned slowly, his eyes darting toward the sound. The shadows between the trees seemed to ripple, as though something moved within them.

"Who's there?" Kai called, his voice firm despite the tremor edging his words.

The forest didn't answer. The wind stilled, and the silence deepened, pressing against his ears like cotton. He squinted into the darkness, every muscle in his body coiled with tension.

A low crunch broke the silence—a sound that didn't belong to the natural creak of the trees or the settling snow. It was deliberate, measured. Footsteps.

Kai took a cautious step back, his boots sinking into the snow as his eyes scanned the treeline. His heart hammered in his chest, his pulse loud enough to drown out rational thought. "If you're trying to scare me, you're doing a damn good job," he muttered, his voice shaking despite his attempt at sarcasm.

The movement came again, closer this time. Kai froze, his breath hitching as a figure emerged from the shadows.

It wasn't human.

The wolf was enormous, its silver fur gleaming faintly in the moonlight, each ripple of its muscles fluid and deliberate. Golden eyes locked onto his, unblinking and impossibly intense. The air around it seemed to shift, the frost curling at its paws as though responding to its presence.

Kai's body refused to move. The sheer size of the creature was enough to root him in place, but it was the intelligence in its eyes that truly unnerved him. This wasn't an ordinary wolf. He could feel it in the way the storm seemed to still, the air holding its breath as they stared at each other.

"You've got to be kidding me," Kai whispered, his voice barely audible. His hand twitched toward the knife strapped to his belt, but he didn't draw it. He wasn't sure why—whether it was fear or the certainty that such a weapon would be useless against this creature.

The wolf didn't move. Its gaze remained fixed on him, as though it were studying him, weighing something unseen. The golden glow of its eyes was mesmerizing, pulling at Kai in a way that made his chest tighten. The pull he'd felt earlier—the strange, unexplainable tug—now surged to the forefront, stronger than ever.

"What the hell is this place?" Kai muttered under his breath, his voice tinged with frustration and unease. His gaze darted over the wolf's massive form, searching for any sign of threat, but the creature remained still, its tail flicking once in what almost seemed like... amusement.

The absurdity of the situation bubbled up in Kai, forcing him to ask, "You're not going to eat me, are you?" The words were out before he could stop them, his tone laced with nervous energy and a touch of sarcasm.

The wolf let out a low, rumbling sound—not quite a growl, but something akin to acknowledgment. Its tail flicked again, and its golden eyes glimmered faintly. Kai blinked, unsure whether to feel relieved or even more unsettled by the response.

"Well, that's reassuring," he muttered, his breath hitching as the wolf took a single step closer. The snow didn't crunch beneath its paws; its movements were silent, almost ethereal. Despite the tension coiling in his body, Kai stood his ground, his gaze locked on the wolf's.

"You're... not just a wolf, are you?" Kai asked, his voice softer now, the question more for himself than the creature before him. The sheer intelligence behind those golden eyes sent a chill down his spine. There was something otherworldly about it, something that didn't belong to this frozen wasteland—or any world Kai had known.

The wolf tilted its head slightly, its ears twitching as though it understood. The movement sent a fresh wave of unease through Kai, but he couldn't look away.

And then, without warning, the wolf turned. It stepped back into the shadows, its massive form disappearing into the swirling snow as silently as it had appeared.

Kai exhaled shakily, his legs trembling as the pull in his chest abruptly vanished, leaving an ache in its wake. "What the hell is going on?" he whispered, his voice barely audible over the faint rustle of the wind.

The forest gave no answer.

His legs finally obeyed, stumbling backward toward the village. The pull in his chest had vanished, but its absence felt heavier somehow, like the weight of the wolf's gaze still lingered.

Are all wolves in this world so large?

Kai reached the door of his cottage, his hands trembling as he fumbled with the latch. The weight of the encounter with the wolf clung to him, his mind racing with questions he couldn't answer. He pushed the door open and stumbled inside, the warmth of the fire licking at his frozen cheeks.

Gerhard was already there, seated on the edge of the table, his arms crossed and his jaw tight. The firelight danced over his features, sharpening the angles of his face and casting his expression into shadow. He turned as the door shut behind him, his sharp blue eyes immediately locking onto hers.

"Where have you been?" he demanded, his voice low but taut with worry.

Kai froze, his pulse quickening. For a moment, he struggled to summon Kai's bravado, but the events of the night had shaken him too deeply. "I needed some air," he said finally, his voice quieter than he'd intended.

"Air?" Gerhard's brow furrowed as he stood, his imposing frame towering over him. "In the middle of the night? In a storm?"

"It wasn't a storm," he said defensively, pulling off the cloak and draping it over a chair. "It was calm. And I'm fine."

Gerhard's jaw tightened, his hands dropping to his sides. "You don't get it, do you?" he said, his voice rising slightly. "They're looking for any excuse to take you. To turn you into their scapegoat. If you disappear in the middle of the night, what do you think they'll assume?"

The words hit harder than he expected. He turned away, avoiding his gaze as he tried to shove down the guilt clawing at his chest. "I can handle myself," he muttered.

"You shouldn't have to," Gerhard said sharply. "And you know it."

Kai whirled to face him, his frustration bubbling to the surface. "What do you want me to say?" he snapped. "That I'm scared? That I don't know what I'm doing? Because fine—I'll say it. But don't stand there acting like you can fix this. You can't."

The silence that followed was deafening. Gerhard's shoulders tensed, his eyes darkening, but the anger in his expression softened almost immediately.

"I know I can't fix it," he said quietly. "But that doesn't mean I'm not going to try."

Kai's breath caught, the raw sincerity in his voice catching him off guard. He opened his mouth to respond, but the words wouldn't come.

Gerhard stepped closer, his movements slow as if afraid he might pull away. "You don't have to go through this alone," he said, his tone softer now. "Whatever happens—whatever they decide—I'll be here. For you."

The heat in his chest was sudden and overwhelming, a confusing mix of gratitude and something deeper that he couldn't quite name. He swallowed hard, his gaze dropping to the floor. "You don't know what you're saying," he murmured.

"Yes, I do," he said firmly.

For a long moment, they stood in silence, the fire crackling softly in the background. Kai's thoughts were a chaotic mess, torn between the impossible weight of his situation and the quiet steadiness of Gerhard's presence.

Finally, Gerhard reached out, his hand brushing against Kai's. The touch was light, tentative, but it sent a jolt through Kai that left him frozen in place.

"Talk to me," he said, his voice low and steady.

Kai looked up, his chest tightening at the concern etched into Gerhard's features. He wanted to tell him everything—that he wasn't really Kai, that he didn't belong in this world, that the Snow King was already reaching for him. Instead, the memory of amber eyes glinting in the shadows surged forward.

"I think I saw a wolf," he said, the words tumbling out before he could stop them.

Gerhard froze, his brows drawing together in alarm. "A wolf? Where?"

"Near the woods," Kai said, his voice steady despite the shiver that ran through him. "It was massive. Bigger than any animal I've ever seen."

For a moment, Gerhard said nothing, his gaze shifting toward the window as if expecting the creature to be staring back at them. When he spoke, his voice was low, almost reverent. "There are stories... about the Snow King's guardian. A wolf of shadow and ice that hunts at his command."

Kai's stomach twisted. "You think it's real?"

"I don't know," Gerhard admitted, though the weight in his tone suggested he believed more than he let on. "But if it is, and if you've seen it..." He trailed off, his lips pressing into a thin line.

"What?" Kai prompted.

Gerhard shook his head, his expression grave. "It means the Snow King's gaze is already on you. Be careful, Kai."

Before Kai could respond, the faint toll of a bell rang out in the distance, its sound low and haunting. Gerhard's expression darkened further. "It's late for a meeting," he muttered, his jaw tightening.

Kai's stomach twisted. The weight of what the bell signified was unmistakable—the elders weren't wasting time.

"I'll go," Gerhard said, his voice grim. He turned toward the door, pausing briefly with his hand on the latch. "Stay inside. Please."

Kai nodded, though his mind was already racing. As Gerhard stepped out into the night, the cold wind rushing in behind him, he knew the respite was over.

The toll of the bell echoed across the village, its somber tone heavy with finality. He paced the length of Kai's cottage, his heart pounding in time with each ring. The fire had burned low, casting flickering shadows on the walls, but he couldn't bring himself to tend it.

He didn't want to think about what was happening in the meeting hall. About Gerhard standing among the villagers, his strong, steady voice likely drowned out by the elders' cold logic. About the decision that was no longer a question but an inevitability.

Kai gritted his teeth, his hands curling into fists. He was *not* going to let himself be led to slaughter like a lamb. Not without a fight.

The door slammed open.

Gerhard stepped inside, his face tight with anger. Snow clung to his dark hair and shoulders, but he didn't bother brushing it off. His jaw worked furiously, and his eyes burned with a fury that sent a fresh wave of unease through him.

"They decided," he said, his voice clipped.

Kai swallowed hard, his chest tightening. "What?" he asked, though he already knew.

He took a step closer, his hands clenching and unclenching at his sides. "The elders. The ritual is going to happen," he said. "And they've named you—" He broke off, his voice cracking. "They've named you as the sacrifice."

The words hit like a physical blow, his stomach twisting painfully. He staggered back a step, gripping the edge of the table for support.

"Of course they did," he said bitterly, the words tumbling out before he could stop them. "Why wouldn't they?"

Gerhard's gaze snapped to Kai's, his eyes narrowing. "You think this is fair?" he asked, his voice low and dangerous. "You think I'm just going to let them take you?"

"I don't think you have a choice," Kai shot back, his frustration bubbling to the surface. "They've already made their decision, Gerhard. It doesn't matter what you or I say."

"It matters to me," he growled, his fists slamming down on the table. The force of it made his jump, but he held his ground, meeting his furious gaze head-on.

"You don't get it," he continued, his voice shaking. "I've watched them push you aside your entire life, treating you like you're less than them, like you're expendable. And now they think they can just—" He broke off, his shoulders heaving as he struggled to rein in his temper.

"Like you said. They're scared," Kai said, his voice quieter now. "And scared people do terrible things."

Gerhard shook his head, his expression hardening. "That doesn't make it right."

The fire in his eyes made his chest ache, a confusing mix of guilt and gratitude swirling through him. He opened his mouth to respond, but before he could speak, the bell rang again—its final toll, deep and resonant, as if sealing the elders' verdict.

The weight of the moment pressed down on them both.

"Fine," Gerhard said finally, his voice quieter now but no less determined. "If they're going through with this, then I'm going with you."

Kai blinked, startled. "What?"

"I'm not letting you face this alone," he said firmly.

His breath caught. The intensity in his voice left no room for argument, but the words hit harder than they should have. He wasn't Kai. He wasn't the person Gerhard thought he was defending.

"You don't have to do that," he said, his voice trembling. "I'll... I'll figure something out."

Gerhard let out a humorless laugh, shaking his head. "You're not running from this. Not without me."

His words sent a jolt of panic through him. He couldn't let him put himself at risk for a lie—for someone he wasn't. But the quiet conviction in his gaze left him speechless.

"Gerhard..." he began, but he cut him off with a sharp look.

"Get some rest," he said, his voice softening. "We'll figure out the next step tomorrow."

Before he could protest, he turned and stepped toward the door.

The cold rushed in as he opened it, snow swirling in the faint glow of the moonlight. He paused, glancing back at him one last time.

"We'll get through this," he said.

And then he was gone, the door shutting softly behind him.

Kai stood frozen, his mind spinning. He wanted to believe Gerhard's words, to let his strength carry him through the suffocating weight of the elders' decision. But all he could feel was the crushing reality of his situation.

The Snow King wasn't a story anymore. He was real, and he was waiting for him.

Chapter 3

THE NEXT MORNING, THE village was alive with a grim energy, the kind that came when people were desperate enough to believe in impossible solutions. Everywhere Kai turned, he saw signs of preparation for the ritual: the elders gathering offerings near the meeting hall, the women working on ceremonial garments, and children peeking out from behind doors, their eyes wide with curiosity and fear.

It all felt surreal, like a nightmare he couldn't wake from.

Kai forced himself to walk through the square, his shoulders squared and his expression carefully indifferent. It was the kind of defiance he guessed the real Kai might have shown—a mask to hide the growing panic in his chest. He kept his gaze fixed ahead, ignoring the weight of the villagers' stares.

"They should've done this sooner," someone muttered as he passed.

"He's always been... different," another voice whispered.

Kai's jaw tightened, but he didn't turn. The words weren't surprising—he'd already learned how the village viewed Kai as an outsider, someone who didn't fit their narrow mold. But hearing their rationalizations now, when they were planning to send him to his death, stung in a way he hadn't expected.

As he reached the edge of the square, a familiar figure caught his eye. Gerhard.

He stood in the shadow of the blacksmith's workshop, his arms crossed over his chest and his expression thunderous. Though his presence was imposing as ever, there was a tension in his stance that spoke of barely contained anger.

Gerhard wasn't helping with the preparations—that much was clear. His refusal to participate in the ritual was a silent but unmistakable statement, one that hadn't gone unnoticed by the villagers. Kai could see the sidelong glances they cast at him, their unease clear in the way they gave him a wide berth.

Their eyes met briefly, and something sharp twisted in Kai's chest. He could see the conflict in Gerhard's gaze—the guilt, the frustration, the helplessness. It was the look of a man who wanted to fight but didn't know how.

Kai turned away quickly, his throat tightening. He couldn't let himself dwell on Gerhard—not now. There were too many other things to worry about.

The door creaked softly as Kai stepped back into the cottage, the warmth from the fire meeting him like a hesitant embrace. He shut the door quickly, leaning against it for a moment to catch his breath. The encounter with the wolf still lingered in his mind, vivid and unsettling.

"You've got to be careful."

The deep voice startled him. Kai's head snapped up to see Gerhard standing near the table, his broad frame casting a shadow that stretched toward the firelight. His arms were crossed, and his jaw was set tight, but his eyes betrayed a mix of worry and frustration.

Kai hesitated, unsure of what to say. The sight of Gerhard—so solid, so familiar—was both a comfort and a sharp reminder of how far out of his depth he was.

"I needed air again," Kai said finally, shrugging off the cloak. He moved to hang it on the back of a chair, his movements deliberately casual.

Gerhard didn't look convinced. "You have a whole village trying to sacrifice you, but you needed air?" he asked, his voice low and edged with disbelief.

Kai turned toward the fire, avoiding Gerhard's gaze.

"You know what the elders have decided. You know what's coming."

Kai stiffened, his grip tightening on the back of the chair. "I don't need a reminder," he said quietly.

Gerhard exhaled sharply, the sound heavy with frustration. "Then why are you acting like nothing's wrong?"

"Because what else am I supposed to do?" Kai snapped, turning to face him. "Beg them to change their minds? Run away and let them blame you instead?"

The words hung in the air, sharp and raw. Gerhard's expression darkened, but his voice softened when he spoke. "You think I care what they blame me for?"

Kai's chest tightened, guilt curling low in his stomach. He looked away, his eyes fixed on the fire as it crackled faintly in the hearth.

Gerhard stepped closer, his voice quieter now. "Talk to me, Kai," he said. "Tell me what the elders said to you."

Kai swallowed hard. He could feel Gerhard's gaze on him, steady and unrelenting, and it made his skin prickle with an uncomfortable heat. He couldn't tell him the truth—couldn't admit that he wasn't really Kai, that he didn't belong in this body or this world.

So he did what he always did. He deflected.

"They didn't say anything you don't already know," he said, forcing a faint smirk. "I'm the sacrifice. The Snow King gets his pound of flesh, and the village gets to sleep a little warmer."

Gerhard's jaw tightened, his hands curling into fists at his sides. "Don't joke about this."

Kai shrugged, his voice light. "Why not? It's funny if you think about it. All this fuss, and for what? To throw me to some mythical king in the hopes he'll let us plant potatoes again?"

Gerhard moved quickly, his hand gripping Kai's chin—not roughly, but firmly enough to make him freeze. The sudden closeness sent a jolt through Kai's chest, but it wasn't fear.

"Stop," Gerhard said, his voice low and steady. "Stop pretending this doesn't matter."

Kai blinked, his breath catching.

"It matters to me," Gerhard continued, his grip loosening but his gaze unwavering. "I don't care what the elders say, or what the village thinks. I care about *you*."

The words hit harder than Kai expected, cutting through his carefully constructed facade. His throat tightened, and he looked away, unable to hold Gerhard's gaze.

"You don't understand," he said softly. *I'm not Kai.*

"Then help me," Gerhard said. His voice was gentler now, but there was a quiet intensity in it that made Kai's chest ache. "Help me understand."

Kai hesitated, his thoughts racing. He wanted to tell Gerhard everything, to let him in on the secret that had been eating at him since the moment he woke up in this body. But how could he? How could he ask Gerhard to believe something so impossible?

Instead, he whispered, "You can't fix this."

Gerhard's hand moved down to grip Kai's neck, the warmth of his calloused fingers grounding him in a way that was both comforting and overwhelming. "I don't have to fix it," he said. "But I'm not going to let you face it alone."

Kai's breath hitched. The sincerity in Gerhard's voice, the weight of his unwavering loyalty—it was almost too much to bear.

For a moment, the room felt impossibly small, the fire's warmth and Gerhard's presence pressing in on all sides. Kai didn't trust himself to speak, so he didn't.

They stood there in silence, the only sound the faint crackle of the fire.

Finally, Gerhard released his hand and stepped back, his expression softening. "Get some rest," he said quietly.

Kai nodded, though his chest felt heavy as he watched Gerhard move toward the door.

"Gerhard," he said suddenly, his voice halting.

The blacksmith turned, his sharp blue eyes meeting Kai's.

"Thank you," Kai said, the words barely above a whisper.

Gerhard didn't respond, but his expression softened, and for a moment, the anger and frustration faded from his face.

As the door shut behind him, Kai sank into the nearest chair, his hands trembling.

Gerhard's devotion wasn't meant for him.

And that was what made it hurt the most.

Morning came with a leaden sky, clouds heavy with the promise of more snow. The frost on the windows had grown overnight, its intricate patterns spreading like veins of ice across the glass.

Kai sat at the table, his hands curled around a steaming mug of weak tea. He hadn't slept—not really. His thoughts had circled endlessly, replaying the events of the previous night, Gerhard's words, and the quiet intensity of the wolf's golden eyes.

The knock at the door startled him.

Kai rose slowly, setting the mug down as the door creaked open. Two of the elders stood outside, their expressions carved from stone. Between them, one of the village women carried a bundle of furs lined with silver embroidery, the ceremonial garment meant for the ritual.

"It's time to prepare," the sharp-eyed elder said, her voice clipped.

Kai bit back a sharp reply, knowing it wouldn't do him any good. Instead, he stepped aside to let them in. The woman set the furs on the table, her hands lingering briefly on the fabric as if she didn't want to let go.

"These are for the ritual," she said softly, not meeting Kai's eyes.

The elders exchanged a glance, their cold, calculating silence filling the room. "You understand your role," the sharp-eyed elder said, her tone leaving no room for argument. "This ritual is for the good of the village. Any resistance on your part will only bring harm to those you claim to care for."

Kai's jaw tightened, anger flaring in his chest. "You've made yourselves clear," he said, his voice sharp. "I'm the sacrifice. Congratulations—you've solved all your problems."

The woman carrying the furs flinched, but the elders remained unmoved. "It is not a question of fairness," the elder said. "It is a matter of survival."

Kai didn't respond, his hands curling into fists at his sides. The silence stretched until the elders turned and left without another word, their boots crunching against the snow as they disappeared into the gray morning.

The woman lingered for a moment, her gaze flicking nervously between Kai and the door. "I... I'm sorry," she murmured before hurrying after the others.

Kai shut the door with more force than necessary, his breath hissing through his teeth. He turned to the table, staring at the ceremonial furs as if they might suddenly explain everything.

The embroidery was intricate, each silver thread catching the faint light from the window. It should have been beautiful, but all Kai could see was a death shroud.

Kai paced the cottage, the fire long reduced to embers. He couldn't shake the feeling that the Snow King's presence had been real, tangible in the frozen air of the woods. His chest ached with the pull that had guided him toward the figure, the hum still faintly lingering in the back of his mind.

The ceremonial furs lay draped over the chair where he had left them, the silver embroidery catching the faint glow of the embers. They felt like a mockery, a reminder of what the village expected of him—of what awaited him.

He had just reached for the tinderbox to stoke the fire when a soft knock echoed through the quiet.

Kai froze. For a moment, he considered ignoring it—pretending to be asleep or not home at all. But the knock came again, firmer this time.

Sighing, he crossed the room and opened the door.

Gerhard stood on the other side, his broad frame silhouetted against the faint glow of the moon. His shoulders were slumped, his expression weary, but his sharp blue eyes were locked onto Kai's with an intensity that made his chest tighten.

"Can I come in?" Gerhard asked quietly.

Kai hesitated for only a moment before stepping aside to let him in.

The blacksmith moved into the room, his presence filling the small space. He didn't speak at first, his gaze drifting over the ceremonial furs and the sword resting near the hearth. His jaw tightened, his hands curling into fists at his sides.

"They're really going to do it," he said finally, his voice low and rough.

Kai swallowed hard, closing the door behind him. "You already knew that," he said, trying to keep his voice steady.

Gerhard turned to face him, his eyes dark with frustration. "Knowing doesn't make it easier," he said. "And it doesn't make it right."

Kai crossed his arms over his chest, leaning back against the door. "What do you want me to say?" he asked. "That I'm fine with it? That I'm not scared out of my mind?"

Gerhard's expression softened, his shoulders relaxing slightly. "No," he said. "I just... I wish there was more I could do."

Kai opened his mouth to respond but stopped, the lump in his throat making it hard to speak. He looked away, his gaze falling to the floor.

"You've already done enough," he said finally, his voice quieter.

Gerhard stepped closer. "I don't think I have," he said.

The words sent a pang through Kai's chest, sharp and unexpected. He looked up, meeting Gerhard's gaze, and for a moment, the weight of everything—the ritual, the village, the Snow King—seemed to fade, leaving only the quiet intensity between them.

"I should've done more," Gerhard said, his voice barely above a whisper. "I should've fought harder. Spoken louder. Maybe if I had..." He trailed off, his hands flexing at his sides.

Kai's chest ached at the guilt in his voice. He wanted to reach out, to tell him that none of this was his fault, but the words wouldn't come.

Instead, he said, "You can't fix this, Gerhard."

"I don't care," Gerhard said, stepping closer. "I'd burn this whole village down if it meant keeping you safe."

The raw emotion in his voice left Kai breathless. He looked away again, his throat tightening. "You shouldn't say things like that," he muttered.

"Why not?" Gerhard asked, his voice softer now. "Because you think I don't mean it? Or because you do?"

Kai's breath hitched, the words striking too close to the truth. He turned back to Gerhard, his heart pounding in his chest.

"I'm not who you think I am," he said, the words slipping out before he could stop them.

Gerhard frowned, his head tilting slightly. "What does that mean?"

Kai hesitated, his thoughts racing. He couldn't tell Gerhard the truth—not now, not when it would only complicate things further. But he couldn't lie to him, either.

"It doesn't matter," he said finally, his voice quieter. "What matters is that you don't destroy yourself trying to save me."

Gerhard stepped even closer, his hand reaching out to brush against Kai's. The touch was brief, but it sent a jolt through him, warmth cutting through the cold that had settled deep in his bones.

"I'd do it again," Gerhard said softly.

Kai's breath caught, his chest tightening with a mix of emotions he couldn't name. He wanted to say something, to tell Gerhard how much his words meant, but all he could do was nod.

For a long moment, neither of them spoke. The only sound was the faint whistle of the wind outside, its low, mournful tone filling the silence.

Finally, Gerhard stepped back, his expression softening. "Get some rest," he said. "Tomorrow..." He trailed off, his jaw tightening again. "Just... get some rest."

Kai nodded, his throat too tight to speak. He watched as Gerhard moved toward the door.

As Gerhard opened the door, he paused, glancing back over his shoulder. "You're stronger than they think," he said. "Don't let them take that from you."

Kai didn't respond, his chest too heavy with unspoken words.

The door shut softly behind Gerhard, and the cottage fell silent once more.

Kai sank into the nearest chair, his hands trembling as he gripped the edge of the table. The frost on the windows had spread further, curling in intricate, otherworldly patterns that seemed to glow faintly in the moonlight.

Chapter 4

The morning arrived bleak and unforgiving, cloaked in a heavy, unnatural silence that pressed against the village like a suffocating hand. The storm swirled above, its winds dragging snow into spiraling chaos that never quite touched the ground. The sky stretched out, a pale, frozen gray—colorless and void—as though the sun itself had abandoned this place.

Kai stood at the edge of the square, staring out at the village. It looked foreign, transformed into something ceremonial and sinister. Torches lined the square's perimeter, their flames fragile against the biting wind, flickering and bending as though pleading to be snuffed out. The light they cast was thin and wavering, leaving pools of darkness at the edges of buildings that seemed to watch, silent and uncaring.

At the center of the square sat the altar. The stone was old and rough-hewn, streaked with faint veins of silver and covered in a crust of ice that refused to melt. The surface glittered with frost as if the storm itself had kissed it in preparation. Kai's gaze snagged on the sight, his stomach twisting into knots, the unease in his chest deepening.

A figure approached him, draping the ceremonial furs over his shoulders. They were heavy, their weight pulling at his frame as though preparing him for a burden he could not yet comprehend. The silver embroidery shimmered faintly in the torchlight, intricate patterns of swirling frost and delicate snowflakes that marked him as the sacrifice. The chosen.

Each step toward the altar felt like walking through water—slow, deliberate, and inevitable. The pull deep in his chest had been growing since dawn. His breaths came shallow, the icy air stabbing at his lungs with every inhale. His fingers curled beneath the edge of the furs, gripping tightly as though the fabric alone might anchor him.

The villagers lined the path leading to the square, silent and unmoving. Their faces were pale in the torchlight, shadows carving lines of fear and sorrow into their expressions. Mothers clutched their children, elders stood rigid, and men who had once greeted Kai with scorn now looked through him as though he were already gone. Whispers rippled through the crowd, soft as falling snow but sharper than any blade.

"This will save us." "The Snow King must be appeased." "It has to be done."

The words were spoken with resignation, a chant of justification. But none dared meet Kai's gaze. None spoke his name.

The snow beneath his feet crunched with a sound that seemed too loud, too real. Kai forced himself to lift his head, to look forward, his pulse pounding in his ears. At the end of the path, beyond the altar, he could see the forest. The trees rose dark and jagged against the pale sky, their bare limbs swaying faintly in the wind as if they were calling him. The storm swirled above them, and for a moment, Kai could almost hear its voice—a low, unrelenting hum that resonated through the marrow of his bones.

He was halfway to the altar when a cold gust of wind cut through the square, making the torches sputter and dim. The flames shrank back as though afraid of what was to come. Kai stopped, the chill wrapping around his ankles like tendrils of ice. He squeezed his eyes shut and exhaled slowly, watching his breath cloud before him.

You don't have a choice, he told himself. *It's already happening.*

When he opened his eyes again, the altar loomed before him—waiting.

The silence was absolute now. Even the whispers had faded. Kai felt every pair of eyes on him as he climbed the three shallow steps that led to the stone platform, his furs dragging across the frost-covered surface.

Turning back toward the crowd, Kai let his gaze sweep over the villagers. For a heartbeat, he searched for a familiar face, for something—anything—that might tether him to this world, but perhaps Gerhard couldn't stomach it.

The wind rose again, pulling at his furs, and Kai looked up. The sky above him seemed closer now, the swirling storm an open eye watching him with interest. Its winds sharpened as they spiraled downward, crystalline snowflakes cutting through the air like glass shards.

He stood still against it, his breath steady now, his resolve hardening as the pull in his chest grew stronger.

Behind him, the sharp ring of a bell shattered the silence, and the first elder stepped forward, her face hidden beneath the heavy hood of her cloak. Her voice rose over the wind, cold and commanding as she began to speak words in a language older than the village itself.

The ritual had begun.

The elder's voice rose in a slow, guttural chant, the foreign words vibrating in the air like a heartbeat—steady, measured, and absolute. Kai could feel the sound rippling through him, sinking into his bones and mingling with the pull in his chest. Each syllable wrapped tighter around him, invisible threads drawing him closer to the altar's purpose.

His breath hitched. **It was already happening.**

The crowd remained deathly silent, their fear deepening as the chant grew louder. It seemed to resonate with the storm itself—the wind rising in harmony, swirling violently as though the sky and earth were answering the ritual's call.

Then, a shout shattered the rhythm.

"Stop this!"

The words rang out like a crack of thunder, jarring and raw. The crowd turned sharply, parting as Gerhard pushed through them. His shoulders heaved with effort, his face pale with fury and desperation. The wind bit into him, dragging at his cloak as though trying to force him back, but he shoved forward, unrelenting.

"You can't do this!" His voice was rough, his words torn from his chest as he broke free of the crowd and staggered toward the altar.

Kai's heart twisted sharply. Gerhard's face was flushed from the cold and his anger, his gray eyes wide and frantic as they locked onto Kai. It was as if the sight of him on the altar ripped something vital from the blacksmith's chest.

The sharp-eyed elder stepped forward, her cloak billowing like wings in the wind. Her voice cut through the chaos, cold and unyielding. "This is not your decision, blacksmith. The winter will not end without sacrifice."

Gerhard ignored her, his hands trembling as he reached for Kai. The storm howled around them, flurries of snow catching on his hair and cloak, clinging to him like frost.

He gripped Kai's arm with calloused hands, his voice breaking. "Kai, listen to me. You don't have to do this. We'll leave. We'll go somewhere they can't find us—somewhere far away."

The desperation in his tone was enough to pull at something deep within Kai. Gerhard's hold was solid and warm, grounding him amid the unnatural cold pressing against him from all sides. For a heartbeat, Kai let himself believe in the offer—a life somewhere else, far from this altar and this storm, a life where no one whispered his name like a death sentence.

But the pull in his chest tightened, and the storm roared louder, as if in answer. Kai's gaze flicked to the swirling clouds, their spiraling movements focused solely on the altar. He could feel it—a purpose written in the wind, something ancient and unrelenting calling to him.

He shook his head slowly, his voice barely audible above the wind. "It's too late, Gerhard. This... this is already happening."

Gerhard's face fell, his expression stricken. His hands slackened around Kai's arm for just a moment before he tightened his grip, his words torn from him like a last plea for salvation. "No. No, it's not too late. Don't say that."

Kai swallowed hard, his throat tight. "Gerhard..."

"I won't forgive myself," Gerhard said, his voice raw and uneven, "if I let them take you. You're not supposed to be here."

Something about the way he said it, the conviction in his tone, cut through Kai. He thought of the nights spent by Gerhard's forge, the quiet hours when the blacksmith would wordlessly hand him tools and let the silence speak for them both. Gerhard, who had been steady where the rest of the village faltered. Gerhard, who was now breaking before him. Did he know that Kai had been switched?

"You've done enough," Kai whispered, his voice steady despite the ache in his chest. "This isn't your fault."

The sharp-eyed elder's voice rang out again, louder this time. "Step away, blacksmith. Or you will join him."

The words carried a dangerous edge, a promise laced with magic. Gerhard flinched, but his grip did not waver. He turned toward the elder, his voice trembling with anger. "You would sacrifice him for this storm? For a god that doesn't even care about us?"

The elder's expression remained impassive, her eyes dark beneath the edge of her hood. "You do not understand the cost of defying him. The Snow King must be appeased."

The crowd murmured faintly, their voices uneasy as the wind tore at their cloaks. Some villagers glanced away, unable to meet Gerhard's gaze. Others clutched each other tightly, as if bracing against the storm's growing wrath.

Kai closed his eyes for a moment, steadying his breath. He could feel the pull in his chest grow heavier, relentless and insistent, like invisible threads wrapping around his heart. When he opened his eyes again, the look he gave Gerhard was soft but resolute.

"Go back," he said quietly, his voice firm despite the tremor in it. "You can't stop this."

Gerhard stared at him, his expression crumbling. For a moment, he looked as though he might argue, might fight against the inevitable. But then his hands fell away from Kai's arm, trembling as they dropped to his sides.

"Kai…" The name came out like a whisper, broken and helpless.

The wind howled around them, drowning everything else out. Kai stepped closer and rested his hand on Gerhard's arm, squeezing it gently. "Please. Stay safe for me."

Gerhard's jaw clenched, his teeth gritting as he looked away, unable to meet Kai's gaze. His shoulders hunched, every line of him radiating pain.

Slowly, reluctantly, Gerhard stepped back into the crowd, his figure swallowed by the swirling snow. But his eyes never left Kai, even as the elder's chant began again, louder now, the words cutting through the wind.

The air seemed to thicken as the sharp-eyed elder stepped forward once more, her heavy cloak trailing behind her like a living shadow. The torches surrounding the square sputtered and dimmed, their flames shrinking as though the very fire feared what was to come. The crowd pressed closer together, their silence absolute as though none dared to breathe.

The chanting began.

It was guttural and ancient, the sound raw and resonant as though dredged from the very earth. It vibrated through Kai's chest, a deep hum that seemed to sync with the pull he felt—unrelenting, ever-present. He swayed where he stood, his knees threatening to buckle as the storm above answered the elder's call. The wind's howl grew deeper, carrying whispers that no human tongue could replicate.

The other elders stepped into the square, their faces hidden beneath their hoods. They formed a circle around the altar, their voices rising in unison. The chant wasn't loud, but it was heavy, the rhythm measured and steady like a heartbeat. Each word they spoke felt like it pressed down on Kai, wrapping tighter around his chest.

Frost crept outward from the altar, snaking tendrils that curled over the stone and spread across the ground. Kai's boots crunched faintly as the ice reached him, the cold biting into him like teeth.

He stood still, his hands shaking as the words continued to weave their invisible web.

Gerhard's voice echoed faintly in his mind—*We'll leave, somewhere they can't find us*—but it was distant now, swallowed by the chant and the pull of the storm.

Two elders moved toward Kai, their figures obscured by the swirling snow. Their hands, clad in rough, lined gloves, gripped his arms with surprising strength. Kai tried to pull back on instinct, but his limbs felt sluggish, his body heavy. The pull in his chest grew sharper now, tightening like a noose.

It's already happening, he thought.

The elders guided him forward, their steps slow and ceremonial. The snow fell in sharp, crystalline shards, swirling unnaturally through the air. It should have melted against his skin, but instead, it burned like sparks of fire.

The stone altar loomed before him, its surface gleaming slick with frost. It seemed larger now, almost alive, its jagged edges sharp enough to cut. Kai felt his pulse thrumming in his ears as he was led up the shallow steps.

The sharp-eyed elder raised her arms to the storm, her voice rising over the wind, each word a command that the heavens themselves obeyed. "In the name of the Snow King, we offer this life to end the winter's wrath. Let the storm take what it is owed."

Her words cracked through the air, and the torches shuddered violently. The flames bowed and guttered until they extinguished altogether, plunging the square into darkness save for the faint glow of the swirling storm.

Kai's chest ached, his breathing ragged. His limbs felt numb as he was guided onto the altar, the cold of the stone sinking into his knees as he collapsed against it.

For a moment, everything slowed. The wind dulled into a distant roar, the chant an echo of itself, as though Kai stood at the edge of two worlds. He stared into the snowstorm swirling above him, the patterns in the clouds mesmerizing and unnatural. They spiraled downward, tighter and tighter, until they seemed to focus solely on him.

The pull in his chest grew unbearable. It was as though something—*someone*—was reaching for him, beckoning him closer. His body trembled violently as his breath clouded before him, ice forming on his lashes.

He couldn't look away from the storm. It watched him, waiting, hungry.

The elder's voice rang out one last time, a declaration that shattered the moment's quiet. "Let the storm take its claim!"

The words echoed through the square like the final toll of a bell.

Kai sucked in a sharp breath and for a moment, there was silence—a stillness so profound it felt as though the world itself had stopped to take a breath with him.

Then the wind roared to life.

It tore through the square with a sound like a thousand voices screaming at once, howling and twisting around the altar. The torches—extinguished moments before—were ripped from their stands, their wooden bases splintering as they tumbled into the snow. Cloaks snapped and whipped against the wind, and villagers stumbled back, shielding their faces as the storm turned violent.

Kai's breath was torn from his lungs, his body jolting against the stone as though struck by unseen hands. He pressed his palms to the altar to steady himself, but the pull in his chest intensified, sharp and unrelenting, as though invisible threads were tearing him apart from the inside. The cold was no longer simply a biting presence—it had weight, pressing down on him, anchoring him in place.

The wind focused on him.

It spiraled into a vortex, snow and ice forming jagged patterns that whipped around the altar in a violent, chaotic dance. Kai felt its power pressing down on him, surrounding him like invisible hands, pinning him to the stone. His arms trembled as he tried to resist, but it was no use. He was drowning in it.

From the crowd, Gerhard's voice broke through the storm, raw and frantic. "Kai!"

Kai lifted his head, straining to see through the snow that cut through the air like glass. Gerhard's figure emerged from the blur of white, his face twisted in desperation. He fought against the wind, his steps slow and laborious as he tried to push closer, but the storm tore at him with brutal, unrelenting force.

Gerhard shouted something else—his voice hoarse, his words almost unintelligible—but the wind swallowed the sound, leaving only a distant, broken echo. Kai's chest ached as he watched, his pulse hammering in his ears. Gerhard looked small and helpless against the chaos, his outstretched hand clawing at the air as though he could pull Kai back from the storm's grip.

I'm sorry, Kai thought, his lips too numb to form the words.

The pull deep inside him grew stronger, sharper, a force he couldn't resist. It felt like being tethered to a star, an unrelenting draw that promised to tear him apart. He gasped as the pressure in his chest became too much, his body arching against the stone as though pulled by invisible strings.

The vortex above him condensed, snow and wind converging into a singular shape—a spiraling column of white that reached down from the storm itself. It moved with purpose, sentient and hungry, its energy vibrating through the air like the hum of an ancient voice.

The villagers cried out, their fear palpable as they stumbled backward, fleeing the altar. They shielded their faces, their silhouettes mere shadows against the storm. Gerhard, still fighting, fell to his knees in the snow, his screams drowned beneath the chaos.

Kai's body jerked violently as the column of snow and wind descended. It wrapped around him like a cocoon of ice, cold and alive, pulling him upward.

The pressure was unbearable. He could feel himself lifting from the stone—his legs numb, his arms weightless—dragged into the storm's embrace. The world tilted wildly, the altar, the village, and Gerhard's desperate figure spinning out of focus, fading into a blur of white.

Pain flared in Kai's chest, and he screamed, though the sound was muffled, swallowed instantly by the wind. His voice was meaningless here, lost in the vortex's power.

What is happening to me?

The storm pressed closer, suffocating and eternal. He felt weightless, untethered to the earth, as though his very soul were being pulled from his body. It was dizzying, the sensation of being everywhere and nowhere at once.

Through the chaos, Kai caught one last glimpse of Gerhard—his figure small and broken in the storm, his hands outstretched and reaching.

Then the world tipped violently, and everything went black.

The world returned in jolts and fragments—a bone-deep cold, the feel of ice seeping into his skin, the harsh scrape of snow against his cheek. Kai stirred, groaning as awareness clawed its way back to him. Each breath stung like needles in his lungs, and his body felt impossibly heavy, as though he'd been buried alive beneath the frost.

When he opened his eyes, he found himself staring at a world smothered in white.

Snow stretched out endlessly around him, soft and pristine, unbroken save for the shallow impression where his body had landed. The storm still raged above, but here in the forest, the winds had dulled to an eerie whisper, winding through the trees like a breath caught on the edge of words. The towering trunks of the trees loomed dark and skeletal against the swirling sky, their branches bare and twisted like claws.

The silence here was thick, pressing in around him. The village was gone—Gerhard's cries, the flames, the chanting elders—swallowed by this unnatural place. Kai pushed himself up onto his elbows, his muscles screaming in protest as he dragged himself out of the snowbank. Frost clung to his clothes, his eyelashes, and his skin, chilling him to the core.

Where am I?

The air here felt different. Alive. Charged. It pressed against his skin like a thousand invisible hands, sinking into his bones. There was no sound save for the faint whistle of the wind and the crunch of snow beneath his trembling hands.

As Kai rose to his knees, swaying slightly, he glanced back in the direction he thought he had come from. There was nothing—no altar, no village—only the empty expanse of the forest. The snow at his feet was untouched, as though he had fallen from the sky itself.

The pull in his chest remained, heavier now, sharper. It tugged at him like an invisible tether, pointing him deeper into the forest. He gripped the edges of his cloak, wrapping the ceremonial furs tighter around himself, as if they could stave off the unnatural cold.

Then he felt it.

A weight.

Eyes.

The sensation prickled across his skin like a chill far colder than any wind. He turned slowly, his breath clouding the air, his heart pounding painfully in his chest.

There, between the trees, **a shadow moved.**

It was massive, larger than anything that should exist in a place like this. The dark outline wove silently through the forest, its steps muffled by the snow. For a moment, Kai could make out the faint gleam of silver fur, so pale it almost seemed to glow in the dim light.

Then the shadow stopped.

Two golden eyes emerged from the darkness, pinning Kai where he stood. They glowed faintly, like twin embers, vibrant and alive in a world of frost and stillness.

Kai froze, every muscle in his body locking into place. The pull in his chest pulsed sharply, as though recognizing the figure before him. The wolf.

The creature stepped closer, its massive paws sinking silently into the snow. With every step, Kai could feel its presence growing—heavy, ancient. Its silver fur shimmered faintly in the dim light, and its eyes never wavered from him, watching, waiting.

The pull in Kai's chest twisted sharply, becoming something deeper, something that seemed to tie him to the wolf itself. His breath came in shallow gasps, his body trembling not with fear, but with something else.

Recognition.

CHAPTER 5

Fenrir stopped a few paces away, the snow between them untouched by either of their movements, as though this place belonged to neither of them. His fur shimmered like frost-forged silk, each strand catching the storm's dim light, making him seem to glow against the dark forest looming far behind him. His eyes were gold—liquid and bright, too intelligent, too knowing. They pinned Kai where he lay, as though the wolf were peeling back his very soul.

Kai tried to move, but his limbs refused to cooperate. He could only watch, wide-eyed and shaking, as the wolf stepped closer.

The snow seemed to retreat from Fenrir's path, the storm bending around him, as though it, too, knew better than to challenge him. When he reached Kai, the wolf lowered his great head until his breath, a sharp and impossibly warm exhale, stirred the frost clinging to Kai's face.

For a moment, the wolf only stared.

Then, in a voice that rumbled low and steady, vibrating the air around them, Fenrir spoke.

"You will not die here. Come."

The words struck Kai like a blow, knocking something loose in his chest. He blinked at the wolf, disoriented, his frozen thoughts unable to reconcile the reality of what he was seeing.

"You... spoke?" His voice cracked, barely more than a whisper.

Fenrir huffed—a sound that almost resembled amusement. He nudged Kai's side with his broad nose, the force of it knocking the wind from him. *"Move."*

Kai gasped, his breath catching as he forced himself upright. Pain lanced through his frozen limbs, his muscles stiff and uncooperative. Every movement felt slow, disconnected, as though he were a marionette with tangled strings. The snow resisted his ascent, dragging at his legs like unseen hands unwilling to release him.

The massive wolf remained at his side, a silent sentinel, his thick silver fur barely shifting in the lingering wind. Even in the stillness, there was something about him—an untamed presence, a force of nature as much as the storm itself.

Once on his feet—barely—Kai swayed, his vision swimming. The muffled roar of the storm pressed at the edges of the world, a distant but persistent hum.

"What..." His voice cracked, his lips numb from the cold. He swallowed, trying again. "What's your name?"

The wolf's golden eyes flicked toward him, sharp and assessing. He studied Kai for a long moment before turning away.

"Fenrir," came the low, resonant reply, spoken not in the rumbling growl of a beast but in clear, deliberate words.

Kai's breath hitched. That was—he was—

Before he could process it, Fenrir glanced back, his gaze commanding. *"Follow me."*

Still shaking, still trying to comprehend what had just happened, Kai stumbled after him.

The forest rose up around them as they walked—a jagged maze of blackened trees weighed down by snow. Their twisted branches stretched toward the sky like skeletal fingers, as if they were trying to tear at the swirling clouds above.

Fenrir led the way, silent and sure, his silver form a beacon against the shadows. Kai stumbled often, his feet catching in the drifts of snow that covered the uneven ground. His breath came in ragged bursts, sharp against his throat, but he forced himself to keep moving.

He didn't trust himself to look back.

The storm was still there, whispering behind them, its distant hum following like an unseen predator. He couldn't see it, but he felt it—watching, waiting. Every step felt like walking a tightrope over something vast and unknowable.

Shadows flickered at the edges of his vision, shifting in the corners of his eyes, darting between trees too quickly for him to catch. The sound of the snow beneath their feet felt too loud, masking the faint whispers that curled through the air like smoke.

They're watching me.

The thought came unbidden, sinking into him like frost. He shivered, his hands clutching the furs tighter against himself as his gaze darted nervously between the trees.

"Are we being followed?" he whispered, his voice trembling.

Fenrir didn't pause or look back. *"No."*

"But there's something out there. I can feel it."

The wolf glanced at him, his golden eyes gleaming faintly. *"This place welcomes you, little warmth. You should be honored."*

Kai swallowed hard, his steps faltering. "Remembers me? What does that mean?"

Fenrir didn't answer.

It started as a shadow—indistinct at first, just a vague dark shape rising beyond the trees. As they moved closer, it grew clearer: sharp spires that pierced the sky like frozen spears, their surfaces glistening faintly with reflected light.

The Snow King's palace.

It rose impossibly large, carved from solid ice that shimmered with faint blue and silver light. Jagged edges and smooth surfaces interwove into an intricate masterpiece—equal parts beautiful and terrifying. The palace looked like it had been pulled straight from a nightmare or a dream, its presence an unnatural scar against the frozen forest.

Kai stumbled to a halt as it loomed before them, his breath catching in his throat. The sheer size of it made him feel small, insignificant. It radiated power, an ancient cold that seemed to seep from its very walls, spreading outward into the land.

"The Snow King lives *here*?" Kai's voice was barely above a whisper.

Fenrir paused, turning his head just enough for Kai to see the faint amusement in his gaze. *"Do you think him a man of modesty?"*

Kai didn't answer. He couldn't.

The closer they moved to the palace, the quieter everything became. The wind faded to nothing, the whispers of the forest falling silent as though the very land held its breath. The snow beneath Kai's feet stopped crunching, the sound swallowed by the oppressive stillness that pressed down on him.

It was as though the palace itself were watching him now. Waiting.

The silence deepened as Fenrir led Kai through the gates of the Snow King's palace. Massive slabs of ice formed the towering arch, their surfaces slick and translucent, like frozen glass. Faint shapes shimmered just beneath—shadows of something long trapped, their outlines fractured and indecipherable.

Kai hesitated, his chest tightening as he stepped past the threshold. The storm, ever-present and furious in the forest, fell quiet here, as though its power stopped at the palace walls. The sudden lack of sound was jarring, the absence a weight that pressed against his skin and squeezed the air from his lungs.

It wasn't peaceful. It was **wrong**.

The courtyard stretched before him, vast and empty. Its surface, once white and smooth, was fractured in places, frost cracked and webbed like glass under pressure. The air felt heavier here, thick with something Kai couldn't name—something more than cold.

Kai's gaze drifted to the shapes scattered across the courtyard, half-buried in the snow. At first, he thought they were statues—works of art carved from ice. But as he moved closer, his steps slow and reluctant, the truth revealed itself, and his heart lodged in his throat.

The frozen forms were people.

Spirits, fae—he didn't know what they had once been—but they stood motionless, trapped mid-movement in poses of agony and despair. Faces contorted, hands outstretched as though clawing for freedom, their bodies coated in thick frost that blurred their features. Some were crouched on the ground, heads bowed, while others loomed taller, arms raised to the heavens as if in prayer or supplication.

The snow had gathered around them, drifts covering their feet and hands like a burial shroud. It was as though they had been swallowed by the cold itself, and Kai couldn't shake the feeling that they had been alive when it happened—that they had felt every moment of their entombment.

His steps faltered. "What... what is this place?"

Fenrir didn't slow, his massive frame moving effortlessly over the broken frost. His voice rumbled, low and steady, though there was something quieter beneath it—something almost mournful.

"The remnants of a kingdom. A graveyard for those who served him."

Kai's breath caught. He forced himself to move, though every instinct screamed at him to run. The air pressed against him like a physical weight, heavy with magic and the echoes of something ancient. The closer he got to the frozen figures, the colder it became—so cold it burned.

One of the forms caught his eye. It was a woman, her arms outstretched as if reaching for someone. Her face was tilted upward, her expression frozen in eternal sorrow. Ice had coated her hair, forming delicate, deadly strands that seemed to ripple like a waterfall. Kai's stomach twisted as he reached out a trembling hand, his fingers hovering inches from her frost-covered cheek.

"Who were they?"

Fenrir stopped, turning his massive head to look back at him. The wolf's golden eyes were unreadable, but Kai thought he saw something flicker there—a shadow of memory.

"They were loyal. They loved him once."

Kai dropped his hand, the cold biting through his skin like punishment for even considering such a gesture. "And now?"

Fenrir didn't answer immediately. When he spoke, his voice was quieter, almost reverent. *"Now they are echoes. They linger because he allows it."*

Kai swallowed thickly, his gaze sweeping over the courtyard. There were dozens of them—more than he could count. A kingdom turned to ice, their lives reduced to sculptures of torment. The thought of it, of being trapped like that forever, made his chest ache.

The Snow King had done this.

Kai's steps were unsteady as he followed Fenrir across the courtyard. The shattered frost crunched beneath his boots, the sound unnaturally loud in the oppressive silence. The frozen figures seemed to watch him as he passed, their eyes invisible but heavy on his back.

The palace walls rose up on either side, massive and shimmering faintly in the dim light. Their surfaces were smooth but imperfect—reflecting warped, distorted versions of Kai as he walked. In one reflection, his face looked hollow, eyes shadowed as though the frost had already claimed him. He turned away quickly, his stomach lurching.

"Why is it so quiet?" he whispered.

Fenrir didn't pause, his deep voice a steady murmur. *"This place remembers its pain. It holds its breath, waiting for what comes next."*

Kai shivered—not from the cold this time, but from the weight of those words. He glanced up at the looming palace entrance, its doors tall and sharp, carved from the same impossible ice. They seemed alive, pulsing faintly with light as though something ancient beat within.

The pull in his chest grew stronger, tugging him toward the palace. Kai pressed a hand to his ribs, trying to quell the sensation, but it refused to ease.

"Do you feel that?"

Fenrir glanced at him, his golden gaze unreadable. *"You hear it now. The castle calls to you."*

Kai's mouth went dry. "Why?"

The wolf said nothing, only turned back toward the massive doors. As they approached, the storm that had raged beyond the palace walls fell even quieter. It was as though the very land feared this place—feared what lay beyond those doors.

When they reached the entrance, Fenrir paused, his great head tilting slightly as though listening for something. Then he looked at Kai, his gaze pinning him in place.

"Do not linger. The King's eyes are everywhere here."

Kai blinked, his heart thundering in his chest. Before he could ask what that meant, Fenrir turned, pressing a massive paw against the doors. They groaned in protest, the sound deep and hollow, like the wail of something ancient and dying.

The doors swung inward slowly, revealing a cavernous darkness beyond—a space vast and empty, swallowing the faint light that tried to touch it. A pulse of cold air swept outward, cutting through Kai's furs like knives.

Kai hesitated at the threshold, his instincts screaming at him to turn back. The courtyard felt like a graveyard, but this... this was something worse.

Fenrir's voice rumbled softly from ahead. *"Come, little warmth. He waits for you."*

The pull in Kai's chest yanked sharply, and he stepped forward into the palace.

The air inside was colder than anything Kai had ever known. The chill sank past his skin, past muscle and bone, and into the marrow of his being, leaving him trembling despite the furs wrapped tightly around his shoulders. It was the kind of cold that felt alive, a presence pressing against him with each step.

The doors groaned shut behind him with a hollow finality, the sound reverberating through the vast chamber. Kai turned, his eyes adjusting slowly to the dim, silvery light that filtered through the ice walls. The ceilings stretched high above, disappearing into shadows that shifted faintly, as though something unseen moved within them.

Fenrir's claws clicked softly against the icy floor as he walked ahead, his massive frame cutting through the pale light like a shadow. Kai stumbled after him, the frost-covered ground slick beneath his boots. The faint pull in his chest grew heavier with every step, its invisible threads tugging him deeper into the labyrinthine corridors of the palace.

The first hall they entered was massive, its walls carved from flawless ice that refracted the faint light into shimmering patterns across the floor. Kai's breath misted before him, his steps echoing loudly in the oppressive silence.

Rows of ice pillars lined the space, their surfaces etched with intricate designs—swirling patterns that might have been vines or rivers or veins. Kai reached out hesitantly, his fingers brushing against one of the pillars. The surface was smooth but burned with cold, and he jerked his hand back.

"What is this place?" His voice sounded too loud, the words bouncing off the walls and returning to him as hollow whispers.

Fenrir paused, his golden eyes glinting faintly as he glanced back. *This is his court.*

Kai's gaze swept the room. It didn't feel like a court—it felt like a tomb.

As they continued deeper into the palace, Kai began to notice the remnants of what this place must have once been.

In one room, a long banquet table stretched out beneath a frozen chandelier. The table was set as though for a feast, each plate and goblet perfectly preserved under layers of frost. The chairs were pulled out, some tilted as though abandoned in haste, while others sat neatly in place.

Kai ran his hand over the surface of the table. Beneath the frost, he could just make out the faint glimmer of gold filigree, intricate and elegant. It reminded him of something alive, as though the room itself had once been vibrant, full of warmth and laughter.

But now, it was dead.

"What happened here?" Kai murmured, his voice low, as though speaking too loudly might disturb the silence.

Fenrir's response was simple, his tone devoid of emotion. *The curse.*

The deeper they went, the heavier the air became. It wasn't just the cold—it was something else, something that made it hard to breathe, as though the palace itself were alive and watching him.

The walls hummed faintly with magic, a low, constant vibration that Kai felt more than heard. It buzzed beneath his skin, making his head throb and his limbs feel heavy.

"Why does it feel like this?" he asked, clutching the furs tighter around him.

Fenrir didn't stop. *"This place was built from magic. Every wall, every pillar, every shadow. It breathes because it cannot die."*

Kai swallowed hard, his gaze darting nervously to the shadows that pooled in the corners of the hall. The oppressive silence pressed against his ears, making even the sound of his breathing feel too loud.

Fenrir stood in the doorway, watching him quietly. *"Do not linger,"* he said, his voice low.

They continued onward, the corridors narrowing slightly as they moved deeper into the palace. The pull in Kai's chest grew sharper now, insistent, as though it were guiding him somewhere. He pressed a hand to his ribs, his fingers trembling slightly.

"Why do I feel this?" he asked, his voice unsteady.

Fenrir glanced at him briefly. "Because fate is impatient."

Kai frowned, his pulse quickening. "What does that mean?"

The wolf didn't answer.

The silence stretched between them, heavy and suffocating, until Kai couldn't take it anymore. "What does he want from me?"

This time, Fenrir paused. He turned, his massive frame blocking the faint light behind him, his golden gaze locking onto Kai.

"You will know soon enough."

The chamber Fenrir led him into was vast and hollow, like the belly of a frozen cathedral. The ceiling disappeared into shadows above, the faint silver light from the walls barely stretching far enough to touch the edges of the room.

His boots slid slightly on the frozen floor, slick and crystalline, but Kai didn't care anymore. Every muscle ached, and his limbs were too heavy, too cold. He stumbled toward the center of the room, swaying slightly before sinking onto a wide, flat surface—what might once have been a bench or a throne, now coated in thin layers of frost.

The moment his body stilled, the exhaustion hit him all at once.

His chest rose and fell with ragged breaths, the ceremonial furs still clinging to him like a shroud. He buried his face in his hands, his fingers trembling as they pressed against his frozen skin.

What is happening to me?

The pull in his chest was quieter here, more like a dull throb than a sharp tug, but it was still there—still present, a reminder that he was not meant to stop. That he couldn't stop.

Fenrir sat a short distance away, the sound of his great form settling against the floor faint but distinct. His golden eyes glowed softly in the dim light, unblinking as they watched. For a long while, the only sounds were Kai's shallow breaths and the low hum of the castle's magic, vibrating faintly through the very ice around them.

Finally, Kai looked up, his voice hoarse. "Why did you bring me here?"

Fenrir tilted his head slightly, the movement graceful despite his size. His voice, when it came, was low and steady. *"Because you are needed."*

Kai barked a bitter, breathless laugh, the sound echoing off the frost-coated walls. "Needed? For what?" He threw his hands out in exasperation, his breath clouding before him. "Do you think I *wanted* to be here? Do you think I asked for this?"

Fenrir watched him calmly, unruffled by the outburst. His golden gaze held a patience that only something ancient could possess, as though he'd heard these words many times before.

Kai's shoulders sagged, his voice quieter now, edged with frustration and something dangerously close to despair. "What does he want from me? What do *you* want from me?"

Fenrir's eyes narrowed faintly. *"I told you before—you will not die here. You were brought because you are different."*

"Different?" Kai echoed, his voice rising again. "Different *how*? I'm just me. I don't have magic, I'm not some hero. I don't belong here!"

The wolf regarded him for a moment longer before speaking again, his voice calm but unrelenting. *"This place says otherwise. The Snow King brought you here, and the castle responds to you because you are not like the others."*

Kai froze, his pulse pounding in his ears. "What others?"

Fenrir's tail flicked, his gaze sharp and knowing. *"You are not the first to stand before the Snow King's wrath."*

The words hit like a punch to the gut. Kai's hands curled into fists against his knees, his nails biting into his palms as he stared at the wolf. "What happened to them?"

Fenrir did not look away. *"They failed."*

The silence that followed was deafening. The word echoed in Kai's mind, sinking into his chest like an anchor. *Failed.*

He shook his head slowly, his voice shaking. "And what? You think I'm supposed to be different? I'm supposed to *succeed* where they didn't?" He laughed again, the sound broken. "I can't even tell where I am, let alone what's happening. You've got the wrong person."

Fenrir rose to his feet, his claws clicking softly against the ice as he moved closer. The wolf's presence filled the space, heavy and unyielding. When he stopped before Kai, he lowered his great head until their gazes were level, his golden eyes burning with something Kai couldn't name.

"Neither did they."

Kai stared at him, his breath catching in his throat.

Fenrir's voice softened slightly, though it lost none of its intensity. *"None who came before you understood their purpose. None believed they could succeed. But unlike those summoned by the Snow King, I have brought you here, little warmth, and I believe you will succeed—where they have failed."*

Kai felt the weight of those words settle over him, a slow, suffocating realization. His heart thundered in his chest as he searched Fenrir's gaze for answers—something, *anything*—but all he found was certainty.

"Why me?" Kai whispered, his voice breaking. "Why would you bring me?"

Fenrir didn't answer immediately. The silence stretched, heavy and deliberate, before the wolf finally said, *"Because you are the first who may be able to thaw him."*

The word *thaw* clung to the air between them like frost, settling over Kai and leaving him shivering.

"You think I can stop this... this curse? Is it a curse?" His voice was unsteady, almost incredulous. "I don't even know what's wrong with him."

Fenrir regarded him steadily, his golden eyes faintly glowing. *"You will learn."*

Kai let out a shaky breath, his head falling into his hands again. The thought of it—the idea that he was here for a purpose that no one could explain—felt like too much to bear. It was absurd. Impossible. He was nothing but a man who had been dragged from his home, thrown into a storm that wanted to devour him.

And yet...

The pull in his chest was still there, constant and insistent, like a compass pointing him deeper into the palace. He couldn't deny that something about this place—about the storm, about the Snow King—**recognized him.**

It terrified him.

Finally, Fenrir moved back a step, his form shifting slightly as though satisfied. He turned his head toward the far end of the chamber, where shadows seemed to stretch and deepen.

The air in the room shifted abruptly, growing colder and heavier.

Kai felt it immediately, the temperature plummeting until the breath in his lungs burned like ice. The frost along the walls began to spread, creeping inward like reaching fingers, and the low hum of magic intensified, vibrating through the air.

Fenrir's voice rumbled, low and warning. *"He comes."*

Kai looked up, his chest tightening as he felt it too—a presence unlike anything he had ever known. It swept into the chamber like a wave of cold power, stealing the very air from the room.

Fenrir stiffened, his golden eyes narrowing sharply. A low growl rolled through his chest, the sound a warning that echoed faintly through the chamber.

Kai's breath caught as he felt it too—**a presence**. It slid into the room like a tide, stealing the warmth from the air, turning the very act of breathing into a painful struggle. Every instinct in his body screamed for him to run, to escape, to *hide*—but he couldn't move. His limbs were locked in place, frozen as surely as the walls around him.

The shadows at the far end of the chamber deepened and began to shift, swirling like ink in water. From within that darkness, something stepped forward. At first, it seemed like the figure moved too slowly to be real, like time itself had bent around him. Then the light caught on flowing robes of ice and frost, the fabric trailing across the floor in a soft hiss, as though the palace itself exhaled at his passing.

And then Kai saw him.

The Snow King.

He emerged from the shadows, his very presence making the air vibrate with an unnatural stillness. His figure was impossibly tall and regal, his long cloak trailing behind him like a frozen river. Silvery hair spilled past his shoulders in sharp, smooth strands, gleaming faintly in the dim light as though etched from starlight and frost. His skin was pale as marble, his features carved to perfection—sharp cheekbones, a strong jaw, and lips set into a line of cold indifference.

But it was his eyes that truly froze Kai in place.

They were ice incarnate—pale, crystalline blue, sharp enough to cut. They locked onto Kai with an intensity that made him feel exposed, as though every part of him was being dissected and laid bare for judgment. It wasn't just that the Snow King *looked* at him—it was as though he could *see* him in ways no one ever had, peeling back layers of his being until nothing remained hidden.

Kai shivered violently, his breath misting in front of him, his chest tight. The Snow King's presence pressed against him like an unseen weight, forcing him to brace himself just to remain standing.

Fenrir growled softly, stepping closer to Kai in a gesture of quiet protection, but the Snow King's gaze barely flicked toward the great wolf before returning to Kai.

For a moment, there was nothing but silence. It stretched endlessly, so heavy that it seemed the entire palace held its breath in anticipation.

Then the Snow King spoke.

"You are not what I expected."

His voice was deep and resonant, rolling through the chamber like a winter storm—soft and deadly all at once. Each word seemed to vibrate with an ancient power that clung to the edges of every syllable, as though the magic within him was barely restrained.

Kai flinched at the sound of it, his pulse pounding in his ears. He tried to speak, tried to answer, but his throat was dry, and the words caught there.

The Snow King's head tilted slightly, his sharp gaze narrowing as he studied Kai further. The faintest twitch of his lips suggested the ghost of a smile—though it held no warmth.

"What are you?"

Kai's voice finally broke free, though it wavered slightly, his words laced with an edge of sarcasm despite the tremor in his knees. He straightened, trying to steady himself. "An uninvited guest, apparently. Do you treat all your visitors like this, or am I special?"

"Hardly." His gaze swept over Kai, cold and assessing. *"You're simply... unexpected."*

He turned then, his cloak flaring slightly with the motion, trailing frost that spread across the floor like lacy patterns of ice. His footsteps were silent, the sound of his movement no more than a faint whisper, and yet his presence left a trail of frozen tension in the air.

Kai remained frozen where he stood, the weight of the Snow King's gaze lingering even as he walked away. Every muscle in his body screamed for him to move, to escape, but his feet remained rooted to the ground.

Fenrir nudged him sharply, his voice a low rumble. *"Move, little warmth. Do not make him wait."*

Kai tore his gaze from the path the Snow King had taken and looked at the wolf, his voice a hoarse whisper. "Wait for what?"

Fenrir's golden eyes narrowed faintly, though his voice remained calm. *"To decide your fate."*

The words struck Kai harder than they should have. He swallowed thickly, his heart still hammering painfully in his chest, before forcing himself to take an unsteady step forward.

Every instinct screamed at him to run. To turn back, to leave the cursed palace and its king to their misery.

But the pull in his chest tightened as he moved, insistent and undeniable. It dragged him after the Snow King, deeper into the frozen shadows of the palace.

CHAPTER 6

K AI FOLLOWED BEHIND, HIS breath ragged and clouding faintly in front of him, the furs around his shoulders doing little to fend off the bitter cold. His limbs felt heavy, the cold dragging at his every step as though the castle itself resented his presence, trying to freeze him into stillness.

The Snow King didn't look back. He moved with the silent confidence of someone who did not care if he was followed. His cloak trailed behind him, a flowing thing of frost and shadow, brushing the icy floor without leaving a mark. It was as if the castle bent itself to him, offering no resistance.

Kai stumbled as the heel of his boot caught on a patch of uneven frost. The sound—small as it was—shattered the silence, and Kai flinched at the echo of it. The Snow King didn't stop. He didn't even slow.

Something about the man's indifference burned at Kai. He clenched his fists beneath the heavy folds of the furs, frustration welling in his chest alongside the chill. "What do you *want* from me?"

His voice rang out sharply, bouncing off the frozen walls. It sounded far too loud, too small and desperate against the vast, endless quiet of the castle. Kai regretted the words the moment they left his mouth, but he couldn't swallow them back.

The Snow King stopped.

The abruptness of it made Kai stumble again, his boots scraping noisily against the slick surface of the floor. The king's figure was still, frozen mid-step, as though time itself had paused for him alone. The silence deepened, stretching into something unbearable, and Kai felt a shiver crawl up his spine.

Slowly, the Snow King turned.

His gaze found Kai, sharp and unrelenting, two pale blue shards of ice that froze him in place. For a long, unbearable moment, he said nothing—he simply looked. It was as though he could see through Kai, peeling back every layer of thought and fear until there was nothing left.

Finally, the Snow King spoke, his voice low and smooth, yet carrying enough weight to cut like a blade. *"Want?"*

The single word hung in the air, chilling and scornful. His head tilted ever so slightly, the faintest motion, but enough to feel deliberate—mocking, even. *"I want nothing from you."*

Kai's pulse quickened, a knot twisting tight in his chest. "Nothing?" His voice cracked, the word smaller this time, almost incredulous. "Then why bring me here?"

The king's lips curled faintly—not a smile, not truly, but something close. It held no warmth. *"You are a curiosity at best, an irritant at worst."*

The words hit like a slap, sharp and final. Kai recoiled instinctively, his expression twisting with confusion and something dangerously close to hurt. His fingers curled tighter into the fabric of his furs, his breathing unsteady.

"You call me a curiosity," Kai shot back, his voice trembling despite the anger he tried to inject into it, "but you dragged me into *this*—your storm, your castle. I didn't ask for this!"

The Snow King's gaze narrowed faintly. The temperature in the room seemed to drop further, the frost along the walls cracking softly as if in response to his displeasure. For a moment, something flickered behind the king's eyes—something sharp and unreadable, an emotion too fleeting to name.

Then he turned sharply, his cloak flaring with the motion like a cascade of dark ice. *"It matters not."*

Kai opened his mouth to respond, but the Snow King was already moving, disappearing into the long corridor ahead, his footsteps eerily silent. His voice echoed faintly behind him, dispassionate and cold. *"Do not follow."*

The words weren't a suggestion. They were a command.

Kai was left standing there, the heavy quiet pressing down on him like a second skin. The frost along the walls seemed to stretch closer now, creeping forward as though eager to reclaim the space the Snow King had vacated.

Kai let out a shaky breath, his chest aching from the effort of holding himself together. The sheer indifference of the king had stung more deeply than Kai wanted to admit. He felt small here—unimportant, insignificant in a palace that did not welcome him.

"An irritant at worst," he muttered bitterly to himself, his voice swallowed immediately by the frozen silence.

His gaze drifted down the corridor where the Snow King had disappeared, the shadows stretching long and endless. Something about the way the man moved—deliberate, distant—had unsettled him. Beneath the cold words and the dismissive gaze, Kai had felt something... else. Conflict, maybe. A flicker of something the Snow King himself hadn't seemed to understand.

But Kai had no chance to dwell on it. He realized now that he was alone—truly alone. The pull in his chest, which had led him so unrelentingly through the storm, was still there, but it had quieted. It no longer pointed anywhere specific, leaving him untethered in this strange and silent place.

Kai turned slowly, looking back down the hallway he had come through. The ice walls shimmered faintly, reflecting his image in distorted ripples—warped versions of himself that stretched and bent as though mocking him. He forced himself to look away.

"Fine," he muttered under his breath, more to himself than anyone else. "If he doesn't want me here, I'll figure things out on my own."

The Snow King's indifference burned in his mind, but Kai refused to let it crush him. He had survived the storm. He had survived being brought here. Whatever this place was—whatever had dragged him into its frozen heart—he wasn't going to let it break him.

As he took a step forward, his boot scraped against the frost-covered floor, the sound too loud in the heavy silence. He glanced down both ends of the hallway, then chose a direction—away from where the Snow King had disappeared.

The palace stretched, vast and labyrinthine, its secrets buried beneath layers of frost. And as he moved deeper into the castle, a strange sense of determination settled over him.

He was here. Alone, unwanted, but here.

So he would find out why.

The castle was beautiful in a way that made Kai's chest ache. It was the beauty of something lost, something abandoned. It wasn't until he entered what looked like a long-abandoned gallery that he realized he was no longer alone. The hall was lined with frozen sculptures—statues of animals and fae creatures, carved in excruciating detail. They stood silent and watchful, their eyes empty and blind, their poses captured mid-motion as though frozen in the middle of something joyful.

But it wasn't the statues that caught his attention.

Something *moved* in the corner of his vision—a flicker of motion in the stillness. Kai stopped, his breath catching as he turned his head.

At first, he thought it might be a trick of the light, but then he saw it: a small creature peering at him from behind a broken pedestal. It was no larger than a housecat, with delicate paws that barely made a sound against the ice. Its eyes were bright—two crystalline orbs that reflected light like captured stars—and its ears twitched as it watched him, curious but cautious.

Kai froze, not wanting to startle it. "What... are you?"

The creature tilted its head, the motion almost comical. Its tail flicked—long and trailing, leaving faint patterns in the frost like a paintbrush dipped in light.

Slowly, Kai crouched, extending his hand in what he hoped was a non-threatening gesture. "Hey there. I'm not going to hurt you." His voice was soft, barely more than a whisper.

The creature blinked at him, its head tilting the other way. Then, to his surprise, it took a hesitant step closer. Kai's heart thudded in his chest as he watched it move, its small paws leaving delicate prints in the snow-dusted floor.

When it reached him, it paused, sniffing at his outstretched fingers. Kai held still, not daring to move.

Finally, the creature nudged his hand with its cold nose.

Kai exhaled shakily, a smile tugging at the corner of his lips. "Well, you're not so scary after all."

The creature tilted its head again, almost as if offended by the suggestion. Kai couldn't help but laugh softly—a sound that felt strange in the empty gallery. It echoed faintly, breaking the suffocating silence, and for a moment, it was as though the room itself exhaled.

The frost fox—because that's what it reminded him of, a tiny, ethereal fox made of snow—stepped closer, circling him briefly before sitting primly at his side. Its tail curled around its paws, its crystalline eyes watching him intently.

"Looks like I've got a shadow now," Kai murmured. He reached out hesitantly, brushing his fingers across its back. The creature was cool to the touch, but not unpleasantly so—like the first snow of winter, soft and fleeting.

The fox let out a faint, chiming sound—somewhere between a hum and a purr—before standing and trotting a few steps ahead, its tail flicking as though beckoning him to follow.

Kai blinked, glancing between it and the empty hall. "You want me to go with you?"

The creature paused to look back at him, its expression—or what passed for one—insistent.

Kai sighed, rising to his feet. "All right. Lead the way, I guess."

He followed the frost fox deeper into the castle, its movements playful yet deliberate, like a guide who had been waiting for him. As they walked, Kai felt something shift within the oppressive silence. It was subtle at first—a faint hum, a soft crackle of warmth—but it was there.

The castle was still vast and empty, its beauty marred by abandonment and decay, but the fox's presence made it feel a little less like a tomb.

By the time Kai found his chambers with the help of the frost fox, exhaustion had set in, dragging at his limbs its faint glow threw shimmering patterns against the walls, the only light in an otherwise endless void of ice and shadow.

The room that awaited him was unwelcoming—small, empty, and devoid of comfort. Frost lined the edges of the windows, thick and opaque, blotting out the world beyond. The bed was more of a slab, draped in threadbare blankets that looked as cold as the stone beneath them.

Kai sighed, his breath clouding faintly in the still air. "Well, this is cozy," he muttered, more to himself than the fox.

The creature responded with a soft chime, curling itself neatly near the edge of the bed as though to keep watch. Its crystalline eyes blinked slowly, glowing faintly in the dim room.

Kai hesitated for a moment, looking around the space. Despite the wolf's cryptic words and the Snow King's dismissal, something had begun to settle inside him—a sense that the castle itself was watching him, waiting. He could feel it, like an undercurrent of quiet energy threading through the walls and floor, subtle but alive.

He shook off the thought and dropped heavily onto the bed, the blankets stiff beneath his touch. Curling the furs around his shoulders, he tucked himself into as small a shape as he could manage, but the cold still pressed against him. The frost in the air clung to his skin, sinking deep, as though the room itself resented his attempts at warmth.

Kai closed his eyes, his body aching. He wasn't sure how long he lay there, teetering between wakefulness and sleep, but at some point, he must have drifted off.

Kai woke slowly, pulled back to consciousness by a sensation he couldn't quite place—something *different*. For the first time since arriving in the castle, the cold wasn't biting at his skin.

The furs around his shoulders had slipped partially away, but the air was... warmer. It wasn't much—just a whisper of heat, faint and delicate—but it was enough for Kai to notice immediately.

His eyes cracked open, and he blinked, frowning as he sat up. The frost fox stirred at the edge of the bed, its ears twitching as it watched him lazily.

Kai rubbed his hands over his face and pushed the furs aside, his bare feet landing softly on the icy floor. Only this time, the floor didn't feel as biting against his skin. He froze, staring down as something delicate bloomed where his feet touched.

Tiny, crystalline flowers.

They spread out in soft ripples, fragile and perfect, their glassy petals glinting faintly in the pale light. Kai gasped, his pulse skipping as he stepped back instinctively, the flowers fading into frost as quickly as they had appeared.

"What...?" He looked toward the frost fox, who stared back at him unbothered, as though this were perfectly ordinary. "Did I...?"

Kai hesitated, then stepped forward again, more carefully this time. The flowers returned, blooming gently beneath his bare feet. They were intricate, tiny things—impossibly detailed—and though made of ice, they seemed untouched by the cold.

Kai crouched down slowly, reaching out to touch one of the petals. The surface was cool, but not icy. It didn't shatter beneath his fingertip as he expected. Instead, it glowed faintly, refracting light like a shard of crystal.

"I don't understand," he whispered, his voice soft as though afraid to disturb the fragile beauty of it all.

The faint warmth in the room drew his attention to the windows next. The thick frost that had once coated the glass had begun to melt, droplets of water pooling at the edges. Through the clearing ice, Kai could see the storm outside—soft now, like a gentle snowfall instead of the roaring blizzard that had brought him here.

Light filtered through the glass, refracted into rainbows that danced across the walls in shimmering arcs. The room looked transformed, the harsh cold tempered just enough to make it... bearable. Almost inviting.

Kai stood there, watching the light for a long moment, his mind struggling to make sense of it. The castle had been lifeless, cold, and unyielding since he arrived, but now it was... changing. Slowly. Subtly.

And he couldn't ignore that the change had started when he arrived.

The frost fox leapt from the bed, landing soundlessly on the floor and padding toward the flowers still blooming beneath Kai's feet. It sniffed at one of them before nudging its nose into Kai's palm, its cool breath brushing against his skin.

Kai laughed softly, the sound almost alien in the quiet room. "You're not going to explain this either, are you?"

The fox blinked, unbothered, before curling up again at the edge of the bed.

Kai sank back onto the blankets, pulling his knees up to his chest as he stared at the faint flowers still clinging to life on the floor. The warmth was fragile, delicate—just like the blossoms—but it was there.

The air thickened before the Snow King entered, a freezing weight that stole the fragile warmth from the room. Kai felt it immediately—the subtle heat that had grown in the air was ripped away, replaced by an icy pressure that made it difficult to breathe.

The frost fox let out a low, musical whimper and darted behind Kai's legs just as the door burst open.

The Snow King swept into the chamber like a storm given form, his long cloak trailing frost behind him in jagged, creeping patterns. His sharp blue gaze locked on Kai instantly, cold and unrelenting. Frost bloomed with every step he took, cracking the delicate flowers underfoot and spreading like veins across the floor.

Kai shrunk into his blankets, his breath hitching in his chest as the king stopped only a few feet away.

"What have you done?" The words were low and quiet, but they carried the weight of something dangerous, barely restrained.

Kai blinked, his pulse thundering in his ears. "I—I don't understand—"

The king's hand rose sharply, silencing him. His piercing gaze flicked over the room, sweeping from the frost-melted windows to the rainbows dancing faintly along the walls, and finally to the fragile ice flowers still blooming on the floor.

His expression hardened. "*This.*"

Kai glanced around the room, confused. "What are you talking about? I didn't do anything! It just—"

"Changed." The king's voice cracked through the air like a blade, his fury vibrating in the frost creeping closer to Kai's feet on the bed. He took another step forward, his presence suffocating. "This place does not change."

Kai shook his head, his frustration bubbling to the surface despite the fear clawing at him. "I guess it does now."

The Snow King loomed closer, his pale features sharp and cold as stone. "You expect me to believe that this—" he gestured sharply at the frost fox, the flowers, the faint warmth still lingering in the air—"is something beyond your control? Do you think me a fool?"

The frost fox growled softly, its crystalline eyes fixed on the Snow King as it edged closer to Kai, brushing against his leg protectively.

Kai shuffled onto his knees, his own anger rising. "Maybe. I don't control it! Maybe this place is just—"

"*Just what?*" The Snow King's voice dropped into a dangerous whisper, his gaze narrowing. "It bends to you. Your warmth infects it, spreading like poison. *You* are the reason it fractures."

Kai stared at him, incredulous. "Fractures? This place was already broken!" He threw a hand toward the cracked frost along the walls, the shattered flowers beneath the king's feet. "You freeze everything you touch. Not to be cliché, but maybe it's not me; it's you!"

The words escaped before he could stop them, sharp and reckless, and the silence that followed was deafening.

The Snow King's jaw tightened, the frost around him cracking audibly as his magic surged. The temperature dropped further, the cold biting into Kai's skin and stealing the breath from his lungs. His voice was soft but laced with venom. "You speak of strange things and as though you understand this place. You do not."

The pull in Kai's chest grew heavier, pressing against his ribs, and his pulse pounded painfully as the king's presence towered over him.

"I never said I understood it. I don't understand any of this—why I'm here, what you want from me—but whatever you're doing obviously isn't working."

The Snow King flinched, so subtly that Kai almost missed it. For a brief moment, something flickered in his eyes—a crack in the icy armor, so fleeting that Kai couldn't name it.

But the moment passed, and the frost along the walls surged outward, reaching toward Kai's feet with sharp, splintering patterns. The Snow King's magic pressed closer, suffocating and oppressive, as he stepped within inches of Kai.

The Snow King tilted his head, his pale blue eyes narrowing. "You believe you can stand here and lecture me about *my* kingdom?" His voice was low, almost a whisper, but it carried the force of a thunderclap.

Kai's pulse raced, but his voice didn't waver. "It's not a kingdom—it's a tomb."

The words hit like a strike of flint against steel. The frost beneath the king's feet crackled sharply, spreading outward in jagged, splintering lines that made the air hum with magic.

"You presume too much. You are nothing here—a fleeting warmth destined to vanish."

"Then why are you so angry?" Kai shot back, his voice trembling with frustration. "If I'm nothing, why does it matter what I do? Why do I matter at all?"

The question hung in the air, heavy and unrelenting.

The Snow King's lips pressed into a thin line, his eyes narrowing further. The pull in Kai's chest throbbed painfully now, a steady, insistent beat that seemed to echo through the room.

"You think you can change this place," the king said, his voice dropping into a deadly whisper. "You think you can change *me?*"

Kai's heart pounded painfully, but he forced himself to meet the king's gaze. His voice was quieter this time, but no less firm. "Maybe I already have."

The Snow King froze.

For a moment, his cold mask cracked—not enough to soften, but enough for something raw and vulnerable to flicker behind his eyes. His lips parted slightly, and the frost in the room stilled, the air growing almost too quiet.

Kai's breath caught as the king leaned even closer, their faces mere inches apart. The frost on the walls shimmered faintly, and the tension between them grew electric.

The Snow King's voice was low, almost a growl. "You don't know what you're playing with."

"Then tell me," Kai whispered, his words trembling but earnest. "Stop hiding behind all of this." He gestured vaguely at the frost and shadows around them. "If I'm really nothing, then why are you still standing here?"

The Snow King's eyes searched his, sharp and calculating, as though trying to decipher a riddle that refused to reveal itself. The frost fox let out a faint whimper, but neither of them moved, the moment stretched impossibly thin.

And then, the crack came.

Within a heartbeat, the Snow King's icy fingers dug into the soft flesh of Kai's neck. But the anger in his grasp swiftly gave way to a different desire as his eyes dropped to the human's lips. With a low growl, he lunged forward, claiming Kai's mouth in a brutal, all-consuming kiss.

Kai gasped, his eyes shooting wide open at the suddenness of it all. Sharp bites of coldness radiated from the Snow King's lips as they pressed hard against his own, a chill seeping into Kai's very core. It was a harsh kiss, one that bordered on violent—but beneath that icy exterior, something warmer lingered, a desperate need struggling to break free.

And then, for just a moment, the crushing cold dissipated. A flicker of heat coursed through Kai's veins as warmth flooded his chest. His heart raced at the sensation of life pulsating between them, something deep and raw that stirred a response within him.

The Snow King pulled back slightly, their heavy breaths mingling in the frosty air. His gaze bore into Kai, filled with longing and lust. "Fuck," he muttered under his breath, his voice strangled with desire. "You're burning me."

The Snow King's lips claimed Kai's with a force that felt inevitable, like frost yielding to flame, like a storm collapsing into stillness. There was no space between them, no hesitation—only the raw, fervent hunger of something neither of them could resist.

His fingers were relentless, tugging at Kai's clothes with a desperation that made the air between them electric. Buttons scattered like tiny stars on the frost-laden floor, and belts slipped free with practiced ease. Within moments, Kai lay exposed, his skin kissed by the chill of the icy chamber, save for the heat emanating from the Snow King's fevered touch.

The king's gaze swept over him, drinking in every inch of Kai's form. His icy blue eyes darkened, sharp with need, as though committing every line, every curve, to memory. "Beautiful," he murmured, the word slipping past his lips like a confession as he leaned down, their bodies coming together in a collision of warmth and cold.

Kai gasped at the sensation, a low, involuntary moan escaping him as the Snow King's frosty skin met his own. The contrast was dizzying, the sharp sting of cold mingling with the heat radiating from where the king's chest pressed against him. It was overwhelming, intoxicating—a paradox that sent shivers racing down Kai's spine.

He arched into the touch, his body craving more of the strange, addictive blend. His breath hitched as the Snow King's hand trailed down his side, the chill of his fingers tempered by a growing warmth that left Kai trembling. He didn't know if he was succumbing to the cold or the heat—or if he even cared. All he knew was that he needed more.

"Please," Kai whispered, his voice rough with desire, and the Snow King growled low in response, pressing closer, their bodies fitting together as though they had been forged for this moment.

The Snow King wasn't done yet. His hands roamed lower, fingers tracing along Kai's sides before cupping his ass and pulling him closer. Their hips collided, and Kai gasped, his breath hitching as he felt the king's hard length pressing against him.

Fuck, he's huge.

A sharp thrill shot through him, tangled with something deeper—hesitation. His body was unfamiliar, the sensations foreign in ways that sent his pulse skittering. His fingers curled against the king's chest, unsure if he meant to push away or hold on. His mind screamed that he should stop, that he wasn't ready, that this wasn't his body, but the heat curling low in his stomach didn't care.

The Snow King sensed the hesitation. His grip didn't loosen, but his lips ghosted over Kai's throat, his voice a low, teasing whisper against his skin. "Second thoughts, little warmth?"

Kai swallowed hard, his breath unsteady as the Snow King's lips brushed over his throat. The contrast of heat and ice sent a shudder through him, his body caught between the sharp edge of uncertainty and the intoxicating pull of sensation. His fingers twitched against the king's chest, his heart pounding as he struggled to reconcile the foreign need unraveling inside him.

"I..." Kai's voice wavered, caught between a protest and surrender. He wasn't used to this, to feeling like this. His past experiences—what few there were—felt distant, belonging to another version of himself, another life. Here, in this body, everything was new. The way his breath hitched when the Snow King's fingers dug into his hips, the way his own arousal throbbed in time with his racing pulse. It was overwhelming, and he wasn't sure if he was ready.

The Snow King stilled, his lips just below Kai's jaw, as though waiting. The weight of his gaze burned even without meeting it. He was giving him space, but only just. Kai could still feel the tension thrumming beneath the king's skin, the desperate hunger coiled tight in his body.

His fingers curled against the king's chest, less a push and more an anchor. "I don't—" Kai sucked in a breath, his mind spinning. "I've never—" He cut himself off, frustrated with his own stumbling words. "Not like this."

The Snow King exhaled slowly, his grip shifting just slightly. Not loosening, but no longer pressing Kai to move faster than he was ready for. His pale blue eyes searched Kai's face, his expression unreadable, but when he finally spoke, his voice was quieter, steadier.

"I won't break you," he murmured, his cool fingers brushing up Kai's spine in a featherlight touch. "But you are mine to claim, when you're ready to be taken."

Kai's breath caught. It should have been a warning, but the way the words rolled over him, possessive and deliberate, sent a sharp pulse of heat straight through him. He didn't resist when the Snow King leaned in, their lips brushing—not demanding, not urgent, just a whisper of contact that sent a new kind of tremor through Kai's limbs.

The king's lips pressed more firmly against his, slow and consuming, coaxing rather than taking. Kai's fingers tightened against the king's tunic, the hesitation in his chest folding under the weight of sensation. It didn't matter who he had been before, what his body had been before. Here, now, this was his to claim too. "Yours," he said, breathless.

A low growl rumbled in the Snow King's throat as his mouth found Kai's neck, trailing kisses that burned hot against his skin. Each kiss sent a cascade of goosebumps racing across Kai's flesh, the contrast between fire and ice leaving him shivering. The king's breath ghosted against his ear, each warm puff igniting sparks in his chest. "I need you," the king whispered, his voice rough and raw, laden with urgency. "Now, while I can still feel—"

Kai's mind raced even as his body arched into the king's touch. The Snow King's fingers were already at the waistband of his underclothes, fumbling with the fabric. The realization hit him like a cold gust of wind—*they needed lube*. It was reckless, dangerous even—but gods, the way the king's body felt against his made him ache for more. He couldn't think, couldn't breathe, couldn't do anything but *want*.

With a shaky breath, Kai reached down and stilled the king's hand. "Wait," he gasped, his voice barely above a whisper. "We need... lube."

The Snow King froze, his sharp blue eyes locking onto Kai's. The intensity in his gaze softened, shifting to something that almost resembled understanding. He nodded once, a silent promise, before lowering himself to his knees in front of Kai.

Kai's pulse thundered in his ears as the Snow King gripped the waistband of his briefs, tugging them down with an excruciating slowness. Every movement felt deliberate, teasing, designed to set his nerves alight. When the fabric reached his ankles, Kai pulled his feet free, his chest rising and falling in uneven breaths.

The Snow King's tongue darted out, tracing a slow, deliberate path up Kai's inner thigh. A groan escaped him as his hands gripped Kai's hips, pulling him closer. His fingers kneaded the flesh of Kai's ass, spreading him open with a gentle yet commanding touch.

Kai gasped as the chilled tongue delved between his cheeks, a rough, exploratory swipe that sent a bolt of pleasure through him. His breath hitched, not just from the sensation but from the sheer unfamiliarity of it. It was different—so different. The way his body responded, the sharp, dizzying heat curling low in his stomach, the sudden sensitivity in places that had never held pleasure before.

His fingers curled against the Snow King's shoulders, not gripping for more but anchoring himself against the overwhelming strangeness of it. His mind struggled to catch up with his body, to reconcile the pleasure with the fact that it felt good in ways he hadn't anticipated. His hips twitched, but hesitation warred with need, leaving him trembling on the edge of uncertainty.

"This feels..." His voice wavered, breathless and unsure.

The Snow King's hands tightened on his hips, firm but unhurried, as if sensing his hesitation. He didn't speak, just pressed another slow, deliberate stroke of his tongue against Kai's entrance, sending another shudder racing up his spine.

Kai let out a ragged breath, his grip on the king's shoulders tightening as his body swayed. It was new, strange, and yet—his chest heaved as he tried to fight the flush of heat rising inside him—it was intoxicating. The uncertainty remained, but it was quickly being drowned out by the way his nerves sang under the Snow King's touch, the way pleasure spread through him like wildfire despite his initial hesitation.

He wasn't just reacting—he was *feeling* this body in ways he never had before. And gods help him, but he wanted more.

Just as the tension coiled unbearably tight in his core, the Snow King pulled back. His lips glistened, his wild eyes dark with lust as he stood, towering over Kai once more. "I need you," he rasped again, his voice raw with need, barely tethered to restraint.

Kai's body thrummed with anticipation, his own breathless words escaping in a soft nod. The king slid onto the bed, his movement charged with purpose, his hands roaming freely, exploring, claiming, *learning*. Every touch felt electric, a connection forged between fire and frost.

The Snow King positioned himself between Kai's legs, his gaze locking onto Kai's, searching for any hesitation. When Kai nodded again—a silent affirmation—the king pressed forward. The sensation jolted through him, an intense blend of pleasure and pain that stole his breath and left him clinging to the king's shoulders.

"Breathe," the Snow King murmured, his voice low and grounding, a rare gentleness woven into his tone.

Kai did, and the tension in his body eased as the king moved slowly, allowing him time to adjust. Each measured thrust sent ripples of sensation through him, the sharp sting fading into something deeper, something that coiled low in his stomach and spread like fire through his veins. Their rhythm built steadily, each motion more desperate, more consuming, until it became a force of its own, something neither of them could hold back.

Everything blurred—the sharp bite of nails against his hips, the cool press of the king's chest against his skin, the way heat and ice tangled between them, leaving him undone. It was too much and not enough, an unbearable, aching need that only grew as their bodies met in a fevered, relentless pace.

As they moved, the push and pull of them felt inevitable, like the meeting of fire and frost, each feeding the other. Kai's mind emptied of everything but sensation, raw and all-consuming. He cried out, the sound lost to the cavernous room, his breathless pleas answered by the king's low, guttural moan.

Their slick bodies pressed together, every thrust an unspoken demand, every answering movement a surrender. And then, with a primal roar that echoed through the frozen halls, the Snow King came undone, and Kai followed, his release crashing over him in a wave so intense it left him trembling in its wake.

In the aftermath, their bodies lay entwined, slick with sweat and panting heavily. The Snow King's frosty exterior had all but melted away, replaced by a sheen of perspiration that glistened in the dim light. As their breaths slowed and the room fell silent once more, Kai found himself lost in the depths of the Snow King's eyes. The man's fingers trailed idly along Kai's spine, his touch lighter than frost on glass.

Kai shivered—not from cold, but from the tenderness in the gesture. The contrast between the man's earlier fervor and this quiet gentleness made Kai's chest ache in a way he didn't fully understand.

"Are you always this quiet afterward?" Kai murmured, his voice thick with exhaustion but laced with a wry edge. He tilted his head just enough to catch the Snow King's expression—or tried to, as the man stared resolutely at the ceiling.

A faint curve of the king's lips betrayed the ghost of a smile. "It is better to be silent than to speak carelessly."

Kai huffed a soft laugh. "I'd take my chances with careless words over none at all."

The Snow King's gaze flickered down to meet Kai's, his icy blue eyes softening. His hand stilled against Kai's back, resting just above the curve of his waist. "Careless words can ruin fragile things," he said quietly, almost to himself.

Kai frowned, shifting to prop himself on one elbow. The weight of the king's words lingered in the space between them, and his fingers twitched with the urge to touch the other man's face, to pull him back from whatever thoughts had taken hold.

"Fragile things like what?" Kai asked softly.

The Snow King didn't answer right away. Instead, he raised his hand, brushing his knuckles lightly over Kai's cheek in a gesture so fleeting it might have been imagined. When he finally spoke, his voice was a murmur, as though the words were meant for the frost-covered walls and not Kai.

"You do not understand what you have done."

The words sent a shiver down Kai's spine—not cold, but something deeper, something that settled into the pit of his stomach. He searched the Snow King's face, but the man's expression was unreadable, his gaze distant.

"What have I done?" Kai asked, his voice barely above a whisper.

The Snow King's hand slid down to rest against the small of Kai's back, his fingers curling faintly as if to hold him in place. He didn't answer, but the slight tension in his grip said more than words could.

Kai sighed, settling back against the man's chest. He didn't know how to respond, didn't even know if a response was expected. Instead, he let his own exhaustion drag him down, his body softening into the Snow King's cool embrace.

After a long, silent moment, the Snow King shifted, his arm tightening around Kai. The faintest exhale brushed against Kai's hair—an almost imperceptible sign of contentment.

Kai didn't know if the Snow King's tension had truly eased or if he had simply walled himself off again, but the steady rhythm of his breathing soon lulled Kai to sleep.

For now, whatever unspoken weight lingered between them could wait.

From the shadows just beyond the doorway, a pair of golden eyes watched—steady, unblinking, and knowing.

Fenrir moved silently, his massive form blending seamlessly into the dim light. He stepped forward just enough that the faint gleam of his silver fur caught the fractured rainbows still lingering in the room. His presence was quiet but commanding, a shadow woven into the frozen stillness of the castle.

For a long moment, he stood there, studying the scene before him. Kai lay sprawled in the Snow King's embrace, his body slack with exhaustion, the traces of vulnerability etched into the soft lines of his face. The boy—no, the man—was so warm, so fragile, yet somehow radiating a strength that had begun to melt the frost-bound silence around him.

Fenrir's gaze shifted to the Snow King. The ruler's hand rested possessively against Kai's back, his expression carved in ice but his eyes betraying a flicker of something deeper. Something uncertain. Something dangerous.

The frost fox stirred faintly at the edge of the bed, its crystalline eyes meeting Fenrir's. The wolf tilted his head slightly, the faintest movement of acknowledgment. The creature's gaze seemed to echo his own thoughts—watchful, protective, and wary of the storm that had begun to gather.

"It begins," Fenrir murmured softly, more to himself than to the room. The words hung in the air like frost, settling over the quiet scene with weight and meaning.

Kai's breathing slowed, his body giving in to the pull of sleep. The Snow King didn't move at first, his gaze lingering on the man in his arms as though caught in some internal war. Then, slowly, he eased himself away.

Fenrir's golden eyes narrowed slightly as he watched the Snow King sit on the edge of the bed, his movements silent. The king dressed with practiced efficiency, his long fingers fastening the folds of his frost-cloaked robes with a precision that betrayed nothing of the turmoil beneath.

Kai stirred faintly but did not wake. The Snow King's icy gaze flickered back to him, lingering for a heartbeat longer than necessary, before he stood to his full, imposing height.

Without turning, he spoke, his voice low and commanding. *"Come."*

Fenrir didn't hesitate. His massive paws carried him forward soundlessly, the frost beneath them crackling faintly in the stillness. The Snow King did not look back as he strode from the room, his cloak trailing frost and shadow in his wake.

Fenrir paused briefly at the threshold, casting one last glance at the sleeping figure of Kai. His golden eyes softened, though his expression remained inscrutable.

The frost fox lifted its head, its crystalline eyes gleaming faintly in the dim light, as though urging Fenrir to stay. But the wolf merely gave a low, almost imperceptible huff before stepping into the corridor and melting into the shadows at the king's heels.

The faint echo of Fenrir's voice lingered behind him, a whisper carried on the icy air:

"The storm will not end gently."

CHAPTER 7

KAI WOKE SLOWLY, THE chill of the room seeping into his skin before his senses fully returned. His first breath hitched, the cold biting sharply at his lungs, and for a moment, disorientation wrapped around him like a second blanket. Then the ache in his chest stirred, dragging with it the vivid, searing memory of the night before.

The Snow King. His touch, his kiss—both fire and frost, consuming and impossible.

Kai sat up abruptly, his fingers clutching at the edge of the thin, frost-covered blanket as though it might ground him. His breath clouded faintly in the air, the room colder than it had been since his arrival. The faint warmth that had begun to creep in, wrapping around him like an unspoken promise, was gone. Ripped away. In its absence was only the emptiness, gnawing at his chest and dragging his thoughts back to the hollow ache of being left behind.

Beside him, the frost fox stirred. It shifted in its sleep, curling tighter into a ball, its small body emitting the faintest warmth. Its crystalline eyes opened briefly, blinking at him with an almost understanding softness before it buried its face in its tail again, retreating into a comfort Kai wished he could mimic.

Kai's hand brushed over the blankets, his fingers tracing the faint imprint where another body had rested. The memory burned, vivid and surreal—how the Snow King's cold lips had melted into something warmer, the way his touch had scorched and soothed, the fragile flicker of connection that felt like it might become something more.

But it hadn't.

"Did that even happen?" Kai murmured to himself, his voice cracking as the words left him.

The room was silent, offering no answer, its stillness pressing against him like a weight.

Kai swung his legs over the edge of the bed, his feet touching the icy floor with a soft, reluctant thud. The frost prickled against his skin, sharp and unyielding. He glanced down instinctively, his stomach twisting when he saw that the flowers that had bloomed beneath his steps the night before were gone.

Shattered. Melted. As though they had never existed.

The realization struck harder than it should have. He ran his hand through his hair, the cool strands tugging against his fingers as his chest tightened. He could feel the absence like a hollow wound, the chill of the room mirroring the one that seemed to spread through his ribs.

The Snow King was gone, and with him, the faint warmth that had begun to feel like something real.

The castle felt different now.

The walls, which had begun to shimmer faintly with warmth and light, were cold and lifeless again. The frost clinging to them was heavier, more aggressive, creeping inward as though reclaiming the space that had briefly slipped from its grasp. The air was sharp and still, pressing against Kai's chest with an oppressive weight.

He glanced at the frost fox, still curled up at the edge of the bed, and whispered, "Was it all just... a dream?"

The fox let out a soft whine, its ears twitching, but it didn't move.

Unable to bear the suffocating quiet, Kai pushed himself to his feet, pulling the ceremonial furs around his shoulders. He didn't know where he was going, but he needed to move—needed to do *something*.

The castle's halls were eerily quiet, the sound of his footsteps echoing faintly before being swallowed by the endless cold. Frost clung to the walls and floors more aggressively now, the shimmering, fragile beauty of the night before replaced with jagged, icy patterns that stretched hungrily toward him.

Kai wandered aimlessly at first, his steps slow and uncertain. But as the silence pressed harder against him, his frustration grew, sharpening into something desperate.

He began searching in earnest.

The throne room was empty, its massive ice pillars looming silently in the dim light. The frost-covered garden, once hauntingly beautiful, was still and lifeless, the frozen trees casting long, jagged shadows across the snow.

There was no sign of the Snow King.

Kai's chest tightened as he moved through the great halls, his breath hitching with each unanswered question that swirled in his mind. The pull in his chest was faint now, quiet and directionless, leaving him unmoored in the castle's endless maze.

The oppressive emptiness gnawed at him, the silence growing louder with every step.

"Where are you?" Kai whispered, his voice trembling as he stopped in the middle of a vast, shadowed chamber. His words echoed faintly, swallowed quickly by the ice.

The frost fox pressed close to his leg, its small body surprisingly warm against the cold biting at his skin. Kai glanced down at it, his anger fading into something quieter.

He had felt something last night—something real, something *alive*. But now it felt as though the castle itself had turned against him, its silence a cruel mockery of the fragile warmth he had thought might linger.

Kai's breath hitched as he pressed a hand to his chest, the pull faint but steady beneath his ribs. He didn't know what it meant, didn't know why it still tugged at him even now, but it was there, a quiet reminder that he couldn't escape whatever had drawn him here.

The silence became unbearable as Kai wandered deeper into the castle's endless halls. His footsteps echoed faintly, distorted by the frost-lined walls until they sounded like whispers in the dark. He wasn't sure where he was going—his movements were aimless, driven only by the gnawing ache in his chest and the faint hope that he might find the Snow King.

But the castle seemed to push back at every turn. The air felt colder here, heavier, pressing down on Kai with a weight that made each step harder than the last. His breaths came in shallow bursts, the frost clinging to his skin like sharp needles.

The frost fox trotted beside him, its bright eyes glinting in the dim light. It let out a soft, chiming whimper now and then, as if trying to guide him, but Kai didn't know where he was supposed to go. The pull in his chest was faint, offering no direction, leaving him adrift in a maze of ice and shadows.

Then he heard it.

Groans—deep, guttural, and unrelenting—filled the icy corridor, reverberating through the frosted walls like an earthquake.

Kai froze. His breath hitched, caught somewhere between disbelief and morbid curiosity. The sounds were unmistakable—raw, primal, and laced with carnal need. They clawed at him, dredging up memories from last night, stirring emotions he wasn't ready to name.

His legs moved before his mind caught up, dragging him closer to the source of the sounds. Each step echoed in the silence, punctuated by the rhythmic grunts and wet slaps that made his cheeks burn. A knot twisted in his stomach, tight and searing, as if his body already knew what his mind refused to accept.

The doorway loomed ahead, carved jaggedly from shimmering ice, its intricate patterns catching faint rainbows of light as he approached. Each swirl seemed to mock him, the cryptic etchings feeling like a cruel riddle he wasn't meant to solve.

And then, he saw them.

The Snow King, regal even now, at the center of the chamber, his figure illuminated by the soft glow of light filtering through the high, frost-covered windows. His broad shoulders glistened faintly, his usually cold and controlled frame writhing against another's.

Another man.

Kai's breath caught painfully in his chest. The man was ethereal—dark-haired and striking, his beauty almost unnerving. His muscled body glistened with sweat, his strong hands gripping the Snow King's hips with bruising force. Their movements were rough, unrestrained, as though trying to carve some unspeakable truth into one another.

The chamber's icy walls reverberated with the sound of skin meeting skin, mingled groans, and the ragged pants of shared pleasure. It was a dance of dominance and need, brutal in its intensity. The Snow King's sharp features, normally unreadable, were twisted in raw ecstasy as his partner thrust into him with relentless precision.

The sight tore at Kai like a blade, sharp and unyielding. His chest tightened, the ache spreading through his ribs until it was almost unbearable. Last night's memories flashed before his eyes—how the Snow King's touch had ignited something fierce and unyielding in him, how for one fleeting moment, he'd felt like he might be special. That he might matter.

Now, all of it seemed like a cruel joke.

His fingers dug into the doorway, his knuckles whitening with the force of his grip. A bitter heat flushed his skin as he fought to tear his gaze away. But he couldn't. The rawness of it held him captive—the sheer animalistic hunger in their coupling, the unapologetic abandon. It was nothing like what he'd shared with the Snow King. And yet, it was everything.

A sharp pang of arousal coursed through him, unwanted and undeniable. His body betrayed him, heating despite the icy chill pressing in from all sides. His lips parted, his breaths shallow and uneven as his heart hammered in his chest. The ache of desire twisted alongside the sting of betrayal, a cruel mix that made his knees feel weak.

You fool, he thought bitterly, his mind spiraling. You thought you were something. You thought this was your story.

The thought lodged in his throat, bitter and suffocating. The Snow King hadn't even looked at him—hadn't even hesitated before moving on to someone else. Kai's fairy tale had shattered, its pieces scattering around him like shards of broken ice.

And yet, his body betrayed him, humming with something traitorous. His eyes locked onto the flex of the Snow King's back, the way his muscles tensed and shuddered with each relentless thrust. The dark-haired man groaned, his voice echoing through the chamber, his hands gripping tighter as he buried himself deeper into the Snow King.

Kai clenched his teeth, biting down so hard he tasted blood. He wanted to scream, to rip them apart with his bare hands, to drag the Snow King away and demand—what? An explanation? A reason? Some cruel reassurance that he had meant something?

But then the truth slammed into him, colder than the frost that had nearly killed him. Hadn't he been asking himself this same question all along? What am I?

He wasn't just another body. He wasn't even *his* body.

This wasn't his life, wasn't his story, wasn't even *his flesh*, and yet here he was—watching, aching, needing. He had wanted. He had hoped. But what did that mean, when he wasn't even the man the Snow King had taken to his bed?

His hands curled into fists.

You know what? Fuck this. Fuck all of it.

He turned sharply on his heel, heart pounding, ready to leave—to go *somewhere, anywhere* that wasn't here, watching this, feeling this. But the realization hit just as fast. Where would he go?

The village that had tried to kill him?

A kingdom frozen in time, where he had no place, no name, no future?

The weight of it pressed down, suffocating.

His steps faltered.

Tears pricked at the corners of his eyes, but he refused to let them fall. He wouldn't give the Snow King—or himself—the satisfaction. Instead, he forced his breath to steady, locking away every tremor, every spark of pain behind a mask of cold indifference.

He turned his back to the scene, his voice low and seething as he muttered, "I'm done."

Kai walked away, his chest hollow, his steps unsteady, his mind a tangled, aching mess of fury and grief.

And as he walked down the hall, leaving the sounds of pleasure behind him, something inside him cracked. Not shattered—no, not yet. But fractured, the edges splintering, leaving behind a hollow that he wasn't sure could be filled again.

The frost fox let out a soft whine, circling his feet anxiously, but Kai barely noticed. The weight in his chest was too heavy, the ache too sharp. He felt like he was splintering, the edges of his thoughts cracking under the pressure of it all.

He stumbled down the corridor, the voices behind him fading into the oppressive silence of the castle. The walls seemed closer now, the frost spreading in jagged lines that mirrored the cracks forming inside him.

Kai's breath came in uneven bursts as he pressed a hand to his chest, his heart pounding painfully beneath his ribs.

I'm nothing.

Just a pawn. A distraction.

The frost fox whimpered again, brushing against his leg as though trying to pull him back, but Kai couldn't stop moving. He needed to get away—away from the voices, the frost, the unbearable weight pressing down on him.

The air grew colder as he stumbled through the halls, his breaths shallow and sharp. The castle, which had once seemed to shift for him, now felt hostile, its silence pressing harder against him with every step.

When he finally reached his chambers, he slammed the door shut behind him, leaning against it as his trembling hands rose to press against his face.

The frost fox brushed against his leg, its faint glow a quiet reassurance, but Kai barely noticed it.

The ache in his chest had grown unbearable, spreading through him like a storm he couldn't escape. His hands trembled as he pushed off the door and stumbled toward the bed, collapsing onto the mass of furs. The frost beneath him seeped into his skin, biting and unforgiving, but it was nothing compared to the cold clawing at his heart.

The memory of the Snow King standing with the dark-haired man replayed in his mind, vivid and cruel. The soft way the man had touched him, the intimacy in their gestures—it was burned into Kai's thoughts, a constant, inescapable echo.

The frost fox leapt onto the bed, curling up beside him with a soft chime. It let out a quiet whine, pressing its small, glowing body against his side as though trying to offer comfort. But even its warmth felt fleeting, insubstantial.

Kai turned his face away from it, squeezing his eyes shut. "Stop it," he murmured, his voice trembling. "It doesn't matter. None of it matters."

The fox whined again, its crystalline eyes watching him with a gentle, almost pleading expression. It nudged his arm with its nose, but Kai didn't move, his body curled tightly as though trying to shield himself from the weight pressing down on him.

The room grew colder, the frost creeping along the walls in sharp, jagged patterns. It spread across the windows, thickening until the light from outside was almost entirely blotted out. The temperature dropped steadily, the air biting and sharp, but Kai didn't care. He welcomed it, the freezing stillness a match for the emptiness growing inside him.

The hours stretched endlessly, and Kai remained curled on the bed, his thoughts circling endlessly through the same maze of hurt and doubt. The frost fox didn't leave his side, its small form a quiet presence against the overwhelming stillness.

But no matter how tightly it pressed against him, no matter how persistent its faint warmth was, Kai couldn't shake the feeling that he was completely alone.

His breaths came slower now, steadier, but the ache in his chest lingered, a dull, constant throb that refused to fade. The frost on the walls glittered faintly in the dim light, beautiful and cruel, a reflection of the castle's unyielding nature.

Kai stared at it, his eyes heavy with exhaustion. For a moment, he considered giving in to the cold, letting it claim him the way it had claimed so much of this place. But then the frost fox nudged him gently, its glowing eyes steady and unwavering, and something in its quiet persistence kept him tethered.

He turned his head toward it, his voice barely audible. "Why are you still here?"

The fox blinked at him, unbothered by the question, and rested its head against his arm. Its warmth seeped into him slowly, subtly, like a reminder that the cold couldn't take everything.

Kai closed his eyes, his body still trembling faintly. He didn't know how long he lay there, caught in the quiet war between the frost and the fox's fragile warmth, but eventually, his breathing steadied, and the tears staining his cheeks began to dry.

The hurt still lingered, sharp and raw, but Kai wasn't ready to give in. Not yet.

The suffocating weight of the castle became too much. Kai couldn't stay inside any longer—not with the frost creeping closer, the walls pressing in, and the silence amplifying the storm of emotions clawing at his chest. He needed air, needed to escape, even if only for a moment.

Wrapping the ceremonial furs tightly around his shoulders, Kai slipped out of his chambers and into the frozen hallways. The frost fox followed at his heels, its small paws silent on the ice. It let out a faint whine as though sensing his turmoil, but Kai said nothing. He couldn't. His throat felt raw, his words too fragile to escape.

The castle doors groaned loudly as he pushed them open, the sound echoing through the stillness. A blast of icy wind greeted him, sharp and biting, but it didn't stop him from stepping out into the night.

The courtyard stretched before him, blanketed in snow that glowed faintly beneath the moonlight. The storm that had raged endlessly above the castle was quieter now, its swirling winds reduced to a gentle hum. But the cold was no less bitter, wrapping around Kai like invisible chains.

Kai's footsteps crunched softly as he wandered into the courtyard, his boots sinking into the untouched snow. He didn't have a destination—he wasn't even sure he cared where he ended up. He just needed to move, to breathe air that wasn't thick with the weight of the castle's silence.

The frost fox trotted beside him, its faint glow casting soft light against the snow. Kai glanced at it briefly, exhaling a slow, visible breath.

"You don't have to follow me," he muttered, voice raw but steady.

The fox blinked, utterly unbothered, then picked up its pace as if it were leading him somewhere.

Kai sighed and looked up at the stormy sky, letting the snowflakes land on his skin and disappear. The cold barely touched him now—his body had adjusted in ways he didn't fully understand. He pulled the furs tighter around himself out of habit, but it wasn't the cold gnawing at him.

It was the nagging, ceaseless pull of everything he didn't know.

"This is ridiculous," he muttered, dragging a hand down his face. His fingers curled into a fist as his frustration simmered. "What the hell am I even doing here?"

The words hung in the air, curling like frost before fading into nothing.

For a while, he just stood there, staring at the snow-covered courtyard. He wasn't about to break down in the middle of it. He'd already had his moment—curled up in bed, feeling lost and overwhelmed, letting himself feel every messy, humiliating emotion he'd tried to keep bottled up.

That was done now. He was done.

"Enough," he muttered under his breath, more to himself than anything. The frost fox flicked its ears as if it had heard and approved.

Kai's jaw tightened as he turned his thoughts over in his head. He didn't belong here. That much was obvious. But was that really the problem? He hadn't belonged back home either. At least here, there was some kind of purpose tangled in the mess—even if he hadn't figured out what it was yet.

And the Snow King?

Kai let out a short, humorless laugh, kicking at a patch of ice with the toe of his boot. He wasn't heartbroken. He wasn't in love. They'd had mind-blowing sex, sure, but he wasn't some tragic fool clinging to the memory of a man he barely knew. It wasn't about that.

It was the fact that he *had* wanted something. And for a moment, he had thought—maybe—that something had wanted him back.

And that? That was what stung.

The sound of approaching footsteps cut through the quiet.

Kai exhaled sharply, straightening his shoulders as he turned, schooling his expression into something unreadable.

Whoever it was, he wasn't in the mood for more surprises.

The sound of footsteps broke through Kai's thoughts—soft, deliberate, and impossible to mistake.

He stiffened, his body coiled with tension as he turned his head. From the darkness, a massive shadow emerged, silver fur glinting faintly in the moonlight.

Fenrir.

The great wolf moved with practiced silence, each step through the snow leaving barely a trace. His golden eyes glowed softly, sharp and unreadable, but there was no judgment in them—only quiet understanding.

Kai exhaled slowly, pressing his hands against his thighs to keep them from shaking. He wouldn't crumble. Not again.

Fenrir came closer, his ears flicking back briefly before he lowered his head, his breath visible in the cold air. Without a word, he placed something before Kai—a bundle wrapped in cloth, the scent of roasted meat and herbs wafting through the bitter chill.

Kai blinked. His stomach twisted—not with hunger, but with something more complicated. Pride, stubbornness, the raw edge of too many emotions scraping against each other. He wanted to refuse, to claim he wasn't weak, wasn't desperate, but his body betrayed him. The sharp pang of hunger coiled low in his belly, reminding him that it had been too long since the last time he'd eaten.

Wordlessly, he reached for the bundle, unwrapping it carefully. Warmth seeped through his fingers, the simple weight of food in his hands grounding him. He swallowed hard before speaking, his voice rough but steady. "Where did you get this?"

Fenrir tilted his head, as if the question itself was unnecessary. *Does it matter?* his gaze seemed to say.

Kai hesitated, then tore off a piece of the meat. The first bite was almost too much—the rich, smoky flavor exploding on his tongue, the heat chasing away the cold that had settled deep in his bones. He hadn't realized how much he needed it until now.

Fenrir sat beside him, his massive frame blocking some of the wind. He said nothing, merely watching as Kai ate. The quiet was different this time. Not oppressive. Not expectant. Just... there.

Kai swallowed, wiping his mouth with the back of his hand. "I'm not falling apart," he muttered, more to himself than to Fenrir.

The wolf huffed—a sound almost like amusement. Then, as though making a point, he pressed his broad head against Kai's shoulder, solid and grounding.

Kai let out a slow breath. He didn't lean into the touch, but he didn't pull away either.

The frost fox curled up nearby, its glowing eyes watching them both with an almost knowing air.

After a long moment, Kai glanced down at the food still in his hands, then back at Fenrir. His jaw tightened, but his next words came easier than expected.

"...Thank you."

Fenrir didn't reply. He didn't need to.

Kai exhaled slowly, the taste of salt still fresh on his lips, the warmth of the food settling in his stomach like a foreign thing. The night stretched endlessly around them, the silence of the snow pressing in, thick and impenetrable. He wasn't sure how long they sat there—Fenrir beside him, the frost fox curled near his legs, the weight of exhaustion pulling at his limbs.

Then, without warning, Fenrir shifted.

Kai felt it before he saw it—a ripple in the air, like the breaking of a spell. A low hum vibrated through the ground beneath him, and the heat that had begun to seep into his bones vanished, replaced by an eerie stillness. He turned sharply, breath catching as the silver fur blurred, dissolving into a thick mist that coiled like smoke.

His pulse slammed against his ribs, his body instinctively tensing, his mind racing ahead of reason. The mist reformed, solidifying into the shape of a man, and in the dim light, Kai finally saw him.

Broad shoulders. Dark hair streaked with silver. Golden eyes that gleamed like molten fire.

Kai staggered back as brutal clarity crashed over him.

The man in the chamber. The dark-haired, wild beauty who had ravaged the Snow King with such unapologetic intensity.

It was him.

"You…" His voice cracked, torn between disbelief and something sharper—something raw and gutting. His hands curled into fists at his sides, fingernails digging into his palms. "You were—" He couldn't finish the sentence. The image of the Snow King, his head thrown back, his body writhing beneath Fenrir's relentless touch, seared into his mind.

Fenrir's lips curved faintly, a quiet, knowing smile that only infuriated Kai more. "You are not alone, little warmth," he said, his voice a low rumble, steady as ever.

Kai gawked at him, emotion flashing violently across his face—confusion, hurt, anger. And, somewhere buried deep, a reluctant ember of arousal that made his skin prickle with humiliation. He took a shaky breath, then shook his head, his fury bubbling to the surface.

"What the hell are you doing here?" he snapped, his voice sharper than the wind slicing through the trees. "You—you're supposed to be helping me, not…" His throat tightened, his voice failing him. *Not fucking him.*

Fenrir took a slow step forward, boots crunching softly against the snow. He crossed his arms over his broad chest, unbothered by Kai's anger. "Helping you and being with him are not mutually exclusive."

Kai let out a sharp, disbelieving laugh, the sound brittle. The sheer audacity of it sent heat surging through him, momentarily burning away the cold that had settled into his bones. "So, what? You're just *his*? Like everyone else in that goddamned castle?"

Fenrir's expression remained infuriatingly composed, but something flickered behind his golden eyes—something Kai couldn't name. "What I am to him is not what you think," he said, his voice calm, unwavering. "And what he is to you… is not what you fear."

Kai recoiled as if struck, his heart hammering against his ribs. "You don't know what I fear."

Fenrir tilted his head slightly, his gaze steady, piercing. "Don't I?"

Kai exhaled sharply, his breath curling into the cold. He wasn't sure what he *felt*—surprise, mostly. Maybe a little humiliated. No one had lied to him, nothing had been promised, and yet the realization still sat uncomfortably in his chest.

He had barely been here *a day*. He'd fallen into this frozen world with nothing, tangled himself in something intense and consuming, and now, *now* he was just starting to realize he had no idea what—or *who*—he was dealing with.

The Snow King had touched him like he *needed* him. Kissed him like he was something rare. But he hadn't been alone in that bed for long, had he?

Kai clenched his jaw, forcing himself to meet Fenrir's gaze. "Tell me now," he said, voice rough but steady. "What the hell is going on?"

Fenrir studied him for a long moment before exhaling slowly, his breath a thick plume in the frozen air. "Walk with me."

Kai hesitated. The rational part of him—the part still smarting from the realization of what he'd walked into—wanted to *not* give Fenrir the satisfaction of an explanation. But he wasn't stupid. If there was even a chance of understanding what he'd fallen into, he needed to hear it.

He nodded once.

The ceremonial furs dragged heavily around his shoulders as he pulled them tighter, and the frost fox trotted beside him, its glowing eyes flicking between the two men as if waiting for something to explode.

It might.

They walked in silence for a while, their footsteps the only sound in the snow. The cold wrapped around them, sharp as knives, but Kai barely felt it. His thoughts were louder.

He was the first to break the quiet. "You could've *said* something before I walked into that."

Fenrir didn't look at him. "Would it have changed anything?"

Kai's first instinct was to snap *yes*, but his mouth clamped shut before the word could escape.

Because the answer was *no*.

He still would have let the Snow King touch him. Still would have *wanted* it. Last night had been raw and intense, something he hadn't been able to pull away from even if he'd tried.

But *knowing*—that would have at least given him a choice.

Kai scoffed, shaking his head. "I don't like being the idiot in the room."

"Then you have a problem," Fenrir said dryly. "Because you've been in this world for less than two days, and that's exactly what you are."

Kai shot him a glare. "Wow. Thanks. Real inspiring."

Fenrir finally looked at him then, his golden eyes sharp but not unkind. "Would you rather I lie?"

Kai exhaled through his nose. "I'd rather not feel like an ass for not knowing *basic* information. I mean, gods, you and the Snow King—" He gestured vaguely, irritation prickling beneath his skin. "That's something I probably should've known before I got tangled up in whatever the hell last night was."

Fenrir tilted his head slightly. "And what *was* last night?"

Kai faltered.

He opened his mouth, then shut it.

It was a *good* question.

Because what *was* last night? A mistake? A moment? Something more? He had no idea. He wasn't *in love* with the Snow King, not even close—but he wasn't *indifferent*, either.

He wasn't sure what to call it, and that bothered him more than it should.

"That's not the point," Kai said instead, bristling at how flimsy that sounded.

Fenrir's lips twitched. "No, I suppose it's not."

Kai groaned, running a hand through his hair. "You're really enjoying this, aren't you?"

"Immensely."

"Great. Love that for you."

They walked a few more steps before Kai sighed, frustration still buzzing beneath his skin. "How long?" he asked, glancing at Fenrir.

Fenrir didn't pretend not to understand the question. "A long time."

The answer shouldn't have stung, but it did. Kai forced himself to shrug like it didn't matter. "And what, you two are just—what, *together*?"

Fenrir's expression didn't change, but there was something in his gaze—something Kai couldn't quite read. "It's complicated."

Kai barked a short, humorless laugh. "Yeah, no shit." He shook his head, exhaling sharply. "This whole thing is a mess."

"It is," Fenrir agreed, annoyingly calm.

Kai shot him a look. "And *you* could have made it less of a mess if you'd just *told me.*"

"Would you have believed me?"

Kai faltered again.

Gods, that was irritating.

"...I don't know," he admitted, kicking at the snow.

Fenrir hummed, apparently satisfied with that answer. "Then it wouldn't have changed anything."

Kai clenched his jaw. "Still would've been *nice* to know."

Fenrir stopped walking then, turning to face him fully. "And now you do." His golden eyes locked onto Kai's. "If you want more, you should be asking the right questions."

Kai frowned. "Like what?"

"Like *who he was before you met him.*"

Something in Fenrir's voice made Kai pause.

Before he could respond, Fenrir nodded toward the tree line. "Come on. If you want the truth, you'll get it soon enough."

Kai hesitated, his stomach twisting—but he followed.

Because *now* he needed to know.

Fenrir led Kai through the darkened forest, his broad shoulders cutting through the shadows like a blade. The frost fox followed close at Kai's heels, its faint glow offering the only light as they walked deeper into the frozen wilderness. The biting wind softened as they moved, replaced by a quiet stillness that pressed in from all sides. Snow drifted gently through the air, catching in the gnarled branches of ancient trees that stood like watchful sentinels.

Kai felt the shift before he saw it. The oppressive weight of the castle was gone, replaced by an eerie calm. The snow beneath his feet shimmered faintly in the moonlight, and the air carried the barest hint of warmth—just enough to make the hair on the back of his neck rise.

Fenrir stopped at the edge of a grove and gestured to a low, sturdy tree. "Sit."

Kai hesitated, his instincts prickling. But he obeyed, settling against the smooth bark, the cold pressing through the furs draped around his shoulders. The frost fox curled up beside him, its soft glow pulsing faintly.

Fenrir crouched nearby, his golden gaze steady.

"The Snow King was not always as he is now," Fenrir began, his voice low, deliberate. "There was a time when the Winter Court thrived—its beauty unmatched, its people devoted. He ruled with grace, his magic a balance of frost and vitality."

Kai frowned, the words jarring against everything he had seen so far. "That's hard to believe," he muttered.

Fenrir's lips twitched faintly. "It would be," he said. "You've only seen what's left." His gaze flicked toward the frost fox before returning to Kai. "But once, he was a man of warmth as much as ice."

Kai hesitated, something uneasy curling in his chest. "And you... you knew him before all that?"

Fenrir held his gaze. "I was his." The words came quiet but firm. "Before the Summer Prince. Before the court froze."

Kai stiffened. His mind latched onto the memory of the man in the chamber—the dark-haired figure wrapped around the Snow King, their bodies tangled together with raw, unrestrained hunger.

"That was you," Kai said, his voice lower now, rough with realization.

Fenrir inclined his head, unflinching. "Yes."

The weight of that admission settled between them, heavy and sharp. Kai swallowed, his thoughts a tangled mess. He wasn't sure what unsettled him more—the fact that Fenrir had been with the Snow King long before him, or the fact that *of course* he had. That last night had been *nothing new* for either of them, except for him.

"Why?" he asked after a long moment. The word was hoarse, quieter than he intended. "Why are you still here?"

Fenrir's expression softened, but his voice remained steady. "Because I loved him," he said. "I still do."

Kai flinched before he could stop himself. He wasn't sure why. Maybe because it was *so simple*—so easy for Fenrir to say what Kai hadn't even begun to sort through.

His stomach twisted. "Then why did he—" He cut himself off, frustration bubbling to the surface. "Why *me*?"

Fenrir's lips pressed into a thin line. "Because he doesn't know what to do with you."

Kai's brow furrowed.

"You're something he cannot control," Fenrir continued. "Something he doesn't understand. And that terrifies him."

Kai let out a sharp breath, shaking his head. "That doesn't explain why *you* were—" His throat tightened around the words, his mind flashing back to the way the Snow King had *held* Fenrir, *touched* him.

Fenrir leaned in slightly, his golden eyes sharp. "Because he needed something familiar. Something he could hold without fear of it slipping away."

Kai's breath hitched.

His fists clenched against his knees. "And you just *let* him?"

Fenrir's expression didn't waver. "I am not your enemy." His voice was calm, firm. "What you saw last night—it wasn't about you. Or me. It was about *him*."

Kai's chest tightened, irritation and something else—something he didn't want to name—clawing at his ribs.

"You think he's cruel," Fenrir went on. "And maybe he is. But he's also *broken*—shattered by the Summer Prince's betrayal and bound by grief he's carried alone for centuries."

Kai stared at him, heart hammering against his ribs. "The Summer Prince," he murmured, the name unfamiliar but thick with weight.

Fenrir nodded. "He came to the Winter Court seeking the Snow King's heart. But his love was possessive. Poisoned by envy. When the Snow King refused to give up his people, the prince cursed him—froze his court, his magic, his heart."

Kai inhaled sharply. The pieces began to fit together—the frozen figures in the castle, the suffocating silence that hung over it all.

"And you?" he asked, voice barely above a whisper. "What happened to *you*?"

Fenrir's expression darkened, a flicker of something almost *human* crossing his sharp features. "I tried to stay." He exhaled, low and slow. "But the curse turned me into something else. The wolf you've seen—that is what remains of the man I was."

Kai didn't speak for a long moment, the wind rushing softly between the trees.

There was too much to process.

Too much that suddenly made *sense*.

He let out a slow breath, dragging a hand through his hair. "And here I thought I had a complicated night."

Fenrir huffed—a sound that might have been amusement if it weren't so tired. "It's only going to get worse."

Kai groaned. "Fantastic."

But despite the weight of everything, the knot in his chest loosened—just a little. Because now, at least, he *understood*.

And that was more than he'd had before.

Kai stared at Fenrir, his mind still reeling. "Why are you telling me this?"

Fenrir didn't hesitate. "Because you've done what no one else could. You've stirred something in him. You've made him *feel* again. And that is both your greatest strength and your greatest danger."

Kai shook his head, his breath unsteady. "I didn't *ask* for this."

"It doesn't matter." Fenrir's gaze was unwavering. "What matters is what you do now."

The frost fox stirred at Kai's side, its glowing tail brushing against his arm. The gesture felt almost reassuring, though it did little to quiet the frustration curling in his chest.

"Do not mistake his desperation for cruelty," Fenrir said, his voice softer now. "He is trying to remember what it means to be whole. And you are the only one who can show him."

Kai scoffed, shaking his head. "You keep saying that like it *means* something. Like I have some kind of power over him." His fingers dug into the furs at his shoulders. "I don't. He barely looks at me unless it's to criticize, and last night—" He cut himself off, jaw tightening. "Last night wasn't about me."

Fenrir watched him carefully. "No," he agreed. "It was about *him*."

Kai exhaled sharply. The words shouldn't have stung, but they did.

Fenrir leaned in slightly, his golden gaze sharp. "Tell me, *when* was the last time the Snow King felt anything at all?"

The question landed like a blow, sharper than Kai had expected. He opened his mouth, but no answer came.

Because the truth was, he *didn't know.*

He thought of the Snow King's cold, cutting gaze—the way it had softened for the briefest moment. The way his touch had burned, as if trying to remember what warmth even felt like. He *had* felt something last night. That much was obvious. But Kai didn't know if it had been *him* or just the desperate act of a man drowning in his own silence.

Kai swallowed hard, his voice quieter now. "But *why me*? I'm not special. I'm just—" He hesitated. "I'm just a mistake. Someone who got pulled into this mess because of some stupid book."

Fenrir's gaze sharpened. "What book?"

Kai blinked, suddenly regretting saying anything. "It's... never mind," he muttered, looking away. "It doesn't matter."

Fenrir studied him, but after a beat, let it go. "There are no mistakes in this world," he said simply. "Whatever brought you here, it did so for a reason."

Kai huffed out a bitter laugh, raking a hand through his hair. "So what?" he asked. "I'm supposed to thaw his heart? Save him like some *fairy tale hero*?" The words dripped with sarcasm, but there was a flicker of something raw beneath them. "That's not me."

Fenrir's brow furrowed slightly. "Fairy... tale?" he repeated, as if turning the phrase over in his mind. "What do fairies have to do with this?"

Kai blinked, caught off guard. He let out a short, exhausted laugh. "It's an *expression*. A story where someone swoops in and fixes everything, saves the day, makes it all better."

Fenrir tilted his head, his golden gaze thoughtful. "If that is what you expect of your story, then perhaps you misunderstand it."

Kai frowned. "What's *that* supposed to mean?"

Fenrir's voice remained steady, but his conviction was clear. "Not all stories are about heroes. Some are about those who *make* things possible for others."

The words settled like stones in Kai's chest, heavy and uncomfortable. He glanced at the frost fox, its crystalline eyes watching him with quiet patience. "What if I don't *want* to be part of this story?" he muttered. "What if I just... want to go home?"

Fenrir's expression didn't shift. "Then that is your choice." A pause. "But know this—those who came before you tried and failed. They left only cold and silence in their wake. *You* have brought something else."

Kai looked up sharply, his breath catching. "I don't even know *how*," he admitted. "I don't know what I'm doing here."

Fenrir's gaze softened just slightly. "Perhaps you don't need to know yet," he said. "Sometimes, simply *being here* is the first step."

Kai hesitated. "Why?" His voice was quiet but demanding. "What makes me different from those who came before?"

Fenrir's golden eyes gleamed in the moonlight, his voice unwavering. "You are light in a world that has forgotten it. You are warmth in a place that has known nothing but cold. Even if you do not see it, your presence alone changes *everything*."

Kai's throat tightened. He didn't *feel* like light or warmth. He felt lost. Small. A stranger in a story that wasn't his.

"I don't want to be a *sacrifice*," he whispered before he could stop himself.

Fenrir's expression didn't waver. "Then don't be." His voice was quiet, steady. "Be a *choice*. Do what only you can."

The frost fox let out a quiet, chime-like sound, pressing lightly against Kai's side. He exhaled shakily, the storm inside him quieter but not gone.

He still didn't know if he was strong enough to face what was ahead. But as he sat beneath the trees, Fenrir's unwavering presence beside him, he allowed himself to believe—if only for a moment—that the choice might *truly* be his to make.

CHAPTER 8

T HE GROVE'S QUIET SERENITY faded as they made their way
back to the castle. The forest stretched out around them,
its jagged trees etched with frost and shadow, their bare branches
clawing at the storm-darkened sky. The crunch of snow beneath
their boots was the only sound, echoing faintly in the stillness.

Kai kept his gaze fixed on the ground, his breath fogging in the
cold air. His mind raced with the weight of Fenrir's words: the Snow
King's curse, the Summer Prince's betrayal, the endless winter that
had consumed an entire court. The sheer scale of it all felt impossible
to comprehend, like trying to hold an avalanche in his hands.

When they reached the massive ice doors, they groaned loudly as
Fenrir pushed them open. The bitter cold inside washed over Kai
immediately, stealing the faint warmth he had carried from the grove.
He shivered, pulling the furs tighter around his shoulders as they
stepped inside.

The frost-lined walls seemed darker now, the faint light barely
enough to cut through the shadows pooling in the corners. The
oppressive silence returned, heavy and suffocating, pressing down on
Kai like a second layer of ice.

He glanced at Fenrir, his voice quiet but edged with frustration.
"And what happens now? Am I supposed to just... fix him? Break the
curse?"

Fenrir's steps slowed slightly, his gaze turning toward Kai. "What happens now is up to you," he said simply, his tone as steady as the cold air around them.

Kai snorted, shaking his head. "That's not an answer."

"No," Fenrir agreed, his lips quirking faintly again. "It is not."

Kai paced the room with restless energy, the frost fox watching him intently from its perch on the bed. Its tail curled lazily, but its crystalline eyes gleamed with quiet vigilance, as though it could sense the unease radiating from him. The air in the chamber was cold, sharp, biting against Kai's skin as if the castle itself refused to let him forget where he was.

Fenrir stood near the doorway, his arms relaxed but his presence unmistakable. He didn't speak, didn't push, but the way his golden eyes followed Kai's movements spoke volumes. There was no judgment in his gaze, only a patient, steady weight that demanded acknowledgment.

Kai stopped mid-step, his breath clouding faintly in the frosty air. "You've been watching me this whole time," he said suddenly, his voice edged with something raw. It wasn't an accusation, not entirely, but it carried the weight of unspoken questions.

Fenrir didn't deny it. "Yes," he said simply. His tone was calm, but there was an underlying sharpness to it, like the edge of a blade hidden in velvet.

Kai's hands clenched into fists at his sides. He exhaled sharply, shaking his head as if trying to rid himself of thoughts too heavy to carry. "Why?" he asked, his voice trembling. "Why do you care? Why does anyone care?"

Fenrir tilted his head slightly, his golden gaze unflinching. "Do you truly believe no one should?"

Kai flinched at the quiet rebuke, the question hitting far too close. He turned away, raking a hand through his hair as frustration boiled beneath his skin. "I don't belong here," he muttered, his voice low but fierce. "None of this makes sense. I'm not... I'm not who you think I am."

"Then who are you?" Fenrir asked, stepping forward. His movements were measured, deliberate, the kind that didn't demand attention but claimed it effortlessly.

Kai hesitated, his throat tightening. His fingers curled around the furs draped over his shoulders as though they might shield him from the weight of his own confession. "I'm not him," he said finally, the words tumbling out like they had been forced through a crack in a dam. "I'm not Kai—not really. I woke up here, in this body, and I don't know why. I don't know what I'm supposed to do, or how to fix it, or... or anything."

The words hung in the air, raw and unpolished. Kai's chest heaved as though speaking the words aloud had drained him, and he braced himself for Fenrir's reaction. Disbelief, rejection, maybe even anger—he expected all of it.

What he didn't expect was Fenrir's silence.

The wolf-man stepped closer, his golden eyes never leaving Kai. When he finally spoke, his voice was quiet but firm, like the first crack of thunder in a distant storm. "I know."

Kai froze, his heart skipping a beat. "You... know?" he whispered, his voice barely audible.

"I have known since I found you," Fenrir replied, his tone as steady as the earth beneath them. "You are not the same as the boy this world knew. Your presence carries a weight that does not belong to this place. I could see it in your every step, your every word."

Kai's breath hitched, the truth of Fenrir's words cutting through him like ice. "Why didn't you say anything?" he asked, his voice breaking.

"Because it was not my place," Fenrir said simply. "The truth was yours to give, not mine to claim."

The frost fox stirred on the bed, its glowing eyes flickering as it watched them both. Its quiet presence was grounding, though it did little to quell the turmoil roiling inside Kai.

"I don't..." Kai faltered, his throat tightening. "I don't know what to do. I don't know how to be... this." He gestured vaguely to himself, his hands trembling.

Fenrir reached out, his hand settling lightly on Kai's shoulder. The warmth of his touch was steadying, a stark contrast to the biting chill of the room. "You do not need to know," he said. "You are here. That is enough. Kai—" He pauses a moment, something flickering in his gaze. "Do you have another name you'd—"

"—No," Kai rushed. "Kai is fine. Good, even. It feels right even if I'm borrowing it."

"Are you?" he asked, his eyes softer now. "Borrowing it?"

"I..." The words seem to stick in his throat as he remembers the real Kai's journal. How desperate he was to escape. "I don't think I am. I don't think he's coming back."

"But do *you* want to go home?" he prompted.

"No," Kai said softly. "I want to stay."

Kai looked up to see Fenrir with a gentle smile. "Then you'll stay. This world does not give answers freely, but that does not mean your presence here is without purpose. Whatever brought you to this place, it chose you for a reason."

Kai swallowed hard, his pulse racing. He wanted to believe Fenrir's words, wanted to hold onto the fragile hope they offered. But the doubts in his mind whispered louder, relentless and unyielding.

The frost fox padded across the bed, pressing its small body against Kai's side. He glanced down at it, its crystalline eyes meeting his with an almost knowing look. He let out a shaky breath, his hands loosening their grip on the furs.

Fenrir's voice broke the quiet, low but resolute. "You are more than you believe yourself to be, little warmth. And whether you see it or not, the castle has already begun to change because of you."

Kai looked up sharply, his eyes searching Fenrir's face. There was no mockery there, no doubt—only the quiet certainty of someone who had seen more than he could ever explain.

The frost fox let out a soft, chime-like sound, nuzzling closer to Kai as though to echo Fenrir's words.

Kai exhaled shakily, his head lowering as Fenrir's steady presence anchored him in a way he hadn't expected. The words from their conversation still rang in his ears, echoing softly in the quiet of the room. For a moment, he simply sat there, his hands resting loosely in his lap, the frost fox's gentle weight pressed against his side.

"I always felt lost," Kai murmured, his voice low, as though admitting the truth would shatter something fragile. "Back home, I didn't know who I was supposed to be. Every day felt... hollow, like I was just passing time until something—anything—changed. But I couldn't have imagined this."

Kai shifted on the bed, his head resting on the thin pillow as his body sank into the uneven mattress. The ache in his limbs from the day's relentless tension made every small movement feel like an effort. The frost fox nestled against his side, its warmth a faint but welcome contrast to the pervasive chill of the room.

Fenrir sat beside him, his tall frame angled casually against the bed frame. Despite his sharp, golden gaze sweeping the room in silent vigilance, there was a calmness to him—a steadiness that Kai found both grounding and maddening. How could he seem so composed in a place like this? A place that felt like it was swallowing Kai whole?

The silence between them wasn't uncomfortable, but it wasn't easy either. Kai's mind churned with words left unsaid, thoughts he couldn't quite pin down. His hands fidgeted with the edge of the furs draped around him, his gaze flicking briefly to Fenrir's broad shoulders before darting away.

He tried to focus on the frost fox's soft warmth against his ribs, but it only reminded him of the last time he'd shared a bed with someone. Gerhard's steady breathing, his broad arms wrapped protectively around him. Kai remembered the way their bodies had fit together, how natural it had felt to be held like that—even if neither of them had said the words they'd both known hung between them.

The ache in his chest deepened.

"You're going to sit there all night, aren't you?" Kai finally broke the silence, his voice quieter than he intended.

Fenrir's gaze shifted to him, his expression unreadable. "I'll remain until I'm certain you're safe."

Kai huffed a humorless laugh, trying to shake the heaviness from his chest. "Safe from what? The furniture?" He turned onto his side, propping his head on his arm. "You're worse than the frost fox."

The creature gave a faint chime-like chirp at the comparison, nudging against Kai's ribs as though offended. Kai smiled faintly, his fingers brushing over its fur.

"You don't have to guard me like some overgrown sentry," Kai murmured, his voice quieter now. "You could just... lay down. Relax, maybe."

Fenrir raised an eyebrow, his golden eyes narrowing slightly. "Relaxation is not a luxury I often indulge in."

Kai rolled onto his back again, letting out an exasperated breath. "Maybe you should try it. Just this once." He hesitated, the words catching in his throat before he finally added, "Lay down. You'll probably enjoy it more than you think."

There was a pause, the kind that stretched just long enough to make Kai feel like he'd crossed some invisible line. He glanced at Fenrir again, his chest tightening as he waited for a response.

Fenrir tilted his head slightly, his gaze flicking over Kai as though assessing him. "And where, exactly, do you propose I lay?"

Kai gestured to the empty space on the bed beside him, trying to sound nonchalant despite the heat creeping up his neck. "It's not like I'm taking up the whole thing. There's room."

For a moment, Fenrir didn't move. His expression didn't change, but there was something in the way his gaze lingered on Kai that felt heavier than usual. Then, slowly, he stood and stared down at the empty space.

"You're certain?" he asked, his voice low but even.

Kai shrugged, though the motion felt stiff. "It's a bed, not a throne. I think we can manage sharing."

Fenrir hesitated only a moment longer before he lowered himself onto the bed with a grace that seemed at odds with his broad frame. The mattress dipped under his weight, and Kai felt the faint pull as Fenrir settled beside him.

Kai stared up at the ceiling, his heart beating faster than he wanted to admit. He could feel the heat of Fenrir's presence next to him, his proximity strangely grounding despite the tension knotting in Kai's chest. But it was impossible not to compare it to Gerhard. His warmth had been different—softer, maybe even gentler. Fenrir's presence, in contrast, was sharp and consuming, like standing too close to a flame.

"I don't bite, you know," Kai said softly, his lips twitching into a faint smile.

Fenrir let out a low hum that might have been amusement. "Good to know."

Kai turned his head slightly, glancing at him in the dim light. "Do you... mind this?" His voice wavered, hesitant.

Fenrir looked down at him, his golden eyes catching the faint glimmer of the frost fox's glow. "If I did, I would not be here."

The simplicity of the answer made Kai's chest tighten. He nodded, letting his head sink back against the pillow. The frost fox shifted against him, its warmth steady, and Fenrir's breathing fell into a calm, even rhythm beside him.

The silence that followed was heavy but not uncomfortable. For the first time in days, the storm inside Kai's mind felt quieter. He let his eyes drift shut, his body sinking further into the mattress.

For a long moment, neither of them spoke. Then Fenrir's deep voice broke the quiet. "Do you miss him?"

Kai blinked, startled by the sudden question. "What?"

"Your friend," Fenrir said, his tone even but laced with curiosity. "The one you left behind. Do you miss him?"

Kai's breath hitched, and his fingers fidgeted with the edge of the blanket. The question shouldn't have made his chest tighten, but it did. "Gerhard," he murmured, the name heavy on his tongue. "Yeah. I do."

Fenrir hummed softly, a sound that vibrated low in his throat. "He must have been important to you."

Kai hesitated, his mind racing. He thought of Gerhard's quiet strength, the way he'd always seemed steady even when everything around them had felt uncertain. "He was the first man I ever slept with," Kai admitted quietly, then rushed to add, "To sleep, I mean. In the same bed."

Fenrir didn't laugh or tease. Instead, he tilted his head slightly, his golden eyes glinting in the faint light. "And did you find it... comforting?"

Kai nodded, his throat tight. "Yeah. I guess I did."

Fenrir didn't respond immediately. The silence stretched, thick and weighty, until the bed shifted beneath them. Before Kai could react, Fenrir rolled to his side, his strong arm sliding around Kai's waist. The movement was slow, deliberate, as though giving him the chance to pull away.

Kai didn't.

Instead, he froze, his breath catching in his throat as Fenrir pulled him back until his body was flush against his broad chest. The heat radiating from him was startling, seeping through the layers of their clothing to chase away the lingering cold.

The frost fox chirped in what could only be annoyance at the disruption. It shuffled under the covers, burrowing down to curl against their feet like a sulking child.

"Did he hold you like this?" Fenrir asked, his voice low and steady, a rumble that vibrated against Kai's back.

"No," Kai choked, his voice barely above a whisper. He could feel his body responding to the immediate warmth of another, his pulse quickening as his thoughts raced. He wasn't sure if it was the closeness or the memory of Fenrir earlier—his sharp, dominating presence, bent over the Snow King—that made his throat tighten.

Fenrir's arm didn't move, his grip firm but not constricting. "A shame," he murmured, his breath brushing against the back of Kai's neck. "You deserve to be held."

Kai swallowed hard, his fingers clutching at the edge of the blanket. He didn't trust himself to respond, afraid his voice would betray the swirl of emotions tangled in his chest—grief, confusion, and a spark of something warmer, something he didn't want to name.

Fenrir's steady presence behind him, the weight of his arm, and the rhythmic rise and fall of his breath filled the room, lulling Kai into a fragile sense of calm.

Fenrir awoke suddenly, his sharp senses dragging him out of a deep, unexpected sleep. For a moment, he lay still, disoriented by the darkness that greeted him. Sleep wasn't something he indulged in often—especially not at night. The hours of darkness were his to roam, to keep watch over the forest and the Winter Court's abandoned outskirts. Yet, here he was, awake from slumber he couldn't remember falling into.

The room was quiet, the faint hum of change brushing against his awareness like a cool wind. He sat up, his golden eyes narrowing as he scanned the chamber. The frost on the walls had softened further, its sharp edges dulled into curved patterns that almost shimmered in the dim light. The once-opaque windows now carried thin streaks of clarity, allowing moonlight to filter through, casting silvery streaks onto the icy floor.

The castle's atmosphere had shifted. He could feel it in the way the air carried a faint energy, softer and warmer than the frigid cold that usually pressed in from all sides. It was subtle, almost imperceptible, but unmistakable to someone as attuned to the castle as Fenrir.

The boy lay still, his breath deep and even, his face relaxed for the first time in days. The frost fox was curled beside him, its soft glow brighter than before, its tiny form rising and falling in time with Kai's breathing. The scene struck Fenrir as... unusual. It wasn't the boy's peace that surprised him, but the ripple of change it seemed to send through the room.

He let his gaze sweep over the faint carvings emerging on the walls—patterns long hidden under layers of ice. The swirling lines caught the moonlight, creating the illusion of movement, as though the castle itself was stirring awake after a long slumber.

It was undeniable now. Kai's presence had taken root, its warmth radiating outward in ways the boy himself couldn't yet comprehend. The castle, frozen in grief and silence for centuries, was beginning to respond.

Fenrir's sharp gaze lingered on the boy, taking in the subtle tension in his shoulders even in sleep. He tilted his head slightly, his expression thoughtful. Kai didn't yet realize the effect he had on this place, on the king himself. But Fenrir could see it clearly.

The frost fox shifted, its ears twitching as it let out a faint, chiming sound. Fenrir glanced down at it, his lips quirking into a faint, fleeting smile. The creature's glow seemed to pulse in rhythm with the soft hum that vibrated faintly through the walls, a quiet acknowledgment of the boy it had chosen to follow.

Whatever Kai had set in motion, it was only the beginning. And for the first time in years, Fenrir felt a flicker of anticipation for what lay ahead.

Chapter 9

KAI WOKE SLOWLY, THE faint warmth he had felt the night before replaced by a bitter cold that made his breath hitch the moment his eyes opened. He sat up, the frost fox stirring beside him. Its glowing eyes blinked up at him, its ears flicking as though it had sensed the same unease now clawing at Kai's chest.

"What's wrong?" Kai murmured, his voice hushed in the stillness.

The frost fox didn't answer, of course, but it shivered faintly, curling tighter against his leg.

A low growl broke the silence, startling Kai. He turned quickly to see Fenrir standing near the frost-lined window, his golden eyes narrowed as he stared out into the swirling storm beyond the glass. His posture was tense, his jaw set, and the sound that rumbled from his chest was quiet but unmistakably wary.

"What is it?" Kai asked, pulling the furs tighter around his shoulders as he swung his legs over the side of the bed.

Fenrir didn't look at him, his gaze fixed on the chaos outside. The storm had grown violent, its winds howling like a living thing. Snow lashed against the castle walls in sharp, chaotic spirals, and the sky beyond the frost-streaked windows was a roiling mass of shadow and ice.

"Someone comes," Fenrir said finally, his voice low and edged with a quiet warning.

Kai's pulse quickened. "Someone?"

Fenrir turned slightly, his gaze meeting Kai's for the briefest moment before returning to the storm. "Stay close to me," he said, his tone leaving no room for argument.

Before Kai could respond, a loud banging echoed through the castle halls.

The sound was deep and deliberate—the heavy pounding of fists against the massive castle doors. It reverberated through the frozen walls, cutting through the oppressive silence like a crack of thunder.

The frost fox bristled, its fur fluffing slightly as it pressed itself closer to Kai's leg. The air in the room seemed to grow colder, the frost along the walls creeping closer in jagged, branching patterns.

Fenrir snarled softly, his fists clenching at his sides. "Stay behind me," he said, moving toward the doorway with slow, deliberate steps.

Kai hesitated for a moment, his chest tightening with unease. Then, as the pounding on the doors grew louder, more insistent, he followed Fenrir into the hall, the frost fox trotting anxiously at his heels.

The sound of the storm grew louder as they approached the great entrance hall, the wind howling through cracks in the massive doors. Snow and ice swirled violently outside, the storm's fury threatening to break through at any moment.

The pounding stopped suddenly, replaced by a tense, unnatural stillness.

Kai's breath caught as Fenrir pushed open one of the smaller doors. The massive doors groaned in protest, the sound echoing through the hall as a rush of freezing wind howled inside. Snow and ice spilled across the floor, carried by the storm's chaotic breath.

And then, through the swirling frost, a figure stumbled inside, his silhouette barely visible against the swirling snow. His cloak was heavy with frost, boots caked in ice, and his breath came in sharp, ragged bursts that fogged faintly in the bitter air.

Kai's heart lurched at the sight of him. "Gerhard!" His voice broke through the icy haze, desperate and filled with disbelief.

Gerhard's head snapped up at the sound, his wide, bloodshot eyes locking onto Kai's. Relief flooded his face, overwhelming the exhaustion that clung to his every step. "Kai!" he shouted, his voice hoarse but clear. He staggered forward, like a man who had fought death itself to get here. "Thank the gods—I thought I'd lost you!"

Kai darted toward him without thinking, the storm's lingering chill forgotten in his need to reach Gerhard. "Gerhard, what are you doing here? You shouldn't have—"

His words cut off as Gerhard reached him, wrapping him in an embrace so fierce it nearly knocked the breath from his lungs. Gerhard's arms locked around Kai, his grip unyielding, as though he feared letting go would make Kai vanish.

Kai froze for half a beat, then melted into the embrace, his hands clutching at the back of Gerhard's cloak. His chest tightened, warmth blooming inside him despite the freezing air around them. "You're freezing," he whispered, his voice trembling. "What were you thinking?"

Gerhard's response came as a muffled gasp against Kai's shoulder. "I couldn't stay—I couldn't leave you here." His voice cracked, raw with emotion. "I thought I'd never see you again."

Kai pulled back just enough to look at him, his own face twisting with a mixture of relief and worry. "You idiot," he choked, brushing the frost from Gerhard's hair. "You could have died out there."

Gerhard's grip on him tightened, his hands fisting in Kai's furs. "I don't care. If you're here, I'm here." His voice was fierce, desperate, and Kai couldn't hold back the small, broken laugh that escaped him.

"You're impossible," Kai muttered, but his arms only circled Gerhard tighter. For the first time since he'd arrived in the castle, the cold didn't seem so unbearable. It didn't matter that the storm raged beyond the doors, or that the icy veins of frost crept along the walls. All that mattered was Gerhard's warmth, his presence anchoring Kai in a way he hadn't realized he'd needed so desperately.

Gerhard buried his face in Kai's neck, his breath hot against Kai's skin. "I'm not letting go," he said hoarsely. "Not ever."

Kai swallowed hard, his chest aching with a mix of relief and something deeper, something he couldn't name. "Good," he whispered, his fingers tangling in the fabric of Gerhard's cloak. "Don't."

The frost fox let out a soft chirp, breaking the stillness. Its glowing tail brushed against Kai's ankle, grounding him further in the moment. But even as the warmth between them grew, the room's temperature dropped sharply.

The oppressive cold that followed was sudden and unrelenting, pressing against them like a tangible weight. Kai's breath hitched, his gaze darting toward the shadows gathering at the edge of the hall.

A presence filled the room—powerful, unyielding, and unmistakable. The Snow King had arrived.

The Snow King stepped silently into view, his figure tall and commanding, the frost trailing behind him like an extension of his presence. His frost-covered cloak glimmered faintly in the dim light, and the air around him crackled with an icy magic that made Kai's breath catch. The frost surged outward, coiling along the walls and floor as if eager to obey him.

Gerhard stiffened immediately, his wide eyes locking onto the Snow King. His face went pale, his breath hitching as he instinctively tightened his arms around Kai. "What..." Gerhard's voice faltered, barely above a whisper. "What is this place? What has he done to you?"

Kai twisted in Gerhard's embrace, placing a hand on his chest as if to steady him. "Gerhard, it's—"

But the Snow King's gaze pinned him in place before he could finish. Pale blue eyes, sharp as shattered glass, slid from Kai to Gerhard, and something dangerous flickered there—a cold, calculating fury layered with something darker, something that made Kai's stomach twist.

"He does not belong here," the Snow King said, his voice low and smooth, but with an edge that cut through the tension in the room like a blade. His eyes dragged over Gerhard's form, deliberate and unhurried, before narrowing. "And yet, here he is. Clinging to what is mine."

The frost fox let out a nervous chirp from its place near Kai's feet, but Kai barely noticed it over the sound of his own racing heart. He pushed himself out of Gerhard's arms, stepping forward to place himself between them. "Leave him alone!" Kai's voice trembled, but he forced himself to hold his ground. "He came for me. He didn't—"

The Snow King's eyes shifted to Kai, narrowing further. "Do not presume to defend him," he said softly, his words carrying the weight of a gathering storm. "He is the one trespassing in my court."

The frost surged again, sharp cracks echoing through the hall as the temperature plummeted. Tendrils of ice crept closer to Gerhard's feet, but the Snow King's focus remained on Kai. His gaze, cold as it was, held a heat buried deep within—a smoldering fire that Kai recognized all too well.

Gerhard, despite the frost encroaching on him, stood tall. His hands clenched at his sides as he met the Snow King's gaze head-on. "I don't care what you are," he growled, his voice rough with defiance. "I won't let you hurt him."

The Snow King's lips quirked into a faint, almost imperceptible smile, though it was devoid of humor. "Hurt him?" he murmured, his tone laced with dark amusement. His gaze flickered back to Kai, lingering on him in a way that made Kai's skin prickle. "I have no need to hurt what is already mine."

Kai's chest tightened, his pulse quickening as the Snow King's attention shifted once more to Gerhard. The frost seemed to pulse with his movements, reaching toward Gerhard like grasping fingers.

But then, to Kai's horror, the Snow King's expression shifted. His icy mask softened just enough to reveal something else—curiosity, hunger, and a dangerous, almost predatory edge. His gaze roamed over Gerhard's broad shoulders, his strong hands, the curve of his jaw.

The Snow King stepped closer. His hand lifted, fingers brushing against the edge of Gerhard's cloak as though testing the warmth he radiated. "Your defiance is admirable," he said softly, his voice a velvety caress. "So much heat in you. I wonder..." His fingers hovered just above Gerhard's chest, close enough to touch but not quite.

"Stop!" Kai's voice rang out, sharp and panicked. He surged forward, placing a hand on the Snow King's arm to halt his movement. His touch burned against the ice-cold skin, and for a fleeting moment, the Snow King stilled, his gaze snapping to Kai.

"You don't get to do this," Kai said, his voice trembling with anger and something else—something hotter, more desperate. "You don't get to act like you own me and then... then *this*." He gestured wildly, the words spilling out before he could think.

The Snow King's eyes softened, his lips curving faintly as he tilted his head, studying Kai with an intensity that made his knees feel weak. "You burn so brightly," he murmured, his voice low enough that only Kai could hear. "I crave it even as it scalds me."

Kai's breath hitched, his pulse hammering as the words settled over him like a challenge. For a brief, dizzying moment, the tension in the room shifted, the frost retreating slightly as the heat between them grew unbearable.

But then the Snow King leaned back, his icy demeanor snapping into place once more. His gaze flicked to Gerhard, sharp and cutting. "You should not have come here," he said, his tone colder than ever. "Take your warmth and leave before it costs you more than you can bear."

The frost fox growled low, and Kai shot Gerhard a pleading look, his chest aching with the weight of the moment. "Please, Gerhard. Just… listen to him."

But Gerhard didn't move. His gaze remained locked on the Snow King, unyielding even as the frost encroached. "I'm not leaving without Kai."

The Snow King's lips curved faintly, a shadow of amusement flickering across his otherwise icy expression. "Such resolve," he murmured. "For a mortal."

Without warning, the Snow King's hand rose, his cold fingers brushing lightly against Gerhard's chest. Gerhard flinched, a sharp breath escaping him, but he held his ground. The King's touch lingered, slow and deliberate, before sliding inside the fur-lined edges of Gerhard's coat.

Kai's heart slammed against his ribs. "Stop—" he started, stepping forward, but Fenrir was faster. The wolf's strong arms wrapped around Kai from behind, pinning him against Fenrir's broad chest.

"You'll make it worse," Fenrir whispered, his voice a low rumble against Kai's ear.

The Snow King didn't even glance in their direction. His hand continued its unhurried path beneath Gerhard's tunic, his cool fingers tracing the lines of the man's burning skin. Gerhard trembled, his breaths coming faster, but he didn't pull away.

"Don't hurt him," Kai begged, struggling against Fenrir's hold.

Fenrir's grip tightened, his voice lower now but no less firm. "Eryon," he murmured, his breath warm against Kai's ear. "His name."

Kai stilled, his chest heaving as he stared at the Snow King. "Eryon, please."

The name seemed to pierce through the ice. The Snow King's head tilted slightly, his pale blue eyes shifting to Kai. For a moment, something flickered there—something warmer, deeper, a glimmer of emotion that didn't fit the cold mask he wore.

His hand, however, didn't stop. It drifted lower, tracing the ridges of Gerhard's abdomen before brushing against the hard line of his arousal through his pants. Gerhard's breath hitched, his knees threatening to buckle as he trembled under the Snow King's touch.

"Eryon!" Kai's voice cracked with desperation. "Please. Don't."

The Snow King's gaze lingered on Kai, his expression unreadable. Slowly, his fingers curled, giving Gerhard a firm squeeze. Gerhard let out a low, shuddering breath, his resistance faltering for the briefest moment before the King finally withdrew his hand.

"It's impolite," the Snow King said, his voice soft and deceptively gentle, "to enter a fae's court without bringing a gift."

Kai's chest tightened painfully. "I'll give one," he said quickly, his voice trembling. "In his place, I'll give you anything."

The Snow King's eyes softened slightly at that, though his lips curved into something that wasn't quite a smile. He stepped back, allowing just enough space between himself and Gerhard to create the illusion of relief.

"Anything?" Eryon asked, his voice carrying a quiet, dangerous weight.

"Yes," Kai said, his words rushing out. "Anything."

The Snow King's gaze dropped back to Gerhard for a fleeting moment, his hand trailing away fully as he gestured with a slight tilt of his fingers. "Kneel," he commanded, his voice smooth and absolute.

Kai froze, his breath catching in his throat. The word hung heavily in the air, its weight undeniable. Fenrir's arms tightened around him briefly—a gentle squeeze that felt more like a warning than reassurance—before the wolf-man released him, stepping back into the shadows.

Kai's legs felt like lead as he stepped forward. His heartbeat pounded in his ears as he came to stand between the Snow King and Gerhard.

Behind him, Gerhard's voice broke, frantic and flustered. "What are you doing? Kai, no. Don't kneel for this fiend!" His words tumbled out, desperate and disjointed, but his body refused to move, frozen in place by the Snow King's magic.

The Snow King's lips curved into a slow, dangerous smile. "Fiend?" he echoed, his tone light, almost amused. His pale blue eyes flicked to Gerhard's trembling form. "And yet, despite your noble outrage, your body betrays you." His gaze dipped pointedly. "So hard already. It's almost sweet."

Gerhard's face burned, his mouth opening and closing as he struggled for a response. "That's—that's not—"

The Snow King silenced him with a raised hand, his icy power radiating through the room. His attention shifted fully to Kai, who was already sinking to his knees. The Snow King's voice dropped, velvet and sharp. "The cold can feel so good, can't it?" He tilted his head, his expression somewhere between cruel and curious. "But there is nothing—nothing—I would enjoy more than a warm mouth."

Kai's cheeks flushed a deep red, the heat spreading down his neck as his hands moved instinctively to the Snow King's belt. His fingers trembled as he worked the clasp, the icy air biting at his skin even as his stomach churned with equal parts shame and arousal. His throat felt tight, his mind racing, but he couldn't stop himself. His mouth watered as he unfastened the King's pants, the weight of his own humiliation pooling in his stomach.

Behind him, Gerhard let out a strangled noise. "Kai, stop! You don't have to—he's—he's manipulating you!"

The Snow King's smile widened, his icy fingers brushing through Kai's hair as if in mock affection. "Manipulating? Oh, human, you flatter me. If anything, your warmth begged for this." He turned his gaze to Gerhard, his tone dripping with mockery. "Tell me, have you ever had one in your mouth before? Have you imagined choking on Kai's member in the dark of night, your hands trembling as you pleasured yourself to the thought?"

Gerhard's face went crimson, his chest heaving as his protests died in his throat. His body remained locked, his eyes darting frantically between Kai and the Snow King. "I—I never—"

The Snow King's laughter was low and indulgent, sending a shiver through the room. "Such lies, human. I've tasted his sinful sweetness," he murmured, his gaze falling to Kai, who had nearly finished unfastening him. "And if you stay, perhaps you'll have the chance to taste a god's ambrosia yourself. Straight from his honeyed depths."

Kai's breath hitched at the words, his hands pausing for just a moment before continuing. His body burned with mortification, his stomach twisting painfully, but there was no denying the heat pooling low inside him, the way his mouth practically watered in anticipation. Even as shame tangled with desire, he couldn't stop.

He glanced up briefly, his eyes meeting the Snow King's for the barest moment before lowering again. His hands worked quickly, exposing the King's arousal, his throat tightening as he braced himself for what was to come.

The Snow King's cold, elegant fingers threaded through Kai's hair, tugging him closer as Kai took him into his mouth. The sheer size of him stretched Kai's lips, the cool, firm weight sending shivers down his spine. The icy chill of the King's touch was tempered by the heat in Kai's chest, a maddening combination that made his head spin.

"Good boy," the Snow King murmured, his voice low and velvety, the tone more sinful than any act Kai could have imagined. "So eager to please. Such warmth in you, Kai. It burns... so beautifully."

Kai's hands rested on the King's thighs for balance, his heart pounding as he fought the instinct to pull back. The Snow King guided him with measured movements, his hand firm but not cruel.

From behind, Gerhard watched, his chest heaving as his wide, disbelieving eyes locked onto the scene before him. His lips moved, but no sound came at first, his voice lost to the tension choking the air. His hands curled into fists at his sides, straining against his invisible bonds as his body betrayed him, hard and trembling.

The Snow King's gaze flicked lazily to Gerhard, his smile sharp and taunting. "Look at him, human," he said softly, his hand tightening slightly in Kai's hair. "So eager, so willing. Did you ever imagine this? Your Kai, kneeling, burning for me."

Gerhard's breath hitched audibly, and he tore his gaze away, trembling. "Please," he finally managed, his voice strained. "Please stop hurting him."

The Snow King chuckled darkly, the sound curling through the room like smoke. "Hurting him?" He tugged Kai free with a deliberate slowness, the act leaving Kai's lips swollen and glistening. He tilted Kai's head back with a firm hand, his pale blue eyes gleaming as he looked down at him. "Tell him, Kai. Am I forcing you?"

Kai swallowed hard, his voice raw and shaky as he answered, "No."

The Snow King's smile widened, his grip tightening just enough to make Kai tilt his head further. "Do you want me?" he demanded, his voice a low purr. "Did you want me last night when you clung to me and begged me to go harder?"

"Yes," Kai choked, his cheeks flushed with equal parts arousal and shame.

"Tell him," the Snow King commanded, twisting Kai's head just enough to make him face Gerhard, who stood frozen, his body trembling with conflict. "Tell him everything."

Kai's chest rose and fell as he struggled to find his voice. "I..." His throat tightened, but he forced the words out. "I want it, Gerhard. So much. I want him. I want you. I—" His gaze flicked briefly to the shadows, where he knew Fenrir was watching. "I want everything."

The Snow King hummed, his thumb brushing over Kai's swollen lips as if in approval. "Hmm. What say you, Gerhard?" His tone was mocking, though the glint in his eyes was sharp as ice. "Are you ready to go home with your tail between your legs? I'll even give you an escort."

Gerhard's breath rushed out of him, his fists clenching as his eyes darted between Kai and the Snow King. His voice broke when he finally spoke. "I... I don't—" He swallowed hard, his words trailing off as he struggled to process what he was seeing, what he was hearing.

The Snow King's smile turned razor-sharp, and his hand drifted back to Kai's hair, gripping it with deliberate possessiveness. "Think carefully, human," he said, his voice cold and smooth. "There is no room for hesitation here."

The tension in the room was electric, a sharp edge to the silence that fell after the Snow King's words. Gerhard trembled, his breath heavy and uneven, his eyes flicking from Kai's flushed face to the Snow King's cold, predatory smile. The sight of Kai on his knees, his lips still swollen and reddened, seemed too much—equal parts devastating and arresting.

The Snow King's grip on Kai's hair tightened slightly, pulling his head back just enough to expose the line of his throat. His pale blue eyes gleamed as he looked at Gerhard, the faintest hint of amusement in his expression. "Well?" he prompted, his voice smooth as ice. "What will it be? Will you fight for him, or will you leave him to me?"

Kai's breath hitched, the position forcing him to meet Gerhard's gaze. "Gerhard," he whispered, his voice raw with emotion, his eyes pleading. "I—"

"Quiet," the Snow King murmured, cutting him off with a gentle but firm tug. His touch was cold and possessive, his gaze never leaving Gerhard's. "This is not your moment, little warmth."

Gerhard's fists clenched tighter, his knuckles whitening as he strained against his invisible bonds. "What do you want from him?" he demanded, his voice cracking under the weight of his frustration. "You've already taken so much—"

"What I want," the Snow King interrupted, his tone deceptively soft, "is exactly what he gives so freely." His gaze dropped to Kai, a flicker of something darker passing through his eyes. "The fire that burns, the warmth that consumes. It is a rare and exquisite thing. And he offers it... willingly."

Kai shivered under the weight of the Snow King's words, his chest tightening as he felt the full force of the King's attention on him. Despite the situation, despite the shame pooling in his stomach, his body betrayed him, a faint flush spreading across his skin as his arousal only deepened.

The Snow King's gaze returned to Gerhard, his lips curling into a faint, mocking smile. "Does it wound you, human?" he asked, his voice like a blade wrapped in velvet. "To see him here, like this? To know that I have tasted what you only dream of?"

Gerhard's face burned with anger and humiliation, but he couldn't tear his eyes away from Kai. His voice was tight, barely above a whisper. "You're cruel."

The Snow King's wicked smile widened. "Cruelty," he said softly, "is a matter of perspective."

He released Kai's hair abruptly, letting his hand drift down to trace the curve of Kai's jaw. "Stand, little warmth," he murmured, his voice low but commanding. "Let him see the truth in your eyes."

Kai hesitated, his heart pounding as he slowly rose to his feet. He felt exposed, his body thrumming with conflicting emotions as he turned toward Gerhard. The Snow King stepped behind him, his presence looming, his cold hands resting on Kai's shoulders.

The Snow King's lips brushed against Kai's ear, his voice a low, dangerous murmur. "Now, Gerhard," he said, his tone laced with a taunting edge. "What will you do? Will you stay, or will you leave him to me?"

Gerhard's chest heaved as he struggled to find his voice. "I…" He trailed off, his gaze darting between Kai and the Snow King, his fists trembling at his sides. "I won't abandon him."

The Snow King hummed, his smile sharp and satisfied. "Good," he said softly, his hands sliding down Kai's arms before stepping back. "Then let us see how far your loyalty truly extends."

"What would you have me do?"

The Snow King's pale blue eyes sparkled with icy amusement as he studied Gerhard. The mortal's words hung in the air like frost, his chest rising and falling as he awaited the King's answer. The King tilted his head, his expression both predatory and elegant. "What would I have you do?" he echoed, his voice a low purr. "Such a question, mortal. And so very open-ended."

"If it will spare Kai, just tell me."

The Snow King let out a soft, humorless laugh, the sound like cracking ice. "Spare him? How noble. How predictable." His gaze flickered to Kai, lingering for a moment on the way the boy knelt before him, his head bowed. "I wonder, do you even know what you are offering? What I might ask?"

"Whatever it is," Gerhard said, his voice steady despite the chill creeping into his bones. "I'll do it."

The Snow King smiled faintly, though it lacked any trace of warmth. He reached out, his long, gloved fingers brushing lightly against Gerhard's chest, just above his heart. The touch was cold, sharp, making Gerhard flinch but not pull away.

"You humans are so predictable in your bravado," the Snow King murmured, his voice soft but cutting. "Always so eager to offer everything, and yet so unprepared for the cost." He leaned closer, his piercing gaze locking onto Gerhard's. "Very well. If you are so insistent, I shall make my demand."

Kai held his breath as the Snow King stepped back slightly, his cloak swirling around him like a curtain of frost. The King's pale lips curved into a cruel smile as his eyes swept over Gerhard's tense frame.

The Snow King's cold eyes glinted with amusement as his gaze flicked between Gerhard's trembling form and Kai. The sight of him, utterly wrecked and so vulnerable with the king's own taste on his tongue, seemed to ignite a cruel spark in the Snow King's frosty demeanor.

"Kiss him," the Snow King commanded, his voice smooth and soft, yet brimming with absolute authority.

Gerhard froze, his expression faltering as his wide-eyed gaze darted to Kai. "What?"

The Snow King tilted his head, a faint smile curving his lips. "You heard me," he said, his tone laced with icy amusement. "Kiss him. Kiss him like you mean it, like you've dreamed of it. Let me see your devotion."

Kai's head snapped up, his flushed cheeks darkening as his eyes met Gerhard's. "You don't have to—"

"Do not interrupt," the Snow King cut in, his voice sharp but calm. "This is between him and me, little flame."

Gerhard's body was taut with tension. He glanced back at the Snow King, his chest heaving with labored breaths. "You're playing games," he spat, his voice low and shaking. "This isn't—"

"Oh, but it is," the Snow King interrupted, his smile widening slightly. "You claim to care for him, to want to protect him. Prove it. Kiss him. Show me the truth of your feelings."

Kai's heart hammered in his chest as he watched Gerhard wrestle with the weight of the demand.

Gerhard's gaze flicked to Kai, his expression a storm of emotion—anger, frustration, fear, and something deeper, something raw and unspoken. He took a hesitant step forward, his hand trembling as it reached out to touch Kai's cheek.

"Kai..." Gerhard whispered, his voice barely audible. His thumb brushed over the flush of Kai's cheek, his calloused fingers trembling as they lingered against the warm skin.

Kai swallowed hard, his body frozen under Gerhard's touch. He didn't know what to say, didn't know how to process the swirling chaos of emotions in his chest. All he could do was stare at Gerhard, his lips trembling as he tried to find the words to break the spell.

But then Gerhard leaned in, his breath hitching as his lips hovered just above Kai's. "I'm sorry," he murmured, the words a quiet plea, before closing the distance.

The kiss was tentative at first, Gerhard's lips brushing softly against Kai's, testing the boundaries of what he was allowed to take. But then, as though something inside him broke free, he deepened the kiss, his hands cradling Kai's face with a fervor that bordered on desperation.

Kai gasped softly, his body melting into the embrace despite the storm raging in his mind. Gerhard's warmth enveloped him, chasing away the lingering chill of the Snow King's touch. His fingers curled into Gerhard's coat, clutching tightly as he surrendered to the moment.

Behind them, the Snow King watched with a faint, satisfied smile, his icy gaze drinking in the scene with quiet amusement. "How touching," he murmured, his voice a low purr that sent shivers down Kai's spine. "Such a display of devotion."

Gerhard broke the kiss abruptly, his breathing ragged as he pulled back just enough to meet Kai's wide-eyed gaze. His hands trembled against Kai's skin, his expression torn between longing and defiance.

"Enough," Gerhard said, his voice hoarse as he turned his glare to the Snow King. "You've had your show. Leave him alone."

The Snow King raised a single brow, his faint smile unwavering. "Leave him alone?" he echoed, his tone light but mocking. "My dear mortal, you misunderstand. He belongs to me." His gaze flicked back to

Kai, lingering on his swollen lips and flushed cheeks. "And now, so do you."

The Snow King regarded the two of them for a lingering moment, his pale blue eyes sharp and assessing. His hand moved with elegant precision, tucking himself back into his pants and fastening them as though the charged atmosphere he'd created was inconsequential.

He adjusted his frost-covered cloak, his expression unreadable but his aura still potent, electric with the control he exuded over the room. "A lesson, little flame," he murmured, his gaze locking onto Kai, whose flushed cheeks and trembling form still bore the marks of their earlier exchange. "Those who enter my court must understand their place. Yours, Kai, is here. Do not forget that."

Kai swallowed hard, his breath catching at the quiet finality in the Snow King's tone.

The Snow King's gaze shifted to Gerhard, a faint smirk tugging at his lips. "And you, human. So protective. So bold." His eyes drifted downward, lingering just long enough to make Gerhard shift uncomfortably. "Don't let your devotion blind you. The fire you feel may warm you now, but in the wrong hands, it will burn."

Gerhard's jaw tightened, but he said nothing.

The Snow King's cold eyes scanned the room once more before stopping at the shadows near the edge of the hall. His gaze softened imperceptibly, and with a subtle tilt of his head, he called out, "Fenrir."

The wolf-man stepped into the light, his broad frame solid and unyielding as he moved with striking ease. His golden eyes glimmered faintly, catching Kai's briefly before returning to the Snow King. Without a word, Fenrir fell into step behind him, his silent presence a shadow at the King's side as they left the hall.

The room fell into silence, the oppressive frost left in the Snow King's wake beginning to lift. Kai stayed where he was, his chest rising and falling as he struggled to regain control of his breathing.

Gerhard, still trembling slightly, broke the quiet. "Kai..." His voice was low, rough with disbelief and something Kai couldn't quite place. "What the hell just happened?"

Kai's lips parted, but no words came. His throat felt tight, and the weight of everything—the Snow King's dominance, Fenrir's silent departure, Gerhard's confusion—pressed against him like a vice.

"I..." Kai started, his voice faltering. He closed his eyes, inhaling deeply before trying again. "It's... complicated."

Gerhard's brows furrowed, his anger and confusion flickering into something softer. He stepped closer, his hand brushing against Kai's arm. "You don't have to explain, not now. Just... tell me you're okay."

Kai opened his eyes, the concern in Gerhard's gaze cutting through the lingering haze of his emotions. He nodded slowly. "I'm okay."

Gerhard exhaled heavily, relief softening his tense posture. "Alright." He glanced around the hall, the frost still glittering faintly against the walls. "Can we... Can we go somewhere warmer?"

Kai hesitated for a moment before nodding again. "Yeah. My room." He turned toward the hall, his steps uneven as he led Gerhard out of the icy chamber.

The warmth greeted them as soon as they entered Kai's chambers. The frost that had once clung to the walls was gone, replaced by smooth, polished surfaces that reflected the soft light filtering through the cleared windows. The air was gentle, carrying a faint hum of life that seemed to welcome their presence.

Gerhard stopped just inside the doorway, his eyes widening slightly as he took in the unexpected coziness of the room. "It's... warm," he said, his voice tinged with surprise.

Kai glanced back at him, a faint, humorless smile tugging at his lips. "The castle... it likes having people here. It wasn't always like this."

Gerhard stepped further inside, his gaze sweeping the space. The frost fox chirped softly from its spot on the bed, its crystalline eyes glowing faintly as it watched the new arrival.

Kai gestured toward the bed. "You can sit. Rest. You've been through enough already."

Gerhard hesitated before sitting on the edge of the bed. He glanced at Kai, his eyes flicking down and then away quickly. "And you? Are you going to rest... like that?"

Kai froze at the question, his mind suddenly hyperaware of his own body—his swollen lips, the rumpled state of his clothes, the way his arousal hadn't subsided. He opened his mouth to reply but found that no words came. How was he supposed to answer that?

His fingers fidgeted with the edge of his tunic, trying to find some way to cover himself better, but it was useless. He couldn't hide the heat still coursing through him or the hardness pressing insistently against the fabric of his pants. "I don't know."

Gerhard's gaze flickered back to him, hesitant but intense. For a long moment, neither of them spoke. The air between them felt charged, heavy with the weight of what had just happened—and the tension that lingered now.

"You're still..." Gerhard hesitated, his voice dropping. "You're still hard."

Kai's cheeks burned, shame and arousal warring within him. "I can't help it," he said, the words tumbling out in a rush. "The whole thing—him, you, everything—it's too much."

Gerhard's jaw tightened, and he looked away for a moment before turning back, his expression conflicted but resolute. "I could help," he said softly, the words cautious but sincere. "If you want me to."

Kai's breath caught, his gaze snapping to Gerhard's. "You want to help me? After... after what I did?" His voice trembled, equal parts disbelief and yearning.

Gerhard leaned forward slightly, his hands resting on his knees as he searched Kai's face. "You think I don't want to? You think I don't want to erase the way he touched you with something of my own?"

Kai's lips parted, his heart pounding as he stared at Gerhard. The man's blue eyes were dark with an intensity that made Kai's pulse race. He wanted to say something, to find the words to explain the chaos in his chest, but all that came out was a quiet, shaky, "Why?"

Gerhard let out a heavy breath, his hand reaching out tentatively to rest on Kai's knee. The warmth of his touch sent a jolt through Kai, and he couldn't stop the way his body leaned into it, craving more.

"Because it's you, Kai," Gerhard said quietly, his voice rough with emotion. "Because I've wanted to touch you for so long, and if this is how I can have you, even just a little... then I'll take it."

The words undid something in Kai, the tension in his chest unraveling all at once. His hands trembled as he reached out, his fingers brushing over Gerhard's. "Even after everything?" he asked, his voice barely above a whisper. "After what he did to me?"

Gerhard's grip on Kai's knee tightened slightly, his expression fierce. "That doesn't change how I feel about you. It never could."

Kai's throat tightened, and for a moment, he couldn't breathe. The storm of emotions inside him—shame, desire, disbelief—crashed together, leaving him raw and exposed. "Please," he whispered, the word slipping out before he could stop it. "Please, Gerhard."

Gerhard didn't hesitate. His hand slid higher, tracing the curve of Kai's thigh with deliberate care. His movements were slow, reverent, as though he were savoring every moment. Kai's breath hitched, his body trembling as he let himself sink into the warmth of Gerhard's touch. Gerhard didn't hesitate.

Gerhard's fingers brushed the waistband of Kai's pants, his palm resting there briefly as if asking permission. Kai's chest rose and fell rapidly, his breaths uneven, but he didn't pull away. Instead, he shifted slightly, tilting his hips up in silent invitation.

Gerhard's hand moved lower, slipping beneath the fabric and wrapping around Kai's aching length. Kai gasped, the sound breaking from his lips unbidden, and Gerhard stilled for a moment, his grip firm but careful.

"Tell me if you want me to stop," Gerhard murmured, his voice low and rough with restraint.

Kai shook his head quickly, his hands gripping the blanket beneath him. "Don't stop," he whispered, his voice trembling. "Please, don't stop."

Gerhard exhaled shakily, his hand beginning to move in slow, deliberate strokes. His touch was warm and sure, each motion sending a shudder through Kai's body. The tension that had coiled tightly in Kai's chest unraveled with every pass of Gerhard's hand, replaced by a heady mixture of relief and desire.

Kai's breaths came faster, his hips lifting instinctively to meet Gerhard's rhythm. The pleasure built steadily, a wave threatening to pull him under, and he couldn't stop the quiet whimpers that slipped past his lips. He bit his bottom lip, trying to stifle the sounds, but they only grew louder.

Gerhard's gaze flicked to Kai's face, his blue eyes darkening as he leaned in. "You're so loud," he murmured, a faint smile tugging at his lips before they pressed against Kai's.

The kiss was firm and grounding, muffling Kai's cries as Gerhard quickened his pace. Kai moaned into Gerhard's mouth, his body arching against him as the pleasure became overwhelming. His hands clutched at Gerhard's shoulders, holding on as though he might float away without the solid weight of him there.

The tension in Kai's body snapped, and he cried out into the kiss, his release spilling hot and thick over Gerhard's hand. His entire body trembled, every nerve alight as waves of sensation rolled through him.

Gerhard's lips parted from Kai's, his breaths ragged as he pressed his forehead against Kai's. He shifted slightly, his hips grinding against the edge of the bed, and a low groan escaped him as his own release followed. His body shuddered, his grip on Kai tightening briefly before he relaxed.

For a long moment, the room was filled only with the sound of their heavy breathing. Gerhard pulled back just enough to meet Kai's gaze, his hand slipping free to wipe discreetly against the blanket's edge.

Without a word, Gerhard lay back and pulled Kai into his arms, holding him tightly against his chest. The steady rise and fall of his breathing calmed Kai, the warmth of his body chasing away the lingering chill of the room.

Kai let his eyes drift shut, his head tucked against Gerhard's shoulder as sleep began to claim him. The frost fox curled at their feet, its quiet presence a faint glow in the dim light.

For the first time in what felt like forever, the storm inside Kai stilled, leaving only the steady beat of Gerhard's heart against his ear.

Chapter 10

KAI STIRRED, BLINKING GROGGILY as the first soft light of morning filtered through the frost-streaked windows. The warmth pressed against his side was immediate and comforting, and for a moment, the events of the night before felt distant—like a bad dream lingering on the edges of his memory.

Gerhard's arm was wrapped around his waist, his hold firm and steady even in sleep. His breath was a soft, even rhythm against Kai's neck, a warmth that Kai leaned into instinctively. He remembered the way Gerhard had clung to him last night, the desperation in his touch, and the quiet vulnerability in his gaze. It had been overwhelming but grounding all at once.

Kai exhaled shakily, his body sinking deeper into the mattress—and froze.

A second weight pressed against him from the other side, larger and heavier, and entirely unexpected. Turning his head, Kai's breath hitched as he came face-to-face with Fenrir.

The wolf-man was sprawled comfortably on the bed, his arm draped loosely across Kai's middle, his broad chest rising and falling with slow, measured breaths. His golden eyes were half-lidded, catching the soft light of the room as they flicked lazily toward Kai.

"You're awake," Fenrir said, his voice low and rough from sleep.

Kai stared at him, his mind scrambling to make sense of what he was seeing. "You... you're here?" His voice cracked slightly, a mix of confusion and disbelief.

Fenrir raised an eyebrow, his lips curving into something that wasn't quite a smile. "Where else would I be?"

That answer left Kai floundering. "I don't know," he muttered, his gaze darting toward Gerhard, who remained blissfully unaware, still deeply asleep. "With the Snow King, maybe? After last night..."

Fenrir tilted his head, his golden gaze sharpening slightly as he studied Kai. "You think I would stay in his bed when I could be here?"

Kai blinked at him, his stomach twisting with a mix of emotions. "I just... I didn't expect—"

Fenrir's arm tightened slightly around Kai's waist, cutting off his words. "You don't expect many things, little warmth," he said, his tone soft but pointed. "But here I am."

The simplicity of the statement struck something deep within Kai. He glanced down, his hands fidgeting with the edge of the furs, unsure of what to say. The weight of Fenrir's presence was tangible, grounding, but it also made his chest ache in ways he wasn't ready to examine.

Fenrir hummed quietly, his free hand reaching to brush a strand of hair from Kai's face. "Your mind is noisy this morning."

Kai frowned at that, heat rising to his cheeks. "How could it not be after last night?" He paused, his voice lowering. "After what he did."

Fenrir's gaze didn't waver. "He is the storm. You are the spark. And Gerhard..." His golden eyes flicked briefly to the man sleeping soundly on Kai's other side. "He is the anchor you cling to. Last night proved that."

Kai swallowed hard, the knot in his stomach tightening. "And you?" The question slipped out before he could stop it, soft and unsure.

Fenrir's lips twitched faintly, though it wasn't a smile. "I am the shadow that watches over you. For now."

The cryptic response left Kai with more questions than answers, but before he could press further, Gerhard stirred beside him, his grip tightening briefly before his eyes blinked open.

Gerhard's gaze flicked between Kai and Fenrir, his expression shifting from sleep-addled confusion to something sharper. "Morning," he muttered, his voice rough.

Kai hesitated, glancing between the two men. "Morning," he said softly.

Gerhard's brow furrowed as his gaze lingered on Fenrir, his posture stiffening slightly. "You're... here."

Fenrir's golden eyes sparkled with quiet amusement. "Indeed."

The tension in the room was palpable, but Kai wasn't sure how to diffuse it. He sank further into the bed, caught between the steady warmth of Gerhard's embrace and the unnerving weight of Fenrir's gaze. The frost fox, curled at Kai's feet, chirped softly as if sensing the charged atmosphere, its crystalline eyes flicking between the two men.

Gerhard shifted, his arm tightening protectively around Kai's waist as his gaze locked onto Fenrir. "Do you always make yourself at home in other people's beds?" he asked, his voice low and laced with irritation.

Fenrir's lips curved faintly, the barest shadow of a smile tugging at the corners of his mouth. "Only when I'm invited," he said smoothly, his golden eyes flicking to Kai, who flushed under the weight of his attention.

"I—" Kai started, his voice catching before he quickly amended, "I thought you'd stay with the king."

Fenrir's gaze softened, though his expression remained unreadable. "I thought it prudent," he said, his tone calm and even. "The castle is not a place to navigate alone. And after last night..." His words trailed off, but the meaning behind them lingered heavily in the air.

Gerhard's brow furrowed as he sat up slightly, his body still partially shielding Kai. "And what exactly are your intentions?" he demanded, his blue eyes narrowing at Fenrir.

Fenrir tilted his head slightly, his golden gaze unwavering. "My intentions are to protect him," he said simply. "Something you should be grateful for, considering the circumstances."

Gerhard's jaw tightened, his hand resting possessively on Kai's hip. "I can protect him just fine."

Kai glanced between them, the tension in the room growing sharper with every exchanged word. His pulse beat a little too fast, his mind working through a hundred different ways this could spiral further. *I don't have time for this. I don't even know what this is.*

"Stop," he said quietly, his voice cutting through the room. "Both of you."

It wasn't loud, but it carried enough weight to make them pause. Gerhard looked at him first, his expression softening just enough to remind Kai of the night before—the way his hands had *held*, not just taken. Fenrir's gaze lingered longer, studying him with something unreadable, like he was looking *through* him rather than at him. It was unsettling.

Kai tightened his jaw and pushed forward. "I don't need this right now," he continued, forcing his voice to stay steady despite the chaos in his chest. "Last night was... a lot. I'm still trying to figure out what it *means*, so can we not turn this into some kind of territorial standoff?"

Because that's what this feels like, isn't it? The tension between them wasn't just about him, but somehow, he'd ended up in the center of it. *Like I've been dropped into the middle of a war I didn't sign up for.*

Fenrir raised an eyebrow, his gaze flicking to Gerhard before settling back on Kai. "Territorial?" he echoed, and there it was again—that faint, maddening hint of amusement. "I think you misunderstand me."

Kai's frustration snapped before he could swallow it down. "Do I?" His voice came out sharper than he expected.

Fenrir's expression shifted, the flicker of humor in his eyes dimming slightly. He leaned back just a little, like he hadn't expected Kai to bite back. "Perhaps not," he admitted after a moment, his tone quieter now. "But you should know this—the storm that surrounds you is not one you face alone. Whether you like it or not, we are all bound to it now."

Kai swallowed hard, a heavy, uneasy weight settling in his chest.

What does that even mean? The words felt too big, too certain, as if Fenrir had already seen where this was going and Kai was the only one left in the dark. He hated that feeling—the sense that everyone else had a script and he was just fumbling his way through the lines, hoping to keep up.

He glanced at Gerhard, whose grip on his hip remained firm—*grounding, possessive, steady*. Then back at Fenrir, whose golden eyes didn't waver. *Unrelenting. Knowing.*

What do they want from me?

The answer pressed against the edges of his thoughts, but he wasn't ready to let it in. Not yet.

Instead, he took a slow, measured breath and lifted his chin. "Then I guess I should start figuring out what that actually means."

Not a surrender. Not an agreement. Just... a step. One he wasn't sure he wanted to take, but the storm was already here, wasn't it?

And there was no walking away from it now.

"The Snow King's emotions are unraveling," he said, his tone edged with warning. "That makes him dangerous—not just to you, but to himself, and to everyone in this cursed court."

Kai's frustration flared. "Then why doesn't he do something about it? Why doesn't he stop being—" He cut himself off, shaking his head as his words faltered.

"Cold?" Fenrir offered, his lips curling faintly, though it wasn't a smile. "Unyielding? Consumed by his grief?"

Kai didn't respond, the words hitting too close to truths he wasn't ready to admit.

Fenrir tilted his head slightly, his gaze piercing. "You misunderstand him, little warmth. He is not simply cold. He is *bound*. Every flicker of warmth you bring, every crack in the ice, pushes against the curse that has defined him for centuries. You do not realize what you are asking of him—or of yourself."

"I'm not a cure," he said quietly, his voice trembling. "I can't fix this."

"No," Fenrir said softly, his tone gentler now. "You are not a cure. But you are not nothing, either. You stir something long buried, and whether you wish it or not, that makes you a part of this story."

Kai's shoulders sagged, his frustration giving way to an exhaustion that went far deeper than the physical. He glanced back at Gerhard, who remained quiet, his eyes watching through lowered lids.

"What happens if I fail?" Kai asked, his voice barely more than a whisper.

Fenrir didn't answer immediately. He turned back to the window, his gaze fixed on the storm that raged beyond the frost-streaked glass. His voice, when it came, was low and edged with quiet certainty. "We don't have the luxury of failure."

Kai flinched, the words sinking into him like ice. The pull in his chest throbbed painfully, a constant reminder of the weight he carried.

Fenrir's gaze remained on the storm, his expression unreadable. "He will not forgive himself if he loses you. If that happens, there will be nothing left to stop the storm."

"I didn't ask for any of this," Kai murmured, his voice barely above a whisper.

"No," Fenrir agreed, his golden eyes softening.

Kai exhaled shakily, his body sinking further into the mattress. The frost fox chirped again, its small body radiating a quiet warmth that steadied him in ways he couldn't explain.

For a long moment, no one spoke. The tension in the room didn't disappear entirely, but it dulled enough for Kai to breathe more easily. Gerhard's hold on him relaxed slightly, and even Fenrir seemed to ease back, his presence less overpowering.

Kai closed his eyes briefly, letting the silence settle over them. When he finally spoke, his voice was soft but steady. "Can we just... stay like this? Just for a little while?"

Gerhard nodded without hesitation, his hand slipping to rest more gently against Kai's side. "Of course."

Fenrir didn't answer immediately, but after a beat, he shifted, leaning back against the headboard with a quiet hum of acknowledgment. "For now," he said, his tone carrying the faintest edge of amusement.

Kai didn't press further. He let his eyes drift shut, the warmth of Gerhard's body against his and the steady presence of Fenrir beside him lulling him into a fragile sense of peace.

Later that morning, the frost fox paced near the door, its crystalline eyes darting toward the frost-lined hallway as though sensing the day's coming weight. Kai stood beside Gerhard, who stretched his arms and rolled his shoulders with a low groan. Whatever weariness the man had carried the night before seemed to have melted away with the warmth of sleep. His movements were strong and steady now, his confidence unshaken.

"You sure you're ready for this?" Kai asked, one brow raised. He crossed his arms, his tone skeptical but touched with humor.

Gerhard shot him a dry look, his lips curving faintly. "I'm not the one who looks like they're about to topple over. You're sure you slept?"

Kai huffed, brushing off the comment. "I'm fine. I've just had a lot of excitement the last few days."

Fenrir leaned casually against the wall, his golden gaze sweeping over the pair with quiet intensity. "The castle is vast," he said, his voice low and measured. "It does not reveal its secrets easily."

Kai rolled his eyes. "Noted. But I'm guessing it's not going to eat us alive since it's seen fit to give me a toasty room."

The frost fox let out a soft chirp, padding closer to nudge at Kai's ankle, its tail swishing anxiously. Kai glanced down at it, his irritation easing slightly. "Alright, alright, we'll be careful."

Gerhard stepped toward the door, the heavy fur-lined cloak he'd borrowed shifting over his broad shoulders. "Then let's go. Sitting around won't answer any questions."

Kai hesitated, his gaze flicking briefly to Fenrir. The wolf-man's posture hadn't changed, but something about the way he watched them felt heavier, as though weighing the potential outcomes of their exploration. "You're not coming?"

Fenrir's lips quirked faintly, the barest hint of a smile that didn't quite reach his eyes. "I will check in with Eryon. Should you need guidance, the castle will tell me."

"The castle will tell you," Kai repeated, muttering under his breath. "That's not cryptic at all."

Gerhard smirked, stepping past him. "Let's go before he gives us another riddle."

Kai sighed but followed, his boots crunching softly against the frost as they stepped into the corridor. The frost fox trotted ahead, its glowing form a small beacon in the dim light. Behind them, Fenrir's steady gaze lingered for a moment longer before he disappeared into the shadows.

The hallway stretched before them, its icy walls shimmering faintly as the faint silver light from the windows filtered in. The frost patterns along the floor seemed to shift subtly as they walked, as though guiding them forward.

"Anything specific we're looking for?" Gerhard asked, his voice low but steady.

Kai shrugged, his hands stuffed into the folds of his cloak. "The kitchen might be nice." He glanced over his shoulder, though Fenrir was long out of sight.

Gerhard nodded, his brow furrowing slightly. "And if we find something we don't like?"

Kai hesitated. "Then we deal with it," he said quietly. "We don't really have another choice."

The frost fox chirped again, its ears twitching as it led them further into the castle. The air around them felt lighter, the oppressive chill that had clung to the walls since Kai's arrival easing slightly. The faint hum of the castle, a sound Kai had only recently begun to notice, seemed to grow stronger as they walked—a quiet vibration that thrummed through the ice and into his bones.

The castle was as cold and vast as ever, its labyrinthine halls stretching endlessly before them. Ice coated every surface, its sharp edges glittering faintly in the dim light. Gerhard shivered with every step, his breath coming in short bursts that clouded faintly in front of him.

"It's like walking through a tomb," Gerhard muttered, his voice low and wary.

Kai didn't disagree. The oppressive silence pressed down on them from every side, though it felt different now—less absolute, less suffocating. There was something else beneath it, something faint and fragile, like the first crack in a frozen lake.

As they walked, Kai began to notice subtle changes. The frost along the walls seemed thinner in places, its jagged edges softening. The biting cold that had once seemed to sink into his bones felt less intense, though the difference was barely noticeable.

Gerhard noticed it too, his steps slowing as he glanced around. "What's with the walls?" he asked, his voice tinged with unease.

Kai followed his gaze to a section of frost where faint patterns had begun to emerge. Swirling shapes and delicate carvings peeked through the ice, their intricate designs catching the dim light.

"I think... the castle is changing," Kai said softly, his voice filled with equal parts wonder and apprehension.

Their path led them to a grand hall, its towering ceilings disappearing into shadow. Massive columns of ice lined the space, their surfaces glittering with frozen light. At first glance, the figures carved into the ice seemed lifeless, their forms still and serene.

But as Kai and Gerhard stepped closer, the hall's oppressive silence felt heavier, charged with something unfamiliar.

The frost fox let out a soft chirp, its crystalline eyes fixed on one of the frozen figures. It was a fae, its delicate features captured in perfect detail. Its expression was one of quiet sorrow, its hands raised as though reaching for something just beyond its grasp.

"They're beautiful," Kai murmured, his breath hitching as he stepped closer.

Gerhard shivered, his gaze darting warily around the room. "They're unsettling," he muttered. "Like they could wake up at any second."

The words barely left his mouth before a faint crack split the air.

Gerhard froze, his eyes widening as he stared at the figure nearest to them. Its surface shimmered faintly, the faintest spiderweb of cracks spreading across the ice.

Kai's chest tightened, his pulse quickening as he stepped closer. His fingers trembled slightly as he reached out, brushing them gently against the frozen surface.

The moment his skin made contact, warmth spread from his fingertips. It was subtle but undeniable, a faint pulse of energy that rippled through the ice.

The cracks deepened, and for a moment, the figure's eyes flickered open. A soft sigh echoed through the hall, so faint it was almost imperceptible.

Kai stumbled back, his heart racing as the figure's eyes closed again, its form returning to stillness. The frost fox pressed against his leg, its body trembling faintly.

"What did you do?" Gerhard asked, his voice sharp with equal parts awe and fear.

Kai shook his head, his breaths uneven. "I—I don't know. I didn't mean to—"

Before he could finish, another crack echoed through the hall, louder this time, as though the castle itself were responding to his presence.

The crackling sound of ice splintering filled the grand hall, faint but distinct. It wasn't loud enough to be threatening, but it was enough to send a shiver down Kai's spine. He exchanged a nervous glance with Gerhard, who was clutching his frost-covered cloak tightly around him, his wide eyes darting toward the frozen figures that lined the walls.

The frost fox let out another soft chirp, its ears twitching as though it, too, sensed something stirring within the ice.

"What is this place?" Gerhard asked, his voice hushed.

Before Kai could answer, the sound of footsteps echoed behind them. They turned to see Fenrir stepping into the hall, his tall frame cutting a striking figure against the frozen backdrop. His golden eyes scanned the room, sharp and knowing, before settling on the closest frozen fae.

"They're waking," Fenrir said softly, his voice low and even. He knelt beside one of the frozen figures. He reached out, his fingers brushing lightly over the cracks Kai's touch had left behind. The ice shimmered faintly under his touch, but it didn't spread or deepen.

Kai stared at the figure nearest him, saddened at the thought of these beings—these fae—trapped for centuries, their lives stolen away by a curse that seemed impossible to break.

Gerhard frowned, his expression a mix of confusion and unease. "Why would the Snow King do this to his own people?"

Fenrir's golden gaze flicked to Gerhard, his expression unreadable. "He didn't. The curse is not of his making, though it is tied to his heart. His grief, his anger—it feeds the ice that binds them. And until his heart thaws, they will remain as they are."

Kai swallowed hard. He glanced back at the frozen figure whose eyes had flickered open—briefly, but undeniably—and felt a pang of guilt twist in his gut.

"So... they're alive?" Kai asked, his voice barely above a whisper. "All of them?"

Fenrir nodded slowly. "Their lives are suspended, frozen in time. Your warmth stirs their slumber, but it is not without risk."

"Risk?" Gerhard asked, his voice sharp with alarm.

Fenrir straightened, his golden eyes locking onto Kai's. "They are fragile in this state. Too much, too soon, and the ice will shatter—not just around them, but within them."

Kai's breath hitched, his gaze snapping back to the frozen fae. The thought of them breaking—of their delicate forms reduced to shards of ice—made his chest ache with a heavy, unfamiliar guilt.

"I didn't mean to—" Kai started, his voice trembling.

"You didn't know," Fenrir interrupted, his tone surprisingly gentle. "And you did no harm. But you must understand what you are."

Kai frowned, his confusion clear. "What I am?"

Fenrir stepped closer, his presence steady and grounding. His gaze was piercing as he said, "A 'little warmth' in a cold, cold place."

Kai's stomach churned at the words, the pull in his chest tightening painfully. "What does that even mean?"

"It means you are not bound by the curse," Fenrir explained, his voice calm but resolute. "Your presence disrupts the ice. You are the first warmth this place has felt in centuries, and it is responding to you."

Kai shook his head, his pulse racing. "But I don't know what I'm doing."

"You don't have to," Fenrir said softly. "You only need to be here."

The frost fox let out a soft whimper, brushing against Kai's leg as though trying to soothe his growing unease.

Gerhard stepped forward, his expression hardening slightly. "But why does it have to be Kai? Why does any of this have to involve him?"

"Because he was brought here from far away," Fenrir said, his tone laced with meaning. "Further than you could imagine."

The words hit Kai like a hammer, his stomach lurching. He felt Gerhard tense beside him, his broad shoulders stiffening at the implication. Brought here. Further than you could imagine.

Kai's mouth went dry. He hadn't told Gerhard. He hadn't told him that the Kai standing here wasn't the same Kai who had grown up in that village. That he wasn't the man Gerhard had known his entire life, the one Gerhard had risked everything to find.

The truth sat like a stone in Kai's chest, heavy and suffocating. His pulse thundered in his ears as his mind raced with what Gerhard might think—what he might feel—if he knew. Would he hate him? Would last night, the kiss, everything, become a cruel betrayal in Gerhard's eyes?

Fenrir's gaze flicked to him briefly, and for a terrifying moment, Kai thought he might say more. But Fenrir's attention returned to Gerhard, leaving Kai to grapple with the revelation alone.

Gerhard's voice broke the tense silence, his tone low and taut with emotion. "Brought here? From where? What does that even mean?" His eyes darted to Kai, confusion and concern mingling in his expression.

Kai swallowed hard, his throat tight as he avoided Gerhard's gaze. The frost fox nudged against his leg as if sensing his distress, but the small comfort did nothing to ease the panic swirling in his chest.

This wasn't just about him anymore. Last night had been proof of Gerhard's devotion to Kai—the man he used to be. And now, the truth threatened to unravel everything.

"Why does it matter where he came from?" Fenrir said evenly, his sharp gaze settling on Gerhard. "He is here now, and that is what matters."

Gerhard didn't look convinced, his furrowed brow betraying the storm of thoughts behind his steady demeanor. "If he's in danger because of this...because of whatever this is—" His voice faltered, and he shook his head. "I just need to know why."

Kai's chest ached, the words trapped behind his teeth like a dam threatening to burst. He clenched his fists, his heart hammering as he forced himself to speak, his voice trembling with the weight of his confession.

"I—" His voice cracked, and he swallowed hard, his gaze dropping to the frost-covered floor. "Gerhard, there's something I need to tell you."

Kai's words hung in the frozen air, each breath clouding faintly before dissolving into the heavy silence. Gerhard's brow furrowed, his concern deepening as he stepped closer.

"What is it?" Gerhard asked, his voice soft but insistent. "You can tell me, Kai."

The sincerity in his tone twisted something sharp in Kai's chest. His pulse thundered in his ears as he glanced at Fenrir, who stood silent but watchful, the frost fox's glowing form brushing against Kai's leg.

Kai drew in a shaky breath, the cold stinging his lungs. "I'm not... I'm not who you think I am."

Gerhard's head tilted slightly, confusion flickering across his face. "What do you mean?"

Kai closed his eyes briefly, his heart pounding as he tried to find the words. "I'm not—" He stopped, shaking his head as his voice caught in his throat. "I'm not Kai. Not the Kai you grew up with, not the one you..." His voice trailed off, his throat tightening painfully. "I don't even know how to explain it."

Gerhard stared at him, his face unreadable for a long, tense moment. "Then try," he said, his voice quiet but steady. "Help me understand."

Kai's chest ached as he forced himself to look at Gerhard, the weight of his guilt pressing down on him. "I'm from... somewhere else. Another place, another world. I woke up here, in his body. Your Kai's body. And I don't know why. I don't know how to fix it."

The words spilled out in a rush, raw and unpolished, but they left Kai trembling, his chest tight as he waited for Gerhard's response.

For a moment, Gerhard said nothing. His gaze searched Kai's face, his jaw tightening as he processed the confession. "Another... world?" he repeated slowly, his tone caught between disbelief and cautious curiosity.

Kai nodded, his hands trembling at his sides. "It sounds insane, I know. But it's the truth. I don't know how I got here. I don't know why. And I know it's not fair—to you, to him—but I'm not your Kai."

Gerhard's brows knit together, his lips pressing into a thin line as he looked away briefly, his hand running through his hair. The silence stretched, heavy and suffocating, until he finally spoke.

"And the Kai I knew... he's gone?" Gerhard asked, his voice tight, as though he was bracing himself for the answer.

"I don't know," Kai admitted, his voice barely above a whisper. "I don't know what happened to him. Maybe he's where I came from?" He stopped, shaking his head. "I just don't know."

Gerhard turned back to Kai, his gaze sharp and piercing. "But you remember nothing about him? About us?"

Kai's breath hitched. "I don't," he said, the words cutting him as they left his lips. "I don't know the things he knew. I don't have the memories you shared. I'm just... me. Whoever that is."

Gerhard studied Kai in silence, his eyes narrowing as though searching for something just out of reach. His jaw worked, tension evident in the tightness of his features. Finally, he exhaled, the sound weary but laced with resolve.

"I suspected," he said softly, his voice steady but laden with weight.

Kai blinked, caught off guard by the quiet admission. "You... did?"

Gerhard gave a faint nod, his lips pressing into a thin line before he continued. "The Kai I grew up with—he loved me like a brother. He was fierce, protective, and never once hesitated to push me away when I got too close." He hesitated, his brow furrowing as he searched for the right words. "But you—you blush just from standing near me. You look at me like you're afraid I'll disappear, like you're... charmed by every little thing I do."

Kai's face heated, and he looked away, his pulse thrumming in his ears. He wanted to say something, to deny it, to apologize, but the words stuck in his throat.

Gerhard's voice softened, the edge of tension in it easing as he stepped closer. "The signs were there, but I ignored them. I told myself it was the same Kai—just shaken by everything that's happened, different because of the ritual. But deep down, I knew." His gaze lingered on Kai's face, the sharpness giving way to something more contemplative. "I ignored it because... because I was charmed by the newness. By you."

Kai's breath hitched at the admission, his chest tightening as he looked up at Gerhard. "But you—he—" He stopped, the words tangling on his tongue. "I'm not him. I can't be what you wanted, what you thought you were saving."

Gerhard's lips quirked into a faint, bittersweet smile. "You don't have to be."

The response struck Kai like a blow—unexpected and grounding all at once. He stared at Gerhard, his heart racing as the older man continued.

"I'll always love the man I grew up with," Gerhard admitted, his voice quiet but steady. "I'll always hold onto those memories, those moments we shared. But that man is not the one who stands before me now. He's not the one I came here for."

Kai's throat tightened painfully. "So why—why did you—?"

Gerhard's hand lifted, brushing lightly against Kai's cheek, the touch both grounding and tender. "Because the man standing here now is worth saving. Worth knowing. Worth loving, even if I don't fully understand him yet."

Kai's eyes stung, his vision blurring as the weight of Gerhard's words pressed against his chest. "You mean that?" he whispered, his voice barely audible.

"I do," Gerhard said simply, his thumb brushing away a tear that slipped down Kai's cheek. "You're not him, Kai. And that's okay. I came here for you, not for a ghost."

Kai let out a shaky breath, his shoulders sagging as some of the tension that had gripped him since his arrival finally eased. The frost fox nudged against his leg, its soft glow flickering faintly in the dim light.

"Right," Gerhard said dryly, though his shoulders relaxed a fraction. He turned his attention back to Kai, a hint of a smile tugging at his lips. "Well, we've hashed out a lot today—life-altering truths, personal confessions... but there's one thing we still haven't managed to find."

Kai blinked at him, caught off guard. "What's that?"

Gerhard raised an eyebrow, his voice taking on a mock-serious tone. "The kitchen. Or even just food. Unless you want to live off cryptic magical energy forever."

The frost fox tilted its head, giving a soft chirp that sounded suspiciously like indignation. Kai snorted, a laugh bubbling out despite himself. "We're in the middle of a cursed castle, and you're worried about food?"

Gerhard shrugged, his grin widening slightly. "Priorities, Kai. Priorities. I'm just saying, a man can only go so long without a proper meal."

From his spot near the wall, Fenrir stepped forward slightly, his sharp gaze cutting through the room. "The castle will not starve you," he said evenly, though there was the faintest hint of a smirk in his tone. "But it may enjoy making you work for what you seek."

Kai raised an eyebrow at him. "That's comforting. Thanks for that."

Fenrir inclined his head slightly, his expression calm but with an undertone of challenge. "You will learn the castle's ways soon enough. It reveals what it chooses."

The frost fox gave another chiming sound, hopping toward the door before turning back to look at them. Its crystalline tail swished expectantly, the faint light it emitted catching the frost that lined the floor. Gerhard chuckled, gesturing toward the fox. "Looks like someone's eager to prove me right."

Kai hesitated, glancing between Gerhard and Fenrir. The weight of their earlier conversation still hung in the air, but the flicker of humor in Gerhard's expression and the steadying presence of Fenrir were enough to coax him forward. He stepped toward the door, the fox trotting ahead with purpose.

Gerhard followed, his tone lighter now. "If we find something edible, I'm claiming the first bite. Fair warning."

Kai rolled his eyes but couldn't help the faint smile that tugged at his lips. "You're impossible."

"And you're starving," Gerhard quipped, shooting him a sidelong grin. "Let's fix that before we both start snapping at each other."

As they stepped into the corridor, Fenrir moved silently behind them, his gaze scanning the frost-covered walls. Kai caught the faintest glint of amusement in his golden eyes and raised an eyebrow at him. "You're coming with us?"

Fenrir's lips quirked faintly. "I remain where I am needed."

"Or where the entertainment is," Kai muttered under his breath, though there was no real bite in his words. The frost fox chirped, and

Kai sighed, following its lead as the trio ventured deeper into the castle, the chill of the air softened by the faint warmth that seemed to emanate from their shared presence. For the first time in days, Kai allowed himself to believe that maybe, just maybe, they could face what lay ahead—together.

The kitchens were nestled deeper into the castle than Kai had expected. The frost fox led the way, its glowing tail bobbing as it trotted confidently through the winding corridors. The air grew noticeably warmer as they approached, and by the time they reached the heavy wooden door, a faint glow seeped through the cracks.

Kai glanced back at the others, his brow furrowing. "Do kitchens usually heat themselves in abandoned castles?"

Gerhard shrugged, but his gaze was wary. Fenrir, however, narrowed his golden eyes, stepping closer to the door. "This is... new," the wolf-man murmured, his voice tinged with something close to suspicion.

Kai pushed the door open, the hinges creaking faintly, and was greeted by a rush of warm, spiced air. The room beyond was expansive and unlike anything he had expected. Long counters stretched across the space, polished wood glinting faintly in the soft glow of the massive oven embedded into the far wall. The oven was alive with heat, its golden light casting flickering shadows over the room. The scent of something rich and savory wafted toward them, making Kai's stomach rumble audibly.

"Well, that's not ominous at all," Kai muttered, stepping inside.

The frost fox darted ahead, chirping excitedly as it hopped onto one of the counters. Gerhard followed cautiously, his eyes sweeping over the surprisingly tidy space. "It's warm," he said, his voice low with surprise. "And it smells... good."

Kai ignored the comment, making a beeline for the oven. His curiosity overrode his hesitation as he tugged the heavy door open. Inside, a large pot simmered over an open flame, steam curling lazily into the air. The rich aroma hit him full force, and he blinked in shock. "It's... cooking something?"

Fenrir stepped closer, his expression sharp as he peered inside. "This is not the castle I know," he said, his voice carrying a faint edge of unease. "The kitchens have been silent for centuries. The fire—" He gestured to the glowing oven. "—should not exist."

Gerhard moved to Kai's side, his brows knitting together as he stared into the pot. "What is it?"

Kai grabbed a ladle hanging nearby and dipped it into the bubbling liquid. He pulled it out, the steaming broth catching the light, and sniffed cautiously. "Soup," he said, though his tone was more bewildered than certain. "It smells like... chicken? Maybe some herbs."

Fenrir tilted his head, his expression unreadable as he studied the pot. "The castle adapts," he said slowly, his tone more thoughtful now. "But this..."

"This is more than adapting," Kai cut in, glancing back at him. "It's like it's... welcoming us."

Gerhard crossed his arms, his gaze flicking to the frost fox, which sat proudly on the counter as though taking credit for the entire display. "The castle's not exactly subtle about its favorites," he muttered.

Kai dipped the ladle back into the pot, this time pouring some of the broth into a nearby bowl. He blew on it cautiously before taking a sip. Warmth spread through him immediately, chasing away the lingering chill in his bones. "It's good," he said, surprised.

Fenrir took a step back, his gaze scanning the room again. "It's a kindness," he said finally, though his tone carried a note of caution. "But kindness is rarely given freely here."

Kai paused mid-sip, frowning at him. "You think it's a trap? What kind of trap involves soup?"

Fenrir's lips quirked faintly, the barest shadow of a smile. "The clever kind."

Gerhard rolled his eyes, grabbing another bowl and dipping it into the pot. "If it's a trap, at least we'll die full."

Kai snorted, handing the first bowl to Fenrir before pouring another for himself. The frost fox chirped impatiently, its crystalline eyes fixed on the pot. Kai sighed, grabbing a smaller bowl and setting it on the counter for the creature, which immediately began lapping at the steaming liquid.

For a moment, the group fell into a companionable silence, the warmth of the kitchen and the simple act of sharing a meal easing some of the tension that had lingered since Gerhard's arrival. Even Fenrir seemed less on edge, though his sharp gaze never stopped scanning the room.

"This is good," Gerhard said after a moment, his voice soft with surprise.

Kai smirked at him over the rim of his bowl. "See? I told you we'd find something edible."

Fenrir tilted his head slightly, his golden eyes glinting in the oven's glow. "Do not grow too comfortable," he said quietly, though there was no malice in his tone. "The castle is ever-changing. What it gives, it can also take."

Kai felt a shiver run through him despite the warmth of the room. But he pushed the thought aside, focusing instead on the rich, comforting taste of the soup. For now, at least, the castle seemed to be in a giving mood—and that was enough.

Chapter 11

T HE SOFT CLATTER OF chess pieces broke the otherwise quiet hum of the room. The fire crackled low in the hearth, its warmth stretching lazily across the frost-lined floor. Kai lounged on the bed, the furs draped loosely over his shoulders as he watched Gerhard and Fenrir play their third match of the evening.

"Do you always take this long?" Kai teased, resting his chin on his hand. "Or is it just because Gerhard's losing?"

Gerhard shot him a look, though his lips twitched as if suppressing a grin. "I'd like to see you try this, *little warmth*."

Kai snorted. "Pass. I'd rather not embarrass you further."

Fenrir, seated across from Gerhard, allowed a faint smile to touch his lips, though his golden eyes remained fixed on the board. "You shouldn't taunt him when he's trying to think. He's struggling enough."

Gerhard huffed a laugh and moved a knight, clearly trying to reclaim some dignity. "Just wait. I've got you this time."

The frost fox stirred at the foot of the bed, stretching languidly before curling into a tighter ball. The cozy scene was a rare reprieve from the usual tension of the castle, and for a moment, everything felt still.

But then Fenrir's hand, poised over his next move, froze mid-air. His sharp gaze darted toward the door, the light in his golden eyes narrowing like a predator catching a scent on the wind.

Kai sat up, his relaxed posture vanishing. "What is it?"

Fenrir didn't answer immediately. His attention remained locked on the door, his body still but alert. Slowly, he rose from his chair, his imposing frame casting a long shadow against the room's frost-covered walls.

"Fenrir?" Gerhard's voice carried a hint of unease as he glanced between his opponent and the door. "What's wrong?"

The frost fox leapt to the floor, its crystalline glow dimming as it let out a soft, chiming whimper. Kai's chest tightened as the warmth of the room seemed to draw back, the air growing colder and heavier with each passing second.

Fenrir's voice was quiet but firm as he finally spoke. "We have company."

Kai swung his legs off the bed, his bare feet brushing against the cold floor. "What kind of company?"

Fenrir didn't answer immediately, already striding toward the door. "Stay behind me," he said over his shoulder, his tone brooking no argument.

Gerhard rose from his chair, his expression hardening as he grabbed the blade he'd laid beside him earlier. "Company doesn't sound like a good thing."

Kai hesitated for a moment before following Fenrir into the hall. The frost fox trotted ahead of them, its glowing tail swishing nervously as if urging them forward. Gerhard stayed close, his grip on his weapon firm but his eyes scanning the dimly lit corridor with wary precision.

The castle's oppressive silence felt suffocating as they made their way toward the great hall. Frost clung to the walls in jagged veins, and the air carried an unnatural stillness, as though the castle itself was holding its breath.

When they reached the hall, the massive double doors shuddered under the weight of another heavy knock. The sound echoed through the frozen expanse, deep and resonant, like the final toll of a bell.

Fenrir stepped forward, his palm brushing against the frost-covered wood as though testing it. His golden eyes narrowed further, his sharp gaze flicking toward Kai briefly. "Stay behind me," he repeated.

The frost fox let out a soft chirp, its ears flattening against its head as the doors groaned open. A blast of icy wind swept into the hall, carrying with it a swirl of snow that spiraled like an ethereal veil.

Three figures stepped inside.

The figures were striking—beautiful but terrible, their presence radiating an unnatural heat that made the frost-laden air hiss and steam. Their golden armor glowed faintly, as though lit from within by an internal fire.

The leader of the group stepped forward, his molten amber eyes sweeping the room with cool disdain. He was tall and regal, his sharp features framed by flowing hair that shimmered like liquid gold. The air around him rippled faintly with heat, melting the frost beneath his feet as he walked.

Kai felt the frost fox bristle against his leg, its crystalline fur fluffing as it let out a low, nervous whimper.

The leader's gaze landed on Fenrir first, his lip curling slightly. "So," he said, his voice smooth and commanding. "The hound still guards his king's broken court."

Fenrir growled low in his throat, stepping protectively in front of Kai. "You would do well to watch your tongue, Summer dog."

The fae's smile sharpened, though it didn't reach his glowing eyes. "And you would do well to remember your place, Fenrir."

Kai's pulse raced as the temperature in the hall shifted abruptly. The biting cold that had defined the castle surged forward, clashing against the heat radiating from the emissaries. The air felt heavy, charged with magic that crackled faintly like distant thunder.

The leader's gaze shifted to Kai, narrowing slightly as his molten eyes studied him with unnerving intensity.

"And who is this?" the fae asked, his tone laced with curiosity.

Kai opened his mouth to respond, but the words caught in his throat as the Snow King stepped into the hall.

The temperature plummeted further as the Snow King appeared, his frost-covered cloak trailing behind him like a shadow. His pale blue eyes were sharp and unyielding as they fixed on the emissaries, the frost beneath his feet spreading outward in jagged veins with every step.

"You bring fire into my court," the Snow King said, his voice low and cutting. "You would do well to tread carefully."

The leader turned to face him fully, his smile fading into something colder, more calculating. He bowed stiffly.

"The Summer King has felt the change in Winter," he said, his tone sharp with disdain. "We bring a message for the one who dares disturb the balance."

The Snow King stood still as stone, his pale blue eyes fixed on the leader. The frost beneath his feet crackled ominously, spreading in sharp, jagged veins that hissed against the heat radiating from the fae.

The leader straightened from his stiff bow, his molten amber eyes glinting with contempt as he met the Snow King's unyielding gaze. "The Summer King grows weary of your neglect, Winter. Your silence fractures the balance we both hold dear."

The air in the hall grew heavier as the fae continued, his tone sharpening like a blade. "The thaw has been felt even in our lands. Your domain warms, your stillness falters, and the frost spreads where it should not. This cannot continue."

Kai stood frozen behind Fenrir, the frost fox pressed tightly against his leg. The words felt like accusations, though the fae hadn't yet turned his attention to him.

As if sensing Kai's unease, Fenrir shifted slightly, his golden eyes flicking between the Snow King and the emissaries. His presence was steady, protective, but there was a tension in his stance that made Kai's chest tighten.

The fae's gaze finally drifted to Kai, narrowing sharply as though drawn by something unseen. He stepped forward, the heat of his presence intensifying with each measured step. The frost on the floor hissed and steamed beneath his feet, leaving a trail of melting ice in his wake.

Kai's breath hitched as the fae stopped in front of him, his amber eyes locking onto his with an unnerving intensity. "So," the fae murmured, his voice a dangerous murmur. "This is the source of the disturbance."

The frost fox growled softly, its crystalline fur bristling as it pressed closer to Kai.

Fenrir stepped forward instantly, placing himself between Kai and the fae. "Stay where you are," he growled, his voice low and threatening.

The fae's lip curled faintly, though he didn't retreat. "Your loyalty is misplaced, Fenrir. This boy's warmth spreads like a disease, unraveling what little order remains in this frozen wasteland. If it cannot be contained..." He leaned forward slightly, his tone darkening. "Then we will shatter the frost until nothing remains but the silence beneath it."

The Snow King's voice cut through the tension like a shard of ice, low and resonant. "You will do nothing."

The temperature in the hall plummeted violently, frost surging across the floor and up the walls. The oppressive cold pressed against Kai's chest, sharp and unrelenting, but he forced himself to stay upright.

The emissaries didn't flinch, their heat blazing against the Snow King's cold with equal ferocity. The leader's expression turned calculating as he turned back to face the Snow King.

"Will we not?" the fae asked, his tone dripping with mockery. "Your court is already fractured. Your kingdom fades with each passing year. Perhaps it is time Summer brought the frost to its knees."

The Snow King's pale blue eyes burned with fury, his frost-covered cloak flaring faintly as his magic rippled through the air. "You dare to threaten me in my own court?"

Kai's heart pounded as he glanced between the Snow King and the emissaries, the tension in the hall stretching to a breaking point.

Fenrir stepped forward, his golden eyes narrowing as he placed a hand on Kai's shoulder. His voice was low but edged with quiet authority as he addressed the emissaries. "You speak of balance, yet your king has burned his own lands in pride. Do not lecture us on what has been broken."

The leader's molten gaze flicked to Fenrir, his expression hardening. "And yet here you stand, guarding a king who cannot save his own court. You call it pride, but we call it necessity. Balance must be restored, but the Summer Soverign's ire grows."

The Snow King stepped forward abruptly, the frost beneath him cracking loudly as his magic surged. His voice was an icy growl, low and dangerous. "Enough."

The great hall trembled as the power of Winter and Summer clashed, the air thick with opposing forces. Frost surged across the floor, crawling up the walls in jagged, crystalline veins, only to hiss and melt under the heat radiating from the emissaries. The tension between the two forces was palpable, each pushing against the other in a deadly harmony.

The Snow King's pale blue eyes burned cold with fury, his voice cutting through the heavy silence like a blade. "Your Summer is a wasteland of ash."

The leader scowls, the heat of his magic flaring. "Then fix it! Or are you just a shadow, Winter—a relic of a time long past."

"You will find," the Snow King said, his voice dangerously quiet, "that this shadow still commands the storm."

A wave of frost burst outward from the Snow King, racing across the floor like a tide. The air grew impossibly cold, frost climbing toward the emissaries with razor-sharp precision.

The leader raised his hand, and a wall of golden fire erupted to meet the frost. The two magics collided with a deafening crack, sending shockwaves rippling through the hall.

Kai stumbled as the ground beneath him shuddered, the frost fox yelping as it pressed against his leg. Fenrir caught Kai's arm, his golden eyes narrowed as he steadied him. "Stay behind me," he growled, his voice low but commanding.

The heat and cold swirled together in the air, spiraling in deadly waves that made it difficult to breathe. The frost on the walls hissed and melted, only to refreeze moments later as the opposing magics fought for dominance.

"You dare to bring your flames into my court?" the Snow King growled, his voice rising with the storm of his magic. "You will not leave here unscathed."

The fae didn't flinch, his molten eyes gleaming with defiance. "And you will not leave at all."

Kai's chest tightened as the air in the room grew heavier, the storm of magic threatening to consume everything. The frost fox let out a soft whimper, its tail curling around Kai's leg as if urging him to move.

Before he could think—before the tension in the hall could snap—Kai stepped forward.

"Enough!"

His voice rang out, sharp and clear, cutting through the roaring magic like a knife.

Silence slammed into the room. The air was thick with frost and heat, the opposing magics pulling back just enough to leave an eerie stillness in their wake. The frost fox chirped nervously at his feet, shifting its weight as if debating whether to flee or stay.

Kai ignored it. He ignored *everything*—his pounding pulse, the tightness in his chest, the way the Snow King's icy gaze burned into him like a warning. Instead, he lifted his chin and met the leader's molten stare with the best unimpressed expression he could muster.

"You want to talk about balance?" He gestured sharply to the shattered ice and curling steam still hissing through the air. "You want to blame Winter for breaking it? *Fine.* But this?" He swept his hand around the ruined hall, his voice dry. "This isn't balance. This is a temper tantrum with extra steps."

A sharp crack echoed through the chamber as one of the emissaries tensed, their magic spiking in warning. Kai barely resisted the urge to flinch.

The Snow King's gaze snapped to him, his expression carved from ice. "You do not speak for me," he said, his tone laced with frost. But there was something else beneath it, something Kai couldn't quite name.

Kai turned to face him fully, squaring his shoulders despite the instinct screaming at him to *shut up and sit down.* "No, I don't," he admitted, flashing the King a tight-lipped smile. "But someone has to speak. *Someone* has to stop this before it turns into a full-blown disaster."

The leader of the emissaries tilted his head, amusement flickering in his molten gaze. "And you believe *you* are that someone?"

Kai swallowed, but if his nerves were trying to strangle him, he *refused* to let them show. Instead, he exhaled through his nose and flashed a lopsided smirk. "I mean, unless *you* have a better idea?" He raised an eyebrow. "Because if the plan is 'fight until everything is broken,' I feel like we've already nailed that part."

A few of the emissaries shifted, exchanging wary glances. Even the frost fox let out a chuff, as if vaguely impressed by his audacity.

Kai turned back to the leader, forcing himself to hold his stare. His heart hammered against his ribs, but he let his voice settle into something almost casual. "Look. I don't *know* what's going on here, not really. But if

I'm the one who set all of this off... then yeah." He squared his shoulders. "I guess that makes me the idiot who has to fix it."

A beat of silence stretched between them.

Then the emissary smiled—slow and sharp, like a blade catching light.

Kai wasn't sure if that was *better* or *worse*.

The words hung in the air, their weight dragging at the tension like an undertow, silent but suffocating.

The hall remained deathly still, the frost and heat curling at the edges of the emissaries and the Snow King—restrained, but only just. Kai swore he could hear the ice cracking beneath his own feet, waiting for the moment everything *snapped*.

His throat was dry, but he forced himself to stand straighter, locking his knees before they had the chance to betray him. His voice wavered, but he held it steady. "The thaw... it's my fault. I don't know *how*, but it is. If someone has to answer for it, then take me."

The frost fox let out a distressed whimper, circling his legs, as if its tiny body could somehow shield him from the storm brewing in the room.

"No."

Fenrir's growl was low, edged with warning. His golden eyes burned with something fierce and *unmovable* as he stepped closer, his broad frame a barrier between Kai and the emissaries. "You don't know what you're offering."

Kai turned to him, matching his stare with quiet defiance. "I know enough." *I know that no one else is going to fix this. I know that if I don't say something, you'll all just rip each other apart.*

A violent *crack* split through the air as frost erupted beneath the Snow King's feet, his magic flaring. The temperature plummeted, sending a fresh bite of cold clawing up Kai's spine.

When the Snow King's gaze snapped to him, it was ice itself—pale blue and *furious*.

"You do not speak for me," he said, each word honed to a blade's edge.

Kai's chest tightened, the weight of that fury pressing against him like a physical force, but he refused to look away. "This isn't just about *you* anymore," he shot back, his voice rising with the weight of everything simmering inside him. "You've kept your silence for centuries, and *look* where it's gotten you. If I can stop this—if I can stop *them*—then I'll go."

The Snow King's cloak flared with the force of his magic, a sharp gust of cold sweeping through the chamber. His fury crackled in the air, raw and brimming with something Kai couldn't quite name.

"You would *choose* to leave this court for theirs?" The words were slow, deliberate, but laced with something sharper, something almost *pained*.

Kai hesitated—just for a moment. Because the pull in his chest *tightened* at that, like something deep inside him recognized the weight of the question. But he forced himself to push through it, meeting the Snow King's gaze without flinching.

"I would choose to stop this before it turns into something worse."

A cruel smile curled at the emissary leader's lips as he stepped forward, his molten amber eyes glittering with amusement. "How *noble*," he murmured, every syllable dripping with mockery. "So you will come to the Summer Court *willingly*? You would place yourself at the mercy of the Summer Sovereign?"

The air around Fenrir *snapped* with restrained fury. His fists clenched at his sides, his body coiled and ready to strike. "You will *not* take him."

The Snow King's voice dropped to a deadly whisper, so cold it cut straight through Kai's skin.

"You will take *nothing* from this court."

Magic detonated like a winter storm. Frost erupted outward, cracks shattering the ice beneath their feet. Heat flared in response, the emissaries' magic rising in defiance, the two forces clashing in a volatile storm of power.

Before it could explode into something unstoppable, Kai *moved*.

He stepped forward, heart hammering, stomach twisting, but voice ringing out with a force he didn't know he had.

"I CHOOSE TO GO!"

The words echoed, slicing through the storm like a blade of their own.

Silence fell like an avalanche.

The frost fox chirped anxiously, pressing closer against his legs as the room fell into an eerie, suffocating stillness.

Kai exhaled, forcing himself to stand tall. He ignored the cold sweat at the back of his neck, the way his limbs shook *just slightly*. He wasn't sure *what* he had just done—if he had just saved them all or signed his own death sentence.

But at least now, they were listening.

Kai's heart pounded in his ears, each beat hammering against his ribs as the weight of his decision settled over him. The Snow King's icy gaze burned into him, cold and unrelenting, but Kai *refused* to look away. His instincts screamed at him to run, to *rethink* everything, but it was too late for that.

The emissary leader's smile sharpened, his tone dripping with mockery. "How *brave*," he murmured, though something in his molten gaze flickered with approval. "Perhaps you are not as insignificant as you seem."

Kai rolled his shoulders, forcing himself to breathe through the tightness in his chest. "Glad to impress," he muttered, deadpan, before turning his attention to the Snow King.

"This is my choice," he said, his voice quieter but no less firm. "You don't have to *like* it, but I'm not going to stand by and let this turn into a war just because no one knows how to *use their words*."

The Snow King's expression remained frozen, unreadable, but the frost beneath his feet pulsed faintly—*retreating*, if only slightly. A hesitation, barely visible, but enough to make Kai wonder if he'd struck something deeper than the surface.

The hall remained thick with silence, but Kai could *feel* the weight of the moment pressing down on him. The frost fox brushed against his leg again, as if trying to remind him he wasn't entirely alone.

Heat radiated from the emissaries in waves, clashing against the biting cold. They were waiting—*expectant*, almost triumphant.

Kai let out a slow breath and turned his head, catching sight of Gerhard in the shadows. His expression was tight, unreadable at first—until Kai looked closer. *Worry.* Anger. Something *else*, something heavier than just frustration.

Kai's fingers curled at his sides. He couldn't leave things like this.

"I have one condition before I go," he said, his voice steadier than he felt.

The Snow King's gaze *snapped* to him, sharp as a blade. "You are in no position to make demands."

Kai squared his shoulders, ignoring the way the frost in the air thickened in response. "This isn't for me," he said, locking eyes with the King. "It's for Gerhard."

The temperature dropped further, the air growing *thick* with something dangerous. The Snow King's magic flared, wrapping around the chamber like a vice.

"You presume much, boy," he said, each word a razor's edge.

Kai forced himself to hold his ground, though his lungs felt tight with the cold. "You've *already* taken enough from him," he said, voice softer but unwavering. "You can't let him freeze while I'm gone. He came here because of *me*—he doesn't deserve to suffer for it."

The air in the hall was suffocating now, the weight of the Snow King's power pressing into Kai's bones.

The frost fox whined, circling him again, its tail curling around his ankle like it could anchor him in place.

The Snow King's lips pressed into a thin line, his expression *tight*, unreadable but undeniably furious. His cloak flared faintly as he turned his back to Kai, his voice clipped and bitter.

"You presume to tell me what my court will endure."

Kai let out a humorless breath, shoving his hands into his pockets to hide the way they trembled. "I'm not *telling* you anything," he said, voice lighter now—*just enough* to mask the weight behind it. "I'm *asking*. Politely, even. Which, I think, is pretty generous considering the circumstances."

A muscle in the Snow King's jaw twitched.

Kai took a slow step forward, the frost crunching under his boots. "Just... don't let him freeze."

For a long moment, there was nothing but silence. The air itself felt brittle, as if one wrong move would shatter it completely.

Fenrir's golden eyes flicked between them, his expression unreadable. Even the emissaries hesitated, their earlier amusement dimming into something more cautious.

Then, finally, the Snow King turned back, his gaze colder than ever.

"A temporary reprieve," he said, each word laced with disdain. "Nothing more."

Kai exhaled, relief and tension crashing into him all at once.

The frost fox let out a soft chirp, nudging against his leg like it *knew*.

"Thank you," Kai said, though he wasn't sure the words carried the weight he wanted them to.

The Snow King's expression didn't soften. If anything, his pale blue eyes burned colder, unreadable as they locked onto Kai's.

"Do not mistake this for mercy," he said, his voice low, dangerous.

Kai forced a smirk, though his chest ached. "Oh, trust me," he murmured. "I *wouldn't dare*."

But as he glanced back at Gerhard—at the anger, the quiet hurt, the tension in his stance—Kai wondered if his own words were more of a warning to *himself* than anyone else.

"I'll come back," he said softly, his voice trembling. "I promise."

Gerhard's expression faltered, the anger in his gaze giving way to something rawer, something more vulnerable. "You don't know what they'll do to you."

Kai placed a hand on his shoulder, steadying him with a faint smile. "I'll be fine."

Fenrir's presence loomed beside them; his golden eyes sharp as he addressed Kai. "You will not go alone."

Kai looked up at him and nodded, the frost fox brushing against his leg as though echoing the sentiment.

The emissaries moved toward the massive doors, their heat trailing behind them like a flame threatening to consume the cold. Kai took a deep breath, the pull in his chest thrumming like a quiet reminder of what lay ahead.

As he followed them toward the threshold, he glanced back one last time.

The Snow King stood in the shadows, his pale blue eyes fixed on Kai with an intensity that sent a shiver down his spine. The frost beneath the king's feet cracked faintly, the sound echoing in the heavy silence.

For a fleeting moment, Kai thought he saw something flicker in the Snow King's gaze—something raw and unguarded.

But then the moment passed, and the Snow King turned away, his voice a whisper that barely reached Kai's ears: "He will not return unchanged."

The emissaries stepped aside as Kai and Fenrir approached, their molten eyes gleaming with faint approval. The leader smirked, his voice smooth and mocking as he gestured toward the storm beyond the gates. "Your chariot awaits."

Kai ignored him, his focus on the steady presence of Fenrir behind him. The storm outside howled fiercely, its winds biting against his skin as he stepped across the threshold.

The gates groaned shut behind them, the sound echoing through the frozen halls like a final farewell.

As the castle disappeared into the blinding snow, Kai tightened his grip on Fenrir, whose golden eyes glowed faintly in the storm's dim light.

"We'll come back," Kai said softly, more to himself than anyone else.

Fenrir's voice was low but firm, cutting through the wind like a steady anchor. "Yes. We will."

The massive doors groaned shut, sealing out the swirling heat and faint echoes of the emissaries' retreating footsteps. For a moment, the great hall was silent save for the faint crackle of frost as it reclaimed the space, filling the void left by the intruders. Gerhard remained rooted in place, his hand still tingling where Kai had touched him, the boy's trembling promise lingering in his ears like a haunting melody.

The Snow King's presence, though silent, was suffocating. His pale blue eyes burned with an intensity that made Gerhard's chest tighten. Without a word, the king turned sharply on his heel and strode toward the shadows, his frost-laden cloak trailing behind him like a living thing. Each step sent a web of ice spidering out across the floor, the tension in the air sharp enough to cut.

Gerhard let out a shaky breath he hadn't realized he was holding, his fists clenching at his sides. He wanted to shout, to demand answers, but the weight of the king's fury was a wall he couldn't breach. Instead, he watched as the Snow King disappeared through the far archway, his form melting into the castle's icy gloom.

Left alone in the hall, Gerhard glanced down at the frost fox, which sat at his feet, its crystalline eyes watching him intently. Its glowing body pulsed faintly, as though mirroring his uneven heartbeat.

"Well," he muttered, crouching to scoop the small creature into his arms. Its warmth was a surprising comfort against his chest, and it let out a soft, chiming sound as it nestled closer. "Looks like it's just you and me now."

The frost fox chirped in response, its tiny head tilting as though it understood more than it let on. Gerhard shook his head, exhaustion creeping into his limbs as he made his way back toward Kai's chambers. The quiet of the castle was deafening, the frost along the walls seeming to press in closer with each step.

When he reached the room, it was exactly as they'd left it: the furs on the bed still rumpled, the faint warmth lingering in the air like a fading memory. Gerhard set the fox down on the bed, watching as it padded toward the pillow and curled into a glowing ball.

"Do you have a name?" he asked aloud, more to himself than the fox. He sat on the edge of the bed, running a hand through his hair. "You seem to know more about this place than I do."

The fox tilted its head, its crystalline eyes blinking slowly. It let out another soft chime, the sound gentle and oddly soothing.

Gerhard chuckled dryly, shaking his head. "Right. Talking to a fox. This place really is starting to get to me." He leaned back, his gaze drifting to the frost-lined ceiling. "Still... you've been with him since he got here, haven't you? Watching over him."

The fox chirped again, its tail swishing faintly before curling tighter around itself.

Gerhard sighed, his thoughts spiraling. The memory of Kai's trembling words—*"I promise"*—echoed in his mind, twisting the knot of worry in his chest. He reached out hesitantly, brushing his fingers against the fox's glowing fur as he thought of the ethereal man that had gone with him, Fenris. He'd been tempted to argue to go in his stead, but he couldn't argue with the power at play.

"Keep him safe," he murmured, his voice barely audible. "Even if I can't be there."

The fox shifted slightly, its small body pressing against his hand as though offering silent reassurance.

The quiet in the room stretched, the faint glow of the fox the only light as Gerhard sat in thoughtful silence.

A sharp crack echoed faintly in the distance, pulling him from his thoughts. His gaze snapped toward the doorway, the unease creeping back into his chest.

The door to Kai's chambers flew open with a sharp crack, the frost around its edges splintering like shattered glass. Gerhard jumped to his feet, startled, as the Snow King stormed inside, his frost-covered cloak trailing behind him like a living shadow.

"What are you doing?" The king snapped, his pale blue eyes blazing with icy fire as they landed on Gerhard. "Why are you still here?"

Gerhard blinked, his confusion evident. "What?"

"You should already be on your way to retrieve him," he hissed, his voice sharp and unyielding. "We cannot waste any more time."

Gerhard frowned, his chest tightening at the intensity of the king's words. "I thought you couldn't leave," he said, his tone careful but firm. "The curse—your magic—doesn't it keep you bound here?"

The Snow King froze for a heartbeat, his expression faltering. His jaw tightened, and the faintest crack of ice echoed through the room as his magic surged, uncontrolled for just a moment. "You are correct," he said finally, his voice low and bitter. "I cannot leave."

His gaze darted toward the frost-lined window, his hands clenching into fists at his sides. For a moment, the icy mask of his composure slipped, revealing something raw and vulnerable beneath. He turned away sharply, his voice clipped. "Then you must go. Bring him back. Now."

Gerhard didn't move. He studied the Snow King carefully, his sharp features, the rigid set of his shoulders, and the way his gaze lingered on the frost fox curled on the bed. It wasn't just urgency driving the king—it was something deeper.

"You really care about him, don't you?" Gerhard asked softly, his voice carrying a weight that made the Snow King's posture stiffen.

The fae's gaze snapped to him, his icy eyes narrowing. "Do not presume to know what I feel."

But Gerhard held his ground, his own jaw tightening. "It's not presumption. I can see it in you. You're angry, but it's not about me being here. You're furious because he's not."

The king's silence was answer enough. His chest rose and fell in shallow breaths, his hands flexing at his sides as though battling some unseen force.

For a long moment, the room was heavy with tension, the frost creeping along the edges of the walls like silent witnesses to their exchange. Finally, the Snow King's shoulders slumped, the fight draining from him. "He is... a disruption," he murmured, his voice quieter, almost broken. "An unbearable one."

Gerhard tilted his head, his brow furrowing. "An unbearable disruption, and yet, you want him here?"

The king's lips pressed into a thin line, his gaze falling to the frost fox. "Yes," he admitted, the word barely more than a whisper.

Something shifted in Gerhard's expression. He straightened, taking a tentative step forward. "Then we wait," he said firmly. "Fenrir's with him. He'll keep him safe. We trust him to come back."

The Snow King's gaze lifted, his icy blue eyes meeting Gerhard's. For a moment, they simply stared at one another, the frost in the room easing its grip as an unspoken understanding passed between them.

Gerhard stepped back toward the small table by the bed, his voice softening. "In the meantime, we can distract ourselves. What do you say to a game of chess?"

The king arched an eyebrow, his aloofness returning like a cloak pulled tight against vulnerability. "A game?" he repeated, his tone skeptical.

Gerhard gestured to the chessboard still set from earlier. "Something to keep us from pacing holes in the floor."

The Snow King hesitated, his icy demeanor flickering for just a moment before he inclined his head, the faintest hint of intrigue in his expression. "Very well," he said, his voice measured but less biting. "But do not think this will absolve you if he does not return."

Gerhard smirked faintly as he reset the pieces. "Wouldn't dream of it."

As they sat across from each other, the frost fox curled at Gerhard's feet, its glowing presence a quiet reminder of Kai's warmth. And though the storm outside had stilled, the tension within the castle remained—a quiet promise that Kai's absence was felt in every corner, by every soul.

Chapter 12

THE MOMENT KAI AND Fenrir stepped beyond the storm's edge, the biting cold that had clung to them for so long vanished abruptly. In its place came a wave of oppressive heat, suffocating and unrelenting. Kai stumbled, his breath catching in his throat as the stark change assaulted his senses.

Sweat beaded on his brow almost immediately, dampening the back of his neck as the sun bore down with an intensity that felt almost personal. The air shimmered around them, heavy and stifling, each breath tasting of dust and dry heat.

"This is not the Summer Court I remember," Fenrir muttered, his voice low and grim. He walked beside Kai now in his human form, his golden eyes scanning the desolate landscape before them.

Kai followed his gaze, his stomach tightening at the sight. The ground stretched barren and cracked for miles, its surface dry and fragmented like the skin of a parched riverbed. Rivers were little more than faint indentations in the earth, their once-strong currents reduced to dusty, empty scars.

Farther ahead, trees stood skeletal and brittle, their branches twisting upward like clawing hands. What little greenery remained clung desperately to life, leaves curled and brown under the weight of the relentless sun.

"Is this supposed to be paradise?" Kai muttered, swiping at his damp forehead.

Fenrir's lips pressed into a thin line, his gaze hard. "Once, it was."

The oppressive heat weighed down on them as they continued their trek, each step kicking up faint clouds of dust that clung to Kai's boots. Sweat soaked through his shirt, plastering it uncomfortably to his skin. He wiped at his face again, his thoughts churning as the full extent of Summer's decay became impossible to ignore.

The palace loomed ahead of them, rising from the cracked earth like a faded monument to a better time. Once magnificent, its golden stone shimmered faintly in the distance, but the grandeur was dulled, its edges softened by neglect.

Ivy clung stubbornly to the palace walls, but even it showed signs of suffering, its brittle vines curling inward as though trying to shield themselves from the relentless heat. The grand fountains that dotted the outer courtyard stood empty, their basins coated with layers of cracked, dried residue.

Kai's steps faltered as they approached the gates. The palace radiated an oppressive presence, its faded beauty and stifling heat combining to create a sense of unease that settled in his chest.

The guards stationed at the gates stood stiff and silent, their bronze armor gleaming faintly in the harsh sunlight. Their helmets obscured their faces, but their eyes—glowing faintly with fire—watched Kai and Fenrir with an unnerving intensity.

The air around them rippled with heat, the oppressive warmth seeming to radiate from the guards themselves. "You are expected," one of them said, his voice deep and edged with an unnatural resonance.

Fenrir's jaw tightened as he exchanged a brief glance with Kai. "Let's get this over with," he muttered, his tone low.

The guards turned sharply, their movements mechanical as they led the way into the palace. Kai followed, leaning into Fenrir who managed to put off a gentle chill that was comforting.

The palace's interior was no better. The golden stone walls glowed faintly, reflecting the sunlight that poured through tall, arched windows. The air was thick and stifling, pressing into Kai's skin like a heavy blanket. Even Fenrir seemed to be uncomfortable.

Sweat dripped down his temples as they passed through grand corridors, their steps echoing faintly against the polished floors. Fountains and basins carved into the walls sat empty, their dry surfaces cracked and crumbling.

Fenrir's expression remained grim as his golden eyes darted around the space. "This is wrong," he murmured, his voice barely audible.

Kai didn't respond. He was too focused on the faint hum of energy that seemed to radiate from the palace itself. It wasn't magic like the biting frost of Winter, but it was no less oppressive. The heat was alive here, pulsing faintly in the air as though it were watching, waiting.

When they reached the massive doors of the throne room, one of the guards pushed them open with a sharp motion. The hinges groaned faintly, the sound swallowed quickly by the oppressive atmosphere as Kai and Fenrir stepped inside.

The throne room blazed with golden light. It reflected off molten amber pillars that rose to meet a vaulted ceiling carved with intricate patterns of fire and sunlight. The heat was stifling, pressing into Kai's skin with every step as though the air itself sought to consume him.

Fenrir walked at his side, his sharp gaze scanning the room. He didn't speak, but his tense posture spoke volumes.

The court was packed with figures dressed in flowing garments of red and gold, pictures of ethereal beauty. But there was an edge to their beauty—predatory, dangerous, as if they would turn on each other at the slightest provocation.

At the center of it all, lounging lazily on an ornate throne carved from what looked like molten amber, sat the Summer King.

He was impossibly beautiful, his sharp features framed by hair that shimmered like sunlight through smoke. His golden eyes glowed faintly, smoldering embers set into a face that could have belonged to a god. The air around him rippled faintly, humming with a heat that felt alive.

A thin, mocking smile curled his lips as his gaze swept over the room, landing on Kai with an intensity that made his chest tighten.

"Winter sends its little warmth to my door?" the Summer King drawled, his voice smooth and smoky. It carried through the throne room effortlessly, settling like ash in the oppressive heat. "How charming."

Laughter rippled through the court, sharp and cruel. The sound grated against Kai's ears, but he forced himself to stand tall, his pulse pounding as he locked eyes with the Summer King.

"Your kingdom is dying," Kai said, his voice steady despite the sweat dripping down his temples. "I thought you might want to save it."

The laughter stilled instantly, cut short by a sharp gesture from the Summer King. He leaned forward slightly, his golden eyes narrowing as he regarded Kai with a faint smirk.

"And you think *you* can teach me how, boy?" he said, his voice laced with amusement.

Kai's jaw tightened, his fists clenching at his sides. The heat pressed harder against him, sinking into his skin like an unrelenting weight.

The Summer King rose from his throne with a deliberate grace, each movement controlled and fluid. He stepped down from the dais, his molten gaze never leaving Kai as the oppressive heat around him seemed to intensify.

"Tell me," the Summer King said, his tone light but dangerous. "What does a boy born of Winter know of fire and warmth? What do you know of power?"

Kai opened his mouth to respond, but the Summer King cut him off with a laugh, his voice echoing through the chamber. The court laughed with him, their sharp, predatory smiles fixed on Kai like circling vultures.

Fenrir stepped closer, his presence a solid wall of protection at Kai's side. His golden eyes narrowed as he growled low in his throat, the sound a quiet warning.

The Summer King's gaze flicked to Fenrir briefly, his lips curling into a faint smirk. "The hound speaks without words," The he murmured, his voice almost teasing. "How quaint."

He turned his attention back to Kai, his features softening into something resembling curiosity. "Do you truly believe you can save us?"

Kai straightened, his heart pounding as he met the Summer King's gaze head-on. "I believe you need help," he said simply, his voice firm. "Your people are suffering, and you're too proud to admit it."

The faint murmurs of the court stilled, the tension in the room thickening like the heat pressing against Kai's chest.

The Summer King tilted his head slightly, his golden eyes narrowing as though considering Kai's words. Then, slowly, he smiled—a predatory thing that sent a shiver down Kai's spine despite the suffocating heat.

"Brave words," the Summer King said, his voice quiet but cutting. He stepped closer, the air around him crackling faintly with heat. "You speak of warmth as though it is a gift freely given. But tell me, boy—do you truly understand the fire you seek to wield?"

Kai's skin burned under the weight of the Summer King's gaze. The oppressive heat in the throne room pressed into him like a living force, unrelenting and suffocating. Every instinct screamed for him to retreat, to escape the smoldering intensity of the Summer King and his court.

But he didn't.

Instead, he stepped forward, his voice cutting through the heavy air. "Your people are suffering because you refuse to share what you have.

Warmth isn't something you hoard—it's meant to bring life, not destroy it."

The murmur of the court returned, their voices low and mocking as they exchanged amused glances. The Summer King's brow arched slightly, a faint smirk playing at his lips as he studied Kai with an unsettling intensity.

"You speak as though you understand power," the Summer King said, his voice a smoky drawl. He began to circle Kai slowly, the air rippling faintly with his heat. "Warmth is not a gift, little one. It is something to be earned—and wielded."

Kai tensed as the Summer King's presence bore down on him. "I don't care how you see it," Kai said, his voice steady despite the heat threatening to overwhelm him. "Warmth can nourish. It can bring life, hope, balance. That's what it's for."

The Summer King tilted his head, his smile widening slightly as he continued to circle. "Do you truly believe that? That balance comes so easily?" He stepped closer, his voice dropping to a near-whisper that brushed against Kai's ears like the flicker of a flame. "Do you think love and life are so freely given?"

Kai's heart pounded, his breath coming faster as the heat pressed harder against him. "I think they're worth the risk," he said firmly, forcing himself to meet the Summer King's gaze.

The oppressive heat in the room sharpened as though the entire palace was holding its breath.

The Summer King stopped directly in front of Kai, his golden eyes locking onto him with an intensity that made the pull in Kai's chest tighten painfully. "And what would you know of risk, boy?" he asked softly, his voice quiet but edged with steel.

Kai's jaw tightened as he struggled to keep his footing under the weight of the Summer King's presence. "I know enough to stand here," he said, his voice trembling slightly but resolute. "And I know enough to see that your pride is killing your people."

A sharp crack echoed through the room as the Summer King's heat surged.

The court recoiled slightly, their mocking smiles fading into wary silence as their ruler's golden eyes burned brighter. The tension in the room thickened, the heat becoming almost unbearable as the Summer King stepped closer.

"Careful, little one," the Summer King murmured, his voice dangerously soft. "You stand in the heart of my fire. Do not presume to tell me what it can or cannot do."

Kai's pulse pounded in his ears, but he forced himself to stand firm. The pull in his chest throbbed like a second heartbeat, grounding him against the Summer King's fury.

"If your fire is so powerful," Kai said quietly, his voice steady despite the sweat dripping down his face, "then why is your court falling apart? Why are your people starving while you sit on a throne made of ash?"

The Summer King's expression froze, his molten eyes narrowing as the air around him seemed to vibrate with restrained magic.

For a moment, Kai thought he'd gone too far, that the Summer King's fury would consume him. But then, slowly, the smirk returned to the ruler's lips, more dangerous than before.

The air crackled faintly as the Summer King stepped closer, his molten gaze fixed on Kai like a predator cornering its prey. The oppressive heat around him intensified, pressing against Kai's skin with an almost physical weight.

The Summer King extended his hand, palm up, the movement slow and deliberate. "Show me, then," he said, his voice low and smooth, yet charged with challenge. "If you would preach of sharing warmth, you must be willing to offer it."

Kai's heart pounded, his pulse thundering in his ears as he stared at the outstretched hand. He could feel the heat radiating from it, fierce and unrelenting, like the surface of a sun.

Fenrir stepped forward instantly, his growl low and threatening as he placed himself between Kai and the Summer King. "You will not touch him," Fenrir snarled, his golden eyes blazing with protective fury.

The Summer King tilted his head, his lips curling into a faint smirk as his molten gaze shifted to Fenrir. "The hound guards his prize so fiercely. I would think he would be accustomed to sharing."

Kai's breath hitched, the words igniting a mixture of embarrassment and frustration that made his chest tighten. He placed a hand on Fenrir's arm, his voice firm despite the nervous flutter in his stomach. "I can handle this."

Fenrir stiffened, his gaze snapping to Kai. "You don't have to prove anything to him," he pleaded.

Kai met Fenrir's eyes, the pull in his chest steadying him despite the tremor in his hands. "I know," he replied softly. "But I need to do this."

For a long moment, Fenrir held his gaze, his jaw tight with reluctant frustration. At last, he stepped back, his presence still looming protectively at Kai's side as he glared at the Summer King.

Kai turned back to the Summer King, his breath unsteady as he reached out, his hand trembling slightly as it moved closer to the ruler's outstretched palm.

The moment Kai's hand touched the Summer King's, the heat surged through his skin like a sun-scorched flame. His breath caught sharply, his fingers twitching as the burn seared through his nerves.

It wasn't unbearable, but it was relentless, and unyielding. Kai's chest tightened as he forced himself to hold still, his fingers curling faintly around the Summer King's hand despite the pain.

The court murmured softly, their voices a faint hum of intrigue and amusement as they watched the scene unfold.

The Summer King's lips curved into a faint smile, his molten eyes gleaming with predatory satisfaction as he stepped closer, his free hand settling lightly at Kai's waist.

The intimacy of the gesture sent a flush to Kai's cheeks, the heat of the Summer King's presence and the weight of his gaze making his pulse race.

"Warmth is dangerous, little one," the Summer King murmured, his voice dropping to a near-whisper that brushed against Kai's ears like smoke. "It burns when not handled carefully."

Kai's breath came unevenly, the searing heat making his head swim. But he steadied himself, his voice firm despite the tremor in it. "It doesn't have to hurt."

The Summer King's brow arched faintly, his smirk deepening as though Kai's defiance amused him. "Doesn't it?" he asked, his tone laced with challenge. "Share your warmth without fear."

The Summer King's molten gaze fixed on Kai, and for a moment, the tension in the room seemed to hold its breath. His hand remained warm and heavy against Kai's, his smirk deepening as he stepped closer, closing the space between them.

The burn from his touch spread further, creeping up Kai's arm like liquid fire, sinking deep into his skin. It wasn't just pain anymore—it was an intensity that curled low in his stomach, pooling there in a way that made his breath hitch.

The Summer King's hand slid from Kai's to his waist, his grip firm but not forceful, guiding Kai closer until they were sharing the same breath. His heat was overwhelming, a scorching halo that made the air shimmer between them. Kai felt his pulse stutter, his knees threatening to give way under the weight of it.

"Curious," the Summer King murmured, his voice low and velvety, brushing against Kai's ear like the whisper of a flame. "You're trembling, little warmth, but you're not pulling away."

Kai's breath hitched again as the warmth shifted, curling and spreading lower, its touch insistent and almost unbearable. His instincts screamed at him to recoil, but instead, he leaned forward, his forehead resting against the Summer King's shoulder. His breaths came in shallow gasps, each one heavy with suppressed sound.

The Summer King's molten eyes widened briefly, his smirk faltering as he regarded Kai's sudden vulnerability. His touch softened, his fingers splaying against Kai's waist, the pressure turning almost... tender. His head dipped, his lips brushing against the curve of Kai's neck.

Kai's eyes fluttered closed, a low sound escaping him before he could stop it. The heat rolling off the Summer King wasn't oppressive anymore; it was intoxicating. It consumed and comforted all at once, leaving him reeling as he clung to the only steady presence in the room.

A low, guttural growl shattered the moment.

Fenrir stood just behind Kai, his golden eyes blazing with barely restrained fury. The sound rumbled through the room like a warning, his broad frame taut with tension. The frost fox at his feet bristled, its crystalline fur flickering as though in response to the charged atmosphere.

The Summer King froze, his lips still hovering near Kai's neck. Slowly, his molten gaze flicked to Fenrir, the corner of his mouth twitching upward into a mocking smile. "Ah, the hound," he drawled, his tone laced with amusement. "So protective. Tell me, is it jealousy I see, or just possessiveness?"

Fenrir didn't answer, his growl deepening as he took a deliberate step closer.

Kai's eyes opened, the sound snapping him out of the heat-induced haze. He straightened quickly, his heart hammering in his chest as he glanced between Fenrir and the Summer King. "Fenrir," he started, his voice unsteady.

The Summer King chuckled softly, the sound low and indulgent as he released Kai and stepped back. The loss of his touch was both a relief and a strange disappointment. He looked at Kai, his molten eyes gleaming with something dangerous and unreadable. "You handle fire better than I expected, little warmth," he murmured, his voice just loud enough for Fenrir to hear.

The throne room felt different now. Though the heat still hung heavily in the air, it was no longer suffocating. The oppressive pressure that had radiated from the Summer King had eased, replaced by a quieter, sharper presence.

The Summer King studied Kai intently, his molten amber eyes lingering on him as though trying to decipher a puzzle. The faint smirk on his lips softened, losing some of its earlier cruelty.

"You are unlike the others," he said quietly, his voice carrying through the now-hushed chamber. "Perhaps there is something to your warmth after all."

The tension in the room shifted as the Summer King finally stepped back, his molten gaze lingering on Kai for a moment longer before he turned away. His movements were slow, deliberate, as he ascended the steps back to his throne.

He lowered himself onto the molten amber seat with a grace that felt almost weary, his features softening ever so slightly as he regarded Kai from above.

The Summer King's gaze lingered on Kai, his molten eyes narrowing slightly, as if weighing an unseen scale. He reclined slightly on his throne, fingers tapping idly against the amber armrest.

Kai's pulse quickened under the intensity of that stare, and he clenched his fists to keep his composure. The Summer King's earlier words still burned in his ears, but the sudden shift in his demeanor left him unsettled. He wasn't sure what to expect next.

Finally, the Summer King spoke, his voice smoother, softer, but no less commanding. "No, little warmth. That is not it."

Kai blinked, startled. "What do you mean?"

The Summer King stood, his movements fluid. The oppressive heat in the room seemed to intensify as he descended the steps of his throne. He stopped a few paces away, his gaze sweeping over Kai and then Fenrir, who still bristled with restrained tension.

"I think I would rather see it for myself," the Summer King continued, his tone laced with curiosity. "Your Winter Court. The cracks in its frost. The changes you've brought. Words are fleeting, little warmth. I would rather bear witness to what you claim."

Kai's breath hitched, his thoughts racing. "You want to come with me?"

The Summer King's lips curved into a faint, amused smile. "Why not? Your presence has stirred more than just curiosity, and I would see if your 'balance' holds when the fire of Summer meets the ice of Winter."

Fenrir stepped forward, his golden eyes blazing. "You cannot—"

The Summer King's hand lifted, silencing Fenrir with a sharp, imperious gesture. "I can and will, hound," he said smoothly, though his molten gaze flicked briefly back to Kai. "Unless, of course, you object."

Kai hesitated, the weight of the moment pressing heavily on him. A part of him wanted to argue, to say no, but he also understood the gravity of the opportunity. The Summer King wasn't dismissing him outright—he was offering something else entirely.

"No," Kai said finally, his voice steady despite the rapid beat of his heart. "I don't object."

The Summer King's smirk widened slightly, and he inclined his head. "Then it is decided. I will accompany you back to your frozen kingdom."

The court erupted into a low murmur, their surprise rippling through the chamber like a wave. The Summer King paid them no mind, his focus solely on Kai.

Fenrir growled low, his voice a rough whisper meant only for Kai. "This is a dangerous game."

Kai glanced at him, his chest tightening. "I know."

The Summer King's molten gaze flickered with amusement, as though he had heard Fenrir's words. "Prepare yourself, little warmth. Fire and frost rarely meet without leaving marks."

Kai met his gaze, forcing himself to stand firm. "Then I guess we'll see who burns brighter."

The Summer King's laughter echoed through the chamber, a deep, resonant sound that sent shivers racing down Kai's spine.

"Indeed, we shall."

Chapter 13

The borderlands were a strange and shifting place, where the relentless heat of Summer met the creeping frost of Winter. Kai's boots crunched against ground that couldn't seem to decide what it wanted to be—hardened frost one moment, slushy mud the next.

The land itself seemed to protest the clash of opposing magics. Snowdrifts melted into pools that soaked into cracked earth, while fragile flowers struggled to bloom through patches of frost. The air shimmered with both cold and heat, creating a distorted haze that stretched across the horizon.

Kai walked in tense silence between Fenrir and the Summer King, both of whom seemed as unyielding as the magic pressing into the land. Fenrir's steps were heavy, his jaw tight as his golden eyes flicked warily toward the Summer King. The wolf's distrust rolled off him in waves, tangible enough to make Kai's chest tighten.

The Summer King, in contrast, strode ahead with a casual arrogance, his molten eyes fixed on the path ahead as though the dissonance of the borderlands was beneath his notice. Wherever he stepped, the frost at his feet hissed and melted, the warmth of his presence clashing violently with the encroaching cold.

Fenrir's growl was low, barely audible, but it carried the weight of his frustration as he muttered to Kai. "This is dangerous. You should not have brought him."

Kai sighed, the weight of it all pressing against him like the chill in the air. "We didn't have a choice, Fenrir," he said quietly, his voice edged with weariness.

The Summer King chuckled softly, his voice curling through the air like smoke. "The hound frets," he said, his tone amused. "Winter has nothing to fear... unless it is as weak as it appears."

Fenrir's steps faltered, his golden eyes narrowing dangerously as his hands curled into fists. "Say that again," he growled, his voice low and lethal.

"Stop," Kai snapped, stepping between them before the tension could erupt. He glanced between Fenrir and the Summer King, his chest tight as he tried to defuse the situation. "Both of you. This isn't helping."

The Summer King smirked faintly, his molten gaze flicking to Kai. "How diplomatic of you, little warmth," he murmured, though his tone carried a faint edge.

Fenrir's growl deepened, but he said nothing more, his sharp gaze flicking to Kai as though reluctant to press the matter further.

As they neared the edge of the borderlands, the cold of Winter grew sharper, sinking into the earth like claws. The snowdrifts stiffened, their edges gleaming with a brittle sheen as frost crept forward, racing to meet and smother the Summer King's presence.

The Summer King paused at the threshold, his molten gaze sweeping the frozen landscape with a faint smile. The frost at his feet hissed and cracked, retreating slightly as his warmth pressed against it.

"How charming," he said softly, his voice laced with faint amusement. "I've missed this place."

Kai shivered, though whether it was from the cold or the tension between the two rulers, he couldn't say.

Fenrir muttered darkly under his breath, his golden eyes fixed on the Summer King with quiet fury. "This will end in ruin," he said, his voice low enough that only Kai could hear.

Kai sighed, the weight in his chest growing heavier as the pull of the Winter Court's magic grew stronger. He glanced between Fenrir and the Summer King, his heart pounding as they stepped fully into Winter's domain.

The gates of the Winter Court loomed ahead, frost-covered and towering against the pale gray sky. The storm had calmed to a low, constant wind, its chill biting through the air like a warning. Kai's breath misted before him as they approached, each step feeling heavier than the last.

Fenrir walked close to Kai's side, his golden eyes scanning their surroundings with sharp vigilance. The Summer King strode ahead with infuriating ease.

As they reached the gates, the ancient iron groaned, swinging open slowly as though reluctant to admit the intruders. A gust of wind tore through the opening, carrying with it a deep, unrelenting chill that sank into Kai's bones.

They stepped inside the courtyard, and the oppressive silence of the Winter Court descended upon them. Frost-covered statues lined the edges of the courtyard, their frozen faces tilted toward the sky as though in silent prayer. The air felt alive with tension, a heavy weight pressing down on everything within the walls.

At the top of the palace steps, the Snow King appeared. The frost beneath his feet bloomed outward in sharp, crystalline veins with every step, the ice crackling faintly in the otherwise still air.

His pale blue eyes burned with icy fire as they locked immediately on the Summer King. His expression was a mask of fury and cold disdain, his sharp features unmoving as he took in the sight before him.

"You dare to bring him here?" the Snow King said, his voice low and cutting. It carried through the courtyard like the edge of a blade, the frost around him pulsing in response to his anger.

The Summer King smiled faintly, his molten amber eyes gleaming with amusement as he stepped forward. "I was invited," he said, his voice smooth and mocking. "You should be grateful, Winter. I come bearing solutions to problems you seem incapable of solving."

Frost erupted across the ground at the Snow King's feet, the sharp cracks echoing through the courtyard. His pale blue eyes narrowed dangerously, the temperature plummeting further as his magic surged.

"You bring nothing but ruin," the Snow King growled, his voice cold enough to freeze the air. "Your presence is an insult to this court."

Before the tension could explode into chaos, Kai stepped forward, planting himself squarely between the two rulers.

The moment he did, the pressure *hit*—a crushing weight pressing into his bones, Winter's bitter frost clashing violently with Summer's suffocating heat. His lungs tightened, breath shallow against the invisible storm raging between them.

Still, he didn't back down.

"*Stop.*"

His voice trembled but held. It wasn't a request.

The Snow King's gaze *snapped* to Kai, colder than he had ever seen it, the icy fire in his pale blue eyes burning with quiet fury. His voice dropped to a low, lethal whisper.

"Why?"

Kai clenched his fists to keep them from shaking, forcing himself to hold the Snow King's stare. *Because I have no other choice. Because if I don't fix this, no one else will.*

"Because we need balance," he said, ignoring the way the magic in the air crackled, sharp and stinging against his skin. "You *both* do. If you keep fighting like this, there won't be anything left to fight *for.*"

A soft chuckle slid through the heavy silence, smooth as molten gold.

"Balance." The Summer King's amber eyes flicked to Kai, amusement curling at the edges of his lips. "Such an *optimistic* notion."

Kai exhaled through his nose, pulse still hammering, but he met that molten stare with dry, unimpressed resolve. "Yeah, well. Call it a bad habit."

The Snow King remained silent, but Kai *felt* the weight of his stare—searching, *unrelenting*. The frost around him pulsed violently, jagged veins of ice crawling further up the walls, thickening as if trying to *force* the Summer King's presence out.

But the Summer King was *comfortable* here. That was the worst part.

He strolled forward, slow and deliberate, like he *belonged* in these halls, like this frozen castle was nothing more than an old relic for him to sift through.

The frost beneath his feet hissed and cracked, trailing his steps in delicate patterns of melted ice. His expression never wavered—calm, confident, every movement carrying the easy arrogance of a man who had *never* been unwelcome anywhere.

Kai followed, keeping pace beside Fenrir, whose golden eyes stayed locked on the Summer King like a blade waiting to strike. Every inch of him was *tensed*—ready for the inevitable.

By the time they reached the grand hall, a new kind of tension settled over Kai's shoulders, heavy and familiar.

Because *he knew that voice*.

"Kai..."

Gerhard's words echoed through the chamber, quiet but weighted, thick with shock and something sharp beneath it—something close to anger.

Kai's stomach twisted.

Gerhard stood at the far end of the room, his face pale, his eyes wide with disbelief as he took in the Summer King standing in the heart of the frozen court. The frost fox darted out from behind him, its small body glowing faintly against the ice-lined walls. It stopped, hesitating only for a second, before sprinting toward Kai.

The little creature weaved between his legs, circling him in frantic, excited loops, its glowing tail brushing against his ankles like it had *thought he wasn't coming back.*

Kai swallowed, reaching down instinctively to brush his fingers over the fox's soft fur before looking back at Gerhard.

The blacksmith's expression hadn't changed.

"What," Gerhard said, his voice steadier now, his jaw tight, "have you *done?*"

Kai let out a slow breath, pressing a firm hand to Gerhard's arm in a quiet attempt to ground him. *Ground himself, more like.*

"It's going to be okay," Kai said, softer now. *Reassuring. Convincing.*

Gerhard's throat bobbed, but his eyes stayed locked on him, heavy with something unreadable.

Kai offered a small, tight smirk. "I promise."

And gods, he *hoped* he wasn't lying.

Gerhard's gaze flicked to the Summer King, his jaw tightening as he stepped closer to Kai. "That's *him,* isn't it? The one who cursed this place."

Before Kai could respond, the Snow King's voice cut through the air, sharp and cold. "Your pride blinds you, Summer. You bring nothing but ruin to everything you touch."

The Summer King turned slowly, his molten gaze meeting the Snow King's with a faint, mocking smile. "And your cold offers nothing but stagnation," he said smoothly. "You cling to your silence and your ice as though they are enough to sustain you. But your court is empty, Winter. Your frost is nothing without the warmth that gives it meaning."

The Snow King scowled. "You speak of warmth as though you understand it," he growled, his pale blue eyes burning with icy fire. "But all you bring is destruction."

The air grew heavier, the tension in the room crackling like the sharp bite of frost meeting flame. The frost fox let out a soft whimper, pressing closer to Kai as he stood frozen between the two rulers.

Kai glanced between them, his heart pounding as the storm of magic swirled around him. He could feel the weight of their power pressing into his chest, the frost and heat warring silently as though the castle itself braced for collapse.

As the tension built, Kai felt a sharp pang in his chest—a deep pull that seemed to reverberate through the frozen halls. It wasn't just the rulers who were at risk. The castle, the court, and everyone within it were balanced on the edge of a blade.

Kai clenched his fists, his voice trembling but loud enough to cut through the storm of magic. "Stop!"

The word echoed through the hall, silencing the clashing powers for a moment. Both the Snow King and the Summer King turned their gazes to Kai, their expressions unyielding.

Kai's breath came fast as he met their eyes, his voice steady despite the weight pressing down on him. "This can't keep happening. If you destroy each other, there won't be anything left—for Winter *or* Summer."

The Summer King arched a brow, his molten eyes glinting faintly. "And what would you suggest, little warmth?"

Kai hesitated. "There has to be a way to fix this," he said softly. "But it won't happen if all you do is fight."

The silence in the grand hall was heavy, the frost and heat warring in quiet tension as Kai's plea hung in the air. The frost fox whimpered softly at Kai's feet, its crystalline fur glowing faintly as though sensing the weight of the moment.

The Summer King broke the silence first, his molten amber eyes gleaming with faint amusement. He stepped forward, and let his gaze sweep over the room before settling on Kai.

"You are right, little warmth," the Summer King said, his voice smooth and almost teasing. "There must be a way to fix this. And perhaps... you are that way."

Kai's chest tightened as the Summer King's golden gaze locked onto him, the intensity in his expression making his heart pound.

The Summer King turned slightly, glancing toward the Snow King with a faint, knowing smile. "He is the bridge between us," he said, his voice carrying through the frozen hall. "A rare warmth that can exist in both our courts."

The Snow King's frost pulsed sharply, the temperature plummeting further as his pale blue eyes burned with icy fury.

"Do not presume to claim what is mine," the Snow King growled, his voice low and cutting.

The Summer King chuckled softly, his smirk widening. "Calm yourself, Winter. I do not seek to *take* him from you—only to borrow him." He turned his attention back to Kai, his molten eyes gleaming with pointed amusement. "To prove our newfound accord, tradition demands a boon. And so, I claim him."

The room erupted into chaos.

Fenrir stepped forward instantly, his golden eyes blazing as he placed himself between Kai and the Summer King. "You will not touch him," Fenrir snarled, his voice low and dangerous.

The Snow King's magic surged violently, frost lancing across the floor like knives. His voice dropped to a deadly whisper, each word sharp as a blade. "You will take nothing from my court."

The frost fox chirped nervously, darting behind Kai's leg as the storm of magic built around him.

Kai's pulse raced, his chest tight as he raised his hands, shouting over the rising tension. "Stop it! I'm not anyone's to claim!"

The Summer King's smirk didn't falter, his gaze lingering on Kai with quiet amusement. "Such fire," he murmured, his voice soft but carrying through the room. "I mean no harm, little warmth. A season in my court is a fair price for saving your king's frozen wasteland, don't you think?"

Kai's breath came fast as he glared at the Summer King, his frustration and unease bubbling to the surface. "I didn't agree to that," he said, his voice steady despite the tremor in his hands.

The Summer King tilted his head, his smile faint but knowing. "Perhaps not yet," he said smoothly.

The Snow King's gaze burned into Kai, the storm behind his icy blue eyes raging with quiet fury. "You will not go," the Snow King said, his voice cold and final.

Kai forced himself to meet the Snow King's gaze. "It's not your decision to make," Kai said, his voice firm despite the weight of the Snow King's anger, frozen in a mask of restrained fury.

The hall felt like it was on the edge of a precipice, the tension so thick it seemed to hold the room itself still. Frost lined the edges of the great chamber, jagged and threatening, while the Summer King's heat shimmered like a mirage over the icy floor. The frost fox pressed against Kai's leg, its soft glow flickering nervously.

Kai swallowed hard, his throat dry. "Is there nothing you can compromise on?" His voice was steady but quiet, like the first drop of water rippling across a still pond. "Something we can trade? Another boon that doesn't take me away from...them?" He gestured faintly to his lovers, standing silently behind him.

The Summer King's molten eyes narrowed faintly, his lips curving into a small, thoughtful smile. "Resources?" he mused, as though testing the word. "Winter could offer a cool front, a reprieve to bring rains back to the scalding heat of my lands. That is tempting." He paused, his gaze sweeping over Kai in a way that made his skin prickle with awareness. "But there's something far more intimate I have in mind."

Kai's breath hitched as the Summer King stepped forward, his presence overwhelming. He reached out, his hand brushing lightly against

Kai's cheek, the heat of his touch both thrilling and terrifying. "One night," the Summer King said softly, his voice smooth as molten gold. "That is my price."

The room froze—figuratively and literally.

"No," the Snow King said sharply, his pale eyes flashing like shards of ice. His frost surged forward as his magic flared, pushing back against the Summer King's heat.

Fenrir let out a low, dangerous growl, his golden gaze narrowing as he stepped closer to Kai, his body tense and protective.

Kai, however, went silent. His breath was shallow, his mind spinning back to the intimate heat that had spread through him the last time the Summer King touched him. His chest tightened as he remembered the way that heat had curled low in his belly, pooling with a dangerous kind of yearning. He glanced down, avoiding the stares of everyone around him.

The Snow King noticed his silence immediately, his jaw tightening as his gaze snapped to Gerhard. "Would you share him with yet another?" he asked, his voice low and laced with thinly veiled rage.

Gerhard swallowed hard, his Adam's apple bobbing as he looked at Kai. His voice, when it came, was soft but steady. "I would do anything for Kai," he said, his tone measured and careful. "But only under my watch."

The Summer King's smirk widened slightly, his molten eyes gleaming with intrigue. "Interesting," he murmured, stepping back slightly. "You would make such an intimate thing... a spectacle. I like that."

The Snow King's lips pressed into a thin line, his icy gaze cutting toward the Summer King. "You're insufferable," he bit out, his voice cold enough to freeze the air. "The audacity to make such a demand after all you've done."

The Summer King took a slow, measured breath, his sharp features softening ever so slightly. "My son was a fool," he said, his voice quieter now, touched with an edge of something close to regret. "I regret the curse I placed on you—on us both. It has cost more than I ever intended."

The Snow King's frost faltered, the sharp edges retreating slightly as the weight of the Summer King's words hung in the air.

The Snow King's icy gaze lingered on the Summer King, his pale blue eyes sharp and searching. The frost beneath his feet cracked faintly, a sound that echoed through the heavy silence of the hall. Slowly, the tension in his frame lessened, the frost softening just enough to show a shift in his resolve.

"Your regret," the Snow King said, his voice low and resonant, "has been a long time coming." He stepped forward, and stopped just short of the Summer King. For a moment, it seemed as though he might strike him, the weight of centuries of anger visible in his tense posture. But instead, his lips pressed into a thin line, his next words cool but measured. "Your apology is accepted."

The court remained silent, the air around them no longer crackling with the clash of frost and fire but heavy with anticipation. The Summer King inclined his head, his molten eyes gleaming with something that looked almost like relief. Yet before he could speak, the Snow King turned abruptly, his attention snapping to Kai.

"And you," he said, his voice a mix of amusement, "is this what you want?"

Kai's breath hitched as the Snow King's pale eyes swept over him, their intensity burning hotter than any frost. "I—I want what's best for both courts," he said quickly, though the trembling of his voice betrayed the weight of the moment. "I want balance."

The Snow King took a step closer, his gaze narrowing slightly as his lips curled into a faint, knowing smirk. "Balance," he echoed softly, his tone laced with quiet mockery. "Such noble words for someone so delightfully unrestrained."

Kai's cheeks flushed a deep crimson, the heat in his chest blooming under the weight of the Snow King's gaze. "I—what are you talking about?"

The Snow King tilted his head, his eyes glittering with a predatory gleam. "You know exactly what I mean, little warmth," he murmured, his voice dropping to a near-whisper that only Kai could hear. "It's written all over you. The way your body trembles, the way you burn when touched. You thrive in the chaos of our courts, don't you? You want this. All of it."

Kai's pulse thundered in his ears, his fingers curling tightly at his sides. He glanced away, his breath shallow as the Snow King's words sank into his skin like shards of ice. "You don't know what I want," he managed, though the trembling in his voice made the words feel hollow.

The Snow King's smile widened slightly, his gaze never wavering. "Don't I?"

The Summer King watched the exchange silently, his molten gaze flicking between them with quiet intrigue. "You should give the boy credit," he said after a moment, his voice carrying a touch of amusement. "He stands between fire and frost and does not break."

The Snow King's smirk softened, though the intensity in his gaze did not. "Perhaps," he said, his voice thoughtful but still edged with teasing. "But I wonder... How much more can he take before he melts entirely?"

Kai's chest tightened, the pull in his chest thrumming louder as he fought to steady his breathing. The frost fox pressed against his leg, its soft glow flickering as though it, too, could feel the tension in the room.

"What I want," Kai said finally, his voice quiet but steady, "is for both of you to stop looking at me like I'm something to conquer." His eyes darted between the two rulers, his hands clenching at his sides. "I'm here because I want to help. Not to be a prize for your games."

The Snow King's smirk faltered for a fraction of a second before he inclined his head slightly, his pale eyes glinting with something unreadable. "Very well, little warmth," he said smoothly. "For now."

The Summer King chuckled softly, the sound low and indulgent as he turned his gaze back to Kai. "You are a curious thing," he said, his molten eyes lingering. "Perhaps this alliance will prove more... entertaining than I anticipated."

The Snow King's pale eyes lingered on the Summer King for a moment longer before he straightened and swept his gaze across the room. His frost-lined cloak flared faintly behind him as he spoke, his voice calm and cool. "Then let it be formal. Welcome to the Winter Court, Sovereign of Summer. May this stay prove... illuminating."

He gestured toward Fenrir without turning. "Show him to quarters befitting such a distinguished guest."

Fenrir raised an eyebrow, his golden eyes narrowing as a sharp grin tugged at the corner of his lips. "You mean your quarters?"

The Snow King's expression didn't flicker, though his gaze shifted briefly toward Fenrir. "Yes," he said simply. "I'll stay elsewhere."

The room went silent for a beat, the weight of his statement hanging in the frost-tinged air. Then the Summer King laughed, a low, smoky sound that curled through the hall like a flickering flame. "Or you could join us," he suggested, his molten eyes gleaming with mischief. "I am rather curious about this 'sharing' your little warmth has introduced me to."

Fenrir's sharp grin faded into a low growl, his broad shoulders stiffening. "My king shares what he chooses," he rumbled, his voice carrying a warning.

The Snow King tilted his head slightly, his pale gaze sliding toward Kai for a fleeting moment before returning to the Summer King. "It is an intriguing proposition," he said softly, his voice calm but laced with something darker. "Perhaps—"

Fenrir's growl deepened, the sound resonating through the room like the low rumble of an approaching storm. "Eryon."

The Snow King cast him a sharp glance, but the faintest hint of amusement glimmered in his pale eyes. Before he could reply, Gerhard cleared his throat, his hand brushing against Kai's arm as he leaned closer. "Wasn't the Summer King's son having an affair with the Snow King what started all of this?"

The Summer King, who had been watching the exchange with evident satisfaction, turned his gaze toward Gerhard. His molten eyes softened faintly, though his lips curled into a small, knowing smile. "My son," he began, his voice low and smooth, "is a selfish flame. He sought what he could not comprehend and, in his folly, ignited a fire that consumed far more than he ever intended."

Kai blinked, his chest tightening slightly as the Summer King continued. "But he has received his punishment. I married him off to a rather brooding autumn fae who keeps him quite... busy." The faint smirk on his lips deepened, and his gaze flicked to the Snow King. "Had the little fool been more understanding, perhaps he might have basked under the attention of two handsome men. But then..."

His molten eyes turned to Kai, the heat in his gaze warming but not oppressive. "None of us would have had the pleasure of meeting you."

Kai's cheeks flushed faintly, his throat tightening as the weight of the Summer King's words pressed against him. The frost fox chirped softly at his feet, brushing its glowing tail against his leg as though sensing his unease.

The Snow King's sharp gaze lingered on the Summer King for a long moment before he turned to Fenrir. "Ensure his quarters are prepared," he said curtly, his voice brooking no argument.

Fenrir's golden eyes flicked between the two kings, his jaw tight as he inclined his head stiffly. "As you wish." His gaze lingered briefly on Kai before he turned and began to stride toward the exit.

The frost fox trotted after him, its glow flickering faintly as the tension in the room finally began to ease. Kai let out a slow breath, his chest still tight with the lingering weight of the conversation.

The Summer King's molten eyes shifted toward Gerhard, his sharp gaze flicking over the man with obvious interest. A faint smirk tugged at his lips, and he tilted his head slightly. "And who is this?" he asked, his voice laced with a subtle teasing warmth. "Another addition to your... entourage, little warmth?"

Kai's face flushed instantly, the heat rushing to his cheeks as he sputtered, "He's not—it's not like—"

Gerhard stepped forward, his broad shoulders squared as he spoke evenly. "I'm Gerhard," he said, his tone firm but respectful. "Kai and I... grew up together."

The Summer King's smirk deepened, his molten gaze sliding between Gerhard and Kai. "Ah," he murmured, his voice smooth and indulgent. "Childhood devotion turned to something more. How delightfully mortal."

Kai stammered, his words tumbling out in a frantic attempt to explain. "It's not—it's complicated! Gerhard is—he's just—"

The Snow King's voice cut through the air like the sharp crack of ice, calm but commanding. "They are all important to me."

The room went silent, the weight of his words settling heavily over the group. The Snow King's pale blue eyes swept over Kai, Gerhard, and even the frost fox before returning to the Summer King. "Each of them," he said evenly, "has earned their place in my court."

Kai blinked, his chest tightening at the unexpected declaration. He glanced between the Snow King and Gerhard, his thoughts racing. He hadn't expected this—hadn't expected the Snow King to lay claim to them all so openly. The quiet tension that had always lingered between Gerhard and the Snow King seemed to have softened, replaced by something steadier, more assured.

The Snow King's gaze flicked to Kai, lingering for a moment before shifting back to the Summer King. "Your curiosity is noted," he said coolly. "But I trust you will respect the boundaries of my court."

The Summer King chuckled softly, his molten eyes gleaming with amusement. "Boundaries," he mused, his tone rich with suggestion. "A curious word, coming from you, Winter."

Before the Snow King could respond, Fenrir's arrival broke the tension. He stepped into the room with his usual quiet presence, his sharp golden eyes flicking to the Summer King with faint disdain. "Your quarters are prepared," he said, his tone clipped. "If you'll follow me."

The Summer King lingered for a moment, his gaze sliding over the group one last time before he inclined his head. "How gracious," he said, his smirk returning. "Lead the way."

As Fenrir turned and began to stride toward the exit, the Summer King followed with an easy, fluid grace. He cast one final glance at Kai, his molten gaze lingering with a faint heat that made Kai's breath hitch.

When the door closed behind them, the room fell into a heavy silence. Kai's heart pounded in his chest as he glanced at Gerhard, the weight of the Snow King's earlier words still settling over him. "What... just happened?" he murmured, his voice barely audible.

Gerhard's expression softened slightly, his hand brushing against Kai's shoulder. "Something important," he said simply, his voice steady despite the lingering tension.

The room remained thick with silence after the Summer King's departure, the tension in the air palpable. Kai stood frozen in place, his mind racing as the weight of everything pressed down on him—the Summer King's teasing words, the Snow King's sudden declaration, and Gerhard's quiet steadfastness.

The frost fox nudged at Kai's ankle, but it didn't break his reverie. His gaze flicked to the Snow King, who was stepping forward with his usual graceful, commanding presence. Kai tensed instinctively, unsure of what was about to happen.

Would he be angry? Aloof? Something worse?

The Snow King's icy blue eyes shifted to Gerhard for a fleeting moment before turning back to Kai. His expression was inscrutable, sharp and focused, but his movements betrayed something fiercer, more urgent.

Before Kai could speak—or even think—the Snow King's hands were on him. His grip was firm as he pulled Kai close, their bodies nearly flush as his lips descended in a fierce, possessive kiss. Kai gasped against him, his knees buckling slightly from the sheer intensity of the moment.

The kiss wasn't soft or gentle; it was a claim, searing and unrelenting, as though the Snow King was trying to remind him exactly where he belonged. Kai's breath hitched, his fingers instinctively clutching at the king's frost-lined cloak as heat and cold surged through him in equal measure.

When the Snow King finally pulled back, his pale blue eyes burned with a mix of frustration and longing. His voice was low and edged with chastisement as he murmured, "Such a wanton little thing you are, to tempt even the Summer Sovereign with your fire."

Kai's face burned, shame and arousal swirling in his chest as he tried to catch his breath. "I didn't—" he started, but the Snow King's cold fingers against his cheek silenced him.

"But you returned," the king whispered, his tone softening, though his gaze remained piercing. "You came back to us, little warmth. To me. To him." He glanced briefly at Gerhard, whose face betrayed both awe and disbelief, before his eyes settled back on Kai. "Do you know how fiercely we missed you?"

Kai's breath caught at the raw intensity in his voice, the vulnerability barely hidden beneath the surface. He felt Gerhard step closer, his steady presence grounding him even as his emotions threatened to overwhelm him.

"We missed you," the Snow King continued, his voice barely above a whisper now. "Your warmth, your fire. Everything about you was felt in your absence like an open wound."

Kai's pulse raced, his cheeks flushed as he met the Snow King's gaze. There was no mistaking the truth in his words, no denying the intensity of the connection between them. He glanced at Gerhard, who nodded faintly, his expression soft but resolute.

Kai swallowed hard, his voice trembling as he finally found the courage to speak. "I missed you too," he said quietly, his words carrying a weight that surprised even him.

The Snow King's lips curved into the faintest hint of a smile—sharp and possessive but tinged with something deeper, something more tender. "Then stay," he murmured, his hand brushing lightly against Kai's cheek. "Stay with us, and let me show you how much your presence is valued."

Gerhard stepped closer still, his arm brushing against Kai's as he added softly, "We'll make sure you never doubt it."

The Snow King's hands lingered on Kai's waist, cool but not biting, a stark contrast to the heat pooling in Kai's chest. His gaze flicked to Gerhard, his pale blue eyes sharp and commanding as he slid his hands up, pushing Kai to turn.

"Face him," the king murmured, his voice low and rich with unspoken intent. Kai obeyed, his breath hitching as the Snow King's cool fingers moved to his shoulders, slipping beneath the edge of his cloak and pulling it free. The heavy fabric fell to the ground, leaving Kai exposed to the icy air of the room.

The king's touch didn't falter. His hands slid under Kai's shirt, his fingers tracing the curve of his back, skimming across his warm skin with deliberate care. Each movement sent a shiver through Kai, his body responding instinctively to the contrast between cool and warm, between commanding and tender.

Behind him, the Snow King's breath was hot against his neck, teasing the sensitive skin there as he leaned in close. His hand rose, gripping the collar of Gerhard's shirt with enough force to pull him forward. Gerhard stumbled slightly, caught off guard by the gesture, until his chest pressed firmly against Kai's.

Sandwiched between them, Kai let out a shaky breath, his pulse racing as the heat of Gerhard's body seeped into his own. The Snow King's lips brushed against his ear, his voice a dark, honeyed whisper.

"Your king wants to see more than a kiss, devoted," he murmured, his cool breath sending a thrill down Kai's spine. His grip on Gerhard's collar tightened, tugging him closer until there was no space left between them. "Show me how you want him."

Gerhard's breath hitched. His eyes locked onto Kai's, searching for hesitation, for resistance, but all he found was the same want reflected in his own. Slowly, hesitantly, he lifted a hand to cup Kai's face, his thumb brushing over his flushed cheek.

"Are you sure?" Gerhard asked softly, his voice trembling with both desire and restraint.

Kai swallowed hard, his lips parting as he nodded. "Yes," he whispered, his voice barely audible but resolute.

The Snow King's hand slid lower, resting possessively at Kai's hip as he smirked against the curve of his neck. "Then let him see," he commanded, his voice low and velvet-smooth. "Let him see how you've wanted this."

Gerhard leaned in, his lips brushing against Kai's in a kiss that started tentative but quickly deepened. Kai gasped into it, his hands gripping Gerhard's shirt as the heat between them grew, his senses overwhelmed by the feel of Gerhard's body against his and the Snow King's presence at his back.

The king's fingers traced lazy patterns over Kai's skin, his breath hot and heavy as he murmured, "Good... now don't stop."

The Snow King's touch grew bolder, his cool fingers tracing Kai's sides before sliding lower, gripping his hips firmly. Kai let out a soft whimper, his lips still locked with Gerhard's in a kiss that had turned heated, desperate. The tension between them buzzed like static, a heady mix of desire and anticipation filling the air.

Behind Kai, the Snow King began to sink to his knees, his icy breath brushing the curve of Kai's spine as his hands pulled gently to guide him. Kai's pulse quickened, his body trembling under the weight of sensation, his mind barely able to keep up.

But before the Snow King could go further, a sharp voice cut through the haze.

"Well, well," Fenrir drawled from the shadows of the hall, his tone laced with amusement. "Are we trying to give the Summer King a show, then? I didn't realize the main hall was the stage."

Kai froze, his breath catching as he turned his head toward Fenrir. The frost fox darted nervously to the side, its crystalline eyes flicking between the figures in the room. Fenrir stepped into the light, his golden gaze sharp and faintly teasing as he took in the scene before him.

The Snow King rose smoothly to his feet, his icy composure slipping back into place even as his pale blue eyes flashed with irritation. "Fenrir," he said, his voice low and cold. "What is it you want?"

Fenrir's lips quirked into a sly smile, and before anyone could react, he stepped forward, gripping the Snow King by the collar and pulling him into a kiss that was all heat and dominance. The king stiffened for the briefest moment, but then he melted into it, his hands moving to Fenrir's arms as though grounding himself.

Kai and Gerhard watched, their breath hitching at the sudden shift in the atmosphere. The kiss was brief but left its mark, the air between the

Snow King and Fenrir charged with unspoken intensity as Fenrir pulled back.

"I think," Fenrir said, his voice smoother now, his golden eyes flicking to Kai and Gerhard, "that this... performance deserves a more private setting." His gaze lingered on Kai, his smile softening just slightly. "Shall we move to your room, little warmth?"

Kai's cheeks burned, his body still thrumming with the heat of their earlier moments. "I—uh—" he stammered, unsure of how to respond.

The Snow King's sharp gaze flicked to Fenrir, his lips pressing into a thin line before he sighed, the tension in his shoulders easing just slightly. "Very well," he said, his tone resigned but still edged with authority. His hand rested lightly on Kai's shoulder as he added, "Lead the way."

Fenrir chuckled softly, his golden gaze gleaming with something playful and dangerous as he gestured for them to follow. "Then let's not keep the Winter Court waiting."

The group began to move, the frost fox trailing close to Kai's feet as they left the grand hall. The tension between them hung in the air like an unspoken promise, each step drawing them closer to the private sanctuary of Kai's chambers and the storm of intimacy that awaited them there.

The air in Kai's chambers was heavy with anticipation, the faint glow of the frost fox casting soft light across the room until it chimed and disappeared. Fenrir moved with the kind of deliberate grace that demanded attention, his golden eyes sharp and commanding as he closed the door behind them. The air felt warmer than usual, the oppressive cold of the castle eased by the charged heat now simmering between the four of them.

Fenrir's presence filled the space, his posture exuding dominance as his gaze swept over the room. He tilted his head, his lips curling into a faint, wolfish grin. "All of you," he said, his voice low and firm, reverberating with authority, "take off your clothes."

Kai's breath hitched at the command, the weight of Fenrir's words sending a shiver down his spine. His fingers trembled slightly as he reached for the edges of his tunic, his pulse quickening. Beside him, Gerhard let out a soft, unsteady breath, his hands already moving to untie the laces of his shirt.

The Snow King stood rigid for a moment, his pale blue eyes narrowing slightly as they flicked to Fenrir. But there was no mistaking the faint flush that colored his usually frost-pale skin. The command clearly affected him too, though he held his composure with icy resolve.

Fenrir's gaze locked on the Snow King, a sharp glint in his golden eyes. "You," he said, his tone darkening, "on your knees. Where you belong."

The sharpness of the command made Kai's knees wobble, a deep pull tightening in his chest. His eyes darted to the Snow King, whose lips pressed into a thin line. For a moment, it looked as though he might protest, but then, with slow, deliberate movements, the Snow King sank gracefully to his knees, his frost-covered cloak pooling around him.

The sight made Kai's breath catch, a heady mix of desire and disbelief flooding through him. Beside him, Gerhard seemed equally affected, his hands faltering as he removed his tunic. His eyes stayed fixed on the Snow King, his chest rising and falling with quickened breaths.

Kai felt Gerhard's warm hands on his waist, pulling him closer. The mortal's lips brushed against his ear as he whispered, "You're so beautiful like this." Kai shivered, his cheeks flushing as Gerhard's hands slid over his bare skin, the heat of his touch grounding him even as his body trembled.

Fenrir's attention shifted to them, his sharp gaze softening slightly as he watched the way Gerhard's hands roamed over Kai's body. "Good,"

Fenrir murmured, his tone laced with approval. "But don't keep him all to yourself, devoted. We're just getting started."

Kai's heart thundered in his chest, his body caught between the commanding presence of Fenrir and the relentless heat of Gerhard's touch. The Snow King remained kneeling, his icy gaze locked on Kai as though daring him to look away.

And Kai, caught in the storm of their collective desire, wasn't sure he wanted to.

The tension in the room was palpable, the charged atmosphere thick with the heat of desire and the weight of unspoken commands. Fenrir's sharp golden gaze flicked between them, lingering on the Snow King, who remained kneeling, his frost-covered form the only barrier between his pride and vulnerability.

"Up," Fenrir commanded, his voice low but unyielding. His hand gripped the Snow King's arm, pulling him to his feet with a strength that was both dominant and steady. The Snow King's pale blue eyes flickered with defiance, but he didn't resist as Fenrir turned him toward the bed.

Kai's breath caught as he watched Fenrir press the Snow King down onto the bed, his movements slow but forceful. The king's frost-covered cloak slid from his shoulders, pooling on the floor as Fenrir held him firmly in place. The Snow King's lips pressed into a thin line, his usual composure now tinged with something more vulnerable.

"You like to command others," Fenrir murmured, his voice dark and edged with amusement. "But tonight, you will obey."

The Snow King's eyes narrowed, his jaw tightening, but he didn't speak. Instead, he allowed Fenrir to slide his hands to his waist, tugging at the fastenings of his tunic. The fabric fell away in pieces, revealing pale, flawless skin that glowed faintly in the flickering light of the frost fox.

Kai swallowed hard, his cheeks flushed as he stared at the Snow King, now stripped bare. His body was a masterpiece of elegant strength, his pale skin unmarred except for the faintest traces of ice-blue veins beneath the surface.

"Devoted," Fenrir said, his gaze snapping to Gerhard, who stood frozen at Kai's side. "Your prince is waiting. Get your mouth on him. Make him come undone."

Gerhard hesitated only for a moment, his cheeks flushing as he glanced at Kai. The heat in his gaze was undeniable, his earlier hesitations melting away as he moved closer. His hands found Kai's hips, his grip firm but reverent as he guided him back onto the bed.

Kai's breath hitched as he felt Gerhard's warm hands sliding over his skin, pulling him down until he was seated on the edge of the bed. "Gerhard…" he murmured, his voice trembling.

Gerhard didn't answer, his focus entirely on Kai as he knelt before him. His hands moved with deliberate care, parting Kai's thighs as he leaned in, his breath warm against Kai's heated skin. The first touch of Gerhard's mouth sent a jolt of pleasure through Kai's body, his head falling back as a low, desperate sound escaped his lips.

Fenrir's golden gaze flicked to the Snow King, a sharp grin tugging at his lips. "Watch him," he said, his voice thick with command. "Watch the way he falls apart."

The Snow King's gaze shifted to Kai, his icy composure cracking slightly as he watched the mortal's mouth work Kai over, pulling him closer to the edge with every flick of his tongue. His fists clenched against the bed, his breath coming faster as Fenrir's hand slid down his back, tracing the line of his spine before moving lower.

The Snow King tensed as Fenrir's fingers found the soft skin between his thighs, brushing lightly against him. The touch was careful, teasing, as Fenrir pressed closer, his other hand holding the king firmly in place.

"You feel that?" Fenrir murmured, his lips brushing against the Snow King's ear. "That's what surrender feels like."

The Snow King's breath hitched, his body trembling as Fenrir's fingers moved with calculated precision, pressing deeper, preparing him for what was to come. His icy blue eyes burned as he watched Kai's body arch, the soft sounds spilling from his lips driving him mad with want and jealousy.

Kai's hands twisted in the blankets, his body trembling as Gerhard's mouth pushed him closer to the edge. The storm of sensation was overwhelming, his moans growing louder with each passing moment. The Snow King's gaze was locked on him, his own composure slipping further with every sound Kai made, every inch of his skin that flushed with pleasure.

Fenrir's grin widened as he continued his work, his fingers pressing deeper as he whispered, "Let's see how long you can hold that icy control, my king."

Gerhard's mouth moved with deliberate care and unrelenting passion, his lips parting around Kai's length in a way that was both reverent and hungry. The wet sounds of his devotion filled the room, punctuated by soft moans that vibrated against Kai's heated skin, drawing desperate cries from the man above him. Kai's hands fisted in the blankets, his knuckles white as he fought to hold himself together under the onslaught of Gerhard's worship.

"Gerhard," Kai gasped, his voice breaking with the weight of sensation. The heat pooling in his core was almost unbearable, each flick of Gerhard's tongue sending shockwaves of pleasure that threatened to unravel him completely.

The Snow King's pale blue eyes were fixed on the scene, his normally stoic features betraying an intense, almost possessive hunger. His breath hitched audibly, his composure slipping further as Gerhard let out a low, wanton moan, the sound muffled but unmistakable as he took Kai deeper into his mouth.

"Beautiful," Fenrir murmured, his voice thick with approval. He shifted his focus to the Snow King, whose body trembled beneath him. Fenrir's strong hands gripped the king's hips, holding him steady as his fingers pressed deeper, the movement firm but unhurried. "Doesn't this make you ache? Watching him come undone for someone else?"

The Snow King's jaw tightened, his fists gripping the edge of the bed as he struggled to maintain control. The sharp cry that escaped his lips when Fenrir's fingers twisted inside him betrayed his inner turmoil. His icy veneer cracked further, his breathing ragged as the pressure built within him.

"Feel it," Fenrir growled softly, his voice low and commanding as he leaned in, his breath warm against the king's ear. "Feel every inch of what you want but cannot take."

The Snow King choked on a moan, his head falling forward as his body bucked involuntarily against Fenrir's hand. His pale skin flushed faintly, a stark contrast to the frost that seemed to cling stubbornly to his presence. "I—" His voice faltered, his words lost in a sharp inhale as Fenrir's fingers pressed against a spot that sent a wave of pleasure through him.

The room was thick with tension and desire, the wet, desperate sounds of Gerhard's mouth working Kai over blending with the Snow King's labored breathing. Fenrir's golden eyes gleamed with satisfaction as he continued to manipulate the king's body, his fingers moving with expert precision.

Kai's cries grew louder, his body arching off the bed as Gerhard's name slipped from his lips in a breathless plea. The heat between them was almost unbearable, every sound, every movement pushing them closer to the edge.

The Snow King's gaze flickered to Kai, his icy eyes burning with a mix of jealousy and longing both men. His lips parted, another choked moan escaping as Fenrir pushed him further, his body trembling as he teetered on the brink.

Fenrir's low chuckle rumbled through the room, his grip tightening on the Snow King's hips as he leaned closer, his voice a dark whisper against his ear. "You're going to shatter, my king. And when you do, I want you to watch how beautifully he breaks."

The Snow King's throat worked, his grip on the bed tightening as he struggled to hold on. His frost-covered body shuddered beneath him, the heat of desire warring with the icy walls he'd built around himself. Within moments, he choked out a plea. "Fen, please. I need you."

Fenrir chuckled darkly, his golden eyes fixed on the Snow King. "I know, my king," he said softly, "let's see how much you can take." His fingers pressed deeper inside the king, pushing against the last barriers of resistance before pulling free with a wet sound.

The Snow King's eyes widened, his body trembling as Fenrir moved between his spread legs and positioned himself. The cold steel of Fenrir's erection pressed against his entrance, taunting and teasing before finally sliding home in one swift motion. The Snow King gasped, his back arching off the bed as Fenrir filled him completely.

Fenrir pulled back almost immediately, his hips rocking forward again in a long, slow thrust that made them both groan. The Snow King's fingers dug into Fenrir's shoulders, nails leaving shallow marks in the golden skin as he pushed back against him. Their bodies moved together now, a symphony of need and power that filled the room with each grunt and moan.

The tension had snapped like a whip, releasing them into a wild dance of desire that left them both panting and trembling on the edge

Gerhard's gaze flicked between them, his eyes burning with a mix of passion and hunger as he watched them move together.

"Gerhard," Kai gasped, his voice thick with desire. "Please..."

Gerhard leaned back, his lips swollen and gorgeous as his lover's cock slid from his mouth, his hand reaching out to stroke Kai's cheek. "I can't look away," he whispered, his voice raw with emotion. "They're so beautiful together."

"Fuck him." Fenrir commanded as his movements became more urgent, his body slamming into the Snow King with rough precision that left their bed shaking. The sounds of skin hitting skin echoed through the room, punctuated by sharp gasps and moans that filled the air.

Gerhard growled and surged from his knees, claiming Kai's mouth and moaning as Kai wrapped both legs around him and pulled him into alignment. As Gerhard thrust inside, Kai couldn't hold back any longer. He arched off the bed, his body trembling as he came hard in between them. He whined and clung to Gerhard as he fucked him through it, oversensitive and writhing. "Gehard, please..."

His eyes flicked to Fenrir and the Snow King, watching as they moved together in a frenzy that left them both shattered in different ways. The way the guard's muscles coiled and rolled as he owned the king who sobbed beneath him, fingers clutching the furs tightly.

Kai flung one hand out to tangle in the king's hair and another to dig into Gerhard's chest, arching his back and clenching tighter to urge his lover to come for him. The king raised his head and the liquid heat in his gaze made Kai moan.

"That's it, my king," Fenrir rumbled, the loud slapping of his thighs against the king's punctuating every word. "Look how even our little warmth twists you around his finger. Did you miss me while I was gone? Or did you let little warmth's Devotion fuck you?"

The words reached their target because both the Snow King and Gerhard groaned, the former trembling as he released onto the bed beneath him and the later froze thrust deep inside Kai as he shuddered through his release.

"Fen, please," the king begged. "Fill me."

Fenris growled, his grip bruising as he chased his own pleasure. *"Eyron, I'm going to—I can't stop it."*

"Yes," he sobbed. "Please."

The wolf's voice pitched high in a whine as he slammed home and then hissed between his teeth as he shot deep inside the king whose grip on the furs tightened further as he took each drop of heat from the wolf.

For a while, they all simply panted and worked to calm themselves, then slowly Gerard shifted and pulled Kai up the bed. Kai held his arms out for the king and Fenrir, whose cheeks flushed but neither moved.

"Can't move," he muttered. "Knotted."

Kai's eyes widened and he looked at the king, who blushed as well. The sight was surreal. *He wasn't even in his wolf form, but he had a....*

The room was thick with the warmth of shared exertion and the faint, lingering glow of magic in the air. Kai let his arms drop as Fenrir and the Snow King remained where they were, their bodies taut and their expressions uncharacteristically vulnerable.

Gerhard shifted to Kai's side, brushing his knuckles against Kai's cheek before tucking the furs snugly around both of them. "Well," he murmured with a grin that bordered on wicked, "I guess we'll just have to keep the two of them company until they can... sort themselves out."

Kai let out a breathless laugh, his head tipping back to rest against Gerhard's shoulder. His eyes flicked to the Snow King, who still looked a little flustered despite his typically regal composure. Fenrir, on the other hand, managed to smirk even in his predicament.

"It's not... permanent," Fenrir muttered, though his voice was tinged with a mix of frustration and faint amusement. "This will pass."

Kai raised an eyebrow, his lips twitching into a teasing smile. "It's kind of endearing, actually. You—so strong, so intimidating—reduced to this."

The Snow King let out a low, exasperated groan, his pale cheeks tinted pink. "Kai," he warned, though the sharp edge was undercut by his obvious discomfort.

Gerhard chuckled, his voice low and warm against Kai's ear. "Careful, little warmth. If you tease them too much, they might find a way to take it out on you later."

Kai flushed, his laughter breaking into a shy grin. "I think they've already done enough for one night."

Fenrir let out a low, amused hum, his golden eyes narrowing playfully. "Careful, Kai. I'm more resilient than you think."

The soft banter eased the lingering tension, and for a moment, the four of them simply existed in the quiet intimacy of the room. Kai's hand found Gerhard's under the furs, their fingers intertwining as the frost fox curled at their feet, its gentle warmth a steady presence.

"Guess we'll wait, then," Gerhard said with a smirk, his gaze sweeping over Fenrir and the Snow King. "Until our regal companions can rejoin us properly."

The Snow King huffed softly, though there was a faint glimmer of amusement in his pale eyes. "Enjoy your moment, mortal," he said, his voice still tinged with regal pride. "But this is far from over."

Kai let out a soft laugh, his head tilting to press a kiss to Gerhard's shoulder. For now, the storm had quieted, and the warmth they shared filled the room with a peace that felt hard-earned and well-deserved.

Chapter 14

T HE MORNING LIGHT FILTERED through the frosted windows, softer and gentler than Kai had ever seen. He stirred slowly, warmth surrounding him from all sides. Gerhard's steady arms held him securely from one side, while Fenrir's solid frame pressed against his other. The frost fox had burrowed under the furs at their feet, its quiet weight a comforting presence.

The quiet of the room was almost surreal, a stark contrast to the stormy tension that had filled it the night before. Kai's body ached, not unpleasantly, and his mind swirled with the memories of heat, possession, and intimacy. The Snow King's absence was noticeable, but for once, Kai didn't feel his absence as a void.

Movement to his right drew his attention. Fenrir stirred first, his golden eyes opening and sweeping the room with sharp awareness. When his gaze landed on Kai, a faint smirk tugged at the corner of his lips. "Still in one piece, I see."

Kai rolled his eyes, but the flush on his cheeks betrayed him. "You're insufferable," he muttered, shifting slightly against Gerhard's chest.

Gerhard groaned softly, his arm tightening around Kai as his voice rumbled sleepily. "You're both too loud for this early in the morning."

Before Kai could retort, the frost fox let out an insistent chirp from the foot of the bed. It wriggled free of the covers and leapt gracefully to the floor, its crystalline tail flicking in what looked like impatience.

Kai blinked after it. "What's gotten into you?"

The answer came moments later. A faint light glimmered through the frost-laden window, casting shifting rainbows across the room. The frost fox padded toward the window, its chirps growing more urgent.

Fenrir and Gerhard followed Kai's gaze to the frost-painted glass. The tension in the room shifted subtly, curiosity threading through the stillness.

"I think it wants us to look," Gerhard murmured, his voice rough with sleep.

Kai slipped from their shared warmth, shivering slightly as his feet touched the icy floor. Fenrir and Gerhard were quick to follow, their shared presence grounding as they approached the window together.

Kai brushed his hand over the frost-lined pane, revealing a clear patch of glass. What lay beyond it stole his breath.

The courtyard was no longer barren. Where once there had been only ice and shadow, delicate frost flowers now bloomed in gentle clusters along the edges of the snowdrifts. Their crystalline petals glimmered with iridescent hues, catching the pale morning light. The snow that blanketed the ground looked softer, almost inviting, and the air beyond the glass seemed to hum faintly with life.

Gerhard inhaled sharply beside him. "That's... new."

Fenrir's gaze remained fixed on the scene below, his sharp features betraying a flicker of something softer. "This is... different," he admitted, his tone quieter than usual.

Kai reached out to touch the glass, his fingers brushing the cool surface as though trying to connect with the change outside. "It's thawing," he murmured, wonder lacing his voice. "The castle... it's responding."

The frost fox hopped onto the windowsill, its glowing eyes wide with curiosity as it chirped again. It swished its tail, its small body radiating a warmth that matched the hope slowly unfurling in Kai's chest.

Gerhard stepped closer, his hand settling on Kai's back. His voice was low, tinged with awe. "You're the reason for this."

Kai turned to him, his heart swelling at the sincerity in Gerhard's expression. "It's not just me," he said softly. "It's all of us. The castle feels us—our warmth, our life."

Fenrir tilted his head, a faint smile curving his lips. "Perhaps. But you are its center."

Kai's breath hitched, and for a moment, he couldn't find the words to respond. He looked back at the courtyard, his chest tightening with a mix of pride and trepidation.

The frost flowers continued to bloom, their delicate beauty a quiet promise of what could be. For the first time since his arrival, Kai felt a flicker of hope—fragile but real.

The soft light filtering through the frosted windows illuminated the room with a faint glow as the Snow King stirred beside them. His frost-lined lashes fluttered open, pale blue eyes sharp despite the lazy, indulgent haze of sleep. His movement made the frost fox chirp softly from its perch on Kai's chest before it hopped down, sensing the shift in energy.

Kai felt the Snow King's cool hand slide down his arm, his touch lingering just long enough to send a familiar shiver through him. "Eryon..." Kai began, but the Snow King cut him off with a low, begrudging murmur.

"If we don't rise now," Eryon muttered, his voice rich and laced with irritation, "the Summer King will likely take it upon himself to find us. I imagine he'd find no small amount of entertainment in discovering us like this."

Kai's eyes widened, the heat of embarrassment flooding his cheeks. He glanced toward Fenrir, who lounged comfortably against the headboard with one arm draped behind Kai's shoulders, and Gerhard, whose hand rested possessively on Kai's hip.

Fenrir chuckled low, his golden eyes gleaming with amusement. "He's not wrong. You know the Summer King would relish the opportunity."

Gerhard groaned, rubbing a hand over his face before sitting up slightly. "We're still sore, and he's already talking about the Summer King?" He gave Kai a soft squeeze and sighed. "Eryon, couldn't we have at least one morning where you don't mention politics or chaos?"

Eryon turned his icy gaze to Gerhard, arching a single pale brow. "Politics and chaos are unavoidable when the Summer King is involved," he said coolly, though his tone lacked its usual sharpness. His lips quirked faintly as he added, "And you, mortal, are far too at ease."

Kai couldn't help but laugh softly, the tension of the moment easing just enough to make room for a lingering warmth. He leaned into Fenrir's solid presence and glanced at Eryon. "Do we really have to get up?" he asked, half-teasing.

The Snow King's gaze softened, though his voice remained firm. "Yes. If only to keep that insufferable flame from barging in."

Fenrir stretched languidly, his golden eyes sliding to Eryon with a teasing glint. "What are you so worried about, Eryon? Afraid the Summer King might charm us all away from you?"

The Snow King's pale blue eyes narrowed sharply, though the faintest pink touched his frost-kissed cheeks. "He's is no threat to me," he said stiffly. Then, with a pointed look at Kai, he added, "But it's not his charms I distrust—it's your inability to resist entertainment."

Kai laughed outright this time, sitting up and running a hand through his tousled hair. "Alright, alright," he said, shifting so the frost fox could jump into his lap. "Let's get moving before the Summer King does something ridiculous."

As they untangled themselves from the mess of blankets and bodies, the Snow King rose with his usual grace, his frost-edged cloak shimmering faintly as he adjusted it over his shoulders. His gaze lingered on Kai for a moment longer than necessary, something unspoken passing between them before he turned toward the door.

"We will meet in the hall," he said simply, his voice carrying a quiet authority. "Don't delay."

As the door closed behind him, Fenrir huffed a quiet laugh and leaned closer to Kai. "He's jealous," Fenrir said, his tone dripping with amusement. "And far too obvious about it."

Kai rolled his eyes, but a smile tugged at his lips as he glanced at Gerhard, who shook his head with a rueful grin. "Come on," Gerhard said, pressing a soft kiss to Kai's temple. "Let's see what chaos awaits us today."

The grand hall loomed ahead, its vast, icy expanse bathed in the faint silver glow that had begun to spread through the castle. Kai hesitated at the entrance, his breath misting in the cold air as he stared at the frozen figures that lined the room.

The fae stood exactly as they had for centuries, their bodies encased in thick layers of ice. Each figure was locked in a perfect, unyielding stillness—faces serene, sorrowful, or hopeful, as if captured mid-thought. The frost clinging to them glinted faintly in the growing light, casting prismatic shadows across the walls.

Kai's stepped forward, his footsteps echoing softly in the stillness. Behind him, Fenrir and Gerhard followed silently, their gazes heavy as they took in the frozen court.

Thin cracks had begun to spiderweb across some of the icy forms, the faint sound of splintering frost breaking the quiet. Light pulsed faintly beneath the surface of the ice, as though something deep within each figure was struggling to wake.

Kai stopped in front of one of the fae—a delicate figure with soft, elfin features and a cascade of hair frozen in mid-flow. He reached out hesitantly, his fingers trembling as they hovered over the frost-coated shoulder. "Do you think we can…"

"Are you sure about this?" Gerhard asked from behind him, his voice low but laced with concern.

Kai nodded slowly, the pull in his chest urging him forward. "If we can, they deserve to be free," he said quietly.

Fenrir's golden eyes softened faintly as he stepped closer. "They will be," he said, his voice steady.

Kai exhaled and brushed his fingers lightly against the fae's shoulder. The frost beneath his touch softened instantly, spreading outward in a ripple of warmth. A sharp crack split the air, and the ice began to splinter, pieces falling away in shimmering shards.

The fae's chest rose sharply as they gasped, their body trembling as the last of the ice crumbled around them. Their wide, tear-filled eyes locked onto Kai's, and without hesitation, they threw their arms around him, their cool skin pressing against his warmth.

"Warmth," the fae whispered, their voice breaking with raw emotion. "I missed the warmth."

More cracks followed, the sound reverberating through the hall as one by one, the frozen fae began to awaken.

Kai stepped back slightly, but the first fae refused to release him, their hands clutching his cloak as though afraid to lose the warmth he offered. Others began to stir, their icy prisons falling away in glittering cascades.

One by one, they turned to Kai. There was no hesitation, no formality. They didn't kneel; they ran to him, their faces lit with joy and relief as they pressed against him in tearful embraces. Cool hands brushed his arms, his back, his face. Fingers tangled in his cloak, and soft voices murmured thanks, each word laced with a reverence that made Kai's chest ache.

"Thank you."

"We thought it was over."

"You brought us back."

The gratitude was overwhelming, raw and unfiltered. Kai's breath caught as he found himself surrounded, their cool skin a stark contrast to the warmth radiating from his chest.

Fenrir stood slightly apart, his golden gaze softening as he watched the court he had once known come alive again. There was a faint smile on his lips, though it was tinged with something deeper—quiet longing, perhaps, or the weight of memories he hadn't yet shared.

Gerhard lingered near the edge of the room, his expression shifting between awe and unease. His strong hands flexed at his sides, as though unsure whether to reach for Kai or stay back.

When one of the fae reached for Gerhard, offering a shy, grateful smile, he stiffened. But their touch was light, unthreatening, and after a moment, he nodded faintly. His guarded posture eased slightly, though his gaze remained fixed on Kai, who was nearly swallowed by the sea of fae pressing close around him.

Fenrir moved to Gerhard's side, his voice quiet but steady. "They've waited centuries for this," he said. "For someone to bring them back."

Gerhard's jaw tightened, but he nodded again, his voice gruff. "I can see that."

The fae continued to wake, their laughter and tears filling the grand hall as life returned to the Winter Court. Kai could feel the pull in his chest growing stronger, a steady rhythm that seemed to echo in time with the renewed energy coursing through the castle.

One of the fae, a tall figure with frost-kissed wings, pressed their forehead lightly to Kai's, their voice trembling with emotion. "You've given us what we thought was lost forever."

Kai's eyes softened and he managed a soft smile. "You're the ones who kept hope alive," he said.

The fae's smile widened, their eyes shimmering with unshed tears as they stepped back to join the others.

The room hummed with warmth and life, the icy walls gleaming with soft light as the fae danced and embraced one another. For the first time, the Winter Court felt whole—alive in a way Kai had never thought possible.

The joyful hum of the grand hall faltered as a new presence entered the room. The laughter and murmurs of the fae quieted, their movements slowing as the temperature in the hall shifted. The air grew cool—not the biting, suffocating frost that had once ruled the Winter Court, but something gentler, calmer.

The Snow King stood at the entrance to the hall, his frost-covered cloak trailing behind him as his icy blue eyes swept across the room. His sharp, statuesque features were unreadable, but there was something in his gaze—something unguarded and raw—as he took in the scene before him.

The fae, alive and laughing, were a stark contrast to the desolation that had plagued his court for centuries. Their joy filled the air, their glowing faces a testament to the warmth that had been absent for so long.

For a moment, the Snow King stood frozen, his pale blue eyes lingering on the fae before shifting to Kai.

The fae hesitated, their gazes flicking nervously between the Snow King and Kai. One of them, a delicate figure with frost-dusted hair, took a cautious step forward. Their hands trembled as they reached out, their voice quiet and uncertain. "My king?"

The Snow King's gaze fell on them, his expression softening imperceptibly. He didn't move at first, as though unsure of how to respond. But then, slowly, he extended a hand, his frost-covered fingers brushing lightly against theirs.

A soft gasp escaped the fae as they stepped closer, pressing their forehead to his shoulder. The Snow King's frost did not harm them, and for the first time, they clung to him without fear.

One by one, the fae approached him, their movements cautious but growing bolder as they realized his frost was no longer a threat. They pressed their faces against his shoulders, their hands brushing his cloak, their whispered words of gratitude barely audible above the quiet hum of the room.

The Snow King's mask faltered, his composure cracking as his eyes softened with wonder and something like relief. His hands, once cold and unyielding, rested gently on the shoulders of those who embraced him.

Kai stepped forward, his chest tight as he watched the Snow King with a mixture of awe and something deeper—an emotion he couldn't yet name. The pull in his chest grew stronger, drawing him closer to the man who had once seemed so unreachable.

The Snow King's gaze shifted to Kai, the icy fire in his eyes dimming slightly as their eyes met. He stepped toward Kai, the fae parting respectfully to let him pass.

When he reached Kai, the Snow King paused for a long moment, his expression unreadable. Then, with a quiet exhale, he leaned forward, resting his forehead lightly against Kai's.

The touch was cool, but no longer frigid. It carried with it a sense of peace, a quiet acceptance that made Kai's chest tighten.

"You have undone what I could not," the Snow King murmured, his voice low and edged with raw honesty.

Kai closed his eyes, his hands resting gently on the Snow King's arms. "You gave me a reason to try," he said softly.

The fae watched in silence, their expressions shifting from awe to quiet joy as they witnessed the exchange. Fenrir, standing near the edge of the hall, let out a faint, approving hum, his golden eyes soft as they flicked between Kai and the Snow King.

The Snow King straightened slowly, his gaze lingering on Kai for a moment longer before turning back to the fae. His voice, though still cool, carried a gentleness that had long been absent. "Welcome home," he said simply.

The fae's joy resumed, their laughter and gratitude filling the hall as they pressed close to their king, their fear replaced with an overwhelming sense of belonging.

As the fae's laughter swirled through the grand hall, Kai caught sight of Gerhard standing slightly apart from the crowd, his broad shoulders relaxed but his posture still bearing the tension of someone who hadn't quite figured out how to feel. He wasn't glaring daggers, though, and his stance lacked the rigid defensiveness Kai had grown used to.

Kai's gaze flicked to the Snow King, who stood across the room. He wasn't looking at Gerhard—not directly—but there was a certain awareness in the way his eyes moved through the space, as though Gerhard's presence tugged at his attention whether he wanted it to or not.

Kai couldn't help the teasing grin that tugged at his lips. He approached Gerhard, his voice light but laced with mischief. "You're not trying to murder each other with your eyes anymore. Should I be worried?"

Gerhard turned his head slightly, arching an eyebrow as though unimpressed by Kai's attempt at humor. "Didn't think anyone had the energy for that after last night," he muttered, but there was a faint blush creeping up his neck.

Kai's laughter came quickly, his grin widening. "Fair point. Still, it's an improvement. What happened? Did I miss the part where you two bonded over how much of a pain I am?"

Gerhard's lips twitched, fighting a smirk. "Something like that," he said, glancing toward the Snow King. "We... talked."

Kai tilted his head, his curiosity flaring. "Talked?" He leaned in, his voice dropping conspiratorially. "About what? How much he secretly loves me? How annoying I am? Don't leave me hanging, Gerhard."

Gerhard let out a soft snort, crossing his arms over his chest. "You think highly of yourself, don't you?" But the teasing edge in his voice softened as he met Kai's gaze. "We didn't talk much about you."

Kai blinked, momentarily thrown off his rhythm. "You didn't?"

Gerhard shook his head, his expression thoughtful. "Well, maybe at first. But afterward, it was... more about what this place does to people. He's colder than anyone I've ever met—literally and figuratively—but he's..." He paused, his words faltering.

Kai waited, his grin fading as he leaned in closer. "But he's what?"

Gerhard sighed, running a hand through his hair. "He's broken," he said quietly. "But he's trying. I don't think I saw that until last night. I mean, I knew he was fucked up but he was ready to follow you to the Summer Court. If it weren't for the curse, I think he'd have waged war for you and I...respect that."

Kai's chest tightened at the admission, his gaze shifting toward the Snow King again. He watched the way the king carried himself—sharp and unyielding, but with a subtle weight in his every step. Something raw flickered beneath his icy demeanor, visible now in a way Kai hadn't noticed before.

Gerhard hesitated, his jaw working as he thought over his next words. Finally, he spoke, his tone gruff but honest. "I think he cares for you. For both of us. He just doesn't know how to say it."

Kai's breath caught, the weight of Gerhard's words settling over him. He turned back to Gerhard, his grin slowly returning. "So, what you're saying is, you like him now."

Gerhard rolled his eyes, though the corner of his mouth twitched upward in a reluctant smile. "Don't push it," he muttered, but his hand brushed against Kai's briefly, a quiet gesture that spoke volumes.

Kai laughed softly, his heart lighter than it had been in days. "Noted," he said, the teasing in his voice tempered by the warmth in his gaze.

The vibrant hum of laughter and joy filled the grand hall as the newly awakened fae reveled in their freedom. The icy walls of the Winter Court glimmered with an otherworldly light, reflecting the warmth and vitality that had returned to the long-frozen kingdom. Kai stood near the heart of the gathering, surrounded by fae who clung to him, their gratitude palpable.

The doors of the hall creaked open, and the warmth of Summer spilled into the room like the first rays of dawn breaking through a storm. All eyes turned as the Summer King entered, his molten amber gaze sweeping over the crowd with a mixture of curiosity and intrigue. His every step seemed to soften the frost beneath his feet, though it did not melt—an unspoken acknowledgment of the fragile balance in the room.

He paused just inside the threshold, his golden presence stark against the Winter Court's shimmering frost. The murmurs of the fae grew quieter, their awe and curiosity palpable as they regarded the intruder who had once been their king's sworn enemy.

Kai approached him hesitantly, his chest tight with uncertainty. "You didn't have to come," he said softly, his voice carrying only to the Summer King's ears.

The Summer King's lips curved into a faint smile, his molten gaze flicking to Kai. "Didn't I?" he replied, his voice smooth and warm. "I wanted to see this for myself—what you've accomplished." His eyes swept the room again, lingering on the laughing fae and the softened frost. "It's... remarkable."

The Snow King stepped forward from the far end of the hall, his frost-covered cloak trailing behind him as his pale blue eyes locked onto the Summer King. The tension that usually bristled between them seemed muted, softened by the energy of the room.

The Summer King inclined his head slightly, a gesture more thoughtful than mocking. "Winter," he said, his tone carrying an unfamiliar gentleness. "Your court is alive again. And it is beautiful."

The Snow King's expression remained stoic, though his gaze flicked to Kai before returning to the Summer King. "It is as it should be," he said coolly, though his voice lacked its usual sharpness.

The Summer King stepped closer, his movements deliberate and unhurried. He stopped near Kai, his molten eyes gleaming with something softer than amusement. "I've heard reports from my own kingdom," he murmured, his voice low enough that only Kai could hear. "Rain has returned to the Summer lands. Gentle showers, the kind that cool the earth and nourish life. It is... unfamiliar. And it is because of you."

Kai's breath caught, his chest tightening as the weight of the Summer King's words sank in. "I didn't—" he began, but the Summer King shook his head, his hand brushing lightly against Kai's arm.

"You did," the Summer King said softly, his voice rich with sincerity. His lips quirked into a faint smile as he leaned closer, his warm breath brushing against Kai's ear. "I heard you last night," he murmured, his tone dipping into something teasing but tinged with genuine understanding. "Through the walls. And now I see why you choose to share. There is... beauty in it."

Kai flushed deeply, his face burning as he glanced away, his mind spinning from the intimacy of the words.

The Summer King stepped past him, his focus shifting to the Snow King. To the shock of everyone in the room, he dropped to one knee, his golden gaze tilting upward to meet the icy fire of the Snow King's stare. The silence in the room was deafening, the fae freezing in place as though the frost itself had reclaimed them.

"I come before you not as a rival," the Summer King said, his voice strong and resonant, "but as a sovereign humbled by what I see here. My court has warmth, but it has lacked balance. I offer my gratitude, Winter. And my respect."

The Snow King's pale eyes narrowed faintly, his frost pulsing as he took in the sight of his once-enemy kneeling before him. "What is it you want, Summer?" he asked, his voice cool but edged with curiosity.

The Summer King's lips curved into a faint smile. "An alliance," he said simply. "And more." His molten gaze shifted to Kai for the briefest moment before returning to the Snow King. "I offer you, and your consorts, a place in my palace should you wish to visit. And I intend to court you properly."

A collective gasp rippled through the room, the fae exchanging wide-eyed looks as the weight of the Summer King's words sank in. Even Kai felt his breath catch, his heart hammering in his chest as he glanced between the two rulers.

The Snow King's icy composure faltered for a fraction of a second, his pale eyes flickering with something unreadable. "You would dare to propose such a thing," he said, his voice quieter now, though no less sharp.

"I would," the Summer King replied smoothly, his gaze steady. "What you've built here is extraordinary. And I wish to be a part of it."

The room held its breath, the tension so thick it seemed to freeze in place. Finally, the Snow King's lips pressed into a thin line, his gaze locking onto the Summer King's with an intensity that sent shivers down Kai's spine.

"Very well," the Snow King said at last, his voice low and deliberate. "You may court us."

The room erupted into hushed murmurs, the shock palpable as the fae exchanged incredulous looks. Kai stood frozen in place, his mind struggling to process what had just happened. He glanced at Gerhard, who looked equally stunned, his brows furrowed as though questioning whether he'd heard correctly.

The Summer King rose gracefully to his feet, his molten gaze gleaming with triumph. "A wise decision, Winter," he said softly, his voice carrying through the room. He turned to Kai, his lips curling into a faint, knowing smile. "And you, little warmth. I suspect you will make this arrangement most... entertaining."

Kai's cheeks flushed anew, his voice failing him as the weight of the moment pressed against his chest. The Snow King stepped forward, his frost-lined cloak flaring faintly as he placed a steady hand on Kai's shoulder.

"Do not make me regret this, Summer," the Snow King said, his voice quiet but firm.

The Summer King chuckled softly, inclining his head. "Oh, Winter. I wouldn't dream of it."

The two rulers stood together for a moment, their opposing magics brushing faintly against each other—fire and frost in a delicate, tentative balance. Then the Summer King's gaze shifted, landing squarely on Kai.

"And you," he said softly, his voice warm and teasing, "are at the heart of it all, little warmth. You've tied us together in ways I never thought possible."

Kai flushed, his words faltering as he glanced between the two kings. "I didn't mean to—"

"But you did," the Snow King interrupted, his pale blue eyes softening as they lingered on Kai. "And for that, we owe you everything."

Kai's breath hitched, the pull in his chest resonating with a quiet, steady hum as he looked at the men who had come to mean everything to him. Fenrir's steady strength, Gerhard's fierce loyalty, the Summer King's teasing warmth, and the Snow King's quiet vulnerability—all of it had led them here, to this impossible, beautiful moment.

The frost fox chirped softly, weaving between Kai's legs before curling at his feet. The fae's laughter and joy filled the hall once more, the tension melting away like frost under the sun.

For the first time in what felt like forever, Kai allowed himself to breathe. To hope. To believe. He sent out a silent prayer that wherever the old Kai was, he was finding his happy ending too.

EPILOGUE

THE WARMTH WAS OPPRESSIVE.

Kai gasped as he woke, his chest heaving, the air too thick and humid for his lungs. He blinked rapidly, trying to make sense of the world around him. Gone was the familiar chill of Winter, the frost that had been as much a part of him as his own breath. Instead, heat pressed down on him like a smothering weight.

He sat up abruptly, the motion unnatural and awkward. His arms—were they his arms?—felt wrong. Slim, delicate, unfamiliar. His pulse quickened as he glanced down, his breath hitching. His hands were pale, soft, and small.

Too small.

"What...?" His voice cracked, higher and softer than it should have been. He clutched his chest, searching for the reassuring breadth of his frame, the roughness of his calloused skin, but found only unfamiliar curves and softness.

Kai scrambled to his feet, his balance unsteady as his legs felt foreign under him. A cracked mirror against the wall caught his frantic movement, and his breath left him in a rush as he stared at the reflection.

The figure looking back at him was small, slight, and undeniably female. Her face was unfamiliar, framed by messy curls, her wide eyes filled with alarm. He staggered back, his hand shooting to his throat as if he could force the foreign voice from his lips.

"This can't be happening," he muttered, the words tasting wrong in this mouth.

A sharp clatter drew his gaze downward. A book—a pale, icy-blue book—had fallen from the nightstand, its cover shimmering faintly in the dim light of the room.

The Book of Midnight Fables.

The sight of it struck him like a blow. He knelt cautiously, his trembling hands hovering above the book as he hesitated to touch it. The last time this cursed tome had appeared, it had torn Mina from her world and thrust her into his. And now...

His fingers brushed the cover, the faint chill of it a sharp contrast to the stifling warmth of the room. The title gleamed faintly, just as it had when Mina first described it. With a shaky breath, he flipped it open.

The first page was filled with familiar script, silvery and elegant, drawing him in immediately. It was the ending of his story—the Snow King's story—written in striking detail.

He read the words numbly:

"The Snow King's throne thawed beneath the warmth of shared love, the Winter Court alive once more. Kai, Fenrir, Gerhard, and the Summer King stood together, fire and frost in perfect harmony, bound by a love that melted even the coldest of hearts..."

Holy hell, Gerard. His hand trembled as he turned the page. The words shifted, the silvery text shimmering as they rearranged themselves into something new. His heart pounded as the next story began to unfold.

"Once, in a world where the sun rose golden and unyielding, a boy called Cassian stood apart from the rest. Disgraced and scorned, his days were filled with whispers and pointed gazes, a life lived in the shadows of what might have been..."

Kai barely had time to process the words before the air shifted violently. The book glowed brighter, its magic thrumming in the stillness of the room.

"No—wait!" he cried, but the pull had already begun.

The book's light wrapped around him, sharp and cold and dazzling. His vision blurred as the room dissolved into a kaleidoscope of colors, the oppressive heat giving way to a familiar chill. For a brief, disorienting moment, it felt as though he were falling through the fabric of reality itself.

And then it stopped.

Kai landed hard on uneven ground, the impact jarring his entire body. He groaned, his hand instinctively going to his ribs. The air was thinner here, cool and crisp, carrying the faint scent of earth and woodsmoke. He pushed himself up slowly, his limbs aching but functional.

He was in a forest. Towering trees stretched toward the sky, their branches heavy with leaves that dappled the ground in shifting shadows. The sun filtered through the canopy in golden streaks, casting a warm glow over the dense undergrowth. It was a stark contrast to the endless winter he had known.

Kai took a cautious step forward, his boots crunching on the leaf-strewn path.

Boots.

He froze, glancing down at himself. Gone was the slight, unfamiliar body from earlier. He flexed his fingers, relief flooding him as he saw callouses and strength once more. His frame was sturdy again, his shoulders broad.

But the sense of comfort didn't last. His clothes were unfamiliar—a patched tunic and worn trousers, both slightly too big for him. A rough leather belt hung loosely at his hips, and a simple satchel was slung over his shoulder.

A new body. A new place.

The weight of it all settled over him, heavy and unrelenting. He was no longer Kai, the outcast of a small, frostbitten village. He wasn't the reluctant savior of the Winter Court. He was someone else entirely now, thrust into yet another story crafted by the book's unrelenting magic.

A faint glow caught his attention. The book, now lying in the dirt at his feet, pulsed softly. He knelt, his hands steady as he picked it up. When he opened it again, a single line greeted him, written in that same silvery script:

"Welcome to your new story."

The words sent a chill down his spine, sharper than any frost. He clutched the book tightly, his jaw set as he scanned the forest around him. Whatever this place was, whatever role the book had written for him, he wasn't going to play its pawn.

"Alright," he muttered under his breath. "Let's see what you've got for me."

The forest seemed to whisper in response, the faint rustle of leaves carrying secrets he couldn't yet hear. With the book tucked under his arm and determination burning in his chest, Kai took his first step into the unknown.

Pact With the Cat King

Coming Soon

KAI NEVER ASKED FOR a second chance—certainly not in the body of a disgraced miller's son, trapped in a world where power is won through cunning and cruelty. But fate, or something far more dangerous, has other plans. Among his meager belongings, he finds an ornate collar, and with it, he unwittingly summons a creature of legend—the Cat King, a silver-eyed demon as sharp-tongued as he is beautiful.

The Cat King offers Kai a bargain: absolute loyalty in exchange for wealth, status, and the means to rewrite his fate. Desperate and wary, Kai agrees, though he knows that magic always comes with a price. What he doesn't expect is the way the Cat King weaves his lies into reality, transforming him into a noble marquis, nor the dangerous attraction that coils between them—an intoxicating mix of seduction, power, and control.

As Kai is drawn deeper into a world of courtly deception and dark magic, he finds himself caught in a perilous game where love and possession blur, and the Cat King's true nature remains a mystery. But when a jealous rival ends up dead and whispers of the demon's obsession turn to something far more dangerous, Kai realizes too late—he may have made a deal he can never escape.

The Cat King always collects what he's owed.

THANK YOU

Writing *The Snow King's Thrall* has been an incredible journey, and I couldn't have done it without the support of so many wonderful people.

First and foremost, *thank you* to every reader who has ventured into this frozen world with me. Your time, your imagination, and your willingness to follow Kai's story mean more than I can ever express. If you enjoyed the book, please consider leaving a review—it helps more than you know and ensures that more readers can find their way into this tale.

A special, *endless* thank you to @arwen.readsbooks. Your thoughtful feedback, cheeky insights, and all-around amazing commentary kept me fueled and motivated throughout this journey. Your excitement for this story reminded me why I love writing in the first place.

To everyone who supported me along the way—whether by offering encouragement, sharing in my enthusiasm (and occasional despair), or simply believing in this book—*thank you*. This story exists because of you.

With gratitude,

Rory

About the Author

Rory West is an author of dark MM fantasy romance and supernatural horror, blending the eerie and enchanting tales that often romanticize and complicate both the heroes and the villains. Rory's debut novel, The Snow King's Thrall, will be released in March 2025, with the epic The Prince of Eldinar soon after. A devoted lover of cats, atmospheric horror films, and happily-ever-afters for the most misunderstood monsters, Rory writes with a passion for stories that embrace both shadow and light.

When not crafting worlds filled with brooding kings, reluctant heroes, and ancient magic, Rory can be found curled up with their feline companions, plotting their next twist-filled tale. With a talent for the unexpected and a heart for the unconventional, Rory invites readers to explore realms where love thrives even in the darkest corners.

www.ingramcontent.com/pod-product-compliance
Lightning Source LLC
Chambersburg PA
CBHW061343310726
48974CB00001B/177